# Where Lady Slippers Grow

## THE MADISON MCKENZIE FILES
### (BOOK 2)

*Bev Freeman*

Jan-Carol
Publishing, Inc
"every story needs a book"

**Where Lady Slippers Grow**
Bev Freeman

Published October 2017
Little Creek Books
Imprint of Jan-Carol Publishing, Inc
All rights reserved
Copyright © 2017 by Bev Freeman

ISBN: 978-1-945619-45-8
Library of Congress Control Number: 2017958224

You may contact the publisher:
Jan-Carol Publishing, Inc
PO Box 701
Johnson City, TN 37605
publisher@jancarolpublishing.com
jancarolpublishing.com

*In Memory of Daddy, Elder Robert (Bob) Clay,*
*who always encouraged me,*
*"If it's worth doing, do it right."*

*Mom, my go-between,*
*thanks for usually talking Daddy into letting me do*
*what I wanted and paving the way for me.*

# Dear Reader

Thank you for your encouraging acceptance of Madison McKenzie as she tested the waters of rebellion, standing up for what she believed, and reaching for her dream. In *Where Lady Slippers Grow*, Madison takes you into the remarkable world of her extra ordinary perception of scenes. She has grown into a self-reliant strong personality. Listen closely to her intuition, she's evolving and she's threatening in criminal pursuit.

If you enjoyed *Silence of the Bones*, you will love *Where Lady Slippers Grow*.

Remember, *The McKenzie Files* is a Trilogy. *Return to Walkers Mountain* is well on its way to debuting in 2018!

With humble appreciation,
Bev

# Acknowledgments

*Where Lady Slippers Grow* came to me not really as a dream, more like a vision when Bill and I visited Amicalola Falls in the mountains of north Georgia. There is a monument signifying the start of the Appalachian Trail. However, the trail doesn't actually begin until Springer Mountain. The access trail as it's called, is such that it would discourage the faint at heart. Up the trail you come to an Inn called the Hike Inn.

That's most likely as far as I'd ever make it. I've lived near an access trail to the AT most of my life, accept in FL. It's as if the trail was always on my mind and I really do admire those who actually accomplish even a partial hike!

Two weeks ago, chasing a promising sunset, Bill, Brian, Mom, and I hiked a very short distance to the top of Beauty Spot, NC where the AT crosses above Erwin TN. Sure enough, there was a lovely sunset that evening. But even better, I talked to two hikers camping on Beauty Spot, who were on their way to VA. One was an exceptionally nice young man from Serbia. His destination at that point was Demakis, VA. His brother was meeting him to return to Atlanta so that he could take his US Citizens test. I felt proud that he had come so far, for such a young and determined man from the country of Serbia and already had weeks of hiking under his belt. I didn't ask his name, but I thoroughly enjoyed our conversation, and the man with him, who had begun the hike at Franklin.

My AT hike has become this trilogy. I'm not as physical, but still as determined as the thru-hikers. Writing is my dream come true, my goal, my choice of expression. That's why these books include a story along or on the Appalachian Trail. I hope you enjoy the journey with me. I so love picking up new friends along the way and hopefully adding new fans.

# Preface

In the dense woods of the Appalachian Mountains, Michael stepped lightly over deadfalls and snags. Even under the weight of a fully loaded pack, his footsteps were silent, and he left few traces of his passing. Keeping out of sight of any hikers, he paralleled the Appalachian Trail toward Springer Mountain.

When he heard the group, he ducked into the shadows of a hemlock tree. *Listen to those noisy fools, tramping through the woods with all that fancy gear, laughing and talking. They think they're communing with nature, but they just don't get it. By now, they've scared off every rabbit and deer for miles around.*

He heard a woman's voice. "Wait up, ya'll. I want to take a picture."

Michael shrank deeper into the shadows of the hemlock. The woman stepped carelessly through the ground pine, caught her toe on a low-lying branch of rhododendron, and almost tripped. She righted herself and pushed spirals of golden hair off her forehead.

Michael got a good look at her face.

*Susan?* He studied the movements as her fingers worked the settings on the digital camera. When she squatted beside a rotting log, Michael gasped and nearly stood up. *There could be a copperhead lurking underneath that log.*

Her every move brought back memories of what he had done. Michael clutched his belly like he'd taken a knife to the gut. His heart pounded so loudly in his ears, he feared the sound would give him away. He squeezed his eyes shut, shook his head to clear the image, and then opened his eyes again. She was still there.

*That can't be Susan. She's dead; I killed her!*

# 1

Madison McKenzie tapped on the door frame of Dr. Gerre Baker's office. The UT Knoxville's Forensic Medicine Department had been her home away from Cold Creek for the last five years.

Baker turned to see her visitor. "Come in, Maddie."

"Hey, are you busy?"

"Never too busy for my best student. What's up?" Baker closed the laptop in front of her.

"I want to discuss something..." Madison dropped into a chair, plopping her forearms onto the desk.

"Sure, what's on your mind?" Gerre leaned forward, her elbows resting on the laptop.

"I'm not taking the summer session." Madison looked down at the small purse she clutched between her hands. "I need time to let the dust settle. These five years have been...well, like a whirlwind."

"It has gone by quickly, and you're only one year from graduating!" In her mid-forties, the doctor didn't look at all her age. She and Madison had a deep friendship, not a professor/student relationship. Gerre patted Maddie's arm. "You've done a remarkable job, and maintained a near-perfect average. I'm proud of you."

"Thank you," Maddie replied. She took a deep breath, and a tear slipped down her cheek. "I don't want to disappoint you, but—"

"No! You can never disappoint me," Gerre interrupted. "You know I'm here for you."

"I thought I wanted to follow in your footsteps, but now I'm not sure. Ever since I took that geology course, I see things differently. I was happy getting up in the mornings, eager to begin digging. I enjoyed finding gems instead of human bones." She raised her head, and her eyes met those of her mentor. "I've felt sad ever since I watched Aunt Denny die in Alaska. I don't know if I'm cut out for your world."

Dr. Baker stood and walked around her desk. "I suspected as much."

Madison accepted a friendly hug. "I hope you understand. My feelings might change, but I want the summer to process things."

"I understand." Dr. Baker sat on the corner of her desk. "So, what will you do?"

"Volunteer work. You know me, I can't stay out of the woods for long."

"Yes, I do know. Take care of *you*. Don't get lost while trying to find yourself."

As Madison drove down the ramp of the parking garage, leaving UT for what might be the last time, she felt a twinge of guilt. Dr. Baker was responsible for the scholarship that made her education possible. She questioned her decision to drop out, but she knew it was only one summer session; the time off would afford her sharper concentration in the fall. *That's all I want, a summer break. I've worked hard. I miss Bud.* Maybe that was it, more than anything else. *I miss my dog.*

The ringer on her phone roused her from deep thoughts. She recognized the tone as Agent Rick Malone, TBI/homicide division. She let the call go to voice mail, thinking she'd call him back when she was out of the Knoxville traffic.

As she was approaching the Strawberry Plains exit, the caller ID announced another call from Rick. Madison took the exit ramp and turned right. Her SUV rolled to a stop in the gravel on the side of the frontage road.

"Hello, Rick," she answered.

"Hey, I just spoke with Gerre. She told me that you're taking a sabbatical. What's going through your head?" Rick sounded too excited to make sense.

"What do you mean? I just want a break." Madison felt irritated, but not quite to the point of rudeness. Yet.

"Where are you?" Rick asked.

"I'm at the Strawberry Plains exit, heading to Cold Creek."

"I just left the airport. Wait for me. We need to talk."

"OK." She surveyed her surroundings. "There's a Cracker Barrel here. I'll be inside."

"Good, I'm hungry."

"Rick, when are you not hungry?"

"This time it's legit; I just flew in from San Francisco. Glad I caught you. Be there in twenty," Rick disconnected the call.

Madison was sipping the last of her iced tea when Rick joined her.

"Thanks for meeting me." He slid into the chair opposite her. "I have an assignment on the AT, so naturally when Baker told me you were taking the summer off, I thought of inviting you along."

"What type of assignment?" Madison leaned forward in her chair.

"There are a couple of hikers missing, one from North Carolina and one from Tennessee. And then this week, another went missing in Georgia. I think she's actually from Florida. Lone women, except the latest one wasn't actually alone. Apparently, she followed a bird and wandered off the trail, getting lost. Her friends fear she might have been taken, like the other two."

"Wow! Taken? You mean kidnapped? But that's not homicide."

"We hope it stays that way. Let's just say suspicious, for now." Rick smiled. "I don't know anyone who knows the woods like you. If there's evidence, you can find it."

"Did you tell Baker you intended to ask me?"

"Yes. Dr. Baker thought it was a good idea, said you were thinking of doing some volunteer work." Rick leaned back in his chair as the waitress approached. "Tea, please, unsweet, with an extra glass of ice."

The waitress nodded, glancing at Madison. "Must be a new trend." She smiled.

"When did you drop the sugar addiction?" Madison laughed.

Rick smiled but said nothing.

The waitress returned with the tea and extra ice. She asked if they needed some time, or were they ready to order. Rick, apparently familiar with their menu, ordered the Old Timer's breakfast. Madison chose a vegetable omelet.

During their meal, Agent Malone shared what he knew about the Trail Stalker, as the press liked to call it. Authorities had not yet found a body, so they weren't saying anything about deaths, just stating that the women were missing.

Madison and Agent Malone had met five years ago when she'd discovered a graveyard of murdered women buried near her home, along the AT in Cold Creek, TN. Her diligence and determination to learn their identity led to solving the crime. When Madison was in a plane crash in Alaska, Agent Malone joined her and brought her back to TN to a hero's welcome. A real friendship grew between them out of a life-changing experience.

By the time they reached their vehicles in the parking lot, Madison had agreed to join the search. She hoped there was a chance they'd find at least one woman alive.

After returning her SUV to Knoxville, the two traveled south on 411, a slow-travel country road, toward the mountains of Georgia and the Appalachian Trail.

Out of Ocoee, Rick used the GPS to follow two-lane back roads that led them to a ranger station, where they met up with their guide.

"Agent Malone, pleased to meet you. I'm Jake." A tall, spindly man in a uniform of khaki shirt and dark green pants stuck out his hand.

"Jake, thanks for meeting us. I brought Madison McKenzie, from UT's Dr. Baker's team."

"Jake," Madison nodded to the ranger, admiring the loose clumps of blond curls protruding from under a dark green cap. "Unfortunate circumstances, but I'm hopeful I can help locate the woman. I'm at home in the woods."

"Welcome, Ms. McKenzie. We're lucky to have a member of Dr. Baker's staff. Baker is a prized asset of the university, and I'm sure you are too." Jake shook her hand quickly and said, "Shall we go?"

"I'll follow you, Jake." Rick moved toward his rental all-wheel drive Subaru. Madison climbed in on the passenger side.

Jake opened the door of a dark green 4x4 Ford pickup truck, hopped into the seat, and steered onto the highway seconds later. Rick and Madison followed closely behind. Soon they turned left onto what resembled a cow path, meandering up the hillside.

Madison tightened up her seatbelt. "Ah, *now* I understand this Subaru, over your standard black sedan."

"Hang on, Kid!" Rick laughed.

The climb on the access road had taken nearly an hour before they arrived at the top of the mountain, where several more of the green vehicles were assembled. Some of the men wore the same ranger uniform as Jake, while others had donned a version which looked more military, and sported a tan cowboy--style hat instead of the dark green ball cap.

Jake introduced his superiors to the team of Malone and McKenzie.

Agent Malone joined the group gathered around a map spread on the tailgate of one of the trucks.

Madison turned toward them. A ranger dressed like Jake abruptly interrupted, introducing himself as Vic, Jake's boss.

Rick stepped between the two of them. "Vic, I spoke with you on the phone a couple of days ago. I'm Rick Malone." He gestured toward Madison. ""My *partner*, Madison McKenzie."

Vic stood his ground. "Come with me, Madison. I'll introduce you to the hikers."

Madison put her hand on Rick's arm. "I'd like to meet them, Rick." Then she winked at him, reassuring him that she could handle the situation.

Rick stepped aside.

Five years at the University of Tennessee afforded Madison the confidence she had lacked when she and Agent Malone first met.

A group of men and women unfolded from a huddle as Vic and Madison approached.

"This is Madison McKenzie, from Dr. Baker's elite group of forensic pathologists at UT Knoxville. She wants to ask you some questions."

"We're happy to have you join the search. I'm Greg Richardson, also of Knoxville, UT—men's track coach." He offered a welcoming handshake.

"I thought you looked familiar." Madison grasped his hand and added, "Your office is two doors down from Dr. Baker. Why is a coach's office located in the medical department?"

"That's funny; I asked the same question. The powers in charge claimed that was the only space available, at the time. It's been three years now. I kind of like it, though. Please don't tell anyone I slipped away early."

"I won't—if you don't tell anyone I'm only one of Baker's students," Madison said.

They laughed together, then Greg introduced the rest of the group.

"These were students of mine years ago, in Florida. Steve, my star runner; Clark, football and women are his interests." Greg put his hand on Leigh's shoulder, "This is Leigh, all-around athlete and the new physical education teacher at their alma mater, Seminole High. And Diane is..." he paused. With a blush, he continued, "the most beautiful Miss Seminole County, Miss S.H.S., Miss Key-Club, Miss FFA, Miss Spanish Club, Miss Trans World Airline, and..." he turned to the group. "Have I missed anything?"

"Just Diane." A red-faced blonde stood eye-to-eye with Madison. "Coach has been reading too much in the social column." She extended her hand. "Welcome, Madison. We need help. Monique wouldn't go off deliberately. Something has happened to her."

"Let's not jump to conclusions, Diane. We'll let the evidence lead us to her." Madison shook the woman's delicate hand and glanced at the faces of men and women her age, or close to it. Their first summer out of college, and they chose to spend time hiking to renew friendships. *How nice it must be to have these lifelong friends.*

Diane pulled her hand back. "I was the last to see her. I should have never let her out of my sight. We were trying to sneak up and get a photo of a deer, down there." She pointed toward a cluster of rocks, big as houses.

"Let's walk, just you and me," Madison said.

Vic stepped close to Madison, walking with his hand under her elbow. "There are no clues, I've looked. I don't mean to tell you your job—"

"Then don't!" Madison's words cut Vic's sentence off. "Why don't you take Leigh and introduce her to Rick?"

Vic stopped in his tracks. He nodded and turned back toward Leigh.

As the two women walked toward the rocks, Diane explained, "We climbed all over those rocks, I'm afraid Vic is right. There was no sign of her."

"Diane, I don't want to seem smug, but I'm trained to see things you and the others would never notice. It comes naturally to me."

"I hope you're right." Diane forced a smile, but Madison could see through her pain.

"You two have been friends for a while, huh?"

"Yeah, since elementary school," Diane said. "We just *have* to find her!"

They stopped at the base of the first rock, and Diane pointed to a trail, leading into the woods and away from the rocks. "The deer was there, but it walked away before we got close enough for a photo. Then she climbed onto this boulder, saying she heard a pileated woodpecker. She hoped to spot him, and maybe the nest."

"Stay there." Madison climbed the steep, uneven surface. When on top, she looked down. "Did Monique go out of your sight at some point?"

"Yes, then she came back. And she said one was higher, so she looked for a place to cross over. See, the larger one rests against the one you're on."

"Yeah, it kind of bridges the gap. It's narrow, but I can do this." Madison stepped gingerly, one foot in front of the other.

"Higher, out of my sight," Diane said.

After a long few minutes, Madison returned to where Diane could see her. "How long did you remain there before you returned to camp for help?"

"Twenty to thirty minutes, I'd guess. It seemed like a long time. Is there a way down on the other side?"

"Not one she took by choice. Did you walk around the perimeter?"

Diane nodded. "Yes, in two groups. We met back here after about an hour." She pointed to a flat rock, where she then sat down. "It makes me sick when I think back. We tried so hard, but found nothing."

Madison sat next to her on the same rock. "Tell me what happened next. Try to recall every detail."

Diane wiped tears from her cheek. "Steve gathered branches for a fire.

Greg placed stones in a circle and raked up pine needles. There," she pointed, "where our camp is now."

Madison waited patiently for Diane to gather her thoughts.

Diane spoke again. "Greg wanted to organize a grid search. He and Steve drew on the ground in that clearing." Her arm went up to sketch the grid in the air, as if she watched a replay. "The fire made enough smoke to give them bearings."

"You didn't go on the search?"

"No, I was to add pine needles and whatever was necessary to keep the smoke visible. Greg gave me a whistle to blow three times if I saw her. I wanted to help search, but Greg convinced me that I needed to stay here."

"Good plan. Unfortunately, she didn't return."

Diane shook her head slowly and continued her account of the day. "Clark and Leigh paired up, taking the south side of the AT, and Greg and Steve branched off to scout this side of the trail. It felt like hours before anyone returned to camp. I was numb, sick to the point of nausea. But I kept that fire going, and the smoke should have been visible for miles."

After a short pause, Diane picked up again. "Leigh wanted to go for help. Steve said he would, because he is the better runner. They went out again and kept searching until sunset; that's when Greg realized the plan wasn't working. Steve planned to leave at daybreak. We set up our tents, built a huge bonfire, and settled in for the first night."

"Are fires allowed on this part of the trail?"

Diane looked puzzled. "We didn't care. I said, 'Let it bring the rangers; the sooner, the better!'"

"Good point. Let's go back now. I'll talk with the rangers, but I need more time on that rock." Madison surveyed the area, taking it all in, breathing the fresh air. *There's no foul smell, no buzzards; there's no decaying body in the area*, she thought.

Rick met her as she rejoined the group. "Anything?"

"Not on my first observation," she said. "I want a small guy to search a short passage I can't crawl through—nor do I want to."

"Jake is the smallest framed. But," Rick rubbed his chin, "that one is shorter, and almost as spindly. I'll get him. What else do you need?"

"You have your usual gear, don't you? I'll look in the vehicle," Madison said, and walked away.

She rummaged through a black duffel bag with TBI lettering. Both hands carrying items she'd picked out, Madison walked back to the men.

"Maddie, this is Trent. He'll be able to assist you, and I'll be there before you two have completed your assessment."

"Thanks, Rick." She looked at the young man. "Trent, thanks; you're just right. Come with me."

"It's my pleasure, Ma'am. I'm a volunteer ranger this summer. I plan to get my degree in forestry over in North Carolina, at the Cradle of Forestry."

"Yes, near Brevard. I've heard of that school, but I didn't realize it was an active training center."

"Oh, yes Ma'am, and I'm enrolled in their fall semester. I'm stoked."

"I understand. I love the forests myself. It's important to love the work you plan to do for the rest of your career. Don't you agree?"

The enthusiastic kid nodded.

"Are you uncomfortable in tight spaces?"

"No, and I'm not afraid of snakes or spiders or anything!" Trent's voice hit a higher octave. "I'm going to be a good ranger."

"You certainly have the spirit. That's a great beginning."

When they reached the crevasse in the rock, Madison got down on her knees to examine it carefully. "Are you sure you'll be OK with trying to get through that?"

Trent nodded as he dropped beside her.

"Here, put these latex gloves in your shirt pocket in case you find anything you suspect could be evidence. Bring out anything that looks out of place, not natural for the area: cloth, blood on a leaf, anything. Do you understand?"

Trent poked the gloves into his pocket and smiled, still nodding. "I am a *huge* fan of all the *CSIs*, *Criminal Minds*, *Unsolved Mysteries*, and any other show having to do with crime investigation. I get it."

"OK, just be very careful. I'll be listening to you, whatever you say. I want to hear what you see. Take this radio." She handed him a walkie-talkie small enough to fit into his other shirt pocket.

Trent started through the opening. He wasn't out of sight yet when he went into a slight crawl. Only his boots were visible, and then they weren't.

# 2

Madison sat down to wait. A few minutes went by; after another three or four, she became worried. "Trent?" she called into the radio.

Seconds ticked by. Just when she was ready to call to him again, he replied, "Yes, Ma'am, I'm here. It opens up a bit. I'm photographing a dead copperhead, thought you might want to see it."

"Be careful; there are probably more!" Madison climbed to her feet, her heartbeat speeding up. She swallowed and then spoke again, trying to sound calm. "Are you able to stand?"

"No, not yet, but I will be in a few feet. Hold on."

Then she could only hear static over the radio. She waited anxiously. Just when she was about to key the mic, she heard a crackle.

"I'm standing in a pocket. I see where the rocks connect overhead. Looks like a narrow bridge."

"I know where that is. I'm climbing up there. Stay where you are." She hurried toward the place where she'd climbed the rock face before. She knelt at the narrow passage that bridged her way earlier. "Wow, you're way down there."

"Yes, Ma'am. The entry went downhill. Here's the snake's head." He lifted the copper-colored reptile. "It's been dead for a while: lost all the reflective color. And it's been cut off clean, with something sharp. No animal did this! Don't worry; I took lots of photos before I moved it. Want me to put it in a bag? I have some in my pants pocket."

Madison lay flat on the surface of the high rock. She heard Trent's words, but could not wrap her mind around what he was telling her.

"You hear me, Ma'am? Are you up there?"

"I'm here, Trent. I, um, just needed to lay flat to see you better." She felt dizzy, her head hurt, and her heart still raced. "Yes, since you have a bag, bring it."

"I'm moving down the passage." Trent went out of sight, and his voice trailed off.

Madison turned to see Rick coming up the rock face.

"Fill me in," he said. "He down there?" Rick looked into the crevasse below.

"Yeah, and he found a dead snake—a copperhead," Madison replied.

"I'm not surprised, but who killed it?"

"Don't know, but they used a sharp knife or something to cut the head off. Trent says the cavern below is cave-like; it goes downhill. He's trying to find another way out."

The two sat in silence for a short time before Trent asked over the radio, "Did she have a camera with her?"

"Yes! You found it?" Madison jumped to her feet.

"It hasn't been here long, so it might be hers. I see some thick rhododendron and light. I've found a way out, east of the large rocks. Meet me there." Trent sounded excited, but gave no other details.

Madison and Rick worked their way down the steep rock and moved east, quickly locating the thick bushes. Trent emerged within seconds of their arrival, with the camera and snake head.

Back in the camp, Diane saw the camera as the group joined the other rangers.

"That's my camera. Monique had it." She stopped suddenly, blood draining from her face. "She isn't..."

Madison quickly grabbed the tall woman's arm, supporting her as her knees buckled. Rick caught her from the other side. "No, we didn't find her; only your camera. Take it easy, Diane. You've been under a tremendous strain."

Greg appeared behind her with a lawn chair, compliments of the Forestry Service. "Have a seat. Don't rush to conclusions, Diane." He placed his hands on both sides of her waistline, guiding her into the chair. "At least we know she was there."

Greg's words of encouragement put a small smile on Diane's face. "For just a moment, it hit me that she might be..." her voice faded away. "I don't think I'd ever let that thought enter my mind before now." Diane's eyes became pools, and tears tracked down her cheeks.

Before the searchers could regroup the rain returned, complete with thunder and lightning. The woods are not a good place to be during such a storm. The trees attract lightning, plus the rain makes for slippery climbing. The rangers retreated and said they'd resume the search the next morning, weather permitting. For now, they'd return to their headquarters in Clayton.

Earlier that morning, the rangers had strung a tarp over the area close to the fire, so they had a dry place to eat. Greg stirred the fire and added dry wood. They needed a hot blaze to warm their spirits.

Rick and Madison remained with the hikers, now gathered under the tarp.

Steve began the discussion he and Coach were avoiding. "We need to make a decision. How long do we plan to search?" He looked around at the drawn faces of Clark, Greg, and Diane. "You know Monique would want us to go on. We can't stay here forever. We have to set a time limit." Still, no one uttered a word. "Come on; we have to talk about the possibility that we might not find her."

"It's too soon to talk that way." Diane jumped up. "She needs us here, right here. She isn't dead! Stop acting like she is!" She ran off to her tent.

Clark spoke, "We aren't experts at this. We might even be in the way. Maybe we should go into town for a while."

Steve turned to Rick. "I don't want to give up on her. But we have to face reality. We might not find her, not for a very long time, so we should have a plan. That's all I was suggesting."

Rick folded his arms. Madison knew he'd been letting the hikers air their feelings before he spoke up.

"Steve is right. You should reach some agreement. I'm not saying quit searching. Heaven knows, the more we have, the sooner we'll cover all this territory. But..." he picked up a stick and messed with the fire. "I don't know if you've heard. There are a couple of other women missing from the AT. No bodies, no real clues, they're just missing. There is a chance it could be a long time before—if we ever—find any one of them."

"How long have the other two been missing?" Greg glanced toward Diane's tent. "She can't handle hearing this," he looked at Clark, "so we won't tell her."

"No, we shouldn't; I agree. How long?" Clark asked.

"Six weeks since the first, and four weeks on the second. But they were lone hikers, on short day-hikes. One from TN and one from NC, same MO. Both had phones, didn't plan on staying but a night or two. But, they were on the same trail. That's why I'm here. That trail is just a day's hike from here." He nodded toward the north. "In both cases, bloodhounds were brought in, but they found no scent trail. I'm not suggesting we have a killer, but possibly there's a stalker."

The hikers gathered close to the campfire and discussed their options. Leigh chose the opportunity to return to Clayton with Vic and Trent. She'd get some needed supplies and return the next day with Vic.

"Speaking of options," Madison said, drawing close to Rick, "where do we sleep?"

"Oh, didn't I tell you?" He turned Madison around to face two tents higher up on the hill, next to a larger tarp covering a couple of camp chairs and a long table. "Take your choice. I had a couple of the rangers set them up for us. You don't mind sleeping out in the woods, do you?"

"Are you kidding me?" She ran to the cover of the other tarp. Rick followed close on her heels. "This is great! Do you know how long it's been since I slept under the stars?"

"I can't supply the stars tonight, but I hoped you'd enjoy this." Rick sat in one of the chairs. "Sorry we didn't get a fire going, but you can roast marshmallows by theirs."

"This is an excellent surprise. Thank you, Rick. I was so afraid we'd have to drive back to Clayton, or even Knoxville." She studied the tents. "I'll take this one, closer to the tarp."

"I'll get our bags from the vehicle, Milady." He ran down the hillside, pulling his cap onto his head as he went.

Madison slipped into the tent. There was a blow-up mattress, already inflated, and blankets stacked neatly on top, next to a pillow. She lay back on the bed, pulling her shoes off and tossing them by the door flap. "Oh, this will be just fine."

"Knock, knock." Rick lifted the flap and peeked in. "How's your room? Suitable, I trust?" He tossed her bag in and slid inside to escape the rain dripping on his back.

"This is great!" She grabbed her pack and pulled out a deck of cards from a side pocket. "If I remember correctly, you owe me a chance to redeem myself, after the last time we played rummy."

"That was months ago. But it *is* only seven thirty. The rain is getting harder. We might as well get comfortable." He started removing his shoes.

"Out there, Agent Malone." She pointed to the door flap. ""There is a good table with comfortable chairs out there, under a dry tarp."

"Right! Of course!"

One by one, the hikers disappeared into their tents—except for Greg. He carried a canvas chair in one hand and a pan of s'mores in the other. "I thought you might like to clean these up. Don't think anyone was really in the mood to eat them this evening."

"Hey, Man, thanks. Pull up your chair. I'm about to beat the lady in gin rummy. Read 'em and weep, Maddie." He spread all of his cards on the table.

"Oh, darn. Loser gets to eat the s'mores!" Madison stuffed her cards back into the deck.

"I know this is an active case for TBI, but can you discuss your thoughts with me?" Greg parked his chair next to Rick.

"Well, we can go over what we know," Rick began. "The camera dropped because the strap broke. She must have tried to find a way down to it. Whether or not she made it, we're not sure. She didn't have a knife, as you said; so, who killed the snake? The photos show drag marks, tracks, were erased. But whose? We don't know. There were no surprise photos on her camera." Rick stopped to let Greg respond.

He nodded slowly. "Monique was a gymnast. Could she have slithered down through the passage from up top?"

"Maybe," Madison answered. "But remember, the camera slid or rolled down the hill, or Monique was trying to get out the way Trent did. Maybe the snake bit her as soon as she landed on the ground. Or maybe she did have a knife, and you weren't aware of it. Maybe she killed the snake, and then made it to the lower elevation in the passage. Where'd she go from there? Why drag a branch to erase her tracks? It doesn't add up. Someone else was in there."

"Let's give the lab a chance to analyze the evidence before we make the call that there was someone with her." Rick looked sternly at Madison.

"Yeah, I guess that's all we have. We don't know much more than we did before. Except the camera proves that she was there." Greg rubbed the back of his neck. "Well, good night, you two. I'm going to check in on Diane. She's torn up, you know." He folded his chair and leaned it against the table. "See you in the morning."

"Good night, Greg," Madison said.

"I hear you build a fire early and make addictive coffee." Rick stood as the coach walked into the pouring rain.

"Up here, any coffee is good in the mornings," Greg said.

Madison stood and stretched her arms above her head. "I'm ready to turn in, too. I'd like to fall to sleep while the rain plays its concerto on my tent. You can have the s'mores. I was only teasing."

"I'll split them with you." Rick reached in and dug out a big glob of the gooey marshmallows and chocolate atop soggy graham crackers. He disappeared in the direction of his tent.

"Goodnight, Rick." Madison ducked into her tent.

She set the pan of sweetness on the floor next to her bed, dimmed the lantern to barely glowing, and pulled off her wet shoes. She rummaged through her pack for a dry pair of socks, then stripped off her knee-length camp shorts and t-shirt. She slipped into a long night shirt, a pair of stretchy cotton shorts, and the clean socks. Madison zipped her tent flap and secured its ties before eating most of the remaining s'mores.

*Water! What was I thinking? I didn't bring in a bottle of water.*

"Madison, are you decent? I brought you a bottle of water." Rick stood just outside.

"You read my mind. Thanks." She unfastened her flap. "Did you go to the bathroom for me too?"

"Sorry, you're on your own there. I don't have the right plumbing." Rick disappeared once again.

*If I just drink enough to wash my mouth out, I'll be OK. But I should have thought of that earlier. Oh, well.*

The tap of the rain on the tent sang to her, a song of dull thuds and a few tinkles. The events of the day rolled in snippets before her closed eyes. She thought of possibilities, things Monique might have felt, seen, and even heard. Fear elevated as she imagined the snake bite. *Folks survive copperhead's venom when treated immediately. If Monique has a bite, she's laying out there somewhere, suffering, if she's even breathing.* In these dense woods, would they even locate her body?

She thought of the skeletons she'd found near the AT five years earlier. The bones spoke to her, and led her to discover the lies that had cocooned her life. An evil that pushed her to fight for the truth, no matter how badly it hurt. Exposing the truth changed her world forever, and directed her to a career in fighting injustice. The last five years, crammed with hours of study and testing, left no time for Madison's personal life.

This summer break was intended as a time for her to unwind: to allow her breathing room, and the opportunity to finish a thought pattern. Was she ready for the life she wanted so badly? The missing hiker was an example of what her life could become. Sure, she hoped to assist in locating the young woman, but what a lonely life this could be. She could not consider marriage, even if she had a boyfriend. She'd be away from home a lot, like Rick. *Rick has a lonely life.* He'd told her that himself, and often. *I guess that's why he's friends with me; I don't have anyone, either. Do I want a life like his?*

It wasn't long before Madison drifted into a hazy dreamland of empty rooms, dark nights, and a feeling of solitude. *I don't want to be alone the rest of my...*

# 3

Bright sunbeams pierced the opening between her roof vent and the rain cover. "Oh, good. The rain stopped." Madison stretched and realized her first order of business had to be a trip to the ladies' tree. She dressed in a bright green pair of camp shorts and a beige low-cut tank top. *I can feel the heat already today. This tank top should be comfortable.*

Madison stuck her head outside to examine the situation. She spotted Diane heading toward her. "Good morning, Diane."

"Oh good, you're up. I was heading to the privy." Diane laughed.

"I'll join you." Madison grabbed a small pouch from inside her pack. "How are you feeling this morning?"

"Better since the rain stopped. Did you sleep well?" Diane's smile looked as warm as the sunshine.

"Oh, it was unbelievable. I haven't camped out in years! Not since I started college, five years ago." Madison walked in long strides, matching Diane's gait. The two were very close in size and weight.

"I'd never camped, until we came on this hike. It was all Monique's idea, you know."

"No; I'd like to hear how this happened. If you feel up to talking." She and Diane walked further into the area of the woods that had been designated "for women only."

After a few minutes, Diane told the story of Monique's hope to get old friends, schoolmates, together for a reunion of sorts.

"We'd graduated college and not seen each other in four or five years. We all thought it was a good idea when Clark suggested we include Greg in our plan. He'd hiked the AT with a group of his friends, and said he'd love to do it again." Diane took a breath and glanced back toward camp before continuing. "I wasn't sure I could do the hike, but Leigh convinced me I could. Anyway, Monique picked us up at the airport in Atlanta, and Coach—Greg—met us at Amicalola Falls. I've been dizzy ever since. I had it bad for him. All the girls in our high school had a crush on him. To my surprise, he had a thing for me, too. But I never knew. Now we are attracted like magnets, and Leigh hates it." Diane stepped behind a laurel bush.

"So, this is the ladies' room?" Madison laughed and took to the bushes on the other side of the unmarked trail.

"There's something I need to tell you, Madison. Last night, I looked through Monique's backpack, just to see if I could find anything that might give me a clue about her state of mind. Sometimes she was out there, in another universe. That isn't the Monique I knew." Diane reappeared from behind the laurel, tucking her shirt into her shorts. "I found something! There's a page from an old Bible, with a news clipping attached. I was shocked to read the handwritten notes from her mother. It said they named her Monique Renée Lawson, but that news article was about a family named Morrel, who went missing somewhere along the Appalachian Mountains in North Georgia or North Carolina in October 1994, and were never found. The mother in the news article was Renée, and the little girl was Monique Lawson."

"Sounds like an odd thing for her mother to keep. What do you think it means?" Madison asked when she returned to the trail.

"I couldn't sleep last night, so I lay there thinking of crazy stuff. I remembered that once she told me her parents were from Georgia, and she thought her dad was a forest ranger. Isn't that nice? They named their little girl after the one that died in the plane crash. She might have even been family. I don't know how old she was when they left Georgia. I just remember we started Rainbow Preschool together. We were in the four-year-old class. But I went there when I was three, too. She must have been four when she moved there." Diane gazed into the thick underbrush. "I can understand why we haven't found some sign of her. Look how thick these bushes are. She could have crawled up under them, and..."

"Don't allow your thoughts to go in that direction, Diane. That is a sad story. You don't think she would go off on her own just to see if she could find the crash site, do you?"

"Oh, no, she wouldn't deliberately worry us. She's such a sweetheart; she'd never do that." Diane started walking toward camp.

Meanwhile, Rick sipped coffee and talked with Greg. The remainder of the hikers were still sleeping, and the rangers had not returned yet.

When the ladies rejoined them, Rick and Greg had breakfast spread on the table under the big tarp, and they tended a new fire pit.

"Finally! I thought you two might have gotten lost. You hungry?" Rick stood.

"You know it!" Madison leaned close to Rick and nudged him. "As long as Greg did the cooking."

"You're in luck. Greg cooked. I just built a fire. At least I can do that." Rick dropped back into his chair.

"Greg is an excellent cook. He's fed us all these weeks." Diane wrapped her arms around his midsection, giving him a gentle squeeze. "We're all pretty fond of him."

Another hour passed, and still no rangers. The hikers were restless, and wanted to set out on their own. Rick suggested they stay close to camp and wait. "The last thing we need is for another of you to get lost, or hurt."

Steve stepped forward. "Look at those clouds. In Florida, we call that a thunderhead. Maybe we have a rainy front heading our way. Last night's rain came out of the east. This rain is northwest of our camp. A larger front will pull a smaller one toward it. It's my guess that the rangers have looked at the weather radar and seen trouble coming."

"Steve is right. We probably should batten down the hatches. Gather extra wood for our fire, secure the tents against high winds, and wait it out," Greg said.

Clark kicked a chunk of half-burned firewood and then set off into the brush.

"Wait up, Clark." Steve called, "Don't go alone. I'm coming."

Two hours passed as the hikers gathered suitable branches and dead tree trunks for firewood. Greg stacked neat piles according to size, kindling, larger branches, and finally long-burning logs to fuel an overnight fire. He dusted his hands off and lifted the lid of one of the coolers, which the rangers had supplied.

"This ice is melting. I think I'll fry up all that bacon and fix us a big breakfast for lunch today. Does that sound OK with everyone?"

"Sure; nobody is turning down bacon," Clark said.

"Too bad we don't have a ripe tomato," Steve added.

"Who wants biscuits and gravy?" Madison opened the second cooler. "I see a bag of mix, cans of evaporated milk, and even a tub of margarine. One of the rangers was planning."

"Is that all you need?" Rick questioned Madison.

She laughed. "I grew up in Shirley's Restaurant, don't forget. I know a few tricks."

The wind picked up, and dark clouds blew in from the west.

"Better hurry; I think that rain is nearly here." Greg busied himself with the bacon over a lower part of the fire. "Madison, you'll find a Dutch oven down there in the tent the rangers used. We can set it right in these embers to cook the biscuits."

"I'll get it," Rick said, already starting down the hill toward the tent. Then he stopped and called back to Greg, "What's a Dutch oven?"

An eruption of laughter echoed across the mountain top. For a moment, the spirits of the hikers lightened at the expense of the city-boy TBI agent.

Clark and Steve cleaned up the cooking utensils, finishing just as the downpour hit. They stacked everything around the campfire and gathered under the large tarp with Madison, Greg, and Rick. It was at that moment that they realized Diane was not present.

"She's probably in the tent," Greg said. He sat in one of the chairs to wait out the rain.

"I'm going to nap while it's raining. Wake me if anything exciting happens." Clark darted toward his tent.

"Sounds like a plan." Steve went off to his tent.

Rick sat next to Greg. "You think she's all right?"

"Diane?" Greg asked. "She's...not taking this well. You know she and Monique have been friends for most of their lives."

Rick nodded.

"I think I'll go to my tent and read. Call if you need me." Madison patted Greg's shoulder as she brushed past him. "She'll toughen up. Diane is stronger than she looks. But you're right. She and Monique are close. That could be a good thing, you know?"

Rain poured down as if the clouds wept for the lost hiker. Madison finished the paperback she had been reading and returned to the tarp, where Rick sat alone. Sliding a chair close, she whispered, "The rain has set in for the night, you know."

"Yeah," Rick examined a stick he'd been whittling. "Too bad we don't have marshmallows." He tossed the stick onto the table in front of him.

The thought of s'mores flashed through her head, and Madison smiled. "Wouldn't that have been nice?"

\* \* \*

Greg found Diane's tent empty. He walked to the rocks where Monique had vanished. "What are you doing?" he asked, staring down at the drenched woman sitting on a tree stump.

Diane raised her head, but didn't look at him. She eyed the rocks ahead of her, lips trembling. "I wanted to feel what she's feeling. Breathe what she breathes. Smell the smells around these rocks, where she was. She's not here. But she's alive; I know it. I feel it. She needs us here. We can't give up on her. She needs us right here!"

Diane lowered her head resting it on her knees. "It's like when my dad died. I knew the very minute he was gone. No one had to tell me, I just knew. I was on a flight back from Italy When I began to lose focus on everything. Finally, I sat down and cried. One of the flight attendants asked me what was wrong. I told her my dad had passed away. An hour later, I got the call. The flight engineer said I had a personal call over the radio. It was the hospital. It happened exactly at the time I said." She raised her head and looked straight into Greg's eyes. "She's alive. I *know* it. I won't leave her up here alone. Let the others leave if they want to; I'm staying."

"And I'm with you. If you feel that strongly about it, I'll stay too." Greg embraced Diane. "Let's get you into some dry clothes. You're shivering."

He gave her his hand and pulled her to her feet. They stood eye to eye for a moment. Greg pressed his lips against her cheek. Warm tears, obviously not rain, rolled down her face. He pulled her into an embrace. "Diane, you have always been special to me. As a student, you were bright and inquisitive, eager to learn. You were every teacher's dream. But my hopes went deeper; you stirred feelings in my heart. And now, you're a woman. What we feel is no longer a forbidden friendship. Five years between adults isn't too far apart, is it?"

Diane's head tilted back. Her shoulders lifted, and she took a deep breath. She said, "I had such a crush on you as our teacher. All the girls did. But mine stayed with me and grew into a dream. I don't want to wake from this dream, Greg. Except that if I do wake, maybe Monique will be back. Maybe she hasn't been missing. Maybe I am still dreaming."

Greg leaned in and kissed her trembling lips. "If I'm in your dream, it must be real. I feel the same way. Monique brought us together to find each other. When we find her, will you still dream of me?"

"Why would I stop? I don't want to be alone." Diane blinked away the pools of tears that had collected in her eyes.

Back at camp, Rick and Madison were surprised to see the two hikers soaked to the skin. "She wasn't in the tent?" Madison asked.

"No, she was not. But I knew where she'd be, and I was right." Greg walked her past them and waited outside the tent until she handed him her boots and clothes. He returned to the shelter of the tarp and spread her shorts and shirt across the table. He set her hiking boots underneath.

Madison handed him a rock wrapped in a towel. "Slip this into one boot. I'll get another."

"Now that's a good idea." Rick rolled a rock away from the fire and picked it up with a towel. "Don't tell me. That's another old trick that city boys don't learn."

Madison and Greg chuckled.

"I need to get some dry duds on, too." As Greg walked away, he said, "Don't feel too bad, Rick. I'd never seen that trick either."

By this time, Diane had joined them under the tarp, barefooted. She laughed when she saw the drying towels in her boots. "Madison, that has to be your idea. You're a genius."

Rick poured steaming liquid into a mug and handed it to Diane. "The pioneer woman made tea from roots she dug up, too. I had some and I'm still alive, so I guess it won't kill you."

Diane smelled the steaming mug. "Sassafras tea! I love it."

Rick turned back toward the fire, setting down the pot. "I should have known. You've been hiking with Greg; he knows all these tricks."

The girls couldn't help but laugh at the city-boy cop.

"We'll know something soon—maybe even tomorrow. I'm sure of it," Diane said. "She's not dead. We'll know that for sure, soon."

Madison exchanged looks with Rick, but neither said anything.

# 4

The rain tapered off overnight. At sunup, Greg and Clark walked down the hill to meet the rangers.

"Clark, you know we need to make a decision today. I think the best thing for us to do is continue our hike. We could join the search party, and forget about going any further."

"Or we could go on with our hike and leave the searching to the authorities." Clark's comment surprised Greg.

"You mean you'd continue the hike?"

"Yeah, I would. And so would Steve. But you're right; we do need to decide today."

Movement in the grass caught Greg's attention.

"Hello?" He darted toward the edge of the field across the old road.

"Monique? Monique, is that you?" Greg cried. "Thank God, it is!"

Clark ran to join Greg next to the figure of a small person lying on the ground.

She attempted to stand. Her body didn't want to cooperate, weaving back and forth in the tall grass.

"Can you hear me?" Greg scooped the frail woman up in his arms.

Clark looked her over for any sign of blood or injury. "I don't see an injury."

Monique opened her eyes and blinked several times, but she didn't speak.

Vic's truck pulled up next to them at that very moment. He and Leigh jumped out. "You found her? Monique, where have you been?" Leigh nearly knocked Greg down when she raced over to them.

"She was right there, in the grass. We were waiting for you, and saw her moving," Clark explained. "Her clothes aren't wet, or even dirty. I don't see any sign of an injury." His voice was shrill with excitement.

"Has she said anything?" Vic asked. "Where has she been?"

"She hasn't said a word." Greg walked toward the back of Vic's truck.

Vic pulled an unfolded pack from the front seat and let the tailgate down. "Here, put her on this blanket."

Greg carefully put Monique's limp body on the bedding. "Monique, can you hear me? It's Greg. Can you hear me?"

"Yes..." Monique's voice sounded weak. She opened her eyes.

"Run back to camp. Get Diane; she's the nearest thing we have to a nurse!" Greg said. "Bring a canteen of water," he called, as Clark sprinted away.

Vic got another blanket from behind the truck's seat. "Here, she might be in shock. We need to keep her warm." The ranger spread the blanket over her still form. He opened the toolbox in the bed of the truck and brought out a thermos of water. "Monique, drink."

She drank only a sip.

"Monique, you have to wake up." Greg sat on the tailgate and lifted her body to a sitting position. He supported her and continued talking. "We've been looking for you. Where have you been? It rained last night, yet you aren't wet. Where were you?"

She opened her eyes again.

"Talk to us, Monique. Are you hurt?" Greg shook her gently.

She shook her head.

"She smells clean. She couldn't have been wandering in the woods all this time," Greg whispered.

"Let's try some coffee." Vic retrieved another thermos from his toolbox. "Here Monique, drink some coffee." He blew on it to cool the hot liquid so it wouldn't burn her. "Just sip."

"Cold," Monique slurred. "Coffee's cold."

Quickly Vic refilled the cup. "Now...try this," he urged. The coffee steamed this time.

Monique drank it. A big smile came over Vic's face. He leaned closer to the weak hiker. "I'm Vic. You sure have given us a scare. How do you feel?" He refilled the coffee cup and offered it to her again.

Without opening her eyes, she turned her lips away from the cup and whispered, "I'm sleepy."

"No, you can't go to sleep yet. We need to know how you are, and if you sleep, we can't learn what happened to you," Greg told her.

"What?" Monique's voice was barely audible.

"Monique!" Diane squealed. She threw her arms around both her friend and Greg. "Are you OK? Where'd you go?" Diane cried, nearly hysterical.

"What?" Monique leaned toward Diane. "What do you mean?"

"Sweetie, you've been missing for ten days," Diane said.

She just stared as though nothing was registering. "What?"

Rick and Madison ran to where they had all gathered around the petite woman.

"Hello, Monique. We're sure happy to see you." Rick said. "I'm Agent Rick Malone; this is Madison, my assistant."

"Agent?" She sat up straight, more awake now. "Agent, like in the FBI?"

"State: Tennessee Bureau of Investigation, not Federal. But yes, like that. You went missing last week. People from all over three states have been searching for you."

Monique frowned and rubbed her leg.

"Is something wrong with your leg?" Madison asked.

"I don't know; I don't remember. How did I get lost?" Monique wiped her eyes. "My leg hurts a little."

"You guys walk around the truck and let me examine her. She could have injuries and not know." Madison pulled the blanket up around Monique's shoulders. ""Help me, Diane. Hold the blanket, and I'll remove her clothes."

Leigh stepped up, "I'll hold it. Give Madison a hand with her clothing."

Diane unbuttoned the clean shirt, then lifted her t-shirt and examined Monique's stomach and breasts. "Not even a bruise. Let us see your back." Diane touched Monique's back lightly, asking, "Is this sore?" She pressed gently on a yellowish-brown area across her shoulders. "Madison, doesn't that look like a bruise that's healing?"

"Yeah. Monique, does it hurt where Diane is pressing?"

"No," she replied.

"You have some bruising, consistent with a fall." Diane unsnapped the hiking shorts. "Can you stand?"

"Maybe." Monique slipped off the tailgate with Leigh's assistance.

Diane loosened the shorts at the waist and dropped them a little at a time. She checked under the back of Monique's panties. "There's another bruise on your hip; it's nearly healed, too." When the shorts dropped past midthigh, Diane gasped. "Monique!"

"That's a snake bite," Madison said.

Diane pulled the shorts down to her knees. "There are no more marks or cuts. Turn around. Nothing on the backs of your legs."

Monique slumped into Leigh's arms.

"Lay her back down." Diane pushed her friend's shorts up as Monique slumped on the soft covers. "Tell me anything you remember," Diane said.

"I can't remember..." she put her hand to her head.

"There's another old bruise; she must have hit her head when she fell," Leigh said.

"Greg, come here!" Diane called out.

Greg ran to the back of the truck, followed by the other guys. "What did you find?"

"Monique, lie still; let them see this." Diane pulled the shorts leg up to expose the bite. "All we found are bruises, aside from this cut over the bite."

Greg pointed to two red marks joining a clean wound. "She has a snake bite, and someone cut the wound to drain it."

Vic said, "That's just like the textbook example they showed us in first aid when a copperhead bit one of our rangers. Punctures like those mean it was a poisonous snake."

"We saw a copperhead: a dead one, remember?" Rick reminded them.

The men exchanged looks, but no other words. Vic went to the front of the truck and radioed the ranger station.

"I'll have an ambulance meet us. We've got to take Monique to Doc Walden's. He's the closest, about ten miles away," Vic said.

Greg picked Monique up and placed her in the front seat. Diane climbed in next to her, then Greg squeezed in. "We'll be back as soon as we can."

"We'll wait here. Hurry, Vic." Leigh hugged the ranger, in a way suggesting they had become familiar with each other on their two-night stay in Clayton.

Madison ran around to the passenger door of Rick's rental SUV. "Well, come on!"

"OK, yeah, we'll follow you," Rick responded to Madison's quick reaction.

\* \* \*

After a bumpy ride to the paved road, the two vehicles traveled only a short distance to a cabin, gray from age with no paint, overlooking a tumbling creek. Two spotted hounds lay sprawled on the porch. An old man with full, white beard pulled suspenders up as he shuffled off the porch to meet them.

Madison had sprung from the car before it came to a full stop behind the ranger's truck.

"Headquarters radioed me you was coming. Bring the patient in here."

Vic emerged from his truck as Madison approached. "Madison, this is Doc Walden."

The doctor appeared clean beneath the roughness of weathered skin. His boots showed wear, but were also clean. The wooden rocker, smooth from years of use, still rocked where old Doc had been.

The inside of the cabin was simple, with no modern conveniences. An oil lantern swung from the rafters over a long, narrow table covered with a clean white sheet. Madison glanced around at the walls, displaying animal furs, a buck's rack above a primitive stone fireplace, and a drop-leaf dark wooden table with enameled plates, cups, and teapot standing in a dark corner.

"Lay 'er up on my examining table. Thur's some hot coffee on the stove, Vic. Help yourself, and then you fellers get out of here. The purty ladies can stay." He laughed as though he'd amused himself.

"Let me look at her." Old Doc pulled the blanket up and dropped it to the floor, then unfolded the second sheet and laid it over the patient. "You's a purty one. What's your name, Child?" He fumbled with a pair of eyeglasses he pulled from the pocket of his tattered denim shirt.

"Monique," she replied.

"Just call me Doc. Everybody does." He slid the sheet up far enough to expose the cut. "That's a snake bite, all right. Copperhead, you say?" He looked toward Madison.

"We don't know for certain. All we saw was a dead copperhead."

"Got any others?" The rough old mountaineer asked.

"No." Diane stepped up, putting her hand on Monique's shoulder.

"Lemme see." Doc looked closely at the incision. He reached up to a shelf high on the wall and brought down an old doctor's bag. "What happened?"

"We don't know. Monique had been missing for ten days when she showed up this morning," Diane explained. "We found where she fell, but can't figure out how she got out, or where she was all this time."

"Hmm, sounds strange, don't it?" Doc rubbed some salve on the wound with a cotton swab. "Hit ain't hot, or hard, or weeping. Someone doctored her; luckily, they knew what they was doing. Not many people survive a copperhead bite up in the mountains."

"What are you saying? That someone helped her? But who? We've all been all over those woods. There was no one else." Diane sounded emotional

Madison stepped closer to Doc. "Who would know what to do?"

"Them mountains is full of hiding places. There's even a whole valley hidden up there. I've never been able to find it. And there's 'at feller the FBI hunted fer, Eric Rudolph; they only found him when he was all tuckered out. Some folks loves them mountains. They won't live with civilized folks, as I do. They want to be alone. If'n they live with the snakes, they better learn how to doctor for 'em." The old timer spoke the truth in his backwoods dialect.

"You's the one from UT, right?" He gestured to Madison.

"Yes, with Dr. Baker's team," Madison said. "Vic told you that?"

"No, I heard on the scanner. I listen to the rangers' channel to know what's going on in my back yard."

At that point, Monique asked, "Do you have some idea who might have treated me?"

"I reckon I do." The old man smiled. "Do you member him?" he asked.

"Maybe...sort of." She hesitated. "I remember the kindest eyes," she closed hers, "but no beard; his face was soothing, and he had beautiful teeth. My memory's fuzzy, though. I'm not sure; I could have even dreamed it."

"I seen him once, last fall. Nice feller, didn't wanna talk. We run into each other on the trail when I was huntin' me a turkey. He knew them woods, and he told me where he thought I'd find ol' Tom turkey. Sure 'nuff, he was right there, and I had myself a Thanksgiving dinner off him. And dinner for the next week, too." Doc reminisced.

"Who is he?" Monique asked.

"Don't rightly know. Reckon he's somebody hiding from something. Probably been up there a couple of years, from looks of him." Doc carefully put away his medicines and equipment as his patient sat up.

"I wouldn't talk 'bout him to outsiders; they'll think you're crazy. Just be thankful he found you, and let him be." Doc offered his hand as she stood. "You feel steady enough to stand up? Not light in the head, are ya?"

"Thanks, I feel OK. Just sort of feel like I've been on a long sleep, you know?" She hugged the old man, then Diane walked with her out onto the front porch.

Madison caught Doc's arm. "Do you mind talking to me?"

"Nothing I can tell you, Ma'am. Don't see how I can help."

"But you saw a stranger. We have a couple of other women missing. You might know something to help us locate them."

Doc removed his spectacles. He looked Madison in the eyes and said, "He's not your man. I know people about good as I know animals, and he ain't who you ought to be hunting. You can believe me on that."

Madison nodded and walked outside. "Agent Malone might not think it's that simple."

Vic approached the doc. "She going to be OK, Old Man?"

"She's got a mark on 'er head, probably got a concussion when she fell. Her memory will likely come back in a day or so. Don't worry if it doesn't; she'll be OK now. Drink lots of water, hear?"

Monique said, "I will, and thanks again."

Vic thanked Doc and promised to get by for a visit again soon. Monique said, "I appreciate your time. And if I'm ever back up your way I'll stop in and see you. What can I bring you from the city?"

"Shucks. The city ain't got nothing I need. 'Cept maybe some o' that cotton candy. You know, the kind they have at carnivals? I'd like me some o' that." He smiled, showing a couple of teeth in the front, but it was apparent he'd lost most of them.

Madison slipped up next to Rick and whispered for a moment. Then she motioned for Diane and Monique to come with her. They walked over to the rental car.

"It'll be less crowded in here with Rick and me. We have to return to your camp to get our things. You're welcome to ride back with us."

"Thanks, Madison. Do you mind if I ask Coach to come too?" Diane asked.

"Sure, that's fine." Madison sat in the SUV.

Rick spoke with the old doc for a few minutes, then returned to the car. Vic and Leigh got in his truck. They waved goodbye to Doc Walden, and Vic led the way back to the gravel road.

Rick looked at Monique in the rearview mirror. "Sure you don't want to get checked out by a real doctor, in town?"

"No, I'm fine. I feel comfortable with what Doc told me. He knows more, I'd bet, than 'them city folks.'" She laughed, and said, "I like the old man. I think he's interesting."

"If you're sure you feel comfortable, we'll return to camp and decide where we go from there," Greg suggested.

"That's exactly what I want," Monique said, with a big smile.

# 5

Back on the trail, Madison and Rick sat away from the others to discuss their ideas about what Doc said concerning the stranger.

Madison studied the interaction between the hikers and Monique. "They all love her. She must be one special friend."

"She reminds me of a gal I met about five years ago," Rick teased, smiling.

"Rick Malone, I was never that tiny!" Madison laughed out loud.

Rick leaned in close to whisper, "But you *are* that loved."

Vic hung around camp long enough to share their lunch, and offered to take anyone into town that might feel the urge to go. The hikers declined, and he said good-bye. "I'll check on you again tomorrow; I don't think Monique is fit to start hiking again so quickly."

As soon as the ranger was gone, the hikers all huddled around their mysteriously returned friend. "OK, let's have the story, what happened to you?" Diane prodded.

"What do you mean?" Monique sounded puzzled.

"You must remember *something*. We thought you just didn't want to talk in front of the ranger," Steve suggested.

"I don't remember, Steve. At least not where I was, or why. I have feelings of someone watching over me." She dropped her head.

Her friends quietly looked on. No one wanted to ask her, but she volunteered some more bits of memory. "It was a man: a very attentive and caring man. He had wonderfully kind eyes. Blue eyes, bluer than the sky." Monique closed her eyes as she recalled. "He was very gentle and kind. I want to find him and thank him."

"Are you sure you weren't dreaming?" Greg asked.

"Did you feel pain?" Asked Diane.

"Where were you during the rain?" Leigh put her hand on Monique's shoulder.

Before Monique could respond to one question, someone proposed another.

"Wow! The questions are too much, too fast. We need to let her rest. She can tell us more as she feels like it," Diane said firmly.

Clark suggested they do some exploring. "Let's look for the hidden valley. It's the most likely place to find someone hiding."

Rick stepped up close to the guys. "I don't think that's a good idea."

"Why not? Old Doc says there's one up here. How hard can it be to find?" Clark asked.

"Yet Doc says *he* can't find it. He's lived in in these woods all his life; if he can't find it, how do you think we can?" Coach stood with Rick.

Steve argued, "I bet there are some caves nearby. Why can't we at least spend the rest of the day looking?"

"I can't tell you what to do. You're all adults. But I say if you intend on hiking further, you should get an early start tomorrow. Don't spend your time here. I'll have a team of agents in these woods by morning. There could be a crime scene here. I can't allow you to roam around this area, possibly obliterating evidence. But at the same time, since we don't have any proof, I can't say leave, either. You decide—but use good judgment, or you could end up losing someone again."

"Rick is right. Let's leave the exploring of these woods to the pros. Are we going on, or calling it quits?" Coach looked around at the faces he loved and was here to lead. "Let's take a vote."

Diane moved next to Greg. "I'm with you. Whatever you decide is fine."

Steve and Clark said together, "We're for going on." They looked at each other and laughed. "Leigh?"

"I guess I'll go on, if Greg and Diane are?" She turned to their leader. "What do you want to do?"

"I want to continue." He wrapped his arm around Diane's shoulders. "Monique, how do you feel? Think you're up to hiking again?"

Monique stood silent for a long while. She turned to face the dark woods, then pivoted back to look at her friends. "I set this hike up under false pretenses. And I'm sorry I didn't tell you the truth." She scuffed one foot along the ground. "No, I don't feel like going on. I'm going to stop here. I'll catch a ride back with Vic, then return to Atlanta. I can't do this any longer."

Monique rushed to the tent she shared with Diane and slipped out of sight.

"What did she mean?" Leigh asked.

"She doesn't know what she's saying. I'll go and talk to her." Diane followed her friend.

Greg set out to gather firewood for a bonfire. Vic had brought hot dogs, so they needed to roast them. "I'll help you, Greg," Leigh said.

"I'll cut some branches to make roasting sticks." Clark took out his knife and examined the blade.

Steve looked at Rick. "Guess you're right, Agent Malone. We want to hike, so we'll head out tomorrow. But it looks like Monique opted out. Maybe she doesn't feel good. Will you follow up with her?"

"We will, Steve. Don't worry about Monique. I'll personally keep tabs on her." Madison folded her arms. "She's grown on me."

"She has that effect on everybody." Steve turned and walked toward Clark.

"Steve's sweet on Monique," Madison observed.

"Yes, and so is Clark." Rick walked back to the chair he'd been sitting in while working on a report on his laptop.

Madison joined him. "I wonder what she meant by under false pretenses."

"Maybe she wanted Coach Greg and Diane to get together. That's what she accomplished. Greg told me he's been in love with Diane for years." Rick stared at his laptop.

"Probably right. Yeah, and maybe Steve and Clark both made a play for her, so she got lost. But where's she been?" Madison looked at Rick, but he didn't acknowledge that he'd even heard her. *I wonder just how much of this she planned.*

\* \* \*

The sun's rays hadn't yet cut through the morning fog as Monique watched her friends disappear up the trail. Madison waited a while before she approached.

"Regretting not going with them?" she asked.

"Not really. Oh, I wanted to go, but I need to find whoever helped me." Monique turned, staring into the dense woods again. "He saved me. I owe him my life. I want to know why he's here alone, in the middle of nowhere."

"Are you sure he's real?" Madison asked.

"He's real, all right," she answered, turning toward her tent.

Madison followed. "Wait, Monique. What did you mean you got your friends on the hike under false pretenses?"

"Oh, nothing. Not really. I just meant..." Monique didn't finish her sentence.

"Well, you did get Diane and Greg together. There's that much."

"Yeah, that's the best part." Monique's smile warmed Madison's heart.

"Tell me the rest, Monique. Maybe I can help you. I'm perfectly at home in the woods. I'd like to see that hidden valley Doc spoke of. Wouldn't you?"

"So you believe me?" Monique spun around.

"Maybe. You didn't plan the copperhead bite, did you?" Madison folded her arms. "Besides, I promised Steve I'd keep tabs on you."

"Really?"

Madison nodded.

"Don't you have to go back to school?" Monique asked.

"Not until this fall, I took the summer off."

"Why would you help me? I thought you'd be helping Agent Malone."

"No, his job is to investigate the missing hiker from Tennessee. You're safe. He'll go back to Knoxville."

"But he said he'd have a team of agents in the woods this morning," Monique recalled.

"They're probably out there. But not Rick. He'll take me back to my car, and I'll go to Cold Creek. That's my home."

"I see. So, what will you do the rest of the summer?"

"Get some more hiking clothes and come up here to find that hidden valley, what else?"

Monique clapped her hands. "I better get packed up. I'm going with you! I mean, if you don't mind."

"Good, that will throw Vic off your trail. I don't know if you noticed, but he has been all up in your business since you said you didn't want to go on with the hike. I don't trust that guy. Get your things. We'll put them in Rick's SUV."

In no time, Monique bounced back down the hill toward Rick's SUV. "I'm all set."

"Good, let's get going," Rick said. "I'm tired of smelling like a campfire. I sure could use a hot bath."

"Trust me, Rick, we know that feeling. Don't we, Monique?"

The unlikely trio started down the rough logging trail toward paved roads and civilization.

A few hundred yards down the hillside, they met Vic, alone, heading up in his truck. He flagged them down.

"Where is everybody? Where are you two—uh, three—going? Monique's in there with you?"

"Yeah. We convinced her to see a doctor in town, just to be on the safe side. She doesn't have all her energy back." Rick made up an alibi on the spur of the moment. "The guys packed up all your tarps and tables. Need me to help you load them?"

"Thanks, Agent Malone. I can handle it," Vic answered, with an edge in his voice.

With those last words, Rick drove on, not giving the ranger a chance to object. After all, it was none of his business. Monique was found, and didn't want to continue the hike; why not pluck her from the wilderness, to be on the safe side?

* * *

The rush hour traffic around UT was already evident when they turned off the Alcoa Highway. Rick pulled in next to Madison's Blazer.

"When are you going to get a new vehicle, Maddie?"

"What's wrong with my Blazer? I like it very much. It gets me where I want to go, and besides, I don't have the money to spare right now."

"It's at least ten years old: not trustworthy to commute to Cold Creek. I'd be happy to sign for you, if you need a co-signer on loan," Rick teased.

"I don't want a loan. Thanks just the same, Rick!"

"You two squabble like brother and sister. Must be nice to have such a great relationship." Monique said. "My only friends just went on a hike without me."

"What about family?" Rick asked, not knowing the circumstances that left Monique on her own.

"Monique's folks died back in the winter, in a boating accident. She has no other family, Rick." Madison filled him in quickly.

"I'm sorry, Monique. Gee, leave it to me to open my mouth and swallow my foot. Hey, I'm sorry," Rick apologized again.

"That's OK, Agent Malone. You couldn't have known. Besides, I'm doing pretty well now. I have my store in Atlanta. I'll go back and lose myself in my books. Well, if it doesn't go under, that is, now that the new Book-Mart opened across the street. They have a cool coffee shop with computers and free Wi-Fi. How could *that* cause me to lose business?" She forced a dry, sarcastic laugh.

"Have you thought of moving your store?" Madison suggested.

"I have."

"Where are you thinking?"

"Knoxville, maybe. I was born here, you know."

"I thought you were from Florida," Rick said.

"I was raised in Florida. But after my folks passed, I found some papers. It was confusing at first; then I figured it out. The papers were an unreported birth, meaning I wasn't born in a hospital. The county records only had my folks' word on when and where I was born."

"That's not even close to legal!" Rick looked at Madison. "Did you know this?"

"Uh huh."

"Are the papers dated?"

"Yeah. They're at my apartment. I can send the papers to you. Does this mean trouble for me?"

"Oh, no, not at all. I just want to check into it, that's all." Rick glared at Madison as if wanting her support.

"OK, Rick. Monique will get them to you. I'm sworn to keep an eye on her for her friends. There's no need for you to worry. Keep me in the loop about the two missing women, will you?"

Madison tossed her things into the Blazer, then reached for Monique's backpack and set it on the floor behind the front seat. "See you later, Rick. We've gotta get going."

"Thanks, Agent Malone, for all you've done for my friends and me." Monique got in the passenger side of Madison's SUV.

"From now on, that's Rick, not Agent Malone. Got it?"

Monique's smile and the nod of her head said she was happy with the first name basis. "Bye, Rick."

"Bye, you two be careful!" He waved as they backed out of the parking space.

"Say! The more I think about moving to Knoxville, the better the idea sets with me. Diane will be here; she and Greg are getting married. That'd be perfect for me, for her too."

Madison smiled as she listened to Monique talking about her friends.

"I love the mountains, and UT is a large school. Best of all, Knoxville is Greg's home. I don't have a reason to remain in Atlanta anymore. My store manager is retiring at the end of the year. She wants to be with her grandchildren. They live in southeast Kentucky; that's pretty close to Knoxville. Say, maybe Claudia will want to move here, too. She was a good friend to my mom, and she came to Atlanta to help me out when I opened my bookstore. Claudia is the closest I have to family, now."

Monique stared out the window, claiming to be watching the mountains they paralleled by driving north on I-81, but Madison heard soft sniffles and recognized she was crying.

"Everything is going to look a whole lot better soon, Monique. You need to hold to that thought."

Monique didn't respond, so Madison focused on the traffic as they approached the I-40 intersection. She stayed left on 81 where I-40 cuts off to the east, toward Asheville, NC.

Madison thought of what Diane had told her, about finding the news clippings and papers in Monique's pack. If they weren't her birth certificate and notice of birth, why keep the clippings? Now she wished she had questioned Diane further. Maybe she'd see if Monique would volunteer some information. *Can't hurt to ask.*

"Monique, you know Diane was worried to the point of desperation when you went missing. You two must be pretty close."

"We always have been, since Rainbow Preschool. She's the best friend I've ever had."

"I have a friend named Holly. I feel the same way about her. When I learned I was adopted, Holly helped me realize how fortunate my circumstances are, and that I shouldn't feel sorry for myself," Madison said.

"You're adopted?" Monique snapped around to look at Madison in surprise. "But you act normal. I thought adoption messed with peoples' heads."

"It can if you let it, depending on your story. My aunt told me my mother had abandoned me. Long story, but as it turned out, Dennie lied. My real father married Momma Shirley, and she adopted me." That was as much of the story Madison chose to tell at this time.

"Where is your mom? Where was she?"

"Dead: murdered before I was walking. I never even knew her at all."

Monique was quiet for a while. Madison didn't push.

"When my folks died in that boating accident, I had to deal with all their stuff. I sold anything I didn't want or need. I kept the personal items, like the family Bible and old photos. There were no baby pictures of me. I always wondered why as I was growing up, and especially when my friends had them in our senior yearbook. Mom said they burned in a fire. She told me she had nothing left of when I was a baby. But when I went through the Bible, I found a stack of news clippings and a dried bouquet of flowers with a story attached to them. I recognized it was Mom's writing. I didn't read it for a long time. One rainy day, I decided to read the articles, since I'd be crying and the sky was too. Just seemed fitting."

Monique paused for a short time and then she told Madison the strangest story. As Madison listened, questions arose in her mind, but she didn't interrupt Monique's story. She opened the console and brought out a box of tissues, handing them to Monique.

She blew her nose a few times and continued. "I looked up the flowers, and they're called lady slippers. And I think they were pink. They can be pink, yellow, or white, according to what I read about them. They're beautiful, but not commonly seen in the lowlands. The pink are more common blooms in the mountains of north Georgia."

Madison nodded.

"So you've seen them?"

"Yes. I always go to the forest in May to find them, around Mother's Day. The pink ones grow on the hillside above my cottage. They are lovely, and one of my favorite blooms in the spring. You know, they're part of the orchid family."

"Yes, that's what I read. So anyway, I figure that's the time of year the plane went down, in the mountains along the Appalachian Trail, somewhere that lady slippers grow."

Madison was bursting with questions, but she waited.

Finally, Monique said, "So, you see, Madison, I'm adopted too. And I don't remember my parents, neither one of them."

"What was your real name? Do you know? And how old you were?"

"I only know they named me Monique; my last name was Morrel. I guess I was two or three, by looking at the pinafore Mom kept, the one covered in blood. But it wasn't my blood."

"Their name was Morrel?" Madison asked. Monique nodded.

Madison took the Johnson City exit off 81 onto eastbound I-26. The drive through Washington County was quiet. When they crossed into Unicoi County, Monique asked how to pronounce the word. But she didn't make any more comments, except to say how pretty the mountains were, and how green it all looked.

"I guess that's why Tennessee is called the 'greenest state in the land of the free,' in that Davie Crocket song." Madison laughed.

Monique watched the roadside as they passed the tiny community of the Town of Unicoi. "It's charming here, Madison. No wonder you want to come home whenever you can. I would too."

# 6

As soon as they rolled into Cold Creek, Madison dropped off some boxes and her suitcase in her cottage. "I want to run out to Holly's to pick up Bud. He stays with her when I'm away at school. I hope you don't mind. He's my best friend!"

"Can I ride with you?" Monique asked.

"Of course! He's my roommate, but the sofa-bed is all yours; he sleeps in my room."

Bud romped with Holly's dog, Bear, in the front yard when they crossed the cattle guard in the driveway. He recognized the sound of her Blazer and came running to meet her.

Bud was six and in his prime. His short legs, from his Blue Heeler half, could run faster than most heelers. The Lab half made his body wide at the shoulders. Bear, a Border collie, can outrun Bud—except when he's running to meet Madison.

"Easy, Bud, you're going to knock me down. You've gained some weight over the winter. It's diet time for you, fella." Madison dropped to her knees to hug her dog. Oh, how she'd missed him! Staying home with him this summer was another excuse for the break. She could take him anywhere with her, except school. They had some catching up to do. Trails waited for their running feet. She'd felt caged at school, and ached for her old routine of trail running. At least by staying with Holly, Bud still had all the running room he needed, and Bear to keep him company. That made leaving him behind a possibility she could handle—barely.

Monique reached down to pet Bud's black coat. "He's a lovely dog. I love the colors on his neck and belly. That must come from the Blue Heeler in him."

"Yeah, and the brown, too. But the black is the Lab. He was a cute puppy, but he's just as pretty as an adult. His colors didn't change. I'm happy about that; I love his tri-color and the merle-colored underbelly."

Holly ran down the steps. "Maddie! Why didn't you tell me you were coming?"

The two women met at the bottom of the steps in a tight hug. "I wasn't sure what time we'd get here. Meet Monique. Monique, meet my friend, Holly."

"Hey, Holly. I've heard great things about you. Happy to meet you."

"It's good seeing you, Monique. Especially considering your ordeal. Are you all right?" Holly grabbed the tiny girl and hugged her like a mother hugs a lost child.

"Yeah, I am. Just a little gap in my memory. You know, like when aliens abduct people."

They all laughed.

"Come in and meet Henry, and my boys. I guess Madison told you I have twins. Double Dennis the Menace! Never a dull moment around this farm with two five-year-olds."

"Oh, my gosh! She laughs just like Dolly Parton!" Monique said.

"Yes, she does!" Madison laughed. "And she used to look a lot more like her."

"Yeah, before I became a Mom! Having two little boys takes all my time. I don't bother to bleach my hair and keep it poufy anymore." Holly walked with her arm around Madison's waist.

\* \* \*

Later in the evening, after supper at Shirley's Restaurant, Monique and Madison walked across the street to her cottage. Bud lay waiting on the porch. He stood and stretched as they approached.

"You happy to be home, or do you miss Bear already?" Madison rubbed his head. "Inside or out?"

Bud didn't hesitate. As soon as she opened the door, he ran in.

"I think he missed you," Monique said.

"No more than I miss him when I'm away. But it would be cruel to keep him cooped up in my apartment while I'm in school and at the lab. He's better off with Holly and Bear."

"What about your parents? Don't they live close?" Monique sat on the sofa.

"Yeah, but they're on vacation in Alaska. They love traveling, now that Ben and Margie run the restaurant."

"That's good. My folks hadn't retired yet..." Her voice trailed off.

"They raised you, Monique; they might as well have been your parents. It's a shame your real folks died young. Time will heal your wounds, but you'll never forget the parents who raised you. You need to mourn, you know."

Monique nodded.

Madison was glad that Monique was eager to go to sleep. She and Bud went to her room, and she closed the door. She opened her laptop, typing *plane crash in the Georgia Mountains* on Google.

She scanned through several articles until one sounded familiar. *Search for a couple and young daughter suspended after two weeks. Authorities fear due to inclement weather the Bonanza might have become disoriented and flown into the ocean off the NC coast.*

Madison shook her head. *Couldn't be that one. That's too far off course.*

Bud curled up on his favorite braided rug in front of the bed and went to sleep. Madison closed her laptop and turned out the light. She thought sleep might be a long time coming, with stories of plane crashes running through her mind.

Her cell phone vibrated, waking her from a dream. It took her a few seconds to realize what was happening. She took the phone from her night table and swiped the screen. Her father's voice came from the speaker. "Hey, didn't wake you, did I?"

"That's OK; I'd just gone to bed. How's Alaska?"

"Fabulous, as always!" Jess said. "We saw the Lady today. Beautiful clear skies, what a view to wake up to!"

"You got a room at the lodge above Talkeetna? Wonderful! Wish I was there."

"So do we," two voices chimed together. "Hi, Honey, how are you?" Shirley took the phone from Jess. "What have you learned about that lost hiker?"

"Not lost anymore. In fact, Monique is asleep on my sofa. It's a huge mystery, but thank God she was all right." Madison hadn't been able to talk to her folks while on the AT; there was no cell signal.

"That's welcome news. But why is the hiker there with you?" Shirley asked.

"It's a long story... I can't begin to go into all of it now. I'll give you the *Reader's Digest* condensed version." She put the phone on speaker. "Her folks died in a plane crash in the north Georgia Mountains," Madison continued.

"When was that?" Jess asked.

"I guess about twenty-three years ago."

"Where was she from?" It was Jess's question.

"That isn't clear at this point: Knoxville or Chattanooga."

"Madison, I remember a man named Bill Morrel, his wife, and daughter all went missing in their small plane, and were never found. They were from Louden, just outside Knoxville. He owned the largest Ford Dealership in Tennessee. The estate is in the courts. Rick should look it up. Who raised her?"

"That's another not-so-clear twist to this story. The couple is now dead, killed in a boating accident. Monique thinks her adopted mom must have been her real mom's sister, because she had custody. She'd never told Monique. She found out by accident after they died. There were news articles and a handwritten letter in the family Bible."

"Talk to Rick. We're coming home next Tuesday. You need to dig deeper into this story. Will you do that?" Jess asked.

"Of course. Why did I never hear about this?"

"You were young, maybe five, then. There was no reason to bring it up."

"Would you happen to remember what type of airplane it was?" Madison asked.

"A Bonanza. I saw it once at the dealership. He had gotten permission to land and then taxi the aircraft across the active runways to reach the dealership. It's located near the end of the runway. I guess he knew influential people. The Bonanza sat there for a week or so, and got a lot of attention to the dealership. It was in the newspapers and on TV. Quite a bold scheme for advertisement. I guess it worked." Jess chuckled. "Got my attention! I bought a truck from him."

"Oh, I have to go back to a story I saw online. It said the plane might have gone into the ocean."

"Yeah, we heard that too." Jess blew out a deep breath. "Call us tomorrow if you learn anything. OK?"

"OK, I will."

Madison opened the article on her laptop and started reading about the family missing in the Bonanza.

Bud nudged her cheek and Madison opened her eyes to see the sun was high enough to shine through her cottage window.

"I must have fallen asleep reading, Bud. Thanks for waking me."

She went into the living room to find Monique watching the *Today Show*, with the sound turned off.

"I didn't want to wake you," Monique said as she rose from the sofa, already converted. The bedding was folded and stacked neatly on one end.

Coffee's aroma led Madison to the kitchen. "Thanks for making coffee. I was up way too late last night. My folks phoned me from Alaska."

"That's one place I have on my bucket list." Monique asked, "Have you been?"

"Oh, yeah; long story. I'll tell you sometime. More coffee?"

"No, I've had two cups, thanks."

"I'll take this one to my room and get dressed. We can run over to the restaurant for breakfast. My cupboard is bare since I've been away at school." Madison opened the front door for Bud to go out, then went back to her room. She'd keep quiet about the story Jess had told her until she talked to Rick.

As soon as Madison opened her bedroom door, Bud ran in. "Ah, you learned how to open the screen door, huh?" She stepped into the living room.

"No, I let him back in. He doesn't want you too far out of his sight. I think he might be afraid you'll disappear again." Monique picked up her pack. "I can't believe how hungry I am before each meal. That's unusual for me."

Madison picked up her keys and a leash for Bud. "I think it's a good sign that you're healing and your body needs fuel. Let's go get some cackleberries and grits."

"I haven't heard that in a while. My dad used to call eggs cackleberries. When I was little, I wouldn't eat eggs—but if he scrambled them with cheese and told me they were cackleberries, I ate them." She laughed at the fond memory of the man she thought of as her father, looking sad at the same time.

"We all have fond childhood memories. Don't try to block them. Enjoy them."

"Yeah, I am. Thanks, Madison. I'm not a basket case, you know?"

"I didn't think you were. Just want you to know, if you ever are, I'm a great sounding board." Madison put her hand on the small woman's shoulder.

During breakfast, Madison explained that the airports, both Asheville and Tri-Cities, had no flights out that afternoon, but Monique could return to Atlanta the next day. "So, how would you like to spend today?"

"I don't care. Whatever you think is fine by me." Monique scratched the healing bite on her leg. "How far is it to a doctor's office? Maybe I should get this checked."

"Oh, we've got a good doctor, and he's a real one, too." Madison laughed "There's none better than our country doctor. He knows more about snake bites than any city doc. I'll take you to meet him."

"Shouldn't we make an appointment?" Monique asked.

"No, his door is always open, and it's first come, first serve. You'll see."

The two women walked onto the sidewalk running down Main Street. They passed the sheriff's office and the old jail, then the hardware store, then turned the corner at the burned-out foundation of her aunt's dental office, and stepped onto the porch of a new brick building. As they walked, Madison explained a version of the story about her Aunt's office burning and the brick building next to it.

"Aunt Denny was our local dentist, and I was her assistant. One day, she stopped taking her meds and lost her mind, burning down her office and her property outside of town, *and* set a forest fire, all to cover up a crime she was an accomplice to." She pointed to the building across the street. "And the doctor's office was an old frame building from the early nineteen hundreds, just like the dental office. After Doc McClellan saw how quickly it burned, he built this new brick building. That's his old office; the town is making it into a museum."

Monique stopped in front of a sign which read, *Walk-in Clinic, Dr. Chip McClellan MD.* "Sounds like good preventive measures."

Bud lay down on the sidewalk next to the door.

Madison dropped the leash and said, "Stay."

The two women went inside, finding Chip, the doctor, sitting at a desk on one side of the pristine room. Half a dozen recliners occupied the other side. A fish tank filled with vibrantly colored tropical specimens divided the room.

Madison moved closer to peer into the tank. "You have a new shark."

"Yes, I had to get rid of Rex; he got too big for the tank. Plus, he kept eating the babies. I just could not break him of that behavior." The doc laughed.

"Monique, meet Chip, or Dr. Chip." Madison waved her hand from Monique to the handsome doctor, now standing in front of the desk.

"Hello, Monique. I heard you might be in to see me." Chip offered his hand.

Monique extended hers and said, "How'd you know?"

"Cold Creek is a small town. We all know what's going on." Chip shook her hand and placed his free hand on her shoulder. "Come in. I understand you had a snake bite."

"Yeah. I think so, at least," Monique said.

"You can come in too, Maddie, I mean, if Monique doesn't object."

"That's OK with me. Your practice is informal. Don't I have to fill out paperwork?" Monique let the doc lead her into the examining room.

"I'll ask you all the necessary questions. Your answers are recorded and typed up before I complete my examination. We might be a tiny town, but we're in touch with the latest technology. Take a seat on this table, please."

Monique sat.

Chip waved his hand in front of a small electronic device on the wall. "Tell me your full name, date of birth, and home address."

Monique replied to the doctor's questions in the order he asked them, and the oral medical records interview continued for about five minutes.

"Now, tell me what part of the body has the bite," Chip asked.

"My right upper thigh, in the front." Monique slid the leg of her shorts up.

"So, just about ten inches above your kneecap, right?" Chip said.

"Yes."

"May I touch your leg?"

"Of course." Monique snickered.

"You'd be surprised how many women don't like to be touched. Not even by their doctor."

"You're kidding, right?"

"No."

Madison sat on a stool in the corner of the examining room, watching as Chip went about his examination. He asked several more questions, then wiped the area with a gauze 2x2 that smelled of alcohol. Then he moved a small lighted instrument from another electrical device over the marks on her thigh. "This won't hurt at all."

Next, he placed the lighted instrument back in its holder and sprayed it with a burst of unscented sanitizer from a small cylinder. He touched a switch; a small screen displayed an image of Monique's thigh, including the bite—which glowed as though activated by the light.

"Ah, yes: one snake bite with little venom. Good, it's been drained. That explains the small incisions."

"There's still some in there?" Monique sounded concerned.

"It's OK. It leaves a trace of DNA, but nothing to be alarmed about. Unless you want to know which snake bit you, we don't even need to be concerned with his DNA."

"We're pretty sure he's dead: beheaded, you know?" Madison said.

"OK, then." Chip offered his hand, and Monique slid off the table.

"You look to be in great shape, considering. I want you to drink plenty of water to flush any trace from your body, for at least a week. No need to take any medication. Eat a regular, healthy diet, and you'll forget this ever happened—except that the marks will always be there."

"Who could care for a wound like that?" Monique asked.

"Anyone who has studied medicine, or been bitten themselves and survived." Chip smiled, then added, "You don't remember what happened, do you?"

"No."

Chip looked at Madison, then turned back to his patient. "Just be thankful this person was there and helped you. Otherwise..." He didn't finish his sentence.

The three walked into the front office. Chip put his arm across Madison's shoulders. "I hear you dropped out of school. What's that all about?"

"Sometimes this little town talks out of turn. I just took the summer off." Madison slipped away from Chip's arm.

"You can always help me out here in the office, if you need a job." He moved toward the desk. The sound of the printer interrupted the conversation. "Ah, here's your report, Monique." He lifted a sheet of paper from the machine and handed it to her.

Monique looked at the page. "Oh, my goodness! I've never seen anything like this. And I go to some sophisticated offices in Atlanta!"

"I don't mean to brag, but I invented that." Chip looked down at his desk. "I'm a medical doctor by choice, kind of my hobby. I studied electrical engineering on the side. *That's* where my passion lies."

"You're unbelievable. You should be in some big city, putting this knowledge to work," Monique said.

"No big city for me. I'm a country boy. I love it here. And it does work for me. You just witnessed that." He folded his arms.

The women headed for the door.

"Wait, I didn't pay you."

"No charge; I didn't do anything."

Madison pulled Monique by the arm, "Come on, before he tries putting us to work." She winked at the country doctor and waved goodbye.

"I don't know what to say." Monique stopped on the sidewalk.

"I have to show you something." Madison led the way toward the old jail.

Inside, they found Sheriff Drew Perry talking on the phone. They waited in the doorway of his office. After a couple of minutes, Drew hung up the phone and came to meet Madison.

"I heard you were in town." He wrapped his arms around her slim body in a bear hug.

"I want you to meet Monique, our hiker, who is no longer missing. This one had a good ending."

"Happy to meet you, Monique. Rick told me all about your ordeal." He shook her outstretched hand.

"I've heard about you too, Sheriff. Rick talked about you a lot on the trip back to Knoxville. I feel like I know you." Monique stuffed both hands in her pockets after the firm handshake.

"Same here." Sheriff Perry motioned toward a couple of straight-backed chairs. "Have a seat. Tell me what Chip said."

Monique threw her head back laughing. "Are there any secrets here in Cold Creek?"

"Not from me," Sheriff Perry said.

"I want to show her the basement," Madison said.

"Don't you mean the *cavern?*"

"Well, yeah," she admitted.

The sheriff told the story of Madison's malicious incarceration, engineered by his former deputy. "Five years ago, Madison and Bud were locked in the basement of the jail. Our feminine MacGyver managed to escape, and in the process, discovered a lower level that only the former sheriff and my deputy knew was there. The tunnel below the basement led to an old silver mine, and a beautiful natural cavern. She and Bud risked their lives via the uncertainty of the water flowing under the cavern wall. They surfaced in a mountain creek running out to the Nolichucky River. It turns out the cavern is under Madison's property."

"You mean there's a cave beneath Cold Creek?" Monique was all ears. "Tell me more!"

"Well, Madison deeded the mine and any silver to the town of Cold Creek. Small veins were discovered, enabling the cavern to become an attraction for the community's income. The Cold Creek Inn, with the mountain backdrop, was erected near the new opening to Cold Creek Cavern. All proceeds are used for the benefit of the residents, maintaining streets, lights, and even medical equipment; conditions were set up when Madison deeded the property. Cold Creek's residents owe a debt of gratitude to her."

"No, I owe the debt. To all the residents, family, and friends who afforded me a lovely, sheltered life growing up."

"I'm especially proud of Doctor McClellan, born and raised in Cold Creek. He's the grandson of the old doctor, who delivered nearly every person living in town. Chip graduated first in his class and completed college in three years, then medical school and an engineering degree in another four years. He returned to town at the perfect time, after his grandfather passed away."

Madison walked to the staircase. "Come on; I want you to see this."

"Madison, did you forget I had that entrance closed?" Sheriff Perry asked.

"I sure did!" She laughed. "OK, to the main entrance then."

* * *

After touring Cold Creek Caverns, Madison, Monique, and Bud went to

Holly's farm for supper. Bud and Bear took off, running up the hillside like they hadn't seen each other in weeks, instead of just a day.

The three women sat on the back porch in the shade as they waited for Henry to come down from the barn. Holly explained how Madison had influenced the design of the backyard flower garden, with its tumbling creek and arched footbridge. The twins played beneath the weeping willow in a sandbox surrounded on three sides by golden marigolds.

"Maddie planted the marigolds to keep the mosquitos off my boys. She's so smart when it comes to nature. I'm happy to have her as my BFF." Holly giggled.

"She's a special lady; I already knew that," Monique said. "This is beautiful country. You've got it all, Holly: the mountains, the creek, these lovely flowers and trees, two precious children... You're a lucky woman."

"Thank you, Monique. I am blessed!"

Just then, a four-wheeler bounced down the dirt trail from the barn. Henry slid to a stop next to the porch. "I hope I didn't keep you waiting too long, Maddie. That cow was having a rough time, and I couldn't leave her 'til her calf came out safely."

"You have a new calf?" Madison jumped to her feet. "I wanna see it."

"After supper!" Holly protested. "Come on, boys, get washed up with your dad. We're hungry, aren't we, Monique?"

"Um, yes, Ma'am," Monique answered.

"Come on, boys. Can't keep these ladies waiting." Henry clapped his hands loudly.

The boys jumped up and dashed to the house, racing Henry up the steps and through the screen door, letting it slam behind them.

Madison put ice in the glasses and poured tea, setting them one by one next to each plate. Holly placed a large bowl filled with green beans and small red potatoes on the table. She went back to the stove for a steaming dish of creamed corn.

"Madison, please get the butter, and that plate of sliced tomatoes from the fridge, will you?" Holly asked, returning to the table with a plate of biscuits.

"Monique, you may sit here, next to me, Madison, there next to Henry."

The twins made a noisy entrance ahead of their dad. "Quiet, you two! We have a guest this evening." Henry caught each boy by the back of the shirt.

"Honey, will you get the roast from the oven?" Holly said as she sat. She nodded to the twins, and they slipped into the two chairs behind the table.

Henry leaned over his wife, kissing her on top of the head, and set a tray piled high with sliced roast beef in the center of the table. Then he sat down

45

at the end of the table. The boys held hands and reached their hands out toward their parents, who took their hands and offered the others to their guests. Madison and Monique responded by holding hands, closing the circle.

Everyone bowed heads, and Henry said, "We'd like to thank you, Lord, for this food from our farm; our boys, who are a gift from you; and for our guests. Forgive our shortcomings and guide us, keeping us safe another day. Amen."

"Amen," the others softly whispered.

"I'm so sorry. Where are my manners? Henry, this is Monique." Holly folded her hands and closed her eyes. "Forgive me Lord, and thank you for returning this poor little girl safely, from whatever happened to her. Amen"

The twins giggled, clapping their hands over their mouths.

"Happy to make your acquaintance, Monique. Welcome to our humble home." Henry lifted the plate of biscuits. "Biscuit?" He nodded to Monique.

"Yes. Thank you, Henry, and I'm honored to share this bountiful meal!" Monique smiled and snatched a biscuit. "Butter, please?" She looked at Madison.

During the meal and light conversation, Monique proposed a puzzling question. "How do you have fresh vegetables this early in the season?"

Henry showed pride in his wife as he answered, "When corn and beans come in, Holly works long hours in this kitchen, canning everything we don't eat immediately. It's hard for her, but she never lets any of our harvests go to waste. You should see our cellar. It's our grocery store. Holly is truly a farm wife, and a good one at that!"

Holly put her hand on her husband's. "Your mom was my mentor. She taught me everything I know about canning vegetables, drying beans and fruit, and the proper way to prepare greens for freezing. I learned all that from her. And she taught me a little about quilting, too."

Madison smiled, "I wish she'd come back. Don't you?"

Henry winked at Holly, "We're working on that."

The evening meal was topped off with fresh peach cobbler and vanilla ice cream.

"Holly, the boys and I will clean up the kitchen. Why don't you show Madison and Monique the latest addition to your quilting room?" Henry returned the ice cream to the freezer and began stacking plates.

One of the twins pulled a chair up to the sink. The other scraped scraps of meat onto a saucer for Bear. Holly told him to get the raw carrots from the counter next to the stove and set it in the mudroom for later. "He and Bud are having too much fun to call him in now."

"Madison, is it OK with you that we feed Bud fresh carrots? They love crunching them, and it's good for their gums and teeth," Holly said, leading the way upstairs. She opened the door to the room where she and the other members of the Quilting Club met.

"Oh, yeah. Bud loves them too. I give them to him instead of those yucky chew things, like pigs' ears and hog knuckles. I don't want that stuff drooled all over my clean hardwood floors. Who knows what it is?"

Monique entered the quilting room ahead of Madison. Madison scanned the room. In only a moment she spotted it. Against the far wall, a strangely shaped machine sat at the edge of a long table.

"Is that a quilting machine?"

Holly squealed, "Don't you love it? Henry surprised me for my birthday. I never thought the other ladies would want to use one, but we all love it! We still do a lot of quilts by hand, but this one is for the king-sized monsters!"

"I must say, I'm surprised. But happy to see you got one," Madison said.

Holly showed them an album she kept. It had a photo of every quilt that had ever been made by the group, who it went to, and how much. Monique turned the pages, looking carefully at all the different designs and colors.

"They're lovely, Holly. I'd like to learn how to quilt. Sounds like a lot of fun, too."

"You can join our group," Holly said.

"I'd have to move here instead of Knoxville."

"What's wrong with that?" Madison nudged her softly on the shoulder. "We're a great bunch of people, more like family. Couldn't you use a family?"

Monique dropped her head, nodding slowly. She handed the photo album back to Holly. "But, you won't be here, Maddie. You'll go back to school in the fall, and then move off to some big city..."

Monique turned and walked to the door. "Shouldn't we be going now?"

"OK." Madison glanced toward Monique, then put her arm around Holly. "Thanks for supper. The food was phenomenal, and so is the company. Love you, Girl."

\* \* \*

Madison's car rumbled across the cattle guard on the lane leaving Holly and Henry's farm. Monique said, "I'm sorry to pull you away from your friends so abruptly."

"That's OK. Holly needed to give the twins their bath and put them to bed anyway. I'm sure they don't usually stay up this late. It was time for us to leave." Madison kept her eyes on the lane and then turned left onto the pavement. The moon was already high above the mountain as they passed the mill Henry used to operate before the tree supply dwindled in the area. Most of the forest was designated as government land, and only selectively harvested.

"Something made you sad about Holly's life. What was it?" Madison finally asked.

"Everything she has is what I always wanted." Monique turned to face the window on her side of the vehicle. "After I found Momma's Bible, I realized something wasn't quite right with my childhood. She had never mentioned that I was adopted. Why would she not tell me that?"

"Oh, boy. Does *that* ever sound familiar..." Madison whispered. She cleared her throat. "When I was just six, I learned I had been abandoned and then adopted. But you know what? That story wasn't true, and maybe you have this one all wrong, too."

"Maybe, but then that would mean she had another little girl. How can I find out?"

"Do the papers have any dates on them?"

"I don't know, maybe."

"We need to see those papers and the Bible. Rick can help. He has every necessary source to figure this out. Don't be depressed. We'll come to Atlanta and see what we can learn." Madison sounded uplifting and optimistic.

"Would he do that for me?" Monique asked.

"We will! I promise you."

Madison wondered after she'd said those words aloud. *Can I get Rick on-board with this, or will he just laugh at me?* The rest of the night she worried. Was she giving Monique false hope?

# 7

Monique's plane landed at Atlanta's Hartsfield-Jackson International Airport. She had no checked baggage, so she quickly made her way to the outside parking area, where Claudia, her store manager, was to wait for her.

Claudia had parked in the short-term garage to be in the shade. As soon as Monique phoned her, she moved the car down to pick up the weary hiker.

"Welcome home. How are you feeling?"

"I'm OK. How are things with the store?" Monique said.

"Don't change the subject. How do you feel?" Claudia pressed.

"I'm sad, Claudia. Sorry that I got snake bitten, sad to leave my friends, and even more pathetic because I know Momma lied to me."

Claudia stared ahead. Her eyes welled with tears. "You didn't tell me you found Jewel's Bible. Why didn't you ask me before you formed an opinion?"

Monique spun her body to face Claudia, as best she could in the grip of the seatbelt. "You *knew*? All this time?"

The trip across Atlanta was long. Traffic backed up around the stadium because of some event. Monique kept quiet as she listened to Claudia's story. When the car turned into the driveway at Monique's apartment complex, she finally commented. "I can't blame you for this; you were her best friend. I just wish you had prepared me before I read the notes." She got out of the car and disappeared from Claudia's sight.

\* \* \*

Later that evening, Monique's doorbell sounded. She was reluctant to allow Claudia's entry.

"Monique, I know you're in there. I have the money and receipts from the store. I'm not taking them to the bank tomorrow. You'll have to go yourself. While you're there, you can open the lockbox Jewels left for you. She made me promise that I'd never mention it unless you learned the truth. I don't know what's in there, so if you want me to go with you, I will. Otherwise, I'll open the store as usual."

Monique pushed the buzzer to let her friend come up to her floor. She waited at the door when Claudia stepped off the elevator. "I need to do this alone, but thank you for the offer. Come in, please."

The next day, Monique was at Georgia First National when they opened. She made the deposit first, then proceeded to the lockboxes. Her heart pounded so loudly as she approached the lady sitting at the desk that she couldn't hear what the woman said.

"I've never done a lockbox before; can you show me what to do?" Monique forced the shaky words out of her mouth.

"Sure, just need to see your ID." The woman's voice was clear now.

Monique withdrew her ID and bank account card, along with the lockbox key. She handed them to the woman and followed her to another room.

"Here it is, Monique. All you need to do is use your key. You'll find a private area through that hallway. I'll copy your ID while you're in here. Buzz when you're ready to come out." The woman turned and retreated quickly.

Monique stood in front of the wall of boxes, all numbered in sequence and shining under the bright lights. The key to 301 turned easily, and the box slid out slightly. She lifted the roughly shoebox-sized metal container and walked to the private area, where she found a small oak table and an elegant chair, upholstered in a golden brocade.

She sat down, carefully placing the box on the surface of the table. Her hand rested on the lid. Her heart raced as blood pumped through her veins. She breathed deeply, blowing her breath out several times. Her head felt light; she shook it off and swallowed hard.

*I wish Madison were with me.* Then she slipped her fingers into the opening, lifting the lid as though something might jump out at her. The irrational thought caused her to laugh nervously.

The lid now all the way back, she saw a plastic bag containing what appeared to be fabric. Maybe a child's dress? She lifted it out carefully, turning it over but not removing it from the bag.

A dark stain covered the back side of the garment. Monique could now see it was a dress. Little pearl buttons closed the neckline below a scalloped, dingy white collar. The top button was stained dark brown. She set the bag aside. Also in a plastic cover was the front page of a newspaper. *Knoxville Sentinel* scrolled across the top, with the date May 15, 1994.

She didn't open that bag, either. Setting it aside, she discovered a bouquet of dried pink lady slippers, secured by time, crushed together by a tiny hand. It was the bouquet she had when she was found after the crash. Momma had saved one in the Bible from this bunch.

Monique felt sick to her stomach. Her head felt light, and for a moment, she thought she'd faint. Closing her eyes and putting her head between her knees helped. But she still felt sick.

She pulled a canvas tote from her purse and placed the plastic wrapped items in the bag. After a few minutes to be sure she wouldn't fall as soon as she stood, Monique replaced the empty lockbox and made her way back to the woman's desk.

"Everything OK?" the lady asked. "You look pale. Sit here for a minute. I'll get you some water."

Monique dropped into the leather chair in front of the desk, the air conditioning cooling relief to her perspiring body.

"My name is Sandra; I don't think you caught that a while ago," she said, as she handed a glass of cold water to Monique.

Monique accepted the glass and gulped a drink. After a moment she said, "I'm sorry, Sandra. That was shocking. I should have had you come with me, I guess." She drank the rest of the water, then said, "My mother left the box, and now she's gone. I didn't know what to expect. I'm OK now. The box is empty. I won't be needing it anymore." She handed over the key and the glass.

"So, you want me to close the account?" Sandra asked.

"Please."

"You'll see a credit for the refund on your bank statement at the end of the month."

"Refund?"

"Sure. It was paid for many years into the future. I guess your mother didn't want to leave the cash." Sandra smiled. "Some folks do that when there is an inheritance."

"What kind of a refund are you talking about?"

"Sizable. But our accounting department will have to figure in the interest; it's pro-rated, so I'm not exactly sure."

Monique nodded slowly. "I'll wait, then, until the end of the month."

She stood up to leave. "Can you tell me what the name is on the account?"

"Why yes, it's Claudia Jewels."

The surprise on Monique's face spoke volumes.

"Sometimes two names are joined to make a new one. It might not be an actual name."

"Oh, yes, it's a name all right. And the name is *Mud.*" She spun and walked out of the bank.

Claudia was standing behind the register when Monique abruptly entered the store. She flipped the OPEN sign to CLOSED as she swept past.

"The back room? Or are you going to club me right here?" Claudia folded her arms.

"When did you learn the truth? That's all I want to ask," Monique nearly choked out.

"I received a package in the mail. It was the first week after you opened the store. Jewels thought I'd read the material, but I didn't. When I followed her instructions—opened the account, paid in advance—and phoned her, she cried. I asked her why she was crying, and she sounded surprised and relieved that I hadn't read the papers. I told her I didn't want to know! And that she should tell you herself, not me."

Monique stood there, momentarily speechless.

"She assured me she'd get around to telling you, but obviously, she never did."

"No, she didn't." There was a long pause, then Monique said, "Do you know what this means?"

"I suspect Jewels wanted you to know who your birth parents were. But honestly, that's all I've ever thought. I don't know what the bag held, except that it looked like a dress. What the significance of the newspapers or the flowers is, I have no idea. We can read them, if you want."

"From the deposit I made this morning, you haven't been busy this week. You might as well lock up and come to my place." Monique's eyes teared up, but she tried to hide her feelings.

"That was everything for three weeks, not just one. Our business has been dead. Until the fall semester, I'd say it's going to be that way. But then the students will come back to you. They always do."

"That was before the Book-Mart opened. I might as well shut down the business. We can have a closing sale. Maybe recoup some of my money. I'll pack up the supplies I want to move to Knoxville with me." Monique walked toward the front door.

"You've decided to move?"

"We can talk about it when you get there. I'll stop and pick us up some lunch." She didn't wait for any more words from Claudia.

An hour later, the two women sat on the floor of Monique's living room, both wearing latex gloved hands so as not to leave new fingerprints. Claudia unfolded the size 24-month baby dress and noticed the dark stains.

"This must be blood. Sure looks like it," she said.

Monique got up and went to the bedroom to get another bag. This one held the Bible from when she had gone through her folks' things. "This is a pinafore mentioned in the letter. I'd guess she bleached it to get the blood out. Let's see how it fits over the dress."

Just as she'd thought, the dress had a clean void where the dingy white pinafore had covered it. And since it was white, bleach had removed the blood but didn't harm the color the way it would have on the dress. That's why the top button had blood on it; the pinafore wrapped just shy of that button.

"Madison will want to give this to Rick. He's the TBI agent. She says he can get all kinds of the tests run to figure this out. The story in the newspaper pretty well tells me what I need to know. I was on that plane when it went down. What happened after that is anybody's guess."

Monique slid back to rest against the couch. She looked at the salad she hadn't even touched. "I have a few things to do tomorrow. You might as well take the salad for your lunch. You can begin marking prices down, relocating the things we should keep in the back room. I'll come in over the weekend and do the rest. I'll get Brian to pack up the fixtures once we get all the merchandise out. Do you think we can advertise the sale to begin on Monday?"

"I think so. There are plenty of boxes in the back room. I'll pack keepers first, then rearrange for the sale. I can keep the store open the rest of this week, just in case we do have some business," Claudia said.

Back in the higher elevations near Blood Mountain, a cold front blew through the forest at sunset. Michael pulled the hood of his tattered sweatshirt up around his ears. His ponytail hung heavily, dripping with rain. His moccasins slipped in the mud, squishing under his feet. He chose his steps carefully. The path was treacherous on a good day; in the rain, it was a death trap.

Michael stopped when he heard a roar coming from the rim of the valley. He pushed the hood back, turning his head toward the sound. *Not thunder, not an airplane... it's a truck engine!* He ran in long strides, leaping over rocks and small blueberry bushes to reach his hideout, concealed by a tangle of laurels. He ducked behind them at the opening, listening. The engine stopped. Two doors slammed, then he heard voices mixing with the rainfall along the ledge.

The voices came closer, but he couldn't make out what they said. He crept out from the laurels and climbed to a rocky outcrop, crouching behind the rocks where he could see. The rain stopped. He hoped it had washed away his tracks. There was someone on the same path he'd just followed. Minutes passed as he anticipated the intrusion. Finally, he saw a flicker of light. As it passed below him, he saw forms of two men carrying a rolled tarp. It looked heavy and awkward. The light was atop one of the men's helmets, like a miner's lantern.

One man slipped, nearly falling, and dropped his end of the tarp. The other cursed and called him a clumsy oaf.

They argued as they made their way across the valley floor to the opposite side. Michael knew there were caves on that side of the valley, but one held sacred bones; it was his ancestors' burial ground. He would never trespass on their soil. The other housed bats and small rodents. He wasn't fond of mixing with them, either. If these men had business on the other side of his valley, it was nothing to him. He remained out of sight, thinking they'd leave soon enough.

After what felt like an hour, Michael noticed the light coming in his direction again. As they drew close, the awkward one turned, shining his light directly in the taller man's face.

The tall man grabbed the helmet off and shined the light up the path ahead of him, saying, "Give me that. My feet are wet and cold! I just want to get done with this."

"You don't know cold! You ain't never been buried up to your eyeballs in snow and left for dead," the clumsy man grumbled.

The tall man kept climbing and yelled, "Shut up about that! I saved your miserable life that day. The warden was hot on your trail, and you were bleeding to death. The snow stopped the bleeding and saved your hide. So shut up—and remember, you owe me."

Michael listened to the voices, drifting out of range. Soon he heard the truck doors slam, and the engine started up. Creeping back to his hiding place and stripping off his wet clothing, he rekindled the fire. The blaze warmed his body, now wrapped in a deerskin blanket. The clothing would be dry by morning. For now, he'd get to the chore at hand; skinning two rabbits and cooking supper.

\* \* \*

Monique woke early the next morning. She threw a change of clothes into her backpack, and left everything else dumped on the bed. She looked in the phone book and called Enterprise Rent-A-Car. An hour later, she was on I-75 heading north.

Something was driving her, some force that she couldn't fight. The rented Jeep could take her back into the Great Smoky Mountains, back to where it all started. She could get in with 4-wheel drive much faster than they had walked. She should be on the old logging road by early afternoon.

She passed the Cleveland, Tennessee exits and began watching for Hwy 129. Monique spotted the billboard for the Lost Sea attraction, realizing she was close to a fork in the road, according to the map. The next turn would be toward the mountains and the AT. The closer she got to her destination, the faster she drove. Adrenaline surged through her body. The road paralleled the

Little Tennessee River, to a T. She hesitated, then she saw a sign pointing to the right. It read *Bly Gap* and *Murphy.* "Yep, this is the right way, I'm sure of it."

The next left was the turn. The steep logging road made the tires spin in the loose gravel. Shifting into 4-wheel drive, Monique drove the Jeep upward into the rough backwoods for nearly an hour. Finally, like breaking out of the clouds, she was on top. For miles, all she could see was wilderness. A smile spread across her face. She was back on the Appalachian Trail.

She set up her tent not far off the trail, shielded by thick hemlocks, near where she had her accident. She didn't know what she expected to find, but felt it might help her memory.

Monique thought a campfire might attract unwanted attention, so she dug in her backpack and pulled out peanut butter crackers for supper. She wasn't very hungry; she'd stopped at a Hardee's back in Chattanooga for a break.

The sunset stained the clouds a hot pink and orange. Monique watched it to the last flicker of light, and then ducked into her tent for a peaceful rest. The sounds of crickets sang her to sleep.

Early the next morning, she loaded her backpack onto her shoulders and walked up the trail until she heard a noise in the brush. She listened. The noise stopped. She then dismissed the thought of someone following her, and continued walking. The rocks ahead looked familiar. It was where she and Diane had seen the deer. Monique walked carefully around the base of the rocks, but didn't climb on them.

As she continued up the trail toward the thick evergreen trees, she heard noises in the brush again. She ignored it and continued walking, but kept her ear tuned for what she thought to be footsteps in the underbrush. *Animals don't make noises like humans.* Monique felt uneasy. The hair stood up on the back of her neck, a fear response she didn't usually have. She sensed danger.

She crossed the small clearing and deliberately walked away from the trail into some dense bush so that she could see if someone crossed the clearing to follow her. She sat in the brush for a while, but no one appeared. A feeling of anticipation gradually replaced the fear. Monique thought it was time to return to her camp and not venture any further away. She circled to avoid the area where she'd last heard the noises. Approaching her camp, she caught sight of a ranger.

"Monique? Is that you? What on earth are you doing here?" A familiar voice called out.

"Hi, Vic! Am I glad to see you! What are you doing?" She waved and greeted the ranger with a big smile.

"I thought I was here to arrest a poacher. What are you doing?" He demanded.

"I was trying to remember details. I thought being here might help."

"Don't you realize you can't have a vehicle up this far?"

"No, I didn't see any signs."

"What about the gate? Doesn't a closed gate mean anything?"

"The gate was open when I came through yesterday. What do you mean? Am I in trouble?"

"Not since it was me, but if someone else caught you up here, you could be fined. Are you alone?"

"Yes."

"Well, the gate was shut this morning when I came through, so someone had to go out after you came in. Did you see anything?"

"No, nothing. I'm sorry, Vic. I didn't mean any harm."

"I know you didn't." The friendly demeanor she remembered the ranger having returned. Vic stretched out his hand to shake with her and asked, "How are you doing?"

"Vic, there's just something I can't explain. Part of me is missing, and I want to know what that something is. Can you understand that?"

"I guess. What about the doctor? You did see another doctor, didn't you?"

"Yes. The wound was clean. Someone had drained it. I didn't imagine that!"

Vic shook his head. He folded his arms and paced without speaking for a minute or two. "There's someone up here, all right, like Doc said—and he doesn't want us seeing him. I think you had better forget your memory returning on site. Follow me out, so you don't get in any more trouble. The mountain is no place for a woman alone. Come on," Vic ordered, again displaying that he was not the friendly guy she'd met a few days ago.

Monique obeyed, swiftly packing up her tent. She followed Vic back to the ranger station. He got out of his truck and walked over to her Jeep. He bent over and rested his arms on her door. "Come in, let me buy you a cup of coffee."

"No thanks, I'm going to see Doc while I'm up this way. Thanks for not arresting me. I won't do that again." She shifted into reverse.

Vic leaned closer, edging into the window. "Come by to see me if you get back up here, will you? We'll hike up together. I want to find that hidden valley." Vic put his hand on her arm as she gripped the steering wheel. "OK?"

She just smiled and backed away. Vic was supposed to be engaged, but his hand on hers gave her a different feeling. She suddenly realized why she had no one in her life. "They can't be trusted, none of them," she said, looking in her rearview mirror. Vic stood waving 'til she was out of sight.

When she pulled into the yard of Doc's house, he came out to greet his company. She reached for a shopping bag she'd picked up in Chattanooga's mall. "I told you I would come back to visit you."

"Yeah, everybody says that, but no one never does. You're the first to keep your word. What's this?" The old man peeked into the bag. "Cotton candy! Well, I'll be!" He hugged his visitor. "You 'membered."

"Yes Sir, I did." Monique hugged the sweet old man. "I wanted to tell you what the city doc said."

"Come on inside; I just brewed a fresh pot of tea. We can talk in there." He pulled out a bright pink ball of cotton candy, which had been sealed inside a plastic bag.

"They have the cotton candy in stores now. I didn't try it, so I don't know if it will be as good as you remember—but it might be." Monique laughed.

"Sweetie, nothing is as good as I 'member it from when I was a boy. But the thought that you brung it for me's worth a whole lot." He tore off a sticky glob of the pink fluff and stuffed in his mouth. "Ah, just like I 'membered it was. Just as good!" He offered her the bag. "Have ya some?"

"OK. I'll taste it, but I want you to enjoy it; it's yours." She took a small pinch and then said, "Chocolate is my flavor of choice. I never cared for the really sweet candy."

"Chocolate's a whole different animal; it's one of them afer-a-desiacs. Know what I mean?" He slaughtered the Queen's English in the best effort he could muster.

"Yeah, I know what you mean."

The two sat in Doc's cabin and talked for hours. She told him about her day with Madison and the town doctor, and they dined on venison stew and a variety of wild greens and ramps, cooked in squirrel broth. Monique had never tasted greens this good.

"You gotta taste my squirrel gravy." Doc bragged about his mountain man menu. "Ya never ate ramps before either, did ya?"

"No, is that what they are? It tastes like onions with garlic. They're good. Thank you for sharing your meal with me." She finished her tea. "The sweetness in this tea is different, too. What is it?"

"Wild honey bees made it. I fetched it myself, out of a big oak tree on the top of yon mountain. I followed a bear to it one day. Do you like it?" The old-timer grinned. "I don't get to town much to buy sugar, but I got me a sweet tooth, so I have to depend on Mother Nature to supply my sweetener."

"Yes. Yes, I do like it."

After a while, Monique said, "It was nice spending the day with you, but I have to get back to Atlanta. Doc, I'll see you next trip. You want to hike up to look for the hidden valley with me?"

"Reckon you can find it?" His eyes light up. "I'd sure like to see her."

"We'll find it if it's real." Monique looked toward the mountain.

"Oh, it's real, just like your memories. That's what you'll be looking for." Doc smiled and winked, looking wise. "It's real. Don't you let nobody tell you it ain't."

"Thank you for your concern. I know I'll have my answers someday. I'll share them with you when I do." She waved bye to the old man and drove back toward civilization.

The feeling of loneliness had left Monique. She had a smile in her heart from her visit with Doc, and the lingering taste of ramps in her mouth. She fumbled in her purse for some gum, but only came up with a peppermint. *Better than nothing, I guess.*

Shadows alongside the road grew long when the rented Jeep made its last turn toward Atlanta. She'd be way after midnight getting back to her apartment. Her thoughts switched to the uneasy feeling Vic gave her.

What was his story? Surely he wasn't overly concerned about her welfare. Why then, was he so annoyed with her being on the trail alone? She knew the answers she needed lay somewhere in those mountains, and she meant to find them. Somehow, she needed to get back up there without coming in contact with Vic or any of the other rangers. Had he been slipping through the underbrush, stalking her, or was there indeed a poacher? She knew for sure that she hadn't opened the gate. The feeling of dread remained her strongest instinct when it came to Vic. There was just something...off about him. She didn't trust that man. "Madison's words... Hmm."

# 9

Earlier that same day, Madison and Rick walked into the bookstore, surprising Claudia. "If I can help you with something, let me know. I'm packing for our move. We're having a big sale next week."

"My name is Madison McKenzie, and this is Agent Rick Malone. We're looking for Monique. Is she here today?"

"No, I'm sorry. She had other business to tend. But I expect her back in tomorrow." Claudia swiped her wrist across her forehead.

"She hasn't answered her phone all day. I've tried several times as we drove down," Madison said.

"Oh? I haven't heard from her either, but I didn't try to call her."

"Can you tell us how to get to her home?" Rick asked.

"Sure. Let me try calling that number." Claudia punched in the number. "Hey, Monique, you have company here at the store. Madison and Agent Malone want to see you. Give me a call as soon as you get back. Or call Madison's cellphone."

"Answering machine?" Madison asked.

"Yeah. She'll call; she doesn't stay out late. Do you know where you'll be staying?"

"We hadn't gotten that far yet. I hoped we could see Monique today." Madison looked at Rick. "Are we going to get rooms and stay tonight?"

"Guess we'll have to," he answered. "Maybe she'll call while we're having dinner."

"Let me give you directions to her apartment, just in case," Claudia offered.

"How about if we find rooms, and when you close the store, you join us for dinner?" Rick suggested.

"I can close anytime. Business is slow. Monique has decided to relocate to Knoxville. But I'd bet you already knew that, huh, Madison?"

"We discussed her moving the store. I wasn't aware she'd finalized the idea."

"I'll finish packing this box and close, so I can go home and freshen up. I've located a lot of dust in the back room today. I'm afraid it's all over me." Claudia handed Rick her business card. "My phone is on there, and I'm not far from Monique's apartment. What time and where should I meet you?"

Rick took the card, then suggested, "Since this is your territory, you select the place: anywhere you like. And this evening is on me, Claudia. We can find a hotel nearby."

The three discussed ideas and settled on Lamplight, across the interstate from the Garden Plaza Hotel. Rick remembered that he'd stayed at that hotel in the past and was familiar with the location.

Considering there was a ballgame in town, the only room the Garden Plaza had available was a suite. Rick paid for the reservation, and the two of them proceeded to the penthouse floor.

"What a view!" Madison stood in front of a window overlooking downtown Atlanta. "This is acceptable." She laughed. "This suite is larger than my cottage!"

Rick smiled. "You choose your room; I'll camp in the other."

Madison walked through the door on the left side of the sitting area. "Hey, Rick. Look! I can see Stone Mountain from *my* room."

"I'll take this one." He carried his bag into the smaller room, overlooking the swimming pool ten stories below.

Madison gazed out the window as Rick brought her suitcase in. "Oh, nice. You do have a great view."

"Can we drive out there while we're in the area?" she asked.

"Sure." Rick returned to the sitting area and plopped down at the desk, where he plugged in his laptop and connected to the hotel's Wi-Fi. "We have a few minutes before we need to meet Claudia. After I check my messages, we should head to the lounge. I'd like a beer."

He waited for a response, but didn't hear a peep from Madison's room. Ten messages loaded into his inbox. He scanned them, answering only the necessary ones, and then walked to the door of her room. Madison lay across the bed on top of the sheets and comforter, propped up on two pillows—asleep.

He pulled her door to and went to his room. He showered and shaved, watching the clock to be sure he didn't take too much time.

Finally, with only fifteen minutes left, he walked back to the sitting area. Madison sat at the desk looking at her iPad.

"Good, you're awake," he said.

"Yeah, I drifted off for a few minutes." She turned to look at Rick. "You changed your clothes. Should I?"

"No time now; besides, you didn't need to shower and shave. I did. Shall we go?"

Madison answered by standing and hooking her arm in his.

They spotted Claudia immediately on entering the Lamplight Restaurant. She stood as they approached the table. "Is this OK? I requested a table with the view."

"It's lovely," Madison said.

Rick pulled out the chair closest to the window. "Here you go, Maddie." He sat across from her. "Great choice, Claudia. What's their specialty?"

"Steak! They have it flown in daily from Kansas. I don't order beef anywhere else in the city." Claudia motioned to a waiter standing nearby.

He approached and took their drink orders.

"Sounds good to me," Rick said. "What about you, Maddie?"

"I'm still looking over the menu. I don't want a big steak."

"They have an amazing southwestern salad. That's what I get for lunch most of the time." Claudia pointed to the salad on the menu. "You can get it with or without chicken. They marinate the chicken in a yummy sauce, making it so tender you don't even have to chew."

"Wow, I'll have that and white wine. Thanks for the recommendation."

"I like their house wine. Amazingly, it comes from Kansas too. It's slightly sweet and fruity, pairs well with the southwestern flavor." Claudia shared her knowledge.

"You must eat here often," Rick said.

"I do. The owner is a great friend of mine." Claudia smiled in a way that said he was a special friend.

"Let me guess; he's from Kansas." Madison laughed.

All three laughed. The waiter brought their drinks and asked if they'd like to order. Madison squeezed the lime she'd requested into her water. "I'm ready; how 'bout you, Claudia?"

Claudia said, "We'll have a bottle of your House Special White, please. Two glasses or three?" She looked at Rick.

"I'm good. This draft is excellent." He tipped it up and took a long drink.

As soon as the ladies ordered, Rick said, "Gotta go with that Big K T-bone, medium rare."

"Excellent choice, Sir," the waiter said, as he gathered the menus.

After they had enjoyed their meals and there was still no call from Monique, Claudia shared her concern. She told them she'd taken the liberty of stopping by Monique's apartment, and had noticed the contents of her backpack strewn on the bed. She also advised them that she had some evidence to share.

"This is so unlike her, to go off and not call. I'm worried about her state of mind. Losing the business here, moving to a city she doesn't even know, and this thought that someone saved her after that snake bite. She's obsessed with finding that man!"

Rick studied Claudia's face, noting the fear he saw in her eyes. "We have a suite with a large sitting room. Why don't we all go back up there and talk?" He looked at a full restaurant, with several tables within earshot of their conversation. "Not here."

Claudia fought tears as she nodded.

They left the restaurant, Claudia following to the Garden Plaza.

The plastic bags, latex gloves, and a camera sat on the long table in front of the couch. Rick read the newspaper article for the third time.

"Someone found this little girl and carried her out of the forest. We need to know who that person was. Claudia, what can you tell me about Jewels' husband?"

"Randy was a kind, generous man, and good to Jewels. He gave her anything her heart desired, except the one thing she couldn't have: a baby. Jewels had been injured as a teenager, and was never able to carry a baby. She was pregnant two or three times, but always lost them in her first trimester. I think Randy heard of the child or found her himself, because he resigned from the forestry service and they moved to Florida. That's when I met them. They had Monique, and she was just two years old. Jewels adored her! She bought more dresses than the child could ever wear. I never saw her in the same outfit twice. Randy took a job with the school system as a janitor. And he worked at night, too, as a security guard at the sugar mill. He was never home. Jewels was lonely, and when I met her we became friends quickly! I worked at the library then, so my hours were short, being part-time. We lived across the street from each other. As soon as she saw me drive in, she'd run over and tell me she had supper on and wanted me to come and eat with them. Randy came home to eat, and then get ready to go back out to the mill for his night shift. I don't think he slept much."

"Monique was a lovely baby, happy and full of energy. She was smart, and had been walking since she was seven months..." Claudia stopped mid-sentence.

"How would Jewels know that, if she wasn't with her at that age?" Madison asked.

"She couldn't. Maybe she made things up, to keep me from questioning her."

"I'd like to take these to our lab to see what they'll discover," Rick said.

"Yes, Monique wanted you to have them. We used gloves to handle them." Claudia folded her arms. "I just wish I knew where she is."

"She'll show up; she's not going to do anything stupid. Monique is intelligent," Rick said. "Let's not jump to conclusions."

Claudia left the hotel around ten. Rick walked with her to her car. When he returned, he found a note taped to his door. *Getting my shower and going to sleep. Goodnight, Rick.*

Rick pulled up records of all forestry employees fitting the time frame of the plane crash. The names Randy Morell, Randal Morrel, and R. More didn't come up. Next, he tried facial recognition on the small family photo Claudia had supplied. He got a hit: Morris Randall. The facial structure matched, and the eyes, but Randall had a mustache and goatee—*simple enough to get rid of.*

Randall had an outstanding warrant, now expired, but it gave Rick reason to fear the worst. Had the ranger discovered the child and kept her? Did he find the plane and see that her parents were dead? Why else would he not report the crash site? And if his wife couldn't carry a baby, it made perfect sense. The child would never know, at her young age. But evidently, his wife had a conscience. Even though she'd fallen in love with the toddler and agreed to go along with the scheme, Jewels had felt remorse.

*That explains the lockbox and the family Bible.* She wanted Monique to know who she was, and that she might still have a family, if something happened to her and her husband. Jewels was a sweet woman, but she was weak. Randall worked two jobs to give her a real life, but didn't spend much time helping raise the child. *How will Monique handle this news?*

# 10

Monique noticed the light of her answering machine flashing when she entered her apartment. She listened to Claudia's message. *Hmm, too late to call tonight. I'll get some sleep and call them in the morning.*

She woke to the full sun shining on her face. She hadn't intended to sleep late, but had neglected to set her alarm. As soon as her feet hit the floor, her home phone rang.

"Good morning, Claudia. I got your message after midnight. I was going to call you as soon as I woke up. I didn't set my alarm."

"I'm on my way to the Garden Plaza Hotel now. Rick and Madison are there. Get dressed and join us for breakfast." Claudia's voice sounded urgent. Meeting for breakfast was not a request.

"Sure, I'll get there as quickly as I can." She hung up the receiver guiltily. *I should have called her last night. She probably didn't even sleep.*

Madison met Claudia at the front of the restaurant, in the lobby of the Plaza. "Good morning, Claudia. Get any sleep?"

"Not much, but I got an answer when I called Monique's phone this morning. She's meeting us here as soon as she can. Says she got in after midnight last night."

"Oh, good. I know you're relieved. I'm glad nothing happened to her. Did she say where she'd been?"

"I didn't give her a chance; I was too upset. I just told her to meet us."

"We have a table back there," Madison pointed toward the windows on the outer wall of the restaurant. "Rick is downing his third cup of coffee. He did some late-night research."

Rick filled Claudia in on what he'd discovered about Randy, Morris Randall, and that he had an arrest warrant for racketeering. "Fine fellow, huh?"

"Oh, my. He was good to Jewels and Monique, I would never have believed he'd be a criminal. Do you intend to tell Monique?"

"Not right away, but I will eventually. Monique deserves to know the truth," Madison answered for Rick.

He looked at Maddie, reaching out to stroked her cheek. "I agree. She deserves to know; everyone needs to know who they are, and where they belong."

Madison's eyes locked on to Rick's gaze. For a moment, there were no others in the room, except the two of them. Madison felt her cheeks burn; she looked away.

Claudia stood, waving toward the entrance of the restaurant. Monique made her way to their table.

"Don't you *ever* give me a scare like that again, Girl—or I won't work for you!" She pulled Monique into a hug.

Madison smiled at the small woman she had recently befriended. "Glad to see you, Monique. You have a wonderful friend, here."

"Claudia is more like family. She looks out for me."

During breakfast, there was no discussion of anything Rick discovered. Monique apologized for worrying everyone. She avoided secrets, too; not one word was spoken about where she'd been.

Pleasantries covered, Rick insisted they all go to Stone Mountain before the sun was high and the temperature elevated.

"I love Stone Mountain. I've been there several times for the laser light show. Especially for the fourth of July; that's a fantastic celebration," Monique declared.

"Does this mean I don't need to open the store today?" Claudia asked.

They all laughed.

Rick drove east out of Atlanta, toward the lone mountain. Claudia sat in the front with Monique, and Madison in the back.

"What pushed you over the edge with your decision to relocate to Knoxville?" Madison asked.

"It just occurred to me that I should. I love the proximity to the mountains, UT is a larger university, and some other things, including Diane. I can't wait to surprise her with my news."

"How far do you think they'll hike?" Rick asked.

"I doubt if they'll even see Virginia." Monique laughed. "I know Steve and Clark want to make it to Roan Mountain, at least. But who knows?"

"Oh, look," Madison pointed out the front windshield, "there's Stone Mountain!"

Once Rick located a parking spot, the four walked to the ticket booth. Monique explained that it was best to go up on the Skyride, and walk down the trail. Madison agreed. She stepped ahead of Rick to purchase the tickets.

"Do all you ladies have suitable walking shoes on?" he asked.

They all did, fortunately. Soon they were headed for the summit on the Skyride, which takes you past the mountain's Confederate Memorial Carving. The massive carving depicts three Confederate Civil War leaders: President Jefferson Davis, General Thomas J. "Stonewall" Jackson, and General Robert E. Lee.

"Wow, that's huge!" Madison commented. "I've read that the workers had a picnic up there—on the back of one of the horses, I think it was."

"Yes, and when you walk around reading all the signs they have posted, there's one with more stories like that. It's for sure some accomplishment," Claudia added.

Once they reached the top, the group walked across the large, bald rock face to the top of the mountain. The view was great due to the clean air toward Atlanta. Monique and Claudia pointed out landmarks of the city.

The 360-degree panoramic view was amazing to Madison. "It's funny; no higher than this stone hill is, you can see forever!"

"Only because the air is clean today. I've been here sometimes when you can't even see Atlanta, except that you know it's somewhere in the thick soup of pollution, hanging like a cloud to the west," Claudia said.

Monique led them to the hiking trail, which descended a path mingling with white pines and large boulders. "Some of these rocks have dates and names carved into them. Once I found one that is believed to have been carved by a Civil War Soldier."

"I've heard of that. Do you think you can find it again?" Claudia asked.

"I'll watch for it, but it was a long time ago, and the people I was with knew just where to find it. It seems to me that we walked off the trail a short distance. I doubt I can find it," Monique said.

The walk gave Madison an opportunity to question Monique about her dad. Monique admitted that she seldom saw him, except when on vacation.

"He made sure we always went on a nice vacation. One summer, we went to Yellowstone, Yosemite, and the Grand Canyon. It took about five weeks," she recalled.

"Is that why your dad worked two jobs?" Rick asked.

"I suppose." Monique continued discussing selected summers she'd particularly enjoyed. "One year, we drove a motorhome to Mexico City, and then all the way to the beach on the west side. We were gone all summer long. We left the motorhome in Mexico City, then flew back to West Palm Beach. Dad said he'd had his fill of camping and driving."

Rick glanced at Madison. "How old were you, Monique?"

"Thirteen, I think... Yes, I was, because I was worried I'd be late starting my freshman year in high school. He assured me that was one more plus for flying home."

"You had a good childhood?" Rick questioned.

"Yeah, I did. Why are you asking me about Dad now?"

"Was he a boater?"

"No, he didn't care for them. But he won a bass boat at the company dinner. The sugar company gave away fantastic prizes. Anyway, since he had one, he and Mom took up fishing. They had only been out a few times when the accident took them."

Monique had never talked about the death of her folks. Madison felt compelled to know the details now. "Just what *did* happen?"

She was silent; it became evident Monique was not ready to talk about their accident.

Claudia spoke up, telling this part of the sad story. "Jewels was the one who enjoyed fishing. She'd caught a five-pound bass just the week before, and wanted to go back to the same area. She hoped that if Randy caught one, he'd feel the same excitement."

She took Monique's hand. "Jewels called me that morning. It was around five a.m. She sounded excited, because she'd gotten Randy a new Shimano reel for his birthday. He always told her that his old reel was no good. She'd paid a lot of money for it, and bought it at Roland Martin's Marina—that's where they kept their boat."

"Later that morning, I was at the store when the call came in. The Clewiston Police Department wanted to speak to Monique. She wasn't there. I pushed the issue, and they told me her folks were dead, that their boat exploded. They were still searching for the bodies at that time."

"And it was a new boat," Rick stated. "Didn't they find that a little odd?"

"Naturally, I questioned the situation and asked to speak with the chief of police. He was on the scene, so he called me back that night. He couldn't talk about the ongoing investigation, but assured me they would be thorough. It was three days before they recovered the bodies. Monique and I were down there by then. The authorities didn't find any signs of foul play. They determined that the motor hadn't been tampered with."

"I'll follow up with someone I know in the area. It might have been just an accident," Rick said. But he didn't sound convinced.

Monique was quiet on the return trip to Atlanta. Madison felt sad that the worst news was still to come. She told Rick she thought he should tell Monique what he knew. If Randy was an alias, she deserved the truth. Rick agreed. He suggested they follow Monique to her apartment.

Claudia elected to go work at the store, not wanting to know all the stuff Rick had learned. She told Monique she had some more things to ready for the sale on Monday. Monique understood, but had no idea of Claudia's ulterior motive for leaving.

Monique asked them to have a seat while she got bottles of water for the three of them. "I know Claudia gave you the contents of the lockbox. Rick, I want you to see what you can find out. Right or wrong, it's time I know—once and for all."

Rick opened his laptop. "Monique, are you ready for some devastating news?"

"Already?" Monique stood directly in front of him.

"I'm afraid so. Sit down, please," he murmured.

Monique sat. Rick first showed her a photo of Morris Randall. She nodded, confirming he was her dad. Rick showed her the name; tears welled up, and she couldn't speak. He continued opening pages in the file, revealing the outstanding warrant and details of her father's ties to Chicago and the Mob.

Suddenly Monique sat forward, touching a photo. "That's Uncle Ralph. The motorhome we drove to Mexico belonged to him."

*Ralph Spencer, deceased.* The file revealed *he was one of the top members of the Chicago connection.* Spencer *died in Juarez, shot by Mexican Police* while attempting to cross into the USA, in the motorhome Monique and her family drove to the resort near Guadalajara.

"So, it was five years after you went to Mexico that your folks died?" Rick asked.

"No, they died after I graduated college: ten years later." Monique stood up. "This is enough for now, Rick. Take the items, find out what you can. Was my mom real, or was she a made-up person too?" She cried.

Madison wrapped her in a hug. ""Come on Monique; you've had enough. Don't even think about who they were; think of how much they loved you. That's all that's important. Jewels loved you with all her heart. Never doubt that!" She guided Monique to the bedroom.

An hour later, Rick and Madison drove to their hotel, having said good-bye to Monique, and planning to return to Knoxville the next morning.

# 11

From Knoxville, Madison drove to Cold Creek, and Rick headed to the Tennessee Bureau of Investigations Lab to have the lockbox items analyzed. He promised to share the info with Madison as soon as he had answers.

A light rain fell as Madison pulled into her driveway at the cottage. She sat in her vehicle, studying her traditional cottage. How to add more space without taking away from the architecture? What if she built a garage with a loft? That would give her storage, at least. *Yes, a detached garage! I'll talk to Henry about that.*

She noticed the door of the sheriff's office stood open, so she opened the car door and dashed to the building next to her property.

"Hey, Maddie. How did things go in Atlanta?" Sheriff Drew Perry sat behind his desk.

"We just managed to open another can of worms. That poor girl is worse off than I was, not knowing who her real parents are." She dragged a seat close to the desk and set it backward, leaning on the back. "Rick is at the lab now, having the items combed for clues. It seems Monique was in a plane crash that killed her folks. The person who found her got his hands on fake adoption papers. Such a cover-up, but hopefully there was no murder involved."

"Wow, you're like a magnet to confusion, aren't you?"

"Looks that way." She blew out a long breath. "Poor Monique—she's a sweet girl, and has a lot going for her. But now she has to erase everything she thought she knew about her life."

"Sounds familiar," Perry said, putting down the pen. "Let's go get some lunch.

I'll bet you haven't eaten today."

"Oh, yeah? Rick can't pass up a Cracker Barrel. We left our hotel early, but stopped in Chattanooga to eat about 8:30. Thanks anyway. I'm going to go out and talk to Henry about a project. I'm thinking of adding a detached garage, next to the cottage."

"You could use the space. Detached, with a breezeway between would look nice, and I don't think it would affect the historical aspect, either. But Henry will know. He's our go-to historian when Jess is out of town." Perry stuffed the papers in his drawer and stood up. "When is Jess coming home? Any idea?"

Madison walked to the door with him. "In the next couple of days, I'd guess."

She waved goodbye to the sheriff and walked home, then phoned Holly to see if Henry was busy. Holly invited Madison to come out and have supper with them in an hour. She called it a picnic on the back porch, because that's what the boys wanted.

When Madison's SUV rumbled across the cattle guard, she saw Bud and Bear racing toward her from the hillside. She parked in front of Holly's steps and waited for the dogs. Bud leaped into her arms, nearly knocking her off her feet. Bear sat waiting for her to pet him. She scolded Bud, but only a little. She understood that he'd missed her the two days she'd been away. But he still needed to remember his manners.

Holly came out the front door, with the twins following. Hugh came down the steps to give Madison a hug. Harry was shy, and clung to his momma's side.

"They're completely different, aren't they?" Madison lifted Hugh onto her hip and walked up the steps. "You better come and hug me, Harry," she said, teasing him.

He hugged Holly's leg tighter, hiding his face in her apron.

"OK, Hugh gets both boxes of raisins." She set the taller twin down and reached into her purse, pulled out small red boxes. She gave them to Hugh. Immediately he handed one to his brother. "Oh, you're such a good boy!"

"Don't open those now, boys. Supper is on the picnic table out back. Scoot, both of you, and wash your hands. Daddy will beat you to the table and eat all the food." Holly laughed.

"Don't scare them like that, Holly!" They both laughed.

Henry joined them at the table in the shade of the back deck. They all joined hands, and Hugh said a short prayer. Then Holly passed the sandwich tray while Henry filled glasses from the pitcher of lemonade. Harry reached for a bowl of homemade potato chips.

"You are such an organized family: very efficient and proper. I'm impressed, Henry. I know you're behind this."

"Thanks, Maddie. My mom was a proper lady, and she taught, or *tried*, to teach us manners. It wasn't until our boys were born that I realized how important those manners are. Children are a gift from God. We should instill his goodness in them, and pray they learn sooner than their dad."

Holly placed her hand on her husband's and smiled sweetly at him. "I haven't told her. I wanted you to do that, Henry."

"Really? OK, you're just in time to help us dig potatoes, Maddie."

"No! Not that! You know what I mean." Holly tightened her lips and shook her head at Henry.

"I know, Honey. I was just teasing." He stood up and wrapped his arms around Holly's shoulders, "My loving wife is going to add another blessing to our family in time for Christmas. We are praying for a girl, so that we can name her Mattie, M-A-T-T-I-E, after her Aunt Maddie." He sat down, picking up his sandwich.

"Holly! That's wonderful! Congratulations, you two! Oh, that's such good news! I don't know anyone who deserves a little daughter more than you and Henry."

"And we 'zerv a sissy!" Harry said, and then turned his face away from Madison.

"Yes you do, Harry! And you too, Hugh. But I don't know about the name."

"No arguing about that! It's a done deal, if it's a girl," Holly said.

"We think my mom is coming home to spend a couple of months with us at that time." Henry sounded proud of that news, too.

Madison waited until Henry finished eating before she mentioned the garage. But when she did, he was all for the idea. He promised to sketch a plan for her approval and get it to her in a day or two. He kissed both boys on the forehead, and then hugged Holly and Madison before he headed back to the field to plow the "tater" patch before dark.

"I'm so happy for you, Holly. Henry has changed—or maybe I just never gave him a chance. I thought he was a bad person when we were in school. I'm sorry I ever gave him an ill thought."

"No, you were right, to a point. Henry drank a lot when he was young. He was intimidated by his dad, and hated life itself. I guess I was the only person who saw through his act. But he was even mean to me when he was drunk. Thank God, he had the strength to recover from his illness. I'm proud of him."

\* \* \*

Madison drove back to town before the sun set. Bud sat in the seat next to her. She quickly ran inside her cottage to change clothes and shoes. That was the signal Bud knew meant they were going for a run. The temperature dropped with the sun, and Madison headed up the old trail she and Bud had run for years. It felt good, getting back into her old territory. Cold Creek was home, and she loved being here.

One of her favorite spots to view the setting sun was high above Cold Creek, at the edge of the Cherokee National Forest. And during daylight saving time, she could still make the run downhill before total darkness. Today, the colors were like an artist's canvas, done in hues of pink, coral, and purple.

Later into the evening, after Madison had fallen asleep, a text message buzz roused her. Thinking it might be Jess and Shirley, she opened it. The message was from Rick: *meet me in Knoxville as early as possible, if you want to go back on the trail with me. We have some action.*

*What does that mean?* She wondered. She tried to go back to sleep, but it was no use She hit # 2 on her emergency call list.

In a matter of seconds, Rick's voice answered, "I hated to wake you, but I thought you would want to go with me on this."

"Tell me more."

"We've got a body; it's the woman from Tennessee, so I have to go."

"Where did they find her?"

"Near the place where we camped with the hikers. Too near; Monique was lucky."

"Does she know?"

"I haven't called her—and don't *you*, either!" he stressed.

"No, I won't. Can I bring Bud?"

"Yes, you can bring our mutt-child. I know Bud misses you, and I miss him. I'll get him a PD vest and badge. Might as well get you one, too. See you in the morning."

"See you in two hours." Madison clicked off her phone. She wrote a message for Jess, in case they returned before she talked to them. She also wrote one for the sheriff. Bud delivered the note to Shirley and Jess's porch. He knew where to put it. When he returned, Madison had their things in her vehicle. She hooked Bud into his seatbelt beside her and drove toward I-26.

Bud showed his excitement when she merged onto the four-lane highway, recognizing this was a long trip. He watched out the front windshield, repeatedly glancing back at Madison. She swore he could smile as well as most humans, and this was a long and happy expression of gratitude.

"I'm glad Rick requested you come this trip." Madison petted Bud's head lightly. His tail slapped against the leather seat.

After an hour of watching the lights of the big rigs and occasional other traffic, he settled into nap mode, sleeping the rest of the way to Rick's apartment.

# 12

Claudia answered her phone while still in the shower, because she saw that it was Monique. "Hey, how are you this morning?"

"I'm OK. That was a lot to take in, but I can't say anything surprises me anymore." She was silent for a moment. "When I got my Mini Cooper, you said you'd always wanted one. Do you still feel that way?" Monique asked.

"I love your Mini; why do you ask?"

"I want to change vehicles, and thought I'd give you first chance at it. I want an SUV. Going with Madison in hers made me realize I need something bigger."

"If you're serious, yes. I'd have to get a loan, but I'm good for it. I can always sell my Toyota."

"I'm heading to the bank now. I'll have it put in your name; it's yours. No money needs to change hands. Consider it your paycheck, until I get the store set up in Knoxville. I hoped you might consider relocating with me. It's closer to your granddaughter in Kentucky," she coaxed.

"I wanted you to ask me, but I'd never have invited myself. Yes, I've always wanted to move closer to my baby and grandbaby. Knoxville is perfect! But I can't accept your Mini. Not without paying you something."

"I just told you, you won't get paid anymore until maybe fall. I feel lucky just to have you. It's the least I can do. Don't look a gift horse in the mouth." Monique laughed and hung up.

She left the bank and caught the downtown bus to the Subaru dealership.

One of the salesmen showed her the new models, but then she spotted one over in the used section.

"How 'bout that dark green one, over there?"

"I don't have any authority to deal with the used vehicles..."

"Thanks for your time. I'm going to talk to someone about the used one."

Monique walked into the air-conditioned building with USED but Not ABUSED on the window. She noticed three cubicles, and went over to a man reading a brochure. The others talked on the phone with their feet propped up.

"Can you show me that green Subaru out there?"

He jumped to his feet, nearly flipping the desk over. "Yes, Ma'am, I sure can. Just let me get the key. My name is Jimmy." He sounded nervous, and dropped the key the instant he took it off the hook next to a bulletin board in the inner office.

"I'm Monique. Thanks for helping me, Jimmy. I had a Mini Cooper, but thought an SUV might be more my style."

They walked to the far side of the parking area. "This just came in yesterday, and it hasn't even been cleaned up yet. I looked it over myself, thinking I might like it, but I don't need a four-wheel drive. I never go out of town, just to school and work."

"Isn't it an *all*-wheel drive?" Monique asked.

"Yeah, that's what I meant to say."

"What year is it?" she asked.

Jimmy looked at the key tab and read off the information written there. "That's all I know right now. Stu, um Stewart, brought it in. You can talk to him, if you want to know anything more about it."

"No, I'll let you tell me all you can, since you've already seen it. Can we take a test drive?"

"Yeah, I think so. I'll call the office and ask." He turned his head away slightly, then said, "You're my first customer. I just started work here two days ago. Please give me a chance to get up my nerve."

"You're fine, Jimmy. Your secret is safe with me. Make that call, now."

He nodded and punched in some numbers. Then he smiled and handed her the key. Monique walked to the driver's side, and Jimmy got into the passenger's side. They rode on the back roads toward the stadium and all around the airport and back to the sales office.

"If you were going to move to the mountains, would you buy this vehicle?" she asked.

Jimmy wiped sweat from his brow. "Yeah, I would. It's low mileage, and still has the extended warranty; it was sold here, just two years ago. That's not many miles for a two-year-old vehicle. You'd be getting a nice ride. When I drove it yesterday, I tried out the four-wheel drive on a dirt road with some steep hills. It did great! But please, don't tell anyone." He smiled. "I'll let you in on another secret; they'll take less than sticker price if you pay cash."

"Thank you. Will you write the contract?" She exited the vehicle and handed the key back. "Did I see a coffee machine in the office?"

"Yes, help yourself. I do know how to write a contract, so I'll get right to it. Thank you, Ms. Monique, I can only hope all my sales will be this smooth." He opened the door for her and followed her into the air-conditioned office.

The other two salesmen hung up their phones when he walked to his desk, tossing the key into the air and catching it with one hand. He showed a new air of authority as he settled into writing the contract.

Monique returned to Jimmy's desk with a steaming cup of coffee. She winked as she sat down, nodding toward Jimmy's coworkers. "They were too full of themselves when I came in; that's why I came to your desk. Keep up your helpful attitude, and you'll go far."

"You ready to make an offer?" He turned the proposal for her to see.

"You think they'll take that?" She had expected a higher price tag.

"Yes, Ma'am. I'd bet you money on it."

Jimmy led her to the sales manager's office, at the end of a short hallway. "Thomas, give Ms. Morrel your full cooperation, will you?"

"Jimmy, I always cooperate with ladies. Come in, Ms. Morrel."

Jimmy returned to his desk in the front office.

In just a few minutes, Monique returned with paperwork in hand and thanked Jimmy for his help. She had opted to forego the cleanup of the vehicle, since she was ready to hit the mountain.

# 13

After a stop at her insurance office and a few minutes at her apartment, Monique was back on the road, heading north. She had driven for two hours before she turned up a small county road beside a sign reading *Cherokee National Forest Access*. The road was narrow and winding, completely unfamiliar. She ran her finger along the highlighted line on the map she'd printed from the Georgia DOT website.

"That must be the one." She pulled onto a gravel side road, studied the map again, and decided she was on the right path.

The gravel road soon became steep, and she was thankful for her all-wheel drive keeping the tires from spinning. This climb continued for nearly forty-five minutes. Finally, she rounded a curve and crested the top of the mountain. For as far as the eye could see, there was a clear view of mountaintops, ridges, and forest. She stopped for a minute to soak in its beauty.

She flipped the map over and read the notes she had scribbled on the back. *Two and a quarter miles along ridge road. Turn left into thickly wooded valley, onto a primitive road, then travel half a mile; turn right at the fork, and cross Moccasin Creek.*

She continued, watching her odometer carefully. Two point five *miles...there it is. Take a left turn onto the first road—more like this* used to be a road. The Subaru slipped in the soft soil. "This could get scary. Hope I can get back out of here," She spoke aloud, but kept going.

She followed the detailed map. Every turn was just as the notes said it would be. Monique felt secure in that at least the map was accurate. *Now if I just end up on the mountain I think this is going to be, it will all be OK, and worth the trouble.*

Monique had copied the old directions onto the map from a journal made by a group of bikers who used this area to ride their trial bikes, practicing for international competition. She knew one of the bikers while she was in college. *Thank goodness I kept my notes.* She'd written an article about the trials competition. The forestry service had been forced to stop the riders from coming here, because—as always—a good thing was abused by the few who had no regard for the preservation of the forest. Some dirt bikers had tried to turn it into a hill climbing competition area. In the process, they had destroyed acres of vegetation and small trees. To add insult to injury, they left a campfire burning and scorched nearly a thousand acres of woodland a few years back. The forest service made the territory off limits to all motorized vehicles as a result.

When she reached the top, Monique realized she was right where she wanted to be, on the southeast side of the AT, within a mile of the area where the hidden valley is supposed to be. *No one approaches from this side. I''s too hard to get to, and Vic would have no reason to look here.* Besides, she didn't have to go through any gates, and hadn't seen any signs posting the land.

The day was nearly gone, so Monique backed her SUV into the thick underbrush, hoping to conceal it from anyone who might happen along the trail. In the morning, she would do some hiking to familiarize herself with the area. She wanted to know her way in and out, in case she had to leave in a hurry.

As darkness fell, the night air grew chilly, so she built a small fire. She made notes of poetry that came to mind. After a couple of hours, she doused the fire. She wouldn't need it in the morning.

The forest grew loud with nightlife. The screech of an owl and crickets dominated, but mingled among the familiar sounds, there was one distinctly unfamiliar. Monique lay still, almost breathless. Her heart pounded as she raised up just slightly to peek out the side window of her SUV. It was too dark; she couldn't see anything. Nothing moved—or at least nothing she could see, anyway. The sound stopped, and she couldn't be sure what she'd heard. A flash of light in the distance made her think it might have been thunder. Before she drifted into a deep sleep, rain fell softly on the roof of her Forester. *Ah, this is perfect.*

No haunting dreams interrupted her rest. Her new vehicle's seats would lay flat, far better than sleeping in a tent in the rain. She liked her choice in this investment.

She readied herself for a hike and set out in the morning sun. Monique thought if she walked straight north, she should encounter the AT before long. She was right; there were the markings along the trail, less than 500 yards from her camp. "Should I go north or south?" She closed her eyes as if to tune in her internal directional gyro, then continued to talk to herself quietly. South, I think; I feel like I'm above the hidden valley. Oh well, we shall soon see."

Monique heard the cry of the pileated woodpecker. He had gotten her into trouble weeks earlier. She watched him flutter from tree to tree, in search of food. The large bird exhibits an unmistakable flight pattern; it's almost like the breaststroke of a swimmer. She ventured closer, recognizing the enormous rocks up the hill. Indeed, she was back at the place where her friends had camped while she was missing.

Monique sat on a stone and sketched the woodpecker. "You, my friend, have to be one of my collection. You're loud, and draw attention to yourself, so you need to be on a birthday card." She spoke as if he were listening. After several views, satisfied with her drawings, she folded the sketchbook closed and stuck it into her backpack. Relocating her store over the summer would be perfect timing for her new line of greeting cards. The more she thought about it, the more positive she felt in her decision.

Also, she felt that if the hidden valley existed, she could surely find it. The underbrush thickened, and evergreen trees towered over the path to her left. She looked closely for signs of anything out of the ordinary. Then she found a few crude chiseled steps. Monique pushed a branch out of her way and dropped to her knees. There before her was the valley. The sun's rays peeked over the trees like a lighted finger pointing the way. She'd never seen it from above, but she remembered being down there looking up. She knew a kind, blue-eyed man lived in the valley, and she had to speak with him.

*Are you down there, or somewhere on this rocky ledge? What must I do to get you to show yourself?* She realized there was a strange sensation in the pit of her stomach: a mixture of fear and excitement battled within. Her curiosity soon got the best of her. She had to climb down there.

There was some semblance of a trail from long ago, obviously not used recently. *There must be another way.* She nearly fell, but managed to catch herself on a branch of laurel. At that moment, she noticed there was a ledge just below her. She placed one foot on it at a time, slowly testing each step to be sure it didn't slide. Finally, she was securely on the ledge. She sat down and looked for her next move.

A cool breeze blew up the face of the rock. She lay on her stomach and slid to the edge, looking over. Below was a waterfall, spewing out between the rocks and falling into the valley. But she could see no way to get down from her position. She pulled herself back against the wall of the ledge. On either side grew strongly rooted laurel bushes. Was it possible to climb among the branches? She had to try, or sit there until someone threw her a line. The very thought made her laugh out loud.

The first move scared her, but she held on tightly and pulled her weight to the next bush. The next one she had to climb upward. Her arms trembled, but she forced herself on. This tiring ordeal was taking a toll on her physically as well as mentally. Even if she did make it down to the floor of the valley, how on earth was she going to get out?

She closed her eyes tightly, forcing tears and sweat to roll down her face. Her hand reached for the next branch. She had to stretch...no, still out of her grasp. She wedged her left foot into a fork in the laurel and lunged, catching the branch—but it ripped from the soil and fell, leaving her hanging by one leg, dangling over the side of the cliff. She held her breath, waiting for her foot to slip; she'd plunge to her death on the rocks below if it did. But her boot stuck in the fork, and she tried to reach up, grasping for the laurel holding her. She wasn't strong enough; her weight tugged, and her foot slipped slightly. With all the strength she could gather, she folded her body up, grabbing her left leg, and pulled herself back to the original spot in the bush.

Still inverted, but at least she was hanging on with both hands again. Her boot tightly wedged, she managed to slip the right leg over the branch next to the fork. That move released the weight from the fork and freed her foot. She felt the skin on the back of her right knee scrape away, leaving an intense burning sensation where it clung to the branch. Her arms burned. All of her muscles ached, but she righted herself. Above her head, she spotted a lonely pine tree. If she could reach its branches, she might be able to climb up or down, one or the other.

The laurel beside her was larger, and enticed her to move into its safety. From there she dropped onto a thick pine limb. She slid toward the trunk of the pine and scaled down the branches, tearing even more skin from her knees and the inside of her arms, hugging the rough bark as she slid. The pine limbs were her savior, leading her to the floor of the valley. The final drop put her into the water at the base of the falls.

To Monique's surprise, the pool was deep. She went all the way under the water. She surfaced and lay on her back floating for a few minutes, taking inventory of her parts to be sure they were all attached. As much pain as she felt, she knew she had to be alive; death wasn't supposed to hurt. And she was hurting all over!

On the bank of the pool, she opened her backpack. Naturally, her sketchbook was wet. She laid it out on a rock to dry flat. Maybe she could salvage some of her sketches.

She sat still, listening to the sound of the waterfall. The valley felt peaceful. Monique closed her eyes; she remembered the sounds and the smells. Something was coming back to her. A voice, deep but not gruff. Hard as she tried, she could remember nothing else.

Her hair dripped, so she pulled the ponytail holder out to let it dry in the sun. She dreaded looking at the scrapes on her legs, but they didn't hurt so much now. She straightened her right leg out to see. It was scratched, but not bleeding. Then she looked at the other. Not so lucky with that one; there were deep gouges in her calf. She pulled out some splinters of bark. That caused the pain to return with a vengeance. Monique unlaced her hiking boots and pulled them off, along with her socks. She slipped her legs into the water and scrubbed away remnants of laurel branches and pine tar. She lay back on the flat rock; tears slid into her hair. *Why am I even here? I don't know who I am, why must I try to find out who he is?*

The sun beat down on her skin, recharging some of the energy she had expelled. She closed her eyes, shielding them with her forearm. In a moment, she heard a voice. Or was she dreaming? Her arm dropped away, revealing the silhouette of a tall figure standing over her.

"Miss Monique, do you have a death wish, or what?"

Shutting her eyes again, she thought she must be dreaming; it was *that* voice, the one she heard in her memory. She opened her eyes again; the man was still there, but kneeling, hand outstretched. She grasped it and let him pull her to a sitting position.

"I know… I remember… It's you. I'm not crazy, I was not dreaming. I remember your face."

"What about my name?"

No response.

"I'm Michael, Michael Ross. Now do you remember?"

She didn't.

"Well, good. At least I know part of the herbs worked."

"You saved me. From the snake. You saved my life, didn't you?" Monique's fuzziness was clearing.

"Yes, I knew your friends couldn't get you to a hospital in time. I'm sorry I had to leave you to face their questions."

"Why? You're here again."

"I live here; what's your excuse? Are you suicidal? How many times must one man save you?"

Thunder sounded in the distance. "Come on, by the time I can hear the thunder rain is already on me." He pulled her to her feet.

81

She winced and turned her calf to see blood running all the way to her ankle. Michael lifted her into his arms.

"My pack, my sketchbook, let me..."

He swooped her down to let her capture the items, then turned, running toward the rock cliff. Rain pelted hard against her face. "Ouch!" she said.

Just inside a dark cave, Michael set her on her feet. "Can you walk?"

"Yeah."

"Come, I need to put something on that cut. You clean it in the water?"

She nodded.

"Good work. That's why it's bleeding so much. It will clot now."

She felt his fingers mash something into the cut. It stopped hurting, too. "Are you a doctor or medicine man?"

"Both."

Thunder cracked, striking a pine tree right outside his hideout. "That's all pines do, draw lightning. That's why I cleared you away so quickly. I watch them go up in sparks like fireworks," he laughed.

Monique stared at Michael Ross. His black hair glistened even in the dim light of the cave. Dark eyelashes outlined sky-blue eyes. His smile, perfect like a toothpaste ad, warmed his hairless face, smooth and soft to her touch. "Oh, I'm sorry, I'm half asleep. I thought I was dreaming." She backed away, nearly stumbling.

"That's all right."

She thought he was blushing. "Why are you here? You're obviously well educated. You're handsome, you're sweet. Why the heck are you hiding in this cave?"

"None of your business. And I don't mean to sound rude. It's my choice."

"Are you American Indian?"

"Cherokee, but only one quarter."

"Michael Ross... Why is that familiar?" She asked.

"Maybe, John Michael Ross?"

"Yes, that's it. Is that why you're here?"

"It was the home of my ancestors. Now it is my home."

The rain stopped as suddenly as it had begun. Monique stepped into the sun. "I'm wet and cold; this feels better."

Michael followed her and took the sketchbook from her hand. "You're a real artist."

"Thank you. I sketch the pictures for a line of greeting cards in my store."

"I remember you talking about your store."

"I don't remember our conversations. But I'm thankful for what you did."

"Where are your friends?"

"They continued the hike. I wanted to stay here. I'm looking for a flower, pink lady slippers. Have you seen them?"

Michael looked toward the east end of the valley, a sheer cliff face. "Yes, over there among the rocks, below those hemlocks. But you'll never be able to climb to them."

"I have to." She gazed in the direction Michael looked.

"What are you looking for, Monique?"

"This is a beautiful place. How did you find it?" She peered at the steep walls of rock. The sweet smell of grass wafted to her nose. The sound of birds singing and the soft tumbling of the water played like music in her ears.

"My great-grandfather brought me here as a child. He was the son of John Ross, the Chief of the Cherokee people." Michael's shoulders squared, holding his head high.

"*The* John Ross?! You're descended from *that* John Ross?" Monique grasped his arm.

"You've heard of him?" Michael answered.

"Greg, our teacher and one of the hikers, told us all about him. He was a great leader. Now my friends have gone on, and I came to find you because I need your help."

"No, you don't need my help. No one needs me." A sadness settled on his face. "I first saw you when you at the beginning of the trail. You took photographs around a big log. I saw your face, and the memory of a patient flooded back to my mind like a tidal wave. You looked just like her—only you were full of life and happy. She was suicidal, and died at my hands." Michael hung his head. "I couldn't get your face out of my mind. I couldn't sleep; just kept wondering who you were. When I saw you on the rocks, and you fell, I knew I was the only one who could save you."

"You *did* save me, so you're not a failure! I was your second chance, and you did it. You're a doctor. You proved that!"

Michael couldn't look her in the eyes. He turned away. "I was, once."

"And you can be again. Whatever it takes, you've still got it. I needed you, and you were there for me. Give yourself some credit. You're still a Doctor. People out there still need you. You've hidden from the world long enough."

Michael took a couple of steps back. "Why are you here? I mean, before the snakebite and your fall, why did you come to this mountain?"

"We were hiking the Appalachian Trail. It passes right through here. Or hadn't you noticed?"

He flashed her a silly grin and laughed. "Yeah, I saw."

"You have it all here. What more could you need?" she asked.

"A little privacy would be nice." Michael's look was stern.

"Well, you can forget that. Now that the park rangers know about it, the valley isn't hidden anymore. I guess that's my fault," she admitted.

"What do you mean? The ranger named Vic knows about this valley. I've had to hide from him more than once."

"You mean, before I came here?"

"Yeah. Long before, and again last night."

"Are you serious?"

"And a short chubby guy, too. They carried something to the burial cave over on the other side the valley."

"Burial cave?" She stopped. "You mean dead *people?*"

"Not just people, *my* people. The Cherokee used it before white men ran them out of their homeland. It's sacred ground. I don't go near it."

"And then they left?"

"Yeah, and it was dark and raining. I nearly froze waiting for them to leave."

"Michael, why didn't you tell someone?"

"Who? He's one of the head rangers. Who would I tell?"

Monique thought about the situation for a while. "Two women hikers are missing. One from Tennessee, and one from Virginia. Could they have been carrying a body?"

Michael laughed. "You've watched too much television. My guess is they were poaching."

"Where better to hide a body than in a burial ground?" Monique popped her fist on her hip. "And I don't watch TV. I read and write, besides my sketching."

"You can tell your friends, the TBI agent and his lady friend. Maybe they'll find something on him, but don't bring them into my valley." His voice sounded stern again.

"What if the two women are in that cave? Do they deserve that? Does their family deserve the pain of not knowing what happened to them?" Monique fired back at him.

"I'll show you the path out. You need to leave." Michael pulled on her arm, leading her toward the waterfall.

She saw where the small ledge had a trail angling up the side of the bushes, further north than where she'd made her way down. She stood, looking up and then back at the valley. Michael turned his back and walked away from her sight.

Finally, she climbed the steep stone pathway and went back to where she was parked. She took out her sketchpad, drawing Michael's face, now etched into her memory. She lost track of time, and suddenly noticed the light was fading.

*I need to get out of here before dark.* One last look in the direction of the valley gave Monique a feeling of loss. "I *will* come back. Michael can't keep me out of this forest."

# 14

Madison and Rick reached the ranger station before daybreak. One dim light shined in the window of the small building. Rick tapped on the door as he opened it. "Anyone around?" he called.

"Yeah, hold on a sec," a voice slurred from a dark corner. "That you, Rick?"

"It's me."

"Man, you're early! I didn't expect you before eight or nine." Trent ran his fingers through his thick hair as a makeshift comb. "What time is it, anyway?"

"Going on five a.m. The sun will be up by the time we get on the mountain."

"OK, let me get my boots on." The young ranger looked around the room, disoriented. Then he stood, and immediately stumbled over his boots, next to the cot where he slept.

"I'll make a pot of coffee. We can all use some." Rick found the light over the small kitchenette.

"Who's with you?"

"Madison and Bud." Rick stopped short of explaining Bud is a dog.

"Oh, OK. OK." The voice sounded disheartened. "Yeah, we will need coffee." He vanished into the men's room, at the end of the hall.

By the time the coffee all dribbled into the pot, Trent returned. Hair wet, but combed neatly. The smell of mint toothpaste and Scope filled the room.

He reached high overhead on a shelf and brought down a large thermos and a stack of Styrofoam cups. "We'll need these." He stuck his hand into a paper bag and came out with a mixture of white and pink sugar packages and a second handful of coffee creamer packets. "And these." He shoved them into a small Ziploc bag as Rick poured up the pot of coffee.

Madison had switched to the back seat with Bud by the time the two men returned to the SUV. When the interior light came on as Rick opened the door, he said, "Trent, you remember Madison. And this is Deputy Bud, our partner."

Bud yelped a greeting, right on cue.

"You don't have to ride back there, Ms. Madison." Trent said, standing beside the passenger door.

"Sure I will. You go on and get in," Madison said.

"I'm glad Bud is a dog. Er, I mean, I'm glad you brought your dog!"

Rick turned his head to keep the young man from seeing his grin. He recognized that Trent had a sweet spot for Ms. Madison.

Nearly an hour later, bright pink and orange glowed in the sky above the ridge. Madison snapped a leash onto Bud's collar, and they stepped out onto dampened grass. Before her, she saw two tents and a small campfire. Parked just off the rough road were a pair of dark green trucks. She recognized the one with a whip antenna as Vic's. The other she had no idea who it belonged to, but judged he was higher up because of the lettering on the door. *Maybe a commander*, she reasoned.

Vic emerged from the smaller tent and walked briskly toward them. "Good morning, Rick, Madison." He nodded to Trent, but said nothing. "Didn't expect you this early. From the color of the morning sky, I'd say it's a good thing. The sooner we get started, the sooner we can get out of here. It looks to me like we're going to have a heck of a storm today."

"Morning, Vic." Rick accepted a cup of coffee from Trent.

"You want some now, Ms. Madison?" he asked.

"Yes, thanks, Trent. And please," she stepped close to whisper, "just call me Madison."

Trent poured the cup too full to add the Creamer. He apologized to her, then said, "I'll give this one to Vic." He set it down on the hood of the SUV and poured another cup, opened two creamer packages into it, and handed the steaming cup to Madison. "Sorry, I didn't think to bring any spoons."

By this time, Vic was at the front of the vehicle. "This one mine, Trent?"

"Yes, Sir."

Vic pulled a map from his back pocket. "Here is where we are. And over there is the location of the body."

"You said, 'is.' Do you mean the coroner hasn't been up here yet?" Rick glared at the ranger.

"No, I haven't called him yet. I was told to wait for you," Vic said.

"You found the body yesterday! What makes you think I have any authority to hold up the proceedings? Do you know how much damage each passing hour causes? Have you ever even dealt with a homicide before?" Rick's voice was sharp and abrupt.

"Hold on there, Agent Malone!" An older man in a ranger uniform walked up from the direction of the larger tent. "I'll have you know, Sonny, I'm Captain Straus, Commander of Eastern Affairs for all the government parks. This is my call! The coroner will be here momentarily. I have the scene under my control. You are only here as a favor to the Tennessee Bureau of Investigations, because your commander called me personally. You settle down, or I'll have you removed from the premises." He stopped with his nose inches from Rick's face. "You got that?"

Rick stood firm, his mouth twitching and gritting his teeth. After a couple of deep breaths, he said, "I got that. And I know who you are—in name anyway. Sebastian Straus, Commander of the U.S. Army Jag unit, *dishonorably* discharged after found not guilty of harassment, but of conduct unbecoming an officer. Oh, yes, I remember that case. You only got off because your father was an honorable general, and commander of the post. He was embarrassed by you; he had a fatal heart attack. Don't talk to me about removing anyone from the premises. You are a disgrace, even to that uniform you're wearing now. You have no jurisdiction here. I'm a *federal* agent; *you* are only an agent of the state. Now, you got *that?*" Rick said coldly.

The tension was high and thick as the fog in the valley below. Rick walked back to his SUV. He retrieved his backpack and leaned close to Madison. "Let's go. I know where the site is on that map. I'd like to be there before the coroner arrives."

"Let me get my pack," Madison said, stepping toward the open door of the SUV.

The two of them walked along the trail until they came to a place where yellow tape marked a tree. They turned left and continued up another trail to a level spot, where a tent had been erected and a ranger stood guard.

"I'm Agent Rick Malone with the TBI. This is Madison McKenzie, my associate. Is the victim in there?" He nodded toward the tent.

"Yes, Sir. I've been expecting you." The ranger stepped back, feet apart, arms behind him. "No one has touched her. That's the way we found her."

Bud sniffed the ranger to check him out and introduced himself by sitting in front of the man and raising a front leg. He held it there until the young man bent and shook the dog's paw.

"Oh, that's Bud," Madison said.

"I thought he was going to tell me there for a minute." Then the ranger knelt, still holding Bud's paw. "My name is Jason. I'm happy to meet you, Bud. Where's your badge?"

Bud yelped once, then stood to survey the surroundings. Madison released his leash. "Stay close," she instructed, drawing a circle in the air with her index finger.

"I see he's had obedience training," Jason said. "Good Boy!"

Rick lifted the flap, easing into the tent. Madison hesitated. She turned to Bud and said, "Sit; stay." She motioned with her palm toward the dog in a stopping motion. Bud sat.

Madison walked up behind Rick just as he lifted the sheet off the form laying on the ground. "Who placed the sheet on her?" He called.

"We don't know, Sir." The ranger answered from outside. "We just put up the tent, to shield her from the elements."

Rick looked at Madison. "You don't have to do this."

"Yes, Rick, I do," she said.

Madison put a dab of VapoRub under her nose, one of the tricks Dr. Baker shared with her students on days they visited the body farm. She pulled on a pair of latex gloves, then her safety glasses. She swallowed hard as she moved into place beside Rick.

"I'll understand if you need to leave." He patted her hand.

Rick carefully pulled the sheet back from the body. The hair, matted with mud, partially lay across her face. Dark red splotches dotted her skin, making it difficult to distinguish between mud and blood. The thick line along her neck was probably COD. The blood had run down the front of the torso, indicating she'd been standing when her throat was slashed.

Madison's eyes surveyed the marks on the woman's right arm. "Ligature marks," she noted.

Rick nodded, after checking the left arm. He pulled the sheet up from the bottom and looked at the woman's ankles. They were still tied together tightly with a hemp-like string, cutting into the skin. Her feet were bare, covered in mud and blood. Deep gashes in the arch suggested she'd walked barefoot through rough terrain.

A large circular pattern of dark blood covered the midsection of her camp shorts. Rick checked closer and found an entry wound through the cotton fabric. He unsnapped the waistline and unzipped her clothing. She had a deep wound that appeared to be from a broad-bladed knife. "She was stabbed before they cut her throat. Painful, and slow to bleed out. Someone felt compassion.

The throat wound took her quicker." He turned to look at Madison.

"How are you doing?"

A weak voice quietly said, "OK."

"Can you take photos?"

"Oh, yeah. Sure." Madison lifted the camera, which hung from a strap around her neck. She fired off several exposures, moving all the way around the corpse. "Tell me where you want close-ups." She looked at Rick.

"I think you've already covered them. Just check to be sure the shots are all in focus; you might be a little shaky." He smiled, only a slight glimmer, then returned to the grim task of swabbing the wounds.

Madison checked the photos. Satisfied they were all clean, she put the lens cap back on and swung the camera over her shoulder. She knelt, looking closely at the soles of the feet. "There's fine gravel in these cuts, like creek rocks and sand. Do you want me to gather samples?"

"Sure, if you'd like." Rick's look told her he was surprised and pleased.

The examination and gathering of evidence went on for a half hour before the coroner arrived.

A senior with white beard and thinning hair stepped into the tent. He looked Madison up and down before he introduced himself. "Dr. Simonson, but you can call me Seth. All my lady friends do." He chuckled with enough force to make his belly shake. "You'll be Miss Madison McKenzie, I'm sure!" He offered his hand.

Madison looked down at the latex on her hands and shrugged her shoulders. "Pleased to meet you, Dr. Simonson, and this is Agent—"

"Yes, I know," He interrupted. "Agent Richard Malone. I've heard all about you, also. Gerre Baker and I are old friends." The laugh was subdued this time, like it was a pleasant but wistful thought.

"Pleased to meet you, Sir." Rick pulled off his gloves and shook hands with the doctor. "We didn't move the body—waiting for you to do that. And we don't know who placed the sheet on her." Rick propped his fists on his hips.

"Whoever found her here first put the sheet on her. The killers wouldn't have done that." Dr. Seth commented. "Don't 'spect she died here: not enough blood." He walked around the body. "You get a liver temp?" He looked straight at Madison.

"Oh, no, Sir." Madison sounded almost insulted.

"Just thought Gerre might have you doing a full workup. No problem, I'll get it."

"How long has this enclosure been around the body?" Seth stuck his head out the door-flap. "Vic! Where'd he go?"

Jason stepped forward and said, "Said he needed to go take a leak, Sir."

"Um," Rick said, momentarily taken aback. Then he asked, "You know how long this enclosure has been here?"

"Since yesterday afternoon. Maybe two or three o'clock," Jason answered.

"When Vic gets back, tell him to check in with me."

"I will, Sir."

"And when my crew gets here with the four-wheel drive, let me know."

"Yes, Sir. But I'm sure you'll hear it." The ranger assumed his at-attention stance.

"Yes, I suppose I will." He returned to the corpse. "Eighteen point eight-eight, ambient temperature. Has this tent made that much difference?" He rubbed his left hand along his chin, scratching at the beard. "Temp should have been lower. She's been dead more than eighteen hours. Probably more like twenty-four hours."

His thoughts were interrupted by the sound of the Argo pulling up outside the tent.

"Come out here and see our new toy, Rick." Dr. Seth exited the tent with Rick on his heels.

Madison knelt close to the victim. "I wish you could talk to me. We will find who did this. Rick and I won't rest until we do. If you have anything you can share with me, do it now. I won't see you after Seth takes you away." She pulled off one glove and touched the hand of the woman who had been kidnapped from the trail, somewhere between here and Tennessee.

She felt the woman's cold fingers. As though the hand relaxed, something fell to the ground. Madison looked among the mix of soil and moss. Finally, she noticed a circular shape. It was a button. She picked it up with her gloved left hand. She saw blood-soaked thread attached. She closed her hand around the button and held it to her heart.

"This is from your killer, isn't it?" She sank down on both knees and closed her eyes. In her mind, she imagined the woman fighting to get away, pulling at anything she could grasp. She could have pulled this right off the shirt of the man who held her. Madison squeezed her eyes tighter, but no face appeared—only the outline of a tall man, as the woman fell to her knees with her hand to her gut. Madison felt the pain from the knife in her stomach. Then she felt a burning in her neck, like the sting of a bee, only it went all the way from right to left. Then she felt nothing.

Rick returned to the tent to find Madison on her knees. He touched her shoulder, "Hey, are you OK?"

She nodded. Then she tried to stand. Rick caught her under her left arm, lifting her to her feet.

"Look," she opened her hand, "she gave this to me."

Rick looked at the button. And then at Madison. "Gave it?"

"I touched her hand, and she released it. It fell to the ground, but I found it. There's still blood on the threads. It's her blood. She..." Madison stopped. "I'll tell you later. Don't mention the button in front of any of the rangers. I'll give it to Dr. Seth."

The outer poles and the sides of the tent had been removed, leaving only the overhead canopy. Two of Seth's crew lifted the corpse to a backboard and loaded it into the rear of the Argo, strapping it into a secure position.

"Seth, I found this," Madison whispered. She slipped a small plastic bag into the medical examiner's hand. "Handle this with care. Could be the clue we need."

"Then give it to Rick. He has more avenues than my office." He winked at Madison and whispered, "Our secret."

Seth climbed into the front seat beside the driver. "I'll keep you posted, Agent. Madison, please tell Gerre she trained you well; I approve. Thanks for your assistance." He waved as the vehicle moved down the mountainside.

Madison called Bud's name, and he happily returned to her side. She lifted a bottle of water and a shallow pan from her backpack. "Thirsty?" She set the pan down, and he lapped up nearly all the water. She took a sip from the bottle, then returned it and the water dish to her pack.

"Jason, did Vic ever return?" Rick asked.

"No, Sir." He continued folding the frame of the canopy. "Think you can give me a hand carrying this back to the truck?" Jason asked.

"Sure, here let me help you with that." Rick pitched in to help with the accordion folding of the aluminum legs of the canvas canopy.

Madison picked up the sides, rolled into carrying bags. "I got this." She headed down the trail with the guys following. Bud led the way, dragging his leather leash.

# 15

Madison was quiet as Rick drove back to the main road. He waited for her to start the conversation. Finally, he noticed she'd fallen asleep with her head against the passenger side window.

*Sleep, Lovely Lady. The further you get into this line of work, the less you sleep. Trust me on that.*

Rick drove straight to his apartment when they reached Knoxville. Shutting off the engine woke Madison. She blinked several times, still breathing deeply, then she looked at Rick. "Where are we?"

"In Knoxville, at my apartment." He smiled as she pulled the keys from the switch. "You must have been tired."

"A little." She looked into the back seat to see Bud was sitting up, ready to go.

"You want to come in? Shower and change clothes before you head home?" Rick opened his door and slid out.

"I'd like that. That way I can check Bud—and me—for ticks."

"What? Since when is the Woman of the Woods concerned about a few little bugs?"

"Since I visited the vet's clinic, where they had seven dogs with Lyme disease." She climbed out of the front seat, dragging her backpack, then opened the back door and retrieved a small duffel bag with a change of clothes and her Blazer keys. Bud was already out the door Rick had exited on the other side.

She walked to her SUV, unlocked it, and put the windows down a few inches before throwing her pack in the back and getting out a pair of sandals. Then she joined Rick and Bud in the lobby, where he introduced Bud as a service dog so management wouldn't object to him going up to the apartment.

"You go ahead and get your shower, and Bud's too. I'll check my messages and see if I need to return any calls. Take your time; I'm all for feeding these poor little bugs. You know, on second thought, I think I'll change and do laps in the pool. That chemical concentration ought to kill anything." Rick disappeared into the bedroom, returning in a pair of swim trunks with a towel around his shoulders. "You OK with being alone up here?"

"Seriously?" She smiled and shook her head. "Thanks, Rick."

"Maybe you'll be ready to talk when I get back." He had closed the door before she could respond.

Madison stood next to the open sliding glass door drying her hair when Rick returned. Bud lay on the balcony in the sun, drying himself.

"Have a good swim?" she asked.

"Oh, yeah. It's a nice pool, especially with no one else in it." Rick went to the bathroom. "Find any bugs?" He laughed.

"No, we were clean." She unplugged the blow dryer and handed it to Rick. "You want this?"

"Thanks." He put the dryer down on the counter and turned back to look at Madison. "I'm pretty hungry. How 'bout you?"

"I guess." She walked out onto the balcony.

Rick closed the door, and soon Madison heard the shower running. *How do I explain that I just don't have an appetite?*

\* \* \*

Calhoun's Restaurant, famous for ribs, is on the Tennessee River not far away from Rick's apartment. Rick parked in a shaded spot, leaving the windows down for Bud.

Madison ordered a wine spritzer. She sipped it as she looked over the menu. Rick motioned to the waiter that they were ready to order.

The spritzer and Rick's beer had both vanished by the time their meal arrived. Rick signaled to repeat the drink order. When the waiter set her second spritzer on the table, Madison looked at him quizzically.

"I thought you could use the second one." Rick smiled and put his hand over hers.

"He was left-handed." She looked out over the river. "Actually, there were two of them. The one who slit her throat was tall and left handed. The button came from the other man's shirt. He stabbed her first. She struggled with him. The button came off his right sleeve as she clutched her gut, trapping it in her hand. Seconds later, the other guy stood behind her. I felt the pain and the burn." She put her left hand to her throat. "I couldn't see their faces. It was dark and raining."

Rick held onto her right hand. "The button was in this hand?"

She nodded.

"I believe you, Madison."

"Thank you. I wouldn't tell anyone, but you. I hoped you'd understand."

Rick motioned to the waiter again.

"Is there something wrong, Sir?" he asked.

"Something's come up. Can we get our meal to go?" Rick asked.

"Absolutely. I'll take care of it for you." The waiter scooped up the plates and disappeared into the kitchen area.

Rick turned his beer up, drinking most of it. Madison picked up her spritzer. She sipped until the waiter brought their dinners in two neatly folded bags.

Bud's nose responded immediately upon their return to the vehicle.

"Wait till we get back to the apartment, Bud. You'll get your treat." Rick placed the bags in the rear of the SUV, all the way in the back. "Not that I don't trust you, Fella, but I don't want to tempt you that much."

He opened Madison's door, and shut it after she slid into the seat.

With no words exchanged until they were in the living room, Rick placed the bags on the bar by the desk and dug out a rib, full of meat. He opened the sliding glass door, and Bud followed on his heels. Bud settled into a sprawled position, securing the bone between his front paws. Rick watched for a few seconds, then returned to where Madison sat.

"I'd like it if you'd stay here tonight. I'll sleep on the sofa; you take my room." He sat next to her. "I don't want you to be alone tonight."

"Thanks, Rick. I'll take you up on that." Madison leaned her head on his shoulder. "I didn't imagine it, you know."

"I know you didn't." He slipped his left arm around her shoulders. They sat for a long time, silently.

Bud fell asleep on the cool concrete of the balcony, content after his treat.

Madison got up and went to the bar. "I need to get my pack from my Blazer. Bud's water dish is in it."

"I'll go get it. Give me your key." Rick sprang up from the couch. "I could use another beer. How 'bout I go to a liquor store, and get us a six-pack and some wine?"

"I'll drink a couple of beers if you'll get cold Budweiser in the bottles. Little ones, if they have them. I can't stand hot beer!" Madison could see her remarks surprised Rick. She tossed him her keys, saying, "You can drive mine."

"Be back in a few," Rick said, and he went out the door.

# 16

Madison's phone rang, and she saw that it was Holly, her friend in Cold Creek. "Hello, Holly."

"Madison, where are you?" Holly asked, but went on talking before Madison could answer. "It's Drew Perry. He's hurt, real bad."

"What happened?" Madison said.

"He fell down the steps at the jail. Oh, Maddie, he's in really bad shape." Holly was sobbing.

"Calm down, Holly. Where is he?"

"In Johnson City, at the Med Center. He's in surgery! Henry is up there, along with half the town. I had to stay home with the twins. When are you coming back?"

"I'll be a couple of hours; I'm in Knoxville. Does Henry have his phone?" She thought calling him might be better than getting the news secondhand from Holly. "I'll call you as soon as I can. I'm going to call Henry now."

"He didn't want me to call you; don't tell him how you heard." Holly sniffled. "Henry's the one that found him."

"I won't, don't worry. I'll call you in a little while. Holly, you need to calm down, or you'll scare the twins. Do you hear me?"

"Yes, but I'm worried."

"That won't help. Be strong in front of your babies. OK, Momma, you can do this."

Rick returned to find Madison ready to walk out the door, with both her bags over her shoulder and Bud on his leash.

"What's going on? I thought you were going to stay." Rick put a brown paper bag on the counter.

"Sheriff Perry has been hurt. He's in surgery at the Johnson City Medical Center. I'm trying to reach Henry. He's the one who found Drew. Holly said he fell down the steps in the jail."

"Well, that doesn't make any sense!"

"I know!" She took her keys from Rick. "I'll call you once I know what's happening." She went into the hallway.

"I should go too," Rick said.

"No, you've got to get that stuff to the lab." She walked to the elevator.

"Madison, wait! I did. That's what took me so long. I went to the lab first. Come back here, and let me get some things together. I'm going with you."

Rick drove Maddie's Blazer out of Knoxville on I-40, heading to Johnson City. Madison connected with Henry on his cell phone, getting the story of what happened and the extent of Drew's injuries. She hung up and then called Holly back.

"Holly, I just spoke to Henry. Rick and I are on our way there now. I'll call you again after I see Drew." Madison listened for a few moments, then said goodbye to Holly.

* * *

Rain was falling by the time Rick and Madison parked near the Surgical Tower, at the back of JCMC. Inside, they found the lower level receptionist was already gone for the day. They entered the elevator and got off on the third floor.

"Can I help you?" A woman who appeared to be in her early twenties smiled as they approached her desk.

"Sheriff Drew Perry was brought in a few hours ago. Can you tell me how we can find him?"

"Let me check..." She scrolled through the info on her monitor. "Yes, here he is; he is just out of surgery. He's been taken to SICU." She flashed a sweet smile at the couple, pointing back to the elevator.

"Thanks," Madison said.

Henry stood in the doorway of the waiting room. "The doctor is with him. I don't think it's good news!" Henry looked pale.

"How did this happen? Where is he injured?" Madison quizzed Henry.

"Nothing makes sense. Drew called me. Said he wanted me to see something, but didn't say what, so I went straight to the jail immediately. I found him at the bottom of the stairs. He couldn't move. Kept asking me if I'd seen who it was." Henry's hand shook as he ran his fingers through his hair. "I didn't see nobody! No one on the street, no other cars, nothing!"

"It takes what, five, six minutes to get from your place to the jail?" Rick asked.

"Took me less than five, I promise you that."

"How long has the doctor been with him?" Madison asked.

"A while. I've not seen Drew yet, except for when he was rolled by on the bed. One nurse said they were hooking him up to a thing that turns him—you know, like a spit."

"He has a spinal injury?" Madison said.

Henry nodded.

A woman in a set of green scrubs approached. "The doctor will come and talk to you soon. Sheriff Perry has a spinal injury; that's all I know."

Madison said, "Thank you, we'll be in here." She put her arm around Henry and coaxed him out of the hallway to the far corner of the waiting area. Rick followed.

Another half hour passed. A lady dressed in a light gray suit came into the waiting area. She had her head lowered and kept her face partially covered with a tissue. She sat on a chair just inside the door. It wasn't until she put the tissue in her pocket that Madison realized she recognized the woman.

"Nell?" Madison rushed to the woman. Nell stood and met her with a hug. "I thought it was you. Where have you been? How did you hear about Drew?" Madison held Nell's narrow shoulders in her outstretched hands.

"I'm so glad to see you, Maddie. I've tried to call you. You changed your number?" Nell looked past her friend to Rick and Henry. "Hey, how are you all?"

Rick and Henry stood and joined the hug. "Good to see you, Nell. Where have you been?" Rick asked.

"I took a job in Seattle last year. In the move I lost everything I had, my phone, laptop, everything but my purse and the clothes I was wearing. It all vanished in one suitcase. I've been busy, and it's a good position, but they keep me running all the time. I know that's a lousy excuse, and I am sorry. I talked to Drew last week. He saw one of my articles and called me. I was so glad to hear from him. And then this." She pulled the bedraggled tissue back out of her pocket.

"But who called you?" Madison asked.

"No one. I had made plans to come here and see everyone while on an assignment in DC. I rented a car and drove down. Drew was expecting me. He didn't tell any of you?"

"Guess he wanted to surprise us," Henry said.

"When I got to town, all the lights were on at the jail, but he wasn't there. He wasn't at his place, either, so I went to Shirley's Restaurant—where else? They told me something had happened, and an ambulance had taken the sheriff to Johnson City." With barely a pause for breath, she asked, "Have you seen him yet?"

"No, they ushered us in here. You?" Rick asked.

"Just for a second, from the door. Drew is on a turning contraption, with all sorts of connections going everywhere. Oh, God; what's happening?" Nell dropped into the chair.

Madison knelt beside her. "We don't know anything yet, other than Henry found him at the bottom of the stairs in the jail. He was in surgery for quite some time. The injury occurred right around noon, right Henry?"

"Yes; well, maybe closer to one. I was about to go up to the barn when I got the call."

"Why did he call you?" Nell looked at Henry in a way Rick didn't like.

"Now hold on, Nell. Henry is our friend. He didn't have anything to do with Drew getting hurt. Don't start laying blame." Rick's voice was stern.

"No! I didn't mean... That came out wrong. I'm sorry, Henry." She buried her face in her hands.

Nell had met Madison and Sheriff Perry five years before, when she'd covered the story of the bones in Cold Creek. She already knew Rick because of her job with the Knoxville TV station, where she worked at the time. Moving on to other jobs, she lost touch with everyone. Drew and Nell had been in a serious relationship previously. Maybe he hoped they could rekindle the old flame, and haven't wanted to share it with anyone yet.

The lady in the green scrubs came back into the room. "You can come in, two at a time." She turned and walked down the hall toward the double doors. She pushed the button on the wall, leaving it to them to decide who went first. Rick started out of the room, saying, "Come on, Madison."

Madison turned to look at Nell. "Go on, let him know you're here. He's going to need all the support you can give him."

"You sure?" Nell asked, but hurried out to follow Rick.

They entered the room, and both caught their breaths but said nothing.

"I'm Doctor Smyth. Are either of you family?"

"Drew doesn't have any family, but we're friends," Rick spoke up. "This is Nell. I think she's the best medicine for our boy right now."

Nell slipped to the side of the bed, if that's what you'd call something that looked like a rotisserie with a mattress. She kissed Drew's cheek. Her tears slid onto his neck. "I'm here, Drew."

Her words surprised Rick. "I'm here too, Sheriff." Rick stood on the other side. "But I'm not going to kiss you."

Drew managed a slight chuckle, barely audible. "Thanks, Rick." The voice was raspy. His body didn't move, not even his hands. His eyes looked sideways at Nell. "How'd you know?"

"They told me at the restaurant."

"Happy you're...here." He barely had the energy to speak.

The doctor spoke next. "Sheriff Perry has a very serious spinal injury. I don't know what we can expect as the prognosis. Mending is going to be a long process, no matter what the outcome. He needs to be immobilized for months, if not years." Dr. Smyth cleared his throat. "However, this is one tough old bird; I have hope he'll eventually make a full recovery. Won't accept any less, will we Drew?"

There was no more energy in the patient for his voice. Just a rumble in Drew's throat.

Dr. Smyth turned to Rick. "You're his next of kin, aren't you? The TBI Agent, Rick Malone?"

"Yes, Sir, I'm Rick."

"Give him room. He can't talk for a while. At least, not as far as answering any questions. You understand me?"

Rick nodded.

"He doesn't know who pushed him. He was able to tell me that much before he'd allow us to sedate him. He says you'll know what to do with the investigation." The doctor turned and left the room.

Rick followed him into the hall. "Tell me what you couldn't say in front of him."

"Nothing. It's all out in the open between my patients and me. I told him from the beginning we'd have a rough road. Neurology has come a long way, my friend. I meant what I said about a recovery. Give him a few days; he'll be able to express himself soon. But until then, I don't want him upset. You *do* understand, right?"

"Of course. I'll pass the word around. Trust me; no one wants the sheriff to get well more than his friends." Rick extended his hand. "Thank you for an excellent job, Dr. Smyth."

Rick returned to the waiting area. "One of you go on down; it's the first curtain on the left."

Madison said, "Go on, Henry."

"I won't stay long." He walked swiftly toward the double doors.

When he returned, Henry said, "He's about to fall asleep. Go on, Madison."

Rick could see that Henry was troubled. "The doc says to give him some time; he'll be able to talk to us later. Right now, his throat is irritated from the tube during surgery. He's going to recover, Henry. We just have to show him we're here for him."

"Yeah, I get that. It's such a shock. Drew is always in motion. Rick, we're going to get to the bottom of this, you and me."

"Yes, we will. I can't imagine Nell leaving his side, so I'm going to round up some food for her, and a pillow and blankets. These recliners are for the family. They won't let anyone in except for every three or four hours. No point to staying. We'll be at the cottage."

Henry patted Rick on the shoulder. "We'll see you tomorrow," he said, and disappeared down the hall.

Rick wondered how this accident had happened—if it *was* an accident. Drew had been unconscious when Henry found him, and never regained consciousness as far as he knew. The doctor told Rick that Drew was awake when he went into surgery.

The rain stopped just as Henry reached the higher elevation near Cold Creek. The moon edged out from behind dark clouds, helping light the dirt driveway that extended a half mile out from the farmhouse to the paved road. He saw that his truck stirred up a lot of dust as he went down the lane. He'd so hoped the rain would make it up to the pastures and the garden. The creek cutting through behind the house didn't hold enough water to reroute it as irrigation. *Maybe tomorrow, maybe tomorrow will bring a good rain to the valley,* he thought, ever hopeful.

# 17

Back at the hospital, Rick sat in the private waiting room, jotting notes in a pocket notebook as Madison returned from Drew's room.

"She won't leave him." Madison sat on a chair next to Rick. "I guess I can't blame her. I'd feel that way if it were…" She stopped herself.

"I know." Rick extended his arm around her shoulders. "I need to gather what I can from the jail, and hope no one has disturbed anything."

"I want to go home. You can stay at the cottage, if you want. Nell and Monique are the only people who've ever slept on my futon; both said it's comfortable." Madison stood up. "I'll help you at the scene; that way we can knock this out quicker."

"I'd appreciate your help." He stood, and they walked down the hall toward the elevator. "Nell has your number, right?"

"I made sure of it. I put it in her phone myself."

\* \* \*

The lights were still on at the jail. Someone had put yellow crime scene tape across the door. Rick ripped it off, and they went inside. A careful and thorough search determined no one was there, so they began processing the scene.

Madison noticed there were six messages on the phone at Drew's desk. "Shall I listen to see who called?"

"Yes, just don't erase anything," Rick said. "Got gloves?"

Madison grinned. Already, he'd forgotten she knew what to do. "Yes, Sir."

Rick was so engrossed he didn't even notice her remark.

She played the messages. The first two were from Nell; the next was Deputy Sparks, in Erwin; Nell again, sounding frantic at that point; and finally, the last two were an open line, but there were no background noises. She strapped a piece of yellow tape across the buttons and marked her initials on it.

She moved to the basement, where Rick stood talking to himself. "Try me; I'll give you feedback."

Rick looked up, "What?"

"You were talking out loud, to yourself," Madison said.

"I was? Oh, OK. Does this basement look a bit too clean to you?" he asked.

She scanned the room and nodded. "Not even a cobweb. That *is* unusual."

"Help me find the Shop-Vac. I know he uses one." Rick opened the door to the lower stairs, leading to the old mine shaft. "I thought he had this closed up."

"He did...or said he did, just the other day when Monique was here with me. I haven't been down here in at least four years. All he has now is those case files." She pointed to a neat stack of three rows of boxes along one wall. Each with name and date, solved on the top row, ongoing middle row, and the bottom level was the cold and unsolved cases. "Since Drew has been sheriff, there are a lot more cases on the top row," she said.

"This is a puzzlement. I just knew there was no access to the shaft below anymore." Rick stared at the steps.

"Might as well check it out." She walked to the stairs. "There are flashlights in his office. I just saw them up there. I'll go get a couple."

"Let me return Sparks' phone call first. He's here often enough, might even know why it's remained open. We can do that check at a later time. Give me a hand; let's slide this desk in front of the door. If anyone is coming in from there, this desk is sturdy enough to stop their entry."

The long green metal desk barricaded the door sufficiently, considering it opened out into the room. No one was going to push it out of the way.

"That's all we can do tonight." Rick looked at his watch. "It's after midnight. Let's get some shut-eye."

"And a shower!" Madison added.

"For real!" Rick laughed. "Do you know where Drew's keys are? We need to keep the door locked at night."

"Yes, I just saw them in his desk drawer. I'll get them." She went upstairs.

Rick had turned out the lights and started up when he heard Madison yell, "They're gone!"

He topped the stairs and ran to Drew's office. "Are you sure you saw them in *that* drawer?"

"Absolutely!" She looked up. "Someone was in here while we were down there. See, here are his house keys, and his Land Rover keys. Drew is very organized. Why would someone take the keys?"

"I'd guess that someone is looking for something in this office, and Drew disturbed them. They'll be back."

Rick walked to Madison's cottage with her, planning to shower while she fixed them grilled cheese sandwiches. He returned to the sheriff's office to sleep; he would change the locks on the door the next day.

Meanwhile, back in Atlanta, Monique and Claudia finished packing up their inventory. The clearance sale had gone very well. As a result, they had fewer boxes to move to Knoxville. For the time being, they stored stock they had left in a Pod until the relocation.

That was Monique's job. She set out early on Wednesday morning and arrived at University Commons just as the business opened at 10:00. She had done some research and noted a small vacant store next to Pet Smart and convenient to the University. Now, if the rent were doable, she'd have her new store by noon.

At 12:35 p.m., she got back into her SUV and headed south on the Alcoa Highway. It was meant to be. The store had less square footage than the one in Atlanta, and that was all right with her. Rent was acceptable, and the deal was signed. Now she was going to make a stop along the AT on her way back.

*Claudia expects me to spend at least one or two days looking for a place to rent, so she won't suspect I have an ulterior motive while in this area.* They had already decided to get the store set up before they located housing. By staying in a hotel for a week or so, they could learn traffic patterns and chose a smart place to rent or buy an apartment. Claudia still had to sell her condo, but that was already in the works. She had her heart set on a tiny home community, and Monique liked the convenience of condo life.

It was late afternoon by the time she found her way back up to the unexplored side of the AT and the hidden valley. Michael had led her to believe lady slippers grew on the north end of the valley above the burial cave. But he made it clear he'd have no part of helping her access that ground, so she'd have to find it on her own. After all, the blooms only show for a very short time, and it was already mid-May. She had to locate them this year or wait until next spring, and she would rather not wait.

She tied her hiking boots snugly and pulled out a backpack from the rear of the vehicle. She'd been careful to put rope and climbing equipment in her supplies this time. If those rocks were large enough to hide an aircraft the size of a single-engine Bonanza, there had to be crevasses. She hoped to find it today, or rule this area out completely. Those pink blooms were vanishing fast, and she didn't want to waste any more time on Michael.

The forest was not friendly in the area of the rocky ledge of the valley. Monique had a rough time making it through the tangled old-growth mountain laurels and rhododendrons. There were fewer pines and way more underbrush on this side. When she came across a rocky ledge, she felt sure she was on the right path. After following it for what seemed like a hundred yards, she saw the towering rocks ahead. They were higher than the ones that had originally gotten her in trouble with the snake. And to be sure, she was keeping her eyes wide open for anything that slithered. She remembered Ranger Vic saying that if you tap the ground ahead of you with a stick, it warns the snakes so that they hide. He stated, "They don't want to encounter humans any more than we want to meet them." Her stick tapped the rocky surface as if it were a white cane, making way for the blind.

Reaching a dead end, she decided rappelling might be her best chance to see into the crevasses. The rappelling classes she'd taken in college for fun were about to come in handy. She removed her backpack, setting it on the ground, then pulled out the rope and carabiners, descenders, gloves, helmet, and rappel kit, including full body harness. Overkill? Maybe, but she'd learned in class that it was better to be prepared than repaired.

She secured the rope around a lonely pine tree and lowered herself into the dark depths. This area didn't prove to be of any value, so she tried the other end of the vast protrusion. At least in that direction, she could lower into the sunshine.

When she reached sound footing and a semblance of a path, she unhooked the rope and made her way toward an opening. Her first view of the sunny ground revealed broad green leaves and beautiful, bulbous pink blooms with yellow or lime throats. She had found the place she'd been looking for: the place where lady slippers grow.

Almost disbelieving, she sat on the ground next to them and picked one.

She held it to her nose and breathed in the sweet aroma. Tears trickled down her cheeks. Was she really this close to finding out about her identity, her destiny?

"Surely you're not so rare that you only hide in this forest, in this valley?" She rested her head on her knees.

"Yes, they are," a voice behind her whispered.

She spun around to see Michael. She jumped up so quickly her head felt light, and she nearly fell. "Not you again!"

"Afraid so."

"You're not running me out. Not this time. I'm *this* close," She said, holding her thumb and forefinger a centimeter apart. "I can feel it. You can't stop me, so don't even try!"

"I won't."

"Really?" She reached into her pack and brought out a bottle of water. "Want some?"

He shook his head. "I think you need it, Monique. I won't even tell you how dumb it is that you're here. But to keep you alive, I'll take you to the crash site."

"You *do* know where it is! You've known all along! Why wouldn't you tell me?"

"What can you do for them?" Michael knelt down and snapped off a sprig of sassafras, popping it into his mouth. He chewed the stem the way some people would a toothpick.

"Maybe nothing for them. But for me, I'll know for sure where I came from, and who I should have been. I should have perished with my folks, but since I didn't, I still want to claim my identity. There has always been a part of me missing. I used to think it was because I never had any siblings. I often thought it was because my dad was so absent in my life, because he worked all the time. But maybe he worked to keep his conscience from eating at him by being around me. Knowing I didn't belong to them, it must have bothered him. It did my mom. That's why she left the notes in the Bible for me. So if something happened to them, I'd know where to turn."

"I see." He stood and began rolling up the line she'd rappelled down. "You won't need this to get back up there. I'll take you out the safe way. I mean, unless you still have a death wish, and want to join the spirits on this land."

"I hope to live a long life, thank you." Monique snatched the length of rope from him. "Just leave that here. Unless you plan to scale the rock face and retrieve the hook-up for me."

"Nope." He turned and walked out the way she'd come in. Back into the shadows which were growing longer by the minute. "You weren't planning on spending the night here, were you?"

She hurried to catch up. "No. I didn't think it would take me this long to get here."

She followed the big silent man back through a maze of rock passages and tunnels of twisted undergrowth. He led her to an outcropping of rock that had settled into jagged columns like leaning pillars. The sun glinted on the side of the fuselage, nestled into the columns. Further below was a shape much like a wing, now draped in kudzu vine.

Monique stared at the crumpled aluminum. One door was off. Darkness settled inside like a thick blanket.

"Have you been closer?" she asked.

"No."

"I need to." She moved forward one step at a time.

"Wait. Let me. You don't need to see skeletons, in case they are your folks. I'll see what I can find. It's going to be dark here in a few minutes." Michael pushed past her and worked his way to the columns. He clung to the sides with large hands, working his way between them.

Once he was out of her sight, she realized he was trying to get to the opposite side, closer to the nose of the plane. She held her breath clenching her backpack and listening to every sound.

Eventually, Michael reappeared. He held what looked to be a leather briefcase. She watched, barely breathing. Then she rushed to him when he climbed back up to the ledge where she stood.

"There are two skeletons, a male and a female. This case was wedged between the front seats, on the floor. I don't think you should open it here. We need to get out of here while we still have light."

Monique nodded, unable to speak. When she turned, she noticed pink blooms of the lady slipper just over her head. She froze. "The ones I picked as a child were pink. I was here. But how did a tiny baby get this far?"

"There's a trail on the other side of the columns. It looks more like a path you might have taken. But a large pine is laying across it now, and also concealing the tail section of the plane. That's why you can't see it from above. It looks as though it's been there for a decade or more. No one is coming in that way."

She eyed the briefcase as she followed closely behind Michael through the tall grass of the valley floor. Inside his cave, Michael stirred the campfire and added kindling to perk up the blaze. Monique sat on the rocks close to the fire, still staring at the briefcase.

"What if it's locked?"

"It is." Michael sat on the ground next to her. He picked up a sharp stick, as if to pry the small locking device. "This is high-quality leather; otherwise, it would have been deteriorated by now."

"Wait." She reached into her jacket pocket and brought out a small key. "Try this; it might work." The lock opened with a small grinding sound when he slipped it into the slot and turned it.

"Where did you get this?" He asked.

"It was in the pocket of the pinafore. Maybe I liked it because it was so small and shiny. I don't know; I guess one of my parents gave it to me."

Monique's hand touched the cold moldy leather, then she slid her fingers along the opening and lifted the lid. She saw papers folded neatly into compartments. She noticed a small pocket with what she assumed were business cards. She slipped one out and read the name. *Laurence Lawson Morrel.* For a second, she felt a hitch in her breath. Then she read it aloud. "Laurence Lawson Morrel. He was my father."

Michael watched as she opened the papers, trying to read through tears. She'd refold them and put them back exactly as she found them. Then she came across a photo of a man, a woman, and a little blonde-haired girl.

She flipped to the back and read, "Larry, Lynda, and Monique Morrel."

"Can I see it?" Michael looked closer at the photo. "The woman looks like you. And see how petite she is. I think that's your mother."

Monique swallowed and tried to say the name again. "Lyn...Lennie, he called her Lennie." She slammed the case shut. "What if this isn't me? What if these aren't my parents?"

"There's one way to find out: DNA. If your folks handled the contents much, maybe they can find some DNA to test yours against." He wasn't going to mention the small bone in his pocket, which came from the pilot—not yet. Just one finger joint that would hopefully provide them with answers.

Monique lay her head on Michael's shoulder. For a long while, neither spoke. The light of day had faded. The fire, now reduced to embers, made the cave very dark.

Michael placed his hands on her shoulders and moved her away just enough to pick up a stick and put it on the fire. "I have a sleeping bag. You can sleep there, and we'll get you back to your vehicle tomorrow."

Monique didn't protest or agree' she just let her body move where he led her. She stared at the fire until finally he noticed her eyes had closed and she breathed in a regular rhythm. He moved to the mouth of the cave, where he sat watch until daybreak.

# 19

Monique opened her eyes, feeling confused about where she was. It took her a few seconds to recall. She saw the crashed plane and now was in Michael's cave. The man who saved her. *Is this real, or just another of my dreams?*

She stood, wrapping her arms around herself. The chill of the cave air hadn't kept her from sleeping.

"Good, you're awake," someone whispered.

"Michael?"

"Shh, there's someone out there." He joined her and put his finger to his lips. "Don't want anyone knowing we're here," he whispered.

They walked one quiet, careful step at a time back toward the cave opening, concealed by a tangle of old-growth rhododendrons. Michael knelt, pulling her down next to him. They watched as two men also dressed in khaki shirts with dark green trousers worked their way across the valley floor.

"Are those forest rangers?" Monique whispered.

"Yeah, seen them before. One is named Vic."

"Vic?!" her voice was a little louder than a whisper.

Michael clasped his hand across her mouth, releasing it when the men didn't turn. "Good thing they didn't hear you." He furrowed his brow. "He's not a good guy. You don't want to mess with that one."

"He was with the search party. He's a friend."

"No, he's not. Trust me, Monique. You don't want him to know you're here."

She stared into the depths of Michael's turquoise-blue eyes, remembering how concerned he had been for her when she had the fever and her leg ached. "How did you happen to get blue eyes if you're Native American?"

Michael looked away. Monique was sure she detected a glow of blush in his face.

"I didn't mean to pry. It's just so unusual."

"It's OK." He breathed deeply and slid down to the floor to wait out the mission of the two men. "My great grandmother had steel-blue eyes. She was Swedish, and so lovely. Granddad wasn't surprised that one of his offspring shared her eye color. But I think some of the sky got mixed into mine, or the oceans she crossed to get here. He said she was kind and tender, like a doe with her fawn. I asked him how she came to marry an Indian, and he laughed and said that Great Grandfather's spirit was lucky. Said he never spoke of how he attracted her, but was happy he had. They had many children. Granddad was the only one I ever knew. He kind of kept to himself. That's why I love being here. Feels like home."

"Thank you, Michael, for telling me. And thank you for helping me get to the plane crash. What should I do? If I don't report it, I'll never be able to prove who I am. If I do, your cover will be blown. Men will come into this valley and take them out."

"I know." He stared toward the cliff where the secrets lie. "Does it matter to you, to know who they were? I mean, will it change your life?"

"Yes."

"Tell me."

"Since they were never found, they had no family—but they had a will, so the state could not take their holdings. The attorney who drew up the will is in charge of their business. If I can prove I'm their daughter, the rightful heir, I gain control of the estate."

"And what if this attorney fights you?"

"I don't think he will. He has never used a dime of the money for himself, only put it back into the business."

"How can you be sure of that?"

"I did my research while I was in Knoxville. It just so happened there was a big writeup in the newspaper a couple of weeks ago. Rick and Madison showed it to me. They believe I am Monique Renée Morrel, with two ls."

"And if you are?"

"Then I own one of the largest Ford dealerships in the country." Monique smiled as if the sound made her feel good.

"Ah, the money."

"No! Not really, but at least not part of a family of criminals, as it turns out my dad that raised me really was. And their accident might not have been an accident, either!"

Michael nodded slowly taking in the comparison. "I guess I do see your point." He looked up and nudged Monique behind him. "They're coming back."

The two sat quietly as the men dressed like rangers drew closer. The chubby one stepped into higher weeds, heading straight for them. Michael and Monique ducked still lower behind the bushes.

"Come on Drake, I gotta get back to work. We need to get out of here. I don't have time to explore the bushes."

"Hold your horses, Vic! I gotta take a leak." He stopped just a few feet away and unzipped his pants. In another minute, he said, "OK, but I'm gonna come back in here tonight and look around. What if there are caves on this side, too?"

"No, there aren't. I've looked," Vic said.

Drake moved away, heading back in the direction they had come from. Michael motioned for Monique to stay, but he stepped outside to be sure they left the valley.

A while later he returned. "Come on, if he's coming back. I want you long gone. We'll go out another way."

Monique was happy to see Michael had another way out, in case he ever needed to hide from the men again. He led her up a narrow ledge along the back wall. They stepped into a low passage that became a narrow tunnel. He shined a bright flashlight ahead, lighting up the walls.

"Are those drawings? Uh, let me see. Shine the light up there." She pointed to the figure of a man with a bow and arrow. Then she saw another figure, and took the light from Michael's hand. "Did you know these were here?"

He nodded. "Grandfather showed me. They have been here for centuries. His people didn't draw them. They have just always been here. Don't really know where they came from."

"That's remarkable artwork! And this tunnel must have been here a long time."

"I guess." Michael recaptured the flashlight and moved away from the drawings.

They traveled up and down in elevation until they came out in dense woods, not far from where her vehicle was parked. She recognized the area. "How did you know I was parked near here?"

"Monique, there's not much goes on in my valley I don't know about." Michael led her right to her green Subaru. "You mean this one? Nice color, well hidden. I like it. Where'd you come up with this one?"

"It's mine. I'm glad you approve. And yes, the minute I saw it I thought of it blending into *your* woods. I just didn't expect you to find me," she said.

"I have to keep an eye on you, or you're going to get yourself killed!" He laughed.

"What should I do, Michael?"

"That's your decision. I cannot make it for you." He turned and headed back into the underbrush.

"Wait!" she called out, but he was gone.

The trip off the mountain gave her time to consider her dilemma. She cared for Michael. As much as she tried not to think about him, he hadn't given her a truly compelling reason to be thoughtful of his situation, but he had saved her life. That was worth something. Why was he there? What was he hiding from? What did he do that was so awful he couldn't face the world? She might never know.

# 20

Rick made a trip to Lake Okeechobee in south central Florida to talk with the city police chief who had investigated the Morrel couple's accident. Arriving at the city hall in Clewiston, he was directed to the small police station down the street and to Chief Lee.

Lee was sitting behind an overburdened desk, stacks of files and papers showing no discernible order. He looked up at the sound of Rick clearing his throat.

"Excuse me, I didn't hear you come in. What can I do for you?"

"I'm looking for Chief Lee," Rick answered.

"That would be me." He stood and extended his hand. "Ron."

"Agent Rick Malone, Tennessee Bureau of Investigation, Homicide." He accepted the handshake. "I'm here about a boating accident last year involving Morris Randall—or as you knew him, Randy Morrel."

"Randy? Morris Randall? Are you sure?" Chief Lee asked.

"How well did you know the man?"

"Our kids played together when I was with the sheriff's department. Fifteen years ago, maybe. We lived across the street from the Morrels."

"So, pretty well?" Rick suggested.

"Not really. He worked all the time. But he always took his family on a nice vacation. He was a security guard for the sugar company. Season goes down in the spring, so he had part-time jobs 'til fall, when the season started back up again. Always seemed to have what they wanted or needed. Hardworking man.

Who is this Randall Morris, anyway?"

"Chicago mob, at least until he went to Georgia and became a forest ranger for a while. I'm guessing he was trying to disappear even then." Rick dropped another file on top of a short stack directly in front of Lee. "He moved here and became Randy Morrel. Wife named Jewels, and a little baby girl..."

"Monique. Yes, she and my Amanda were great friends."

"He found Monique wandering the Appalachian Trail as a toddler, survivor of a plane crash that killed both her parents. My guess is he wanted a kid, so he kept her and moved here, changing his name."

"That's quite an assumption, Agent Malone. Do you have anything to back your theory?"

"I hoped you could help me with that. Do you have anything here that might have DNA?"

"I can go you one better. I have an eyewitness. Sean Martin, son of the Angler, Ronald Martin. He was the first on the scene. He saw the couple just moments before the explosion." Chief Lee stood with his feet apart and hung his thumbs in his belt. "We're not just local bumpkins here, Agent."

"No, Sir. I never suggested you were. Can you get in touch with Sean for me? I'd like to talk to him."

"Yeah, if he's in town. He does all the bass fishing tournaments, you know?" He picked up the phone, punched in the number from memory, then said, "This is Chief Lee. Is Sean in today? Thank you, I'll hold."

After a couple of minutes, he said, "Hey, Sean. How 'bout lunch? Good. I've got a TBI Agent from Tennessee wants to speak with you about the boating accident last year. Yeah, the one that killed Randy and Jewels. OK, see you then." He hung up, looking at his watch. "How's about lunch at the Marina, about one fifteen?"

Rick drove with Chief Lee's directions along Highway 27 to the last traffic light at the south end of town and turned left. In about three-quarters of a mile they turned right, passed a block of pristine two-story condo units, and then parked in front of Martin's Marina. Behind the Galley Restaurant, Rick saw yachts of all sizes lining the dock.

Inside, there was an impressive display of fishing hardware and clothing. A handsome, tanned young man approached immediately, smiling.

"Hi! I'm Sean Martin. Welcome to Lake Okeechobee, Agent."

"Rick Malone." Rick accepted the handshake. The thought that Madison wasn't with him gave him a sigh of relief. "Glad to meet you in person, Sean. I'm a fan of yours and your dad."

"Man, I love those big striped bass you all have in Tennessee. 'Bout time for me to get back up there for a tournament, you know?"

"I sure do!"

"Sorry, Chief. It isn't every day I met a real Tennessee Bureau of Investigation agent." Sean shook Lee's hand.

"Now, Sean, that's a good thing. Don't you think?" Rick laughed.

Sean led them to a table overlooking the water in the open atmosphere of the tiki bar. A soft breeze blew through the palm trees standing in large pots along the dock. Rick noticed the thatched roof of a Seminole chickee, at the side of the building.

"This looks authentic," Rick gazed at the brown, intertwining palmetto fronds.

"It is." Sean assured the Agent. "We have lots of well-crafted shelters on our property. Friends, real Seminole Indians, maintain them."

"OK, that was a foolish statement. The weaving is beautiful." Rick hoped his face hadn't turned as red as the stinging suggested.

A fabulous lunch of gator tail, swamp cabbage, grilled beans, and hush puppies was served with pitchers of sweet tea. Rick wanted to request unsweet, but was afraid of insulting his host.

*A little sugar, in moderation, never hurt anyone—especially considering I'm in sugar country.*

During the meal, a police officer came in to tell the chief he was needed at the station. Chief Lee apologized and excused himself, asking Agent Malone to touch base with him later.

Alone now with Rick, Sean leaned in close and commented with enthusiasm, "I didn't feel free to talk in front of the Chief; I'm glad he left."

"So, you think the accident was suspicious?"

"I do."

"Tell me your recollection. Any detail you remember, whether you feel it's relevant or not." Rick poured himself a refill of tea.

"We had a tournament that weekend, so the marina was crowded. Mostly people I recognized, some I knew well. But there was this one boat that stood out to me as odd, just not a usual occurrence here on the lake. At the time, I was so upset about Randy and Jewels dying that I was mostly angry. But, it haunted me all that week. I told the chief, but he shrugged it off."

"As familiar as you are with your surroundings, I get where you're coming from. Can you start at the beginning? Tell me word for word what you experienced that day." Rick leaned back in his chair, feeling no guilt for drinking the sweet tea. *What Madison doesn't know won't hurt her.*

"When I host a tournament, I don't compete. But I do mingle with the fishermen. I was out on the rim canal, by myself, cruising along and enjoying the cool morning air. As I passed the Monkey Box, I noticed only one boat, and it wasn't until after I passed it that I realized it was Randy's boat. It was the brightest orange color on the entire lake. I whipped around and turned out the path through the hyacinth, getting close enough to speak. I saw that Randy was using his new rod, so I asked how it was working for him."

Sean reached for his tea glass and took a couple sips. "Jewels had bought it the day before. I showed her the one I thought was best for him. She was excited about surprising him."

After another pause to drink, he cleared his throat and continued. "Randy signaled with a thumbs-up and I turned to go. Didn't want to interfere with their fishing. In a couple of minutes, I passed an older bass boat that I recognized as a rental from Uncle Joe's Fish Camp. I threw my hand up, but they were having trouble with their gear, so they ignored me. I slowed enough to see if they needed a hand, but they said they'd be fine. The strangest part is I saw that one of the men was wearing dress slacks and wingtips. I mean, to each his own, but I never saw anybody go fishing in wingtips! You know, it just didn't set right in my mind."

"I went on, but kept thinking that was out of character for any serious fisherman—or even one with any clue at all. Well, it was about ten minutes after that when I slowed to speak to one of the tournament contestants, and we felt the explosion. And then we saw the smoke, back toward the Monkey Box. I raced back immediately, passed the Uncle Joe's boat headed back in. I ignored them at that point, and went straight to the smoke. There was nothing left: little bit of the hull, bright orange, nothing else. I dove in the water, looking for survivors, didn't see anyone. By the time I got out of the water, other boaters were coming in. I guess it was close to an hour that the Freshwater Fish Commission showed up. It was Tony, a guy I knew from town. I was really angry. I couldn't believe their boat just exploded! I'm not sure what I did, but I left and went flat out on the rim canal. Stupid of me, I know, but I was emotionally charged and that was my release. I finally turned back, and when I went by Uncle Joe's I decided to cut into the river there, and see if that boat had returned."

"So, this didn't make any sense to you the whole time?" Rick asked.

"I was born in a boat, just about. Mom is an angler, and so is Dad. I've been fishing since before I could walk. Never in my entire life have I seen a boat just explode. Dad said he hadn't, either. It's just too strange, but they ruled it accidental!"

Rick thought Sean was emotional again, so he changed the subject for a while, giving the young man a chance to recover.

"Can you take me out to this Uncle Joe's?" Rick placed a fifty on the table and stood up. The two men walked along the dock for a few minutes, then left in a metallic-red Ranger bass boat.

They went through the open locks and turned west in the Intercostal Waterway, a rim canal that surrounds Lake Okeechobee and connects the Atlantic to the Gulf Coast by waterway canals and the Caloosahatchee River.

Sean continued telling his story, how he questioned the worker at the docks of Uncle Joe's Fish Camp about the rental boat and the two men. After speaking with the old man, he became even more suspicious. When he told the chief what he suspected, he still took no action to follow up.

Rick was about to reach the conclusion that Chief Lee either didn't do his job or he was paid not to investigate the tragedy.

They costed up next to the tattered-looking dock and Sean jumped out to secure a rope. "It's safe, Rick. I know it looks shaky, but it's secure." He laughed.

As it turned out, the old dock-hand had vanished over the months following the tragedy, and Uncle Joe being just a name for the old marina, there was no one present who had been on the scene that day.

Sean asked the boy behind the counter to call the owner, a man he knew well that lived in the nearby town of Moore Haven.

"Hey, Gene, it's Sean. How you doing?" He laughed with the man on the phone, then asked, "Do you have your receipts from last winter, when that boat exploded in the Monkey Box?" He listened for a while, then gave the phone back to the attendant.

The stringy-haired young man bent down and pulled a book from the bottom drawer of an old desk, handing it to Sean. Sean thumbed through several pages before turning the page around toward Rick. "Here it is."

Rick used his phone to photograph the signature and photo ID of the man who paid cash for the boat rental, and the deposit return signature. He pointed to a comment written in squiggly handwriting by the man who had recorded the transaction. *Strange characters, them two*, written next to the piece of paper taped into the ledger book.

"Thank you." Rick handed the book back to the boy, along with ten dollars, folded neatly. The young boy grinned and tipped his hat, but said nothing.

Back at the marina, Sean and Rick exchanged business cards. Rick explained that if the two men were brought to trial, he'd be expected to testify. After all, Sean was the only person who could place them in the area at the time of the suspicious explosion. Sean readily agreed, and they said good bye.

Rick had one more stop before he could make his connection at the Palm Beach International Airport.

When he walked into Chief Lee's office, a female officer relayed a message from Lee. "Chief Lee said to please tell you, he's sorry he couldn't be here. He had a prisoner exchange he had to do himself in LaBelle, our county seat." She handed Rick a card. "He wants you to call and keep him up to date on what you learn about this case."

"Thank you, Officer. Assure Chief Lee that I absolutely will keep in touch. Thanks." Rick left for the airport, wheels in his mind turning.

What can of worms was he opening? Had that old man who commented about his suspicions disappeared because he was a witness? Were Chief Lee's hands dirty too? One thing he didn't want to think was that Monique might not be out of the woods herself. After all, as a child she had been witness to a number of trips made under questionable circumstances. If the Chicago gang had taken out her parents, would they try to take her out too?

# 21

Meanwhile, Madison drove west toward Knoxville and cut south on the back roads to Maryville.

*I can't let Vic see me. I don't trust him. But I do know one person I can trust.* She continued past the rangers' office and found her way to the old doc who had examined Monique.

*Doc Walden must know a way up on the mountain that doesn't involve the rangers.* She stopped next to his shack over the creek. Just as he had been when they arrived with the snake-bitten patient, he sat on the porch in that old rocker.

*I'm glad I remembered that he loved cotton candy.* The stop at Walmart had been fruitful. She carried a white plastic bag onto the porch.

"Howdy." The old man kept rocking.

"Hey, Doc, I'm glad I found you at home." She handed him the bag. "When I was here before with the hiker who was snake bitten, you said you loved cotton candy. So I brought you some." She shook his outreached hand. "Madison McKenzie; remember my face?"

"I sure do." He accepted the bag and opened the candy. "Boy, that smells just like I 'membered it." He snagged a chunk with two fingers. "Tastes the same too. How 'bout that?"

"I'm happy it agrees with your taste. A lot of things from our childhoods just are not the same. Like watermelon. Did you ever taste one that was as good as when you were a young boy?"

"No Ma'am, I ain't, that's for sure."

He motioned to another rocker. "Sit a spell and tell me about the patient. Did she get OK?"

"Yes, she did. You mean she hasn't been back up here to see you?" Madison thought sure she remembered Monique saying she was coming here to see the old Doc.

"I ain't seen no one, 'cept for that aggravating ranger."

"You mean Vic?" she asked. *I wonder why he said he hadn't seen her.*

"Yeah, Vic. He stopped by here the other day, wanting to know if you or that FBI feller had been by here. I told him I ain't seen you."

"Really? Wonder why he'd ask you about us."

"I don't pay him no mind. He and some other ranger, in a dirty uniform, was messing in the creek down there. It looked to me like they were a washing something off that other feller's pants."

"Hmm." Madison considered what the rangers might be doing. "Well, unfortunately, I need to get back up on that mountain, but I don't want nosy Vic knowing I'm there. What can you tell me?"

Doc had a handful of blue and pink cotton. "I know a way." He finished what he had in his hand, then said, "I don't tell everything I know." He grinned.

"No, Sir, I didn't think you had. You know where the hidden valley is?" she asked.

"Maybe." He stood up and teetered toward the door. "Let me change my boots. You wanna come in?"

"I'll just wait out here with your dog."

In a few minutes, Doc returned, all laced into hiking boots and carrying a walking stick. "Your vehicle got four-wheel drive?"

"Yep, it sure does," she stood and walked with him to her Blazer.

With the old man's poor eyesight, she was nearly past the turn before he recognized it.

"That's our turn." He looked up the rough grass-covered road as they came to an abrupt stop. "Ain't got no gate, has it?"

"No, I don't see any part of a gate. Are you sure that's a road?" Madison backed up and turned left onto the so-called road. "I'll put it in four-wheel drive, or we won't get up the hill, with all that grass."

"I'm purty sure this is it. I'll know in a minute." He squinted through the front windshield.

After a while, they came to a fork, with a trail even less traveled than the one they came up.

"Go to the left." Doc pointed. "There's a creek just on the other side o' that rise."

Sure enough, there was a rocky creek. Madison stopped. "Let me look at that. I hope it isn't too deep." She opened her door and stepped out.

"Been another car through here in the last day or two." She reported when she got back behind the wheel. "Let's hope it was Monique."

"You expect her to be up here?" The old man frowned. "What reason would she have?"

"She's unaccounted for going on forty-eight hours, and, I can't think of anyplace else she'd be. She's looking for the man who saved her life." She drove slowly across the ford in the creek. "Well, it's a safe crossing at least."

Madison proceeded to tell the story of what she and Rick suspected had happened to Monique, and about her folks in the plane crash

Doc listened carefully, and when she finished, he said, "I 'member that night. It come an awful storm. I was out hunting. I heard a plane engine cutting in and out. Then it got to sputtering, but I didn't see it; the rain was coming down too hard. I found me a cave to take shelter in 'til it let up. Next day, I heard they were a looking for the plane. Never did hear of 'em finding it."

"That's because they didn't. But apparently, a ranger found the little girl. He quit this job and moved to Florida, raised her as his own, and never told anyone. At least that's the story Monique's notes and the family Bible tell. That's why she won't stay away from here."

"That's sad. I wish I had looked for it. Maybe I'd have found the little girl."

The old doc turned his face toward the passenger window, staying quiet for a long time. Madison broke the silence when they came to what seemed to be the end of the road.

"Is this what it's supposed to look like?" She parked the Blazer.

"Yep. We're here, all right. You can back into the bushes. I'll get out and guide you over the smallest, so you won't hurt your vehicle none." He opened his door and walked toward the small saplings, waving his hand for her to follow.

Madison pulled her shifter down into reverse and watched as the old man waved her into an unlikely hiding place. She heard the brushing of the little trees against the SUV. Most that she saw were sassafras and spindly pines. When the pines surrounded her Blazer and the ones behind her stood higher than Doc's head, he held his hand up for her to stop.

"OK, you were right; it makes an excellent hideaway." She put her windows up and shut off the ignition. "Now which way?" She opened the back door to retrieve her backpack.

"Around that stand of trees, there's a big pile of rocks. If Monique is up here, her car might be near the rocks." Doc started walking away.

"Wait a minute!" Madison called out, hurrying to catch up with him. "Where do you think you're going? You are only along to show me the way. You're staying right here!"

"No, Ma'am; I ain't! You can forget that idea."

"No, seriously, I'm grateful for your guidance, but I can't let you go any further. I might run into some trouble."

"All the more reason I'm going. You can't fight off two or more bad guys alone. If little Monique ain't back, its 'cause she's in trouble. I know it, and you know it."

Madison stood looking toward the thick woods for a few seconds before turning back to Doc. "I'm not going to talk you out of this, am I?"

A grin spread across his face, and he turned, walking away into the woods without a word.

When they came to the rock pile, just like Doc had said, there sat Monique's vehicle, wedged in between a boulder as big as a house and tall, wide-based white pines.

"I've never seen pine trees this large. They have to be some of the oldest trees in this area."

"They are. When I was a young boy, they were the biggest around. Paw said they was big when he was a youngun. I expect they've been around here a few centuries."

"At least! That must be what the California redwoods look like," Madison said.

"Nope, they're even bigger!"

Doc stepped onto a rocky ledge leading around the side of the boulder as if he'd been there before. Madison followed closely. She feared his old boots might slip, but who was she to tell Doc to be careful? She paid close attention to her own feet and watched as the valley floor fell away into a tangle of rhododendron below.

The ledge widened as it approached the top of the rock. Doc placed his feet one at a time into shallow indentations that didn't look wide enough for his boots. In a matter of seconds, he stood on top, looking down at Madison.

She took a deep breath and moved up the way she had watched him go. When she reached the last foothold, Doc's hand had reached down to pull her up the rest of the way. Madison felt his grip and realized this old man was not as frail as he appeared.

Doc lay flat and belly-crawled toward the edge of the protruding overhang. "Well, come on up here, if you want to see the hidden valley."

Madison dropped to her knees, then all the way down on her stomach before crawling to Doc's side. She felt a hitch in her throat, but tried not to let him know she was scared by the distance to the bottom. "So that's the hidden valley." She looked down at what appeared to be a couple of hundred feet below. "It's bigger than I thought it might be. Why, that's at least a quarter of a mile."

"More like a half mile, I reckon." Doc lay still, watching Madison take in the vista. "Paw told me those caves has Indian writings and pictures on the walls."

"You've never gone down in it?" she asked.

He shook his head. "Didn't see no need. I like looking from here, and I don't have to get tired-out climbing back up." He laughed.

"Where are the caves? I don't see any." Madison strained to look directly underneath where she was.

"Careful!" Doc grabbed Madison's shoulder. "Don't scare me that way."

"I'm not going any further. I bet the caves are on this side. Because that side surely doesn't have any—unless they're well hidden. Look! That little creek runs out from under those bushes. It might be a camouflaged cave."

She reached into her backpack and pulled out a small pair of binoculars. Looking straight across from where they lay, she scanned the cliff. She snapped her gaze back and adjusted the focus. "I see somebody, there," she pointed, "next to that pool of water. It's a woman; maybe it's Monique." She offered the glasses to Doc.

"Don't need those to see them men coming down the path," he pointed to a switchback of trails on the steep wall above the woman. "That's Vic and that other ranger. If he's even a ranger."

Madison locked in on the pair. "Yep, that's Vic. But I've never seen the other guy, and I met a lot of rangers when Monique was missing." She turned her attention back to Monique. "She's just sitting there. Oh! Her hands are tied, and maybe her feet, too."

Madison slipped back from the edge of the overlook. "I need to get down there."

"Not without me, you don't." Doc slithered past her and worked his way down the backside of the rock.

Madison caught up with him and carefully slipped her feet into the indentions, inching back to the ledge. "OK, we need a plan." She reached into the backpack, and her hand came out with a small revolver. "Do you know how to shoot?"

"Got one of my own," Doc grinned and pulled a Colt 45 revolver from his bibbed overalls. "I could shoot an eye out of a squirrel from fifty yards by the time I was five!"

"Uh, why would you?" Madison shuddered.

"To eat! If you shoot 'em in the body, it tears up a big piece of meat. But not if you hit the head." Doc shook his head and stared at her. "Where would you shoot one?"

"I wouldn't!" She turned and walked back toward the giant pines.

"That's not the way down," Doc called out.

"Shush, they might hear you," she whispered. "I saw the way down."

"Not the way we're going. It's this way." Doc stepped between two small boulders and looked back to her. "You coming with me?"

Madison followed closely, watching her step. She felt this rocky trail was a perfect place for snakes, specifically copperheads. And she did not want to meet up with them.

Doc moved as she'd never have believed he could. He was as agile as a young boy. Was it because he was in his element, in the woods and rocks?

By the time Madison and Doc reached the valley floor, the two men were leading Monique across the tall grass, disappearing from view now and then. Monique's hands were still tied, but her feet were free. They came closer; Madison crouched behind a boulder, but Doc had gone out of her sight around a stand of pines. She hoped he'd remember not to get into a crossfire situation with Monique between them.

The second man, the one she had not recognized, shoved Monique down and told her to sit on the rock. It was the same rock Madison was hiding behind. Then the man walked over to Vic. They seemed to be arguing about something.

Madison pulled a small knife from her hiking boot. She would cut the rope securing Monique's hands. "Don't turn around," Madison whispered. "I'm going to free your hands."

Monique slipped closer to the edge of the rock.

"Sit right there, and keep your hands behind you. I'm slipping the knife into your right hand. Hold on to it until you get a chance to use it. Can you do that?"

Monique nodded.

Vic turned toward the pine trees. "Listen," he said. "Thought I heard something."

"You're paranoid, Vic," Drake grumbled.

"That guy could slip up on us, and you'd never know it."

*What guy?* Madison thought maybe they were holding Monique to draw her imaginary friend out. She slipped closer to the two men. At that moment, she saw a movement just over Vic's head. It was Doc, ready to drop onto the men. Then she saw it was not the 45 in his hand, but a snake! He threw it down on the fat man's shoulders.

"Hands up, Vic!" Madison stepped into the open, her Sig pointed toward the tall ranger. "I'm an excellent shot, so don't push your luck."

Drake dove toward the rocks, trying to escape the rattlesnake. A pistol shot rang out, striking him in the left leg. The rough-looking man bellowed like a hound on a hunt.

"Hands on the back of your head, Vic. Drop to your knees," Madison stepped closer, looking at the guy on the ground. "You'll live, unless you move!"

The snake vanished into the high grass. Vic moved cautiously, placing one hand on the back of his neck; the other edged slowly toward his lower back. Another shot rang out, and Vic's hands both jerked to the top of his head.

Doc slid off the overhead perch and grabbed the gun from Vic's belt. He shoved him to his knees and wrapped a piece of rope around both his hands, tying it quickly. "Recon I didn't tell ya I used to rope calves, did I?" He laughed like he was pleased with his action.

"You did great, Doc!" Madison leaned in and kissed his cheek.

Next Doc tended to the wounded guy laying on the ground. "You're OK, feller. It went clean through. You might live!" He rolled the moaning man onto his belly, and secured his hands behind his back with a second piece of rope.

"We make a great team!" Madison turned to Monique. "Are you all right?"

"Yes, thank goodness you showed up! I thought they were going to kill me and dump me in that cave." Monique flung her arms around Madison.

"I wouldn't let them hurt you, Monique." A deep voice sounded from the shadows of the cave. In a second, the form of a dark-haired man emerged.

Madison couldn't help noticing the piercing blue eyes. "It's you!"

"Michael!" Monique ran to his side. "See, Maddie, I told you he was real!"

"Yes, and you didn't exaggerate, either," she smiled. "I'm Madison, and I think you've met Doc." Madison offered her hand.

"You're the one with the TBI," Michael said as they shook.

"Not exactly; I was with Agent Malone, but I'm only a student." Madison felt diminished as he looked down at her. "I knew Monique wouldn't stop looking, and I'm happy she found you. But what would you have done?"

"Protect her." Michael stepped next to Vic. "I'm here now, you want to pick on a man instead of a kid?"

Vic looked up into the face of hate and vengeance.

"What was in that tarp, anyway? A woman?" Michael looked at Madison. "Can you reach your friend? He might find the other missing hiker in that cave."

"I don't have a cell signal. We'll have to load these characters up and drive them out to the authorities. Can you help me get them out to my vehicle?"

Michael nodded. "But then I'm out of here. I'm not sticking around for the cops."

Monique tilted her head as if to study his face. "Where will you go?"

Madison thought she heard a tremor in Monique's voice. "Let's get started. I'm not looking forward to climbing out of here with these two."

During their climb, Monique stuck with Michael. They whispered occasionally. The wounded prisoner fell repeatedly, causing Michael to have to help him up. Monique finally gave up on getting the answers she needed. She dropped back to bring up the rear with Doc.

"That was some quick thinking with the rattlesnake," Monique said. "Weren't you afraid of handling it?"

"Heck no! I'm a tough old buzzard. That snake was more scared of me than I am of a snake." Dock laughed enthusiastically. "Worked, didn't it?" He laughed even longer.

"You're enjoying this way too much," Monique said.

As soon as they were all on top of the mountain, Madison checked her phone. "I have a signal here!" She called Rick's cellphone. "Rick, where can I take these crooks?" She went on to explain where she and Doc found Monique after Vic and his buddy kidnapped her, how Doc enlisted the aid of a rattlesnake to take down one of the bad guys, and that Michael was a real, live human being.

"You met this blue-eyed ghost?" Rick chuckled loudly. "That valley must have some strange water flowing through it."

"We'll talk later, Agent Malone," Madison was not laughing.

Madison led the way, with Vic securely tied up in her back seat. Drake was tied in the back of Monique's Subaru, and Doc rode shotgun to keep an eye on him. Michael promised he'd wait for the sheriff's department to show them how to find the cave with the tarp, which most likely contained a body.

She drove to the local ranger station, where they met the sheriff and some top officials of the ranger division. A couple of the rangers joined a team of deputies going back up the Appalachian Trail to locate Michael and the cave. Just in case the blue-eyed ghost vaporized, Doc asked if he could join the rangers. They indicated they'd be pleased to have him show them the way.

Jake came to meet Madison. "You rounded up the bad guys! I wish I had been with you, Ms. Madison."

"I just did what I had to. Monique was in a bad position, and I knew she might get hurt. I had to do what I could to free her. I suspected that Vic was dirty. That other ranger is even worse, I think."

"Oh, he's not even a ranger. He's Vic's half-brother: broke out of jail a while back. He's wearing Vic's clothes," Jake explained.

"Oh, that reminds me. Sheriff, check his left sleeve to see if it's missing a button," Madison said.

The sheriff unrolled the sleeve. Sure enough, there was blood on the cuff and the button was gone, along with a piece of the shirt sleeve. "How'd you know?" he asked.

"Test the blood. I'll bet it matches the woman you have in the morgue. And I'll bet he's a leftie." Madison felt sure he was the man who slit the woman's throat.

"You can't pin that on me! Vic was the one that killed her! He's left hand-ed, not me!" Drake was ready to spill his guts. "He traded shirts with me when he had to go into his office yesterday."

"Shut your mouth! They ain't got nothing on us!" Vic barked from the back of the sheriff's department cruiser.

"I'll keep them separate 'til we get their stories. My opinion is they'll both sing like canaries once I get them behind bars. Thank you, Madison. You and Doc did a good job. The county is beholden to you!" Sheriff Pete then drove away with Vic, and the head ranger hauled in Drake in the back of his pickup truck.

Monique looked up toward the mountain, "I wonder if I'll ever see him again."

"Maybe. Who knows what Michael is hiding? In time, he might forgive himself for whatever he's done and look you up."

Trent smiled and tipped his hat toward the women. "Be seeing you, both, I hope, someday."

"Thanks, Trent. Or you can call whenever you come to Tennessee. Mo-nique and I will be both be happy to see you," Madison said as she climbed into her Blazer.

"Be safe, Maddie. Thanks for your help!" Monique started her vehicle.

"You keep in touch. I mean it! And no running off to find a ghost. OK?"

"OK, I promise!" Monique laughed.

They went different directions as the sun dropped behind the mountain.

# 22

Madison drove slowly north through the rolling hills of the countryside leading through the back roads of Tennessee on Highway 411. She often took the county roads instead of the interstate so she could relax and have time to sort things out in her life.

Even though Madison had felt scared when she realized Monique was in trouble, she realized that her blood flowed with adrenaline when she and Doc made the plan to take down the two men. She hadn't hesitated to fire off a couple of warning shots, which had persuaded Vic to respect her orders.

The more she thought about the events of the day, the better she felt about the results. Her phone rang, breaking her train of thought.

"Hello, Rick. No, I'm not passing through Knoxville—"

"They found the second hiker. She was in the cave, like Michael said."

"Oh, I so hoped he was wrong about that." Madison was quiet for a time. "Rick, they didn't take Michael into custody, did they?"

Rick didn't answer right away.

"They did, didn't they?" She answered her question.

"How'd you know?" Rick asked.

"I just did." She waited for Rick to say something, but when he didn't, she said, "I better call Monique. She'll want to know."

"Are you going home or back to Atlanta?" Rick asked.

"Home. Dad and Shirley will be back in a few days. And I want to check in with Nell at the hospital."

"Oh, good news; Drew is at home, and Nell is there with him. They have a nurse coming in twice a day, but he's doing amazingly well," Rick said. "I'll be over later tonight or early in the morning. I'll see you then."

"I'm shocked he's home! Is he still on the turning thing?" she asked.

"No. Our sheriff is in a regular hospital bed, with one of those jell-filled mattresses that moves every few minutes. Guess he's tougher than we thought."

"Great! I can't wait to talk to him. If I'm not at my cottage, I'll be at his apartment." She paused for a moment. "How did they get him up those steps?"

"I thought you'd never ask. They didn't have to, Drew and Nell are in the downstairs bedroom, where Henry's dad slept. It was Holly's idea. As soon as she heard that he could be released, she cleaned up that old man's room, and even painted it. She put up new curtains and blinds, plus she added a bed for Nell. I've never been in that part of the house, but Henry says it's a huge room with a private bath. I guess it was the master suite back in the day."

"Henry and Holly are saints! Oh, my. What will they do next?"

"It's amazing. And to think the sheriff and I thought Henry was rotten like his old man. He's a sweet guy, though. And we both know how special Holly is, don't we?"

"Oh yeah, I've known that most of my life." She waited a few seconds and then added, "I'll see you later Rick. Let me go now, so I can try to reach Monique."

"Sure, we'll talk later. See you."

Madison listened as Monique's phone went to voicemail.

"Monique, I hoped you'd answer. Please call me as soon as you get my message!"

As her Blazer approached I-40, Madison took the turn, putting her on the interstate. She was eager to get to Cold Creek, and by taking 40 to I-81, she could drive much faster and possibly even make it before dark.

In just over an hour, Madison turned down the gravel lane toward the yellow farmhouse where Holly often provided a dog-sitting service for Bud, and now even a convalescent home for Sheriff Drew Perry.

Bud and Bear lay on the front porch when she pulled into the circular driveway. Bud didn't come running to meet her like he usually did. Madison worried he was pouting, since she'd left him behind again while she went back to Georgia.

"Bud, you'd better come see me," she said as she got out of her SUV. Bear wiggled all over, but Bud just raised his head and then laid it back down on the porch. "Are you OK, Buddy?" She rushed up the steps and ran to him.

He raised his head again, and she could see his front leg was swollen and had blood on it. "What *happened* to you?" Madison felt sharp tears forming.

"We think he and Bear got in a tangle with a bobcat. He's OK, nothing broken. He's scuffed up a bit, but he defended our Bear. He didn't get a scratch." Henry lay his hand on Madison's shoulder. "I'm sorry, Madison, but he isn't hurt badly. I promise."

"Oh, I trust you, Henry. I'm just sorry he is hurting. He's my baby, you know." She wiped her eyes on her sleeve.

"No, he's not hurting. After I had gone all over checking for injuries, I gave him Bute, a pain med for animals. I got it from the vet when my coonhound was injured. He's just sleepy. He'll be better by tomorrow." Henry stepped back, holding Bear to keep him out of Madison's way.

"Madison, I didn't know you were coming home tonight. Why didn't you call me? I left two messages on your phone." Holly came onto the porch.

"I'm sorry, Holly. I didn't have a signal on my phone most of the day, and when I did, I didn't think to check messages. It's been an exciting day, trust me. I'll tell you all about it." Madison stood up. "How is your patient?"

"He's doing great! I mean, he's still badly injured, but at least he's in a bed, and has 'round the clock care. I guess Rick told you he came here?" Holly hugged her friend. "We're sorry Bud got hurt. We had no idea there was a bobcat on the property."

"I don't blame you guys. Shucks, Bud's been curious about bobcats ever since he was a puppy. I told him never to tangle with one, but he obviously didn't listen." She laughed.

"Come on in and see Drew before he goes to sleep. He's been asking about you." Holly pulled Madison toward the screen door. "You too, Henry. That way we can all hear what Madison has done. Let Bud sleep a while longer. Bear won't leave his side!"

Holly led the way down a hallway Madison had never been. At the back of the house was a double door that opened into what looked like a study. There were shelves full of books high up the walls on two sides, with an arched doorway leading into another room.

Drew sat with his head propped up on a couple of pillows. The head of the bed was raised just enough not to lay flat. He smiled as Madison walked in. "Hey, Maddie. Thanks for coming."

"How do you feel? You sure look better than when I saw you last week. But should you be raised up like that?" She leaned over and kissed his forehead. "Hi, Nell."

Nell moved to the opposite side of the bed and adjusted Drew's pillow so that he didn't have to turn his head to look at Madison. "There, that's better.

So, Maddie, I hear you are officially in law enforcement now!"

"What? What do you mean? Just because I rescued Monique?"

"And captured those two killers! That was a brave thing you did." Nell propped her fists on her hips. "You should be very proud."

"I just did what I had to, at the moment. Monique was held prisoner to draw out Michael. Doc helped me. I was never in any danger."

"Except when Ol' Doc threw that rattlesnake down," Drew said.

They all laughed.

Drew reached for Maddie's hand. "I've turned in my letter of resignation to the county. I recommended they replace me with you. You have more experience than I had when I first started with the department."

"Oh, no you don't, Drew. I'm not sheriff material," Madison said.

"You are more experienced and educated than anyone I know. The town needs you, Madison."

"There are deputies in Erwin who have been with the department for decades. They need to choose one of them."

"Why do you think I never brought one up to Cold Creek as my deputy? They're not qualified, and you are!" Drew's breathing became labored.

"Well talk about this another time. You need to rest now," Nell said.

"Nothing more to say. Henry, convince her! We need her now, not later."

Madison tried any angle she could think of to decline the offer. She even declared she had to return to school in a few weeks, and the town just needed to hold an election. She was sure that was the end of the discussion.

The evening was wearing on Drew. His voice became weak, and Nell suggested he go to sleep. Madison and the others left the room, saying goodnight to both Drew and Nell. On the way out, Madison noticed a second bed next to the doorway.

"I never realized there was a room this large downstairs. Was this Henry's dad's?"

Holly answered, "Yes, and I was never in there, except after he passed away. I didn't know myself. There's even a bathroom through that other door; you might think it's a closet."

"Hmm. Funny how we didn't know what was right under our noses," Madison said.

"And that's not all. Across the hall is another door. It goes into the basement. That's where he kept his moonshine. I found it quite by accident. I was looking for his clothes closet to find a suit to bury him in. Henry said he'd only been down there one time," Holly whispered.

Madison sat at the table when she and Holly got to the kitchen. "Did you ever find his clothes closet?"

"It's in the room with the books, but you'd never see it behind the book-case. Like in your... Uh, I mean, Denny's house, you know: secret passages. For weeks Henry and I looked for hidden doors, but didn't find any."

"They did have some strange secrets in their lives, didn't they?" Madison looked at her watch. "I better get going."

Just at that moment, Henry walked in with Bud and Bear following him. Bud limped a little, but he came right to Madison and laid his head on her lap.

"You ready to go home, Sweet Boy? You look pitiful!" She smoothed the hair on his neck. "Thanks for taking care of him, Henry. I appreciate it."

"No problem. I'm sorry Bud got hurt. I never dreamed a bobcat could get the best of a dog this big. Must be one big cat!" Henry got a beer from the re-frigerator. "Beer, Maddie?"

"Oh, no thanks, Henry. I think I'll take my baby home and fuss over him a while." She and Bud made their way to the porch ahead of Henry. Holly fol-lowed along with Bear.

"I guess the twins are in bed, huh?" Madison asked.

"Yeah. I need to rest, so I get them to bed as soon as they get their bath."

"And she bathes them in that lavender-smelling stuff, so they'll relax and get sleepy." Henry laughed and hugged his wife.

"Oh, that's just plain dirty! Does it work?" Madison asked.

"Sometimes," Holly said. "I think I'm ready for a lavender bath."

"Oh no you don't!" Henry objected.

"Goodnight, you two!" Madison helped Bud into the floor of the Blazer, and he climbed on his own up into the seat. As she drove away, she adjusted her mirror and saw Henry pick Holly up and carry her into the house. "They're happy, Bud. I'm glad Holly has him."

# 23

The next day, Henry stopped by to see Madison. She and Bud sat on her porch. He told her the town council had called an emergency meeting, due to Sheriff Perry's injury and resignation letter.

"Going with me to the town hall?" Henry asked.

"Oh, is that why there are so many people going into Shirley's this time of day?" Madison laughed. "I didn't realize it had been dubbed the town hall. But I guess it always was!" She stood up and told Bud to stay, then said, "Yeah, I'll walk over with you."

The room erupted in applause when they walked in. Madison stopped cold in her tracks. Mr. Olsen, Mayor of Cold Creek and the owner of the hardware store, approached her.

"Madison, we polled our residents; out of the three hundred fifty within our town limits, three hundred forty-nine voted for you to replace Sheriff Perry." Mr. Olsen smiled and placed her hand in his. "Will you do us the honor of being our sheriff?"

Madison felt nervous. Her stomach flip-flopped. She swallowed hard, then spoke. "Three hundred forty-nine out of three hundred fifty? Wow, one person in their right mind. Who's the holdout?"

"You. What do you say?" Dr. McClellan stepped close to Madison. "You have proved at least twice that you are brave enough to handle the job. We all know you're trustworthy and honest. You have a better education than Perry, even, so how can you not take the offer? It just makes perfect sense to all of us."

Madison stepped over to a nearby stool and sat down. Ben was behind the counter. "Need a drink?" he laughed.

"I don't think you have anything substantial enough to change my mind, Ben," she said.

Mr. Olsen sat beside her. "That's something else we will discuss at our next meeting, but right now we need to know your serious answer. Your town needs you, Maddie. You and that Rick fellow are already trying to find out who did this to our sheriff. Why not make it an official title? You're perfect for our needs. And I get the feeling that you need us, or else you'd be in the summer session back at UT. Am I right?"

Madison didn't know what to say. Ben handed her a bottle of water. The entire room was filled with her friends and neighbors, all gathered close around her. *No pressure here.*

It felt like an eternity before she finally said, "I'll do it. If you will put out a notice for an election and get others to run, I'll take it, but only until someone else can be elected."

The room sounded like UT had scored a touchdown. The hoots and hollers and clapping brought a nervous smile to Madison's face.

Mr. Olsen held up one hand to silence the crowd. "We need to go to the sheriff's office and swear you in."

"You mean, right now?" Madison gulped a drink from the water bottle.

"Why not?" Henry placed his arm around her shoulders. "No time better than the present. And we have a nice crowd to cheer you on."

"OK, let's go." Madison stood on shaky legs, but she tried hard not to let anyone see her nerves. "Henry, you bring my deputy, Bud, OK?"

The crowd gathered on the sidewalk in front of the old jail. Only a handful of the town council members could fit inside the office. Mr. Olsen pulled the sheriff's badge out of his coat pocket, and a small Bible. He knew the words without looking at any cue cards. Maddie held up her right hand and repeated after Mr. Olsen. Instead of pinning the badge on, she clipped it to her belt on her jeans.

"I guess I can't wear jeans as my sheriff attire, can I?" she asked, looking at the council members.

"As long as your colors are black and gold, or tan, you can wear whatever you want, aside from Daisy Duke shorts," one of the men said.

"What's wrong with Daisy Duke shorts, Slim? I think Madison could get better cooperation from you old fellas in them. She's got the build for it!"

"No Daisy Dukes! I can promise you that!" Madison lowered her head at Mr. Tittle. "And I won't tell Sally you suggested it!"

The guys began leaving the office until only Henry, Mr. Olsen, and Dr. Chip remained. "Thank you, Maddie. You already apprehended the worst criminals we had in Cold Creek; what could you possibly be worried about?" Mr. Olsen started for the door.

"Oh, please don't say that! I'm not worried about trouble, just hope I don't let anyone down. I will need your guidance and counseling, Mr. Olsen."

"You'll do fine, my dear. I always knew you'd be the best thing ever to come from this town." With that, he disappeared into the street filled with residents.

"Doc, you are the best thing to come from this town; he didn't mean that." Madison apologized for Mr. Olsen's remark.

"No problem, Madison... Er, Sheriff McKenzie. I don't have a problem with what he said. In fact, I agree with him. Don't you, Henry?"

"I sure do." Henry sat on the edge of Sheriff McKenzie's desk. "I'm proud of our hometown heroine."

Doc left, and Henry asked Madison if she wanted help rearranging anything. When she declined, he told her goodbye and left.

Madison sat behind the desk she'd looked up to as long as she could remember. Of the men preceding her, she only recognized Sheriff Franks Sr. and Drew Perry. *I hope I can do this job justice. I'll certainly give it my best effort, until they elect another person.*

With that thought, she looked for the new keys that Rick had put in the desk drawer when he replaced the locks. Rick had purchased a decorative key, green with rhinestones. As she compared them, she realized the two were the same. She separated them and put one into a file in the cabinet and the other in her pocket. *What was he thinking, getting a green sparkly key? It isn't like he knew I'd end up with it...or did he?!! I'll kill him!*

The next morning, Madison drove Bud out to visit Bear for the day, while she ran into Johnson City to the Mall. Belk's carried her favorite jeans, and she felt sure she'd find a suitable shirt to use as a uniform.

She located the Gloria Vanderbilt jeans in khaki, but only one pair in size eight. She looked through the blouses and tops, not seeing anything suitable, then she spotted a button-down shirt across the room on the wall. The long-sleeved black shirt had the perfect amount of stretch. It fit her perfectly, so she looked for a short-sleeved version. She chose a similar style that had roll-up sleeves with loops that buttoned to secure them for summer. Taking them to the register, she asked the sales clerk if she had more of the jeans in khaki in her size.

"There are some on another display over there, did you see them?"

"I missed that table; thanks." Madison came back with one more pair.

"What about the blouses? Any more in black?" she asked *Mary*, as she saw on the woman's tag.

"Black? Hmm... I think there are more in the back. I'll check."

Mary returned with two short-sleeved and one long-sleeved. "This all I have in your size. But I can call the store at the Pinnacle, in Bristol. If they have them, they can ship them right to your home."

"That would be great. I'm using khaki and black for a uniform. I ordered the patches from the county for the shirts. They're gold with black lettering. Don't you think that will look nice?" Madison gave Mary her name and address a little at a time, as Mary typed the information into the computer register: Sheriff Madison McKenzie, 101 North Main Street, Cold Creek, TN, 38040. Then she smiled; it was the first time she'd used the title sheriff.

"Oh, my! You're the sheriff *Johnson City Press* featured this morning! I'm thrilled to meet you!" Mary squealed and clapped her hands together.

Madison felt her cheeks burn. "I, uh, didn't see the paper." She looked around to see if anyone heard the clerk. Luckily, she saw that no one else was close enough to hear Mary's excitement.

"Sheriff McKenzie, I hope I didn't embarrass you. It's just that...well, I've always wanted to be in law enforcement. And when I saw your story, it made me want it even more."

"There's no reason you can't. You can contact Dr. Gerre Baker at UT, and she'll help you choose your classes." Madison recovered quickly from the shock of Mary's reaction. It made perfectly good sense, after hearing why Mary reacted the way she did.

On her drive home, Rick's ringtone brought her phone alive. She answered, "Sheriff McKenzie."

Rick sounded disappointed. "Oh, come on! You spoiled my line."

Madison laughed.

"Where are you?" Rick asked.

"Heading home from the mall in Johnson City."

"I'm heading up from Asheville. See you in town?" Rick asked.

"Good, we'll go out and visit Drew." Madison disconnected the call.

Forty-five minutes passed while Madison waited in her new office for Rick. She looked through a stack of law enforcement bulletins sent from surrounding towns and counties. She found one story that drew her attention, sent from Smyth County Virginia. The flyer gave information about a nine-year-old boy named Nicholas Cameron. The date was back in February. She called the Smyth County Sheriff Department for more information.

"Hello, this is Sheriff Madison McKenzie in Cold Creek, Tennessee. Can you give me an update on the nine-year-old boy missing from your area?" She listened a moment and then said, "Yes, Nicholas."

After speaking for a while with Smyth County's office, she learned that the boy was still missing. Countless leads had been dead ends. The boy had just vanished from his school one afternoon, and had never been seen again.

Madison thanked the woman on the phone and asked that she be updated if there was any change in the case. She also requested a photo, since there was none on the flyer. In a moment her phone vibrated, signaling a text. It was a picture of Nicholas, a dark-haired boy with green eyes behind black-rimmed glasses. He had dimples in both rosy cheeks, and his smile showed a mix of permanent and deciduous teeth. *A handsome little guy*, Madison thought.

She called about all the bulletins from the last six months, and was pleased to learn only Nicholas was still missing. She felt this was a good starting point in her new job as sheriff of Cold Creek.

Madison busied herself making sure all the windows were locked. Then she saw Bud jump up and go into his all-over body wiggle, signaling Rick had arrived. She walked to the door and opened it just as Rick was reaching for it. "You must have been in *south* Asheville."

"I was leaving from the airport—just flew in from Atlanta."

"Where'd you park?" She looked out on the street.

"At the restaurant. Come on, I haven't eaten all day." Rick stepped off the sidewalk after greeting Bud with his usual scratching behind the ears.

"Porch, Bud. Stay." Madison pointed to her cottage and joined Rick. Bud went straight to the steps of her porch. He understood that he was 'on guard.'

Dinner didn't take long. Madison and Rick both ordered that night's special: baked country ham, sweet potato casserole, and fresh steamed green beans. Shirley's was still the only eating establishment in Cold Creek.

As they came out of the restaurant, Rick whistled for Bud. He raced to join them. Madison heard the door locks click in a white SUV, so she walked to the passenger side of the vehicle. Rick opened the door to allow Bud to get in. He also slipped the dog a bite of ham.

"I saw that, Rick Malone!" Madison knew he always managed to sneak a treat for Bud, and she didn't mind.

The twins met them as soon as the rental SUV stopped in front of the yellow farm house. Hugh rattled off, "Daddy's got his gun and went to the barn, hunting that bobcat. He got Mommy's chickens!"

"Oh, no!" Madison said.

Harry said, "Come on Bud. Bear's in the house. Daddy didn't want that cat to eat him."

"You visit with Drew. I think I'll go to the barn and find Henry. Thanks, boys. You keep Bud safe with Bear, OK?"

"We will, Miss Maddie," they said together.

Madison walked around the house, passed the willow tree, and started up the steep path to the barn. She caught a movement in her peripheral vision, drew her Sig from the shoulder holster, and turned to see a bobcat ready to spring at her. She squeezed the trigger, getting a shot off just in time. The cat turned in mid-air as the bullet grazed his shoulder. He fell just six feet from her beside the path. She froze. The largest bobcat she'd ever seen lay there looking up at her. She felt tears welling up. She'd never missed a target, and this time she was sorry for her good shot. The cat attempted to get up. He was suffering, and Madison wanted to help. Suddenly she was aware of Henry beside her.

"That was a great shot, Maddie, I thought he had you."

"He's just winged, Henry. He could survive." She slid her Sig back into the holster. "What do we do with him?"

Henry raised his rifle, "I'll take care of him."

"No!" She grabbed the barrel of the 22. "You have a muzzle for your hounds. Can't we use it, and then sedate him? I know you have the medicine."

"Are you kidding me?" Henry's voice was stern.

"I'll take him to the vet. He's beautiful, just misplaced. He deserves a chance at life. I won't let you kill him."

Henry stomped toward the barn, mumbling something under his breath. He soon returned with a blanket, a muzzle, and a syringe filled with medicine. "Hold this." He thrust the plastic syringe into Madison's hand. He dropped the blanket over the cat's head, then reached for the medicine, popping the sedative into the cat's rump. This action caused the cat to squall, but the drug worked quickly. In just a minute, he appeared lifeless. Henry didn't waste any time wrapping the back and front legs with rope and tied it snug. He slipped the muzzle on the cat's face, not a good fit, but he tied it in place anyway. "That should hold."

Madison wrapped the blanket around the cat as soon as Henry lifted him up.

"Gosh! He weighs more than my hounds!" Henry carried him to the back porch.

Holly stood in the doorway. "What will you do with it?"

"Please bring me Bear's kennel, and hurry," Henry said.

"He's not dead? I heard a shot." She ran into the house. And in just a few minutes she returned with the dog kennel.

"I just wounded him," Madison said. "And I couldn't let Henry kill him.

He's too pretty."

Henry placed the cat in the kennel and secured the door. "I'll call the wild-life preserve, see if they have someone on call."

"Do you mean Bays Mountain?"

Henry nodded. "Seems to me I've seen a night-call number in the phone book, just for such instances like this."

Holly returned to the porch with the phone in her hand. "I've got them. Can you meet this fellow in Johnson City?"

"Sure, where?" Henry asked.

Holly continued talking to someone as Henry and Madison loaded the kennel into the back of his truck. Henry closed down the tonneau cover and then kissed Holly good-bye.

Madison climbed into the passenger's side. "I'm going with you," she said.

"OK with me. That is your cat back there," Henry laughed.

By the time they reached the meeting place the bobcat was starting to come out of the sedation. The vet checked him over and thanked Henry for treating him with compassion.

"He's a beautiful specimen. I've never seen one so large. I think he's going to be just fine. It's nice that you kept him warm. That may have saved his life." The vet and the wildlife officer shook both their hands and invited Henry and Madison to come to visit their cat at Bays Mountain in a week or so.

"Oh, I will. You can count on that," Madison thanked the men for meeting them.

On the way back to the farm, Madison reminded Henry about her thoughts of adding a detached garage at her cottage. Henry hadn't had time to do the sketches they'd talked about yet; he promised to research plans and let her know what she could do. He agreed that since she'd be a year-round resident again, she needed a garage.

"Let's not jump to conclusions, Henry," she said. "I'm not sure about that decision."

Once Madison and Rick were back in Cold Creek, they stopped in at the jail. They found a couple of notes on the door and a vase of fresh cut flowers sitting on the stoop. Madison lifted the card and read aloud, "Congratulations, Maddie. We are so proud of you! Best wishes, Ben and Margie."

"That's sweet of them," Rick said. "The notes are from Mr. Olsen, and Jack Kelly, both saying they wish the best for you."

"Oh, I didn't even see Mr. Kelly tonight. He's an old fishing buddy of Jess'."

"Henry told me there were a lot of people standing outside the restaurant, waiting to see what you would say when Mayor Olsen asked you to fill the position."

Madison smiled. Inwardly she felt dread and uncertainty, but she had felt that before and learned to overcome it. She'd do it again.

She unlocked the door and carried the flowers inside. Rick followed her, the smile on his face telling Madison that he, too, was proud of her.

Rick leaned in and kissed her forehead, "You're right where you need to be."

"I know. I only hope I can do the job justice."

"You will." Rick went to the stairs. "Beginning with solving your first case."

Madison followed him to the basement. The two combed the room again, just in case they had missed even so much as a fleck of dust or a hair. But they found nothing. Rick opened the door that had supposedly been sealed shut. He pulled a small penlight from his pocket and carefully made his way down the old wood steps. Madison lifted a spotlight from the metal desk and followed him. The door at the bottom felt as if it was sealed shut. But with one swift kick from Rick, it swung open.

When he inspected the frame, he found nothing more than a small wooden latch, like one you might find on an outhouse door: not very secure.

Madison stepped into a space that had once held chains in the walls and bloodstains on the earthen floor. A former sheriff had used it to tame wild women—or so the story goes.

"Look; there was no straw here before. Someone brought it in, like to sleep on." She walked to the barricade blocking access to the tunnels leading to Cold Creek Caverns. "Someone loosened these boards, and has been crawling through." She looked toward Rick. "I'm going in. You with me?"

Rick answered as he passed her, "I'll lead. You follow." Bud darted ahead of both of them and into the tunnel. "Well, whatever you say, Deputy Dawg."

In minutes, Bud stopped and growled as though he heard or smelled someone he didn't like.

Madison said, "I've only seen him do that when one person was around."

"Franks!" she and Rick said simultaneously.

Rick continued, "I thought he left town."

"Me too." Madison and Bud started forward again. Soon they came to a fork in the tunnel; Bud went to the right, not the left as she expected. She knew the right was a dead end—or was it?

Bud sniffed all around the ground and then turned his head up. Madison lifted her light and illuminated a ladder, hanging on the wall a few feet off the floor. "*That* wasn't here before," she said.

"You sure? 'Cause it looks timeworn. And you said your lantern was nearly out by the time you made it here." He tested the ladder to see if it would hold his weight.

"I'm sure," she insisted. "Where do you think you're going?"

"To see where it leads."

Madison shined her light as he climbed high over her head. Then he stepped out of her sight.

"There's a room here, and someone's using it as a bedroom. Franks is the only person I can think of who would know about this." Rick climbed back down to the floor. "And here are Drew's keys. I guess Willie Franks is back in town."

"Ah, I do *not* need this!" Madison groaned.

"We'll catch him, Maddie. Don't worry." Rick led the way back to the basement.

"That old cell door is iron. We can get Henry to bring his portable welding machine, and mount it at the bottom of the stairs. We can use a padlock to secure it from this side. Nobody can get in here then. If he wants to die in the tunnel, that's his business. But I've had enough of Willy Franks." Madison aired her thoughts.

"Good idea. I'll call Henry to see when he can do it. It would be nice if it's while I'm here to help him. I think there are enough iron bars to build the framework, too. Didn't Drew say that things had been disappearing around here for a while?"

"Yes, and it makes sense; Franks knows his way around. He was raised in this jail when his dad was sheriff."

After talking with Henry, Rick went next door to Olsen's Hardware. He knew the store used to be connected to the tunnels, too. He wanted Mr. Olsen to be aware of what had taken place at the jail.

Madison sat organizing her desk when Rick returned. "You know, Drew was pretty well organized, for a guy. I changed a few things around. I also wrote my first report," she said.

"You sound as if that pleased you." Rick laughed. "Will you send Mr. Olsen down when he comes in?"

"Sure, MacGyver, can I help you?" Madison asked.

"No, I'm going to see what ideas I can conjure up. Henry will be here soon."

Madison took some rags and a jug of bleach into the bathroom, expecting a job to do. She was surprised to see how clean Drew had kept the toilet and sink. Even the floor had a shining wax job on it. Evidently he had made things spick and span for Nell's visit.

143

As she returned the bleach to the closet, the desk phone rang. *My first official call.* She answered, "Sheriff McKenzie."

"Oh?" the voice on the line sounded like Rose Barnett. "Where is Sheriff Perry?"

Madison was sure it was Rose, now. "Rose, it's me, Madison McKenzie. Sheriff Perry was injured. The town council voted me in as interim sheriff."

"Madison? I thought you were away at school."

"Yes, Ma'am, I was. I recognized your voice. How can I help you?"

"Well, last night George didn't come home. He always comes back in time to watch *Survivor*, but he missed a good tribal council last night."

"Really? Shucks, I missed it too." She didn't feel this was an emergency. "Where is George? And when was the last time you saw him?"

"He's up on Unaka Mountain, hunting 'shrooms. He left after church on Sunday."

"'Shrooms? Isn't it a little early for morels?" Madison asked. She still wasn't thinking this was a real emergency.

"With all the rain we've had, they're early this year. But not many folks know that, so George wanted to get ahead of the scavengers."

Madison said, "And he left on Sunday? I better see if I can locate him. Do you have any idea what part of Unaka he hunts?"

"No... As I said, he left after church Sunday. I ain't heard a word from him. I even plucked one of my young setting hens for dinner last night. She's never laid a single egg anyway. And you know how good the young chickens taste."

"Yes, Ma'am. OK, let me make some calls, see what I can come up with. I'll stop by your place for a while on my way up the mountain." Madison's chest tightened as the news resonated in her mind. "You call my cell if he comes home." She repeated the number a couple of times to be sure Rose had it right.

# 24

Madison walked over to the hardware store to ask Mr. Olsen if he had any idea where George might be looking for morel mushrooms.

Mr. Olsen suggested she look around Red Fork Falls. "I remember him telling me it's the perfect environment, and that there's an old hunting shack on top of the hill, overlooking the falls. He also said it's extremely dangerous up there. That's why most folks won't look on that side of the hill, 'cause it's so steep and rocky."

Madison thanked him and returned to the jail just as Henry arrived. "He's in the basement. Can I help you carry anything?"

"No, I got this. Thanks." Henry answered as he lifted a small but heavy-looking machine from the back of his truck.

Madison led the way to the steps and called down for Rick to give Henry a hand.

"Oh sure. Thanks, Henry." The guys carried the cumbersome welding machine downstairs. "I've got an idea to run by you."

Madison called out, "I've got official business. I'm going to Limestone Cove. George Barnette hasn't been home since Sunday, and Rose is worried."

"George is always in the woods this time of year. Surely you're not going alone?" Henry asked.

"No, I'm sure he'll show up. I'm going to take Rose's statement."

"You ought to call Mr. Brummet, if you do go to the woods. He knows the area like the back of his hand," Henry said.

"OK, thanks. I will if it comes to that. But it's going to get dark soon."

Madison drove her Blazer across the county to Limestone Cove. Rose waited on the porch in her rocker. "Thanks, Sheriff Madison." She laughed, "This is going to take some getting used to: a woman sheriff."

"How do you think I feel?" Madison reached to shake the lady's hand. "Any word from George?"

"No, and I'm anxious. Georgie doesn't have a cell phone; won't get one. But most likely he'd not get a signal up in the woods anyway."

Madison took a seat in another rocker and wrote down what Rose told her. She said she'd asked him not to go, due to the temperature dropping, and besides, he'd have been back home if he'd gotten a good supply of mushrooms by now.

"How about if I take a drive up the mountain before it gets dark?" Madison stood and walked to her Blazer with Rose looking on.

"Take care, Madison. Don't you get lost." Rose called across the yard.

Shadows were long as she drove toward the Unaka Mountain turnoff. Bud watched out the passenger side window. Occasionally they saw a house and a yard filled with kids, and several dogs passed his view. He turned his head to watch the scene go out of sight. The winding road grew steeper, with fewer sights of interest, until nothing but trees going by the window.

Madison turned off the main road onto the narrow, newly paved one running next to a rocky creek. They continued winding upward, gaining altitude on horseshoe curves twisting between tall poplars and sycamores with wide girths. Small rays of light pierced the tops of the trees overhead.

At last the road widened to a pull-off, with steep banks running up both sides. She parked her vehicle as far off the pavement as possible. Rose had given her a cap, which George normally wore around the house. Madison put the hat under Bud's nose. "Sniff, Bud. Rose gave me George's cap; smell him? Remember that scent, and find George and Rex." She folded the hat and tucked it under her belt.

A trail led down from the parking area to a valley with two creeks flowing through it. The previous times she'd been to Red Fork Falls, the creeks had been small enough to step across. Today they were swollen to more than double their usual size. Bud waded into the shallow water and out the other side. He sniffed the ground both up and down the stream. Then he waded back to where Madison stood.

"I guess this means you didn't find a scent." She petted Bud's head. "Good boy. Let's see if there's a narrow place to cross." They walked to where the two creeks joined, but it was still too wide to pass without Madison getting wet.

"Let's try the higher route."

She led the way back toward the Blazer. Bud walked around the SUV sniffing, and then he ran up the steep bank above the road. Madison followed. "Careful, this is dangerous territory, and it's getting darker by the minute." No sooner had she said it than her feet slid out from under her.

With the help of a walking stick, she made her way to the top of the slippery surface. Bud was nowhere in sight. "Bud," she called, then whistled.

Bud barked twice, answering her. She followed his sound, but the laurel thicket was impassable. She searched the edges of the hill and found something that vaguely resembled a trail. It was still a struggle for her to push through. Bud barked again, sounding closer than when she first heard him. Once she saw an opening, she found him standing next to a high rock face.

"Did you find something?"

Bud darted around the side of the rock, right through a patch of briars. Madison combed the edge of the thorny bush until she saw where someone else had passed. Stepping carefully and watching out for snakes in this ideal hiding place, she listened to rustling in the bushes. *I hope that's my dog.* She called Bud's name again and again. Suddenly, a dark shape larger than Bud walked out of the thicket. Madison shined the light, expecting a bear, but it was Rex. "Oh, Rex. You scared the life out of me!"

He licked her hand and then ran in front of her. Soon she realized a wooden structure was just ahead. Bud emerged from the bushes again, but instead of coming to her, he went around the side of the old cabin with Rex.

Finding the door, she shined her penlight in, and there on the floor lay George! Bud licked his hand.

"George, can you hear me?" She felt for a pulse. It was weak, but he had one. His skin felt clammy. "Mr. Barnette! George!" She patted his cheeks, trying to wake him.

Rex barked loudly, and the old man opened his eyes. "Rex, you came back." George's voice was very shaky.

"George, its Madison McKenzie. Can you hear me?" she repeated.

"Madison? What are you doing up here?"

"Looking for you; Rose is worried. Can you walk?" She put her arms under his and lifted slightly.

"No, but I can sit up, if you help." Just those few words left him out of breath.

"Here, sit up. I have a bottle of water." She assisted him to an elevated position. "Where are you hurt?"

"Ankle..." He reached for the bottle of water and sipped.

147

"Take it easy. How long have you been here?" Madison asked.

"Don't know; what day is it?" His voice was barely audible.

"Thursday."

"Two days, I guess." He drank another sip of water.

"I have some peanut butter crackers. You're not allergic to peanuts, are you?"

He shook his head. Madison opened the crackers and gave him one. She could see he was having trouble swallowing. "Drink again."

After a couple of bites, he took the crackers from her. "Thanks, Madison. How'd you find me?"

"Pure luck!" she said. "Maybe divine intervention? Bud must have caught Rex's scent. He led me here. Rex has been in the creek; his feet are wet. Too bad he couldn't bring you some water."

"I slipped on wet rocks. Rex helped me in here, out of the rain. That was Tuesday morning."

"Is the ankle broken?" Madison asked.

"Pretty sure it is. I heard a loud crack." George finished the crackers, then drained the water bottle. "Thank you for coming after me."

"I have no cell signal up here. I'll have to leave you to get help. Bud and Rex can keep you company. Don't you go passing out on me, you hear?"

"No, I'm awake now. My blood sugar is low, but I'm feeling better."

"I'll be back as quickly as possible. Promise!" She turned to Bud. "Stay; on guard, Bud. You too, Rex."

With those comforting words, she left the cabin and made her way back toward the Blazer. When she got there, she discovered Rex had come too. "OK, I'll take you to Rose. I probably can't get a signal here anyway. At least she has a house phone. Come on, get in." She opened the back of the SUV and Rex, one of the tallest Australian shepherds she'd ever seen, jumped in. No doubt driven by hunger, he was ready to go home.

Madison watched her phone for a signal as she drove back down the mountain. But nothing, not even as she pulled into the Barnetts' drive. Rose came onto the porch as she and Rex exited the Blazer.

"We found him. He's pretty weak, and might have a broken ankle. I couldn't get him to my car." She rushed onto the porch. "Gotta call nine-one-one, but I have no cell signal."

Rose pulled her portable landline from her dress pocket. "Here," she said, thrusting the phone into Madison's hand. Rose knelt to pet Rex, saying, "You must be starving." She stroked his head, then said, "Come on in, let's get you fed."

Madison explained to the dispatcher how to locate George, then added, "I'll meet them up there."

Rose came back onto the porch, "Want me to go with you?" She pulled a long-sleeved denim shirt over her dress. There was already a chill in the night air.

"Sure, that will comfort your husband. Do you have an extra flashlight? My penlight is too small to see much. I could clear some of the overgrowths with a machete, if you have one."

"Yep, I'll go get it. We also have a big spotlight!" Rose darted back into the house, returning quickly. She closed the door behind her, leaving Rex inside.

As soon as they arrived at the pullout, Madison got a hiking stick from her back floorboard. "This will come in handy for you; it's terribly slick up that bank." Madison led the way and swung the machete steadily, cutting through the entanglement to allow room for the EMTs to bring in the stretcher. The two women made it to the shack and found George sleeping. Bud licked his face, but the old man did not move.

"George Barnette, you wake up right this *minute!*" Rose said, in a demanding but loving tone.

"Rose? Is that you?" Her husband reached for her familiar face. She dropped next to him and kissed him.

"Good thing the sheriff found you. It's getting cooler by the minute. You might not have woken up in the morning!"

"No, the sheriff didn't find me, it was Madison McKenzie and Bud," he said.

"Yeah, well, that's how much *you* know. *Sheriff* Madison McKenzie found you!" Her smile brightened George's face.

"I hadn't told him, Rose. There was time for that later." Madison heard the sound of an engine coming up the mountain road. "I better guide them in. Here, trade your spotlight for my penlight for now. Stay, Bud." Madison ran toward the flashing red lights down on the road. She stayed up on the bank, holding the spotlight steady. "This way, Guys."

An hour later, Madison and Rose followed the ambulance to the Erwin Hospital. They took George in through the ER. After a few minutes with the patient, the attending physician suggested he remain overnight, to allow for rehydration and blood work. George objected, but when the doctor reviewed the x-rays, he saw that the fibula and tibia bones were both broken. There was no more discussion; George was not going home anytime soon.

Madison said, "Rose I'd be happy to take you back to your house. You could come right back in your car."

But Rose declined, saying Rex had food and everything would be OK at home. She'd call her grandson later, and they would take turns staying with George. She insisted Madison go on back to Cold Creek.

Madison and Bud returned to her office to write up the report of the events that afternoon. She smiled as she signed the last page. *I'm glad this was a successful rescue. Rose and George are good people.*

As she finished up the paperwork, a vehicle pulled up out front. The way Bud reacted, she knew it was Rick. Madison turned off the desk lamp, leaving the hall light on. She pulled the door closed gently, locking it with her green jeweled key.

She and Rick walked to her cottage as Bud ran ahead to the front porch. "He's proud of himself. He and I had our first official rescue this afternoon."

"Oh, really? Bud, you must tell me all about it." Rick laughed as he went up the steps behind Madison.

She unlocked her cottage door, causing a surprised look on Rick's face. "I'm trying to be a realist. Times have changed, even in my hometown, so I need to change my habits. Don't you agree?" She stepped inside her cottage.

Rick nodded. "Unfortunately," he took a deep breath. "Sad, isn't it? Cold Creek was a fairytale town just a few years ago. Everyone was safe and carefree."

Madison didn't comment.

# 25

Madison went into the kitchen, filled Bud's bowl with dry dog food, and gave him fresh water. "I bought the ingredients for pizza. How does that sound to you, Mr. TBI?"

Rick grinned. "Fine, as long as I get to toss the dough up and spin it!"

"Oh no you *don't*! I remember where it landed last time—on the floor!"

Madison prepared the pizza and put it in her small oven. Henry had found her an iron stove at an antique shop; it was perfect for the old look of the cottage, and it didn't take up much room in her tiny kitchen. He adapted a gas element and turned the old wood-burning stove into a gas model. He welded two gas burners under the top surface openings, transforming them into raised burners. Madison had been pleased to see how efficiently it worked, while remaining antique in appearance.

"You watch the pizza while I shower, and put Bud in for a bath, too. We both got pretty muddy today." Madison walked down the hall and Bud followed.

By the time she rinsed her hair, the tub had filled with soapy water. She stepped out with her hair in a towel and another wrapped around her body. She slid a stool over, and Bud carefully stepped into the warm water.

Madison hurried into fresh clothes, returned to check on Bud, then went to the kitchen to test the pizza.

"The timer hasn't gone off yet. I'm watching it." Rick stood in front of the glass door of the pot-belly stove.

"OK, but don't let it burn," she said. "Oh, and there's a six pack of Ultra in the refrigerator. Help yourself."

Bud had enjoyed his bath a little too much. Madison removed the towel from her hair and dropped it on the floor to soak up the splashed water. "Pull the plug, Bud." She pointed. He turned his head and whined.

"OK, I'll let you stay a while longer. Madison pulled the shower curtain closed and returned to the kitchen. Rick had the pizza out of the oven and sitting on a cooling rack on the table.

"Looks good, smells better," Madison said as she opened the refrigerator. It was more like what had been referred to as an icebox back in the day, another of Henry's great adaptations.

The small refrigerator had been used in Mr. Olsen's hardware store to keep soft drinks cold since the early forties. There was a small compartment that held a block of ice and a small motor—a fan, really—that circulated the cold air over the drink bottles. Henry had added a real refrigerator motor and other parts, and the compartment that once held ice was perfect for a couple of ice trays. It made an efficient, frigid refrigerator and freezer. The only problem was that it had to be defrosted the hard way: all food removed, and a pan of hot water set inside to melt the icy buildup. And this needed doing about once a month, or it would freeze up completely.

Madison and Rick ate the pizza quickly. Hearing no more splashing from the bath, she returned to shower Bud off. Rick came to see what kind of mess was to be cleaned up. Knowing Madison was tired, he offered to take over for her.

"He doesn't make a mess. See? One towel is enough to catch the splashes." She laughed and took a deep breath. "I'm out of shape now that I don't run every day. I'm not happy that a little hill climbing makes me this tired." She slid down the wall and sat on the floor.

"Well, then let's start shaping up in the morning. We can run out to see Drew and back." Rick adjusted the water to cool it down, and turned it off in a few minutes.

He wrapped the large towel Madison held around Bud. The dog stood perfectly still, as if waiting for instructions.

Madison stood up, patting the side of the tub, Bud put his front feet up, and she dried his belly. Then she wrapped the towel tightly around his body and told him to step out. He put his front paws on the little stool and then hopped up with the back legs on the side. "See, he knows how to get out without hurting himself."

"Did you ever consider changing to a walk-in shower?" Rick stepped onto the porch behind Bud. "OK, fella, now you can shake to your heart's content."

"I like the tub for myself. Plus, Bud enjoys the deep warm water. Can you blame him? Would you want to always bathe in a cold creek or river?"

Bud shook himself, then ran off the porch and across the yard. He knew not to head for the dirt of the driveway.

Madison and Rick sat on the porch swing while Bud did his business. Rick placed his arm across the back of the swing and leaned in against Madison's shoulders. "If you're worried about people thinking badly of me staying here, I can stay at Drew's apartment. He gave me the key last time I was here."

Madison was silent for a second, then said, "That would probably be more comfortable for you. I know my sofa isn't the best sleeper, especially for a man of your size. Maybe you should. I'm not worried, but someone could get the wrong idea." She looked into his jade green eyes. "Thank you for being considerate of my reputation, Rick. I would never have said anything—nor would anyone else, for that matter. But it's probably best."

"Aren't your folks coming home this week?" Rick asked.

"Ah, you're afraid of *Jess*! Now I see." She laughed and stood up. "Come on, Bud!" She clapped her hands. "Well, where did he go? He was just right there." She stepped off the porch and called him again.

"Here he comes. He was at the jail," Rick said.

Bud stopped as soon as he reached Madison, but his fur was up. He growled, looking toward the back of the jail.

"Someone is out there. Bud acts aggressively with someone around that he either doesn't know, or doesn't like," Madison said.

"Let's go take a look," Rick pulled a penlight from his pocket.

"Let me get my spotlight. Wait a sec," Madison said, running into the cottage.

The two walked across the field behind the old jail. Mr. Olsen's grandson kept all the grassy areas near the buildings mowed closely to minimized hiding places for snakes. The town, nestled below the rock face of Unaka Mountain, had a reputation for housing many varieties of snakes—including copperheads and rattlers. The shorter the grass, the less likely snakes would enter or stick around.

After walking the length of the town, across vacant lots, and around the buildings, Madison suggested they check on Drew's apartment.

Inside, they found one small light burning. There was a blanket on the floor, next to the bed. Madison opened the refrigerator and saw the milk carton was outdated, so she removed it. There were several plates in the sink. She ran water to let the food soak off. Then she noticed a couple of plastic Coke bottles in the trash, along with some paper plates. She removed the bag and asked Rick to run it down to the can by the back of the building.

When Rick returned, he said, "Did you notice those Coke bottles?"

"Yeah, and Drew doesn't drink Cokes or any other soda. He only drinks water or beer. Maybe he had company?" Madison shrugged her shoulders and went back to the kitchen sink.

"I found the bedroom window open. Since it doesn't have a screen, I thought it best to shut it." Rick turned on the TV.

"No screen? Why, that can't be. Drew just bought all new screens for these windows. Mr. Olsen's grandson installed them for him."

They both walked into the bedroom. Madison confirmed that there was no screen. She looked at the other windows. All had the new screens but that one. "I wonder why," she said.

Rick looked in the closet and under the bed. "Here it is. But why leave that one off?"

Madison opened the window and looked outside. There was a tree branch not two feet from the window. She noticed there were scuffs in the bark, like someone had been using the limb to climb on. "Rick, look here. Does that look as if someone has been climbing on this branch?"

"Yeah, it does. And look at the base of the tree; there's a barrel with foot-prints on it." He ran outside and down the stairs to check the prints. "They're small, like a woman's foot—and tennis shoes, I'd say. From out here, I can see mud on the siding. That looks like footprints, too."

Madison leaned out the window to look at the mud. "I see." She ducked back inside.

Rick returned. "I'm calling Drew's cell."

"But he'll be asleep by now. Let's wait until morning, and go out and talk to him. You're sleeping here tonight; no one will come in with you here. Besides, we can't say for sure that Drew didn't lock himself out and leave those prints himself."

"I'm pretty sure his shoe size is bigger than those prints," Rick said. "I'll walk you home, and we'll wait 'til tomorrow."

As they passed the jail, Madison noticed there was no light coming from the hall. "That's strange; I distinctly remember leaving the hall light on when you drove up."

Rick pulled out his pistol. "Someone is messing around here, that's for sure. Unlock the door."

Madison opened the door and let Rick step inside first. Bud growled just like he had back at the house. Madison flipped the lights on as Rick walked toward the stairs. She took her Sig from her holster and walked to the bathroom. The door was now shut, and she'd left it open. It was locked. She slid over to the stairs. Rick was going into the basement. He looked her direction, and she put her index finger to her lips.

Madison stood where she could keep an eye on the bathroom, and glanced down at Rick. When he came back up the steps, she whispered, "Bathroom door is locked."

Rick stepped close to the door. "Who's in there?" he called out. He turned the handle; it opened, and he shoved it back. When he clicked on the light, they saw no one. The window was open, and there was mud on the wall above the toilet.

Madison looked at him and said, "It was locked. I turned the handle."

"How about the window?" He stepped aside allowing her to see.

She took a deep breath. "It was closed, and locked. The security camera! Let's check it." She rushed back to her desk. "It's shut off!"

"Someone is too smart, or so they think!" Rick said. He reached onto a shelf filled with law books and pulled out a recorder. "But I'm one step ahead of them." He rewound the tape and played the audio. They heard Bud's toenails tapping the wood floor, followed by the creaking of the sheriff's old leather chair. And finally, a click of the desk lamp, as Madison went out and locked the door behind her. There was a pause, and then the sound of footsteps again, but softly, as if smaller. The chair creaked, and they heard the drawers open and close. The chair creaked again, and the file cabinet opened, then closed. They heard the footsteps walking away, barely making a sound. Another pause, and they heard whistling, poorly done but a distinct tune. The whistling stopped when they heard the key in the front door. "That's when we returned," Rick said. There was a quick scuffle of shoes down the hallway, and the bathroom door slammed... Bud's growl...the light switch... footsteps and Bud's toenails, then Madison's boots as she walked to the bathroom.

"Someone was in here, and we scared them out the bathroom window. But why unlock the door?" Madison pondered aloud.

"To buy time. When you walked away, the intruder had a moment to open the window. They unlocked it and then climbed out." Rick rewound the tape to listen again.

"It's someone small. A child or a woman. I'm sure of it." Madison opened the door and let Bud out. He ran straight to the back of the jail, barking. She followed with the spotlight, but saw nothing.

Rick had played the security camera. There was some footage, but whoever turned it off knew where the camera was and avoided it. All he saw was a small hand reaching toward the controls. "Here is their hand. But it isn't clear in the dark. It's difficult to say if it's an adult or a child. Small adult, maybe," Rick suggested.

Rick insisted Madison check the locks on all her doors and windows, and said he'd see her in the morning. She knew he had a spare key, so she wasn't worried about him coming in early if he woke up before her. Rick has terrible sleeping habits.

* * *

The next morning, Madison awoke to the smell of coffee. She rolled over to find a mug on her nightstand. Bud was gone, and her bedroom door was ajar. She dressed and carried her coffee into the living room. There was no sign of Rick or Bud, so she went to the porch swing and waited, enjoying her coffee.

The coffee gone and hunger pangs erupting, she went to the kitchen. There she found a note on the table, written and signed by one paw print stamped in jelly. *Oh Rick, my gosh! What are you teaching my dog?*

The note read, *Thought we'd let you sleep while we run out and help Drew take a shower.*

Madison ate a bowl of Cheerios with a banana, then walked to her office. She compiled a list of items she needed at her desk. A noise coming from the bathroom distracted her. She investigated, and saw a can of Lysol was tipped over on the floor. The window was open again.

She went to the supply closet and located a nail and a hammer, then tapped the nail in at an angle to keep the window from being raised.

"Someone will be desperate to open it now!" She walked back to the closet to put up the hammer. That's when she noticed cracker crumbs on the floor. Peanut butter cracker chunks were spilled all around. She even found the wrapper on a shelf, with two crackers still inside. *Do I have a rat? I bet it only has two legs.*

She cleaned up the crumbs and threw the wrapper, crackers and all, in the trash. She checked the messages on the phone, wrote down a couple of numbers she'd need to call at some time today, and erased them.

Mr. Olsen was just unlocking his store, so she went to see if he carried anything she had on her list. To her surprise, he did; he'd added to the store and widened his inventory since she'd been away. Now he offered a little bit of just about everything, including office supplies, not just hardware and electrical supplies.

"We live twelve miles from Walmart. To keep folks from making so many trips, I added a few necessities," Mr. Olsen said, walking to the back to flip on the lights.

"By the way, have you noticed anything missing from your inventory?" Madison asked.

"Always have a few items turn up missing. But folks usually recollect that they were talking and walked out without paying. Then they pay the next time they come in. You know, that kind of thing," he said.

"I think we have someone breaking into the jail, and even over at Drew's apartment. Rick is staying there, and he and I noticed something is out of place. And Drew's bedroom window was open, and the screen under his bed." She looked up and down the isles for her list items.

"Well, you know, now that you mention it, I did have a few Cokes and a box of peanut butter cheese crackers missing off my shelf last week. I figured I might have misplaced them at first, but I never found them." Mr. Olsen scratched his head.

"I thought so. And I think whoever it is doesn't live here; might even be a kid. Have you seen anyone you didn't recognize?" She asked.

"No, don't reckon I have. How old?"

"Maybe about nine or ten. Gotta be small, but stout enough to pull up their weight into that big tree next to Drew's window." Madison suddenly had a thought. "I'll be right back, Mr. Olsen; I've gotta look something up."

She returned to the office and located the flyer from up in VA, then checked her phone for the picture of the missing boy that she'd received in a text from Smyth County. Then she went back to the hardware store.

"Have you ever seen this kid?" She turned her phone so Mr. Olsen could see the photo.

"No, can't say that I have. Who is this boy?"

"A missing boy from up in Smyth County VA. I just thought he might be hiding around here. If you see him, let me know?"

"OK, I will. Do you want this totaled up and put on the sheriff's office bill?" Mr. Olsen looked over his glasses.

"We have a bill? How much is it?" she asked, pulling some money from her pocket. "Add them together; I'll take care of all of it."

"OK." He pulled out a ledger for the previous balance, then added it to her purchase. "That will be thirty-seven dollars and forty-two cents."

She handed him two twenties and told him to keep the change. She thanked him and returned to her office. After putting away the items, she looked at the flyer again. *Nicholas? Maybe I should leave him a note, just in case it is him getting in here. He's just looking for a place to sleep, poor kid. I want to help him, if it is him, before he gets hurt.*

Rick and Bud walked through the open door.

"While I was talking with Drew, he reminded me that Franks is afraid of the dark. He says he'd never sleep in the tunnels. He doesn't think Franks is in the area, and neither does Henry. Maybe we've been looking at the evidence all wrong." Rick sat in the chair across from Madison.

"Well, I have been giving this a lot of thought, too. He has no reason to come back here, unless..." She shook her head. "Nah, he'd never succeed." She put the flyer in her top drawer. "How is Drew?"

"Better every time I see him. He said the shower made a new man out of him. I don't know why he's complaining. With Nell to bathe him, he just doesn't know how lucky he is!" Rick declared.

"Now you sound like Henry." She laughed.

"Well, it's true. Having a beautiful woman to take care of him, he's a lucky guy. I guess that's why they're getting married."

"What did you say? *Married?*" Madison leaned forward on her elbows.

"Yep, next weekend. So you have to take me shopping; I need a new suit." Rick smiled as if he was making fun of the idea.

"Are you for real?"

"Yes, and Nell wants you to be her maid of honor. I'm going to be the best man." Rick leaned closer to Madison.

"No, I'd have to be a bridesmaid, since I'm single. And you *are* the best man!" Their eyes met, but Madison blinked. Her phone rang; it was Holly.

"Hi, Holly. Is Rick telling me a tale, or are Drew and Nell getting married?"

"They surprised all of us. What do you think of the plan?" Holly asked.

"I don't know, I guess it's a good thing. I mean, they do love each other; that's plain to see. But what about Drew's health?" Madison sounded concerned about her friends. "I guess they're responsible adults who know what they want."

"Oh, Madison, you really should give them more credit. They want to be together, no matter if Drew never walks again. I think it's romantic!" Holly scolded her best friend. "I won't tell them what you said."

"Anyway, why did you call, Holly?"

"I wondered if you think Ben and Margie might cater the dinner here. It will be a small group, maybe twelve people. And who can I get to make the cake? Nell wants bright greens and yellows. Are you going to get a new dress? I don't have anything nice for a wedding. Henry's suit doesn't fit him anymore. The twins don't have suits—"

"Hold on, Holly. You're rambling. I'll talk to Ben and Margie; I'm assuming you want a sit-down dinner? And Mrs. Olsen makes lovely wedding cakes, if she's still doing it. I'll talk to her, too. You and Nell should get someone to stay with the twins and Drew, and we can run to Asheville, whatever day you can arrange it. I'll get the flowers in Erwin. I'll call the Flower Palace as soon as we hang up. Who will be performing the ceremony? Do they have their licenses?" Madison was thinking out loud.

"Now you're rambling. Let's make a list, both of us. Then you can email yours to me, and I'll email mine and Nell's to you. That ought to cover it. Bye!" Holly disconnected.

"We've got some work to do. How are you going to be sure you're off next weekend?" She turned around to see Rick was on his phone.

He hung up and smiled at her. "Just took some vacation time. Now, where do we start?"

Madison stood frozen in place.

Rick put his hand on her shoulder. "Are you OK?"

"I feel like crying," she said as she stood up. "I've got some calls to make. What are you going to do?"

Rick's phone rang. "Hey, Claudia. What's up?" He listened for a while and then he told her he'd come by the store next week. He told her about the upcoming wedding.

After Rick had put his phone away, Madison asked if things were all right with Claudia and Monique.

"Yeah, she said she ran across something in the move that I need to see. I told her I'd drop by next week," Rick said. "I'm going to have a talk with the guy over at the caverns, see if he's seen anyone suspicious hanging around. You don't mind if Bud goes, do you?"

"No, that's OK," she answered, but didn't even look at Rick.

"Come on, Bud." Rick said, and he and Bud left.

*Why am I this sad, when two of my friends are so happy? What's wrong with me?*

# 26

The weekend went smoothly, in spite of Madison's bouts with tears. She and Holly found eyelet lace knee-length dresses at a bridal shop in Asheville. Holly looked best in the green, so Madison chose the lemon yellow. Together, they were the colors of a spring tulip in bloom.

Nell's dress was a soft peach linen, also knee length. They had shoes dyed to match, which were to be shipped the next day to Holly's farm.

Drew requested the guys wear jeans with gingham shirts to match the women's dresses. The twins were dressed the same. One would wear a green gingham shirt, the other a yellow one. All the shirts were also ordered from the bridal shop and arrived on time, a pleasant surprise.

Mrs. Olsen created a lovely peach colored basket-weave cake with daffodils on top. Marjorie and Ben posted a *Closed* sign listing the hours through breakfast and lunch so the restaurant could get the banquet prepared and set up for the afternoon wedding and dinner.

Marjorie had some unexpected help from Jess and Shirley, who returned home just in time. Shirley mixed a beautiful fruit-filled punch and ice ring for refreshment. The guests turned out to be 23, counting Ben and Marjorie, Jess and Shirley, and Mr. and Mrs. Olsen. It was only fair to include them; they had done most of the work.

After dinner, Drew was tired out so Henry and Rick put him in his hospital bed. Drew insisted Nell stay with their guests. She peeked in once to check on him, and found him sound asleep.

She and Henry danced while Holly put the twins to bed. And then Henry took Holly into his arms and danced the next three slow songs.

Madison watched them with envious eyes. She wanted so much to find the love that Holly and Henry felt for each other. At that moment Rick slipped his hands around her waist and escorted her to the dance floor: the living room, minus the furniture.

Madison liked the feeling of Rick's hands guiding her movement. She was very conscious of her cheeks burning, but she didn't really care. This was a feeling she'd longed for since the first time she saw Rick Malone, over five years ago. She felt her body melting into his as he pulled her close and guided her across the floor. It was as though she was floating. Her feet didn't feel the floor; she was drifting on a cloud. The music swayed her, following Rick's every movement. You would have thought they'd danced together for years. But in fact, it was their first dance. Her left hand on his neck, his hand low on her back and the other holding her right hand, tucked against his chest, as if it was precious.

Madison closed her eyes, breathing in his scent, feeling his thighs pressing against hers as he moved her backwards. She imagined this was what irresistible physical attraction felt like. Never had she ever wanted to feel more. Never had she wanted a kiss so badly. Never had she realized she was falling in love with Rick. Was that why she'd cried when she learned how happy Nell and Drew were? Was that why she felt so good now? Was this the real feeling between lovers? Between her mother and Jess? Suddenly Madison felt light headed. She went limp in Rick's arms. She was falling, and she could not catch herself. Rick held her tight, lowering her to the floor.

The next thing she knew she was on a sofa, with a cold cloth on her head. Holly and Shirley were fanning her and talking right in her face. Madison thought they sounded far away; she could not understand what they said. Finally, Holly pulled back and Shirley patted her cheeks, calling her name. "Madison, are you all right? What have you eaten today? I didn't see you eat a thing at dinner. Did you eat?"

"I don't know; don't remember. I'm sure I ate something..." she answered.

"Here, Maddie. Drink this." Holly had brought her a cup of fruit punch.

Rick knelt next to Madison. "You nibbled from my plate, but you never did sit down and eat anything of your own. What are you feeling now?"

"I'm OK. You just took my breath away, Agent Malone." She sat up and took several deep breaths. "I haven't done that in a long time. Maybe I've been distracted this week, and not eating right."

"Let's get some fresh air. With so many people in this room, it's become a little stuffy." Rick helped Madison to her feet.

"I need to help Holly," she argued.

"No, you don't! Go out on the back porch with this handsome man, Girl! What's the matter with you?" Nell shooed them out the back door onto the decorated back porch area. She and Holly had draped the posts in soft white mini-lights and fresh flowers, all yellow. "You haven't even seen this yet! Go on now, and while you're at it," she pointed to the walkway over the creek, "show him your bridge. It's beautiful by the light of the moon." Nell winked at Madison.

For a while, Rick walked with his shoulder against Maddie's. Then he took her hand in his. "They did a nice job of decorating. I bet Nell was hoping to spend time with Drew out here. Too bad he ran out of energy."

"And the twins would have loved it, too. Maybe Holly will let them stay up later tomorrow night so they can play under the lights," she said.

"What did Nell mean by saying *your* bridge?" Rick asked.

"Holly, Henry, and I were out here messing in the creek one day. We dammed it up, and I suggested he build a bridge across to the willow tree, and add a flower garden. Henry did just that. He really loves Holly. She's—no, *they* are lucky to have each other."

When the couple reached the stairs, Rick put his arm around Maddie's waist and held her as she took the three steps. He left his arm around her and pulled her closer against his side. They followed the lighted pathway to the little bridge, stopping at the top of the arch to take in the dim glow of the porch with all its flowers. Rick leaned against the rail, pulling her thin body against him. He pushed one side of her hair back off her neck and leaned in to kiss it.

Madison breathed deeply and pulled back, but he held her firm. She stood eye to eye with him in her heels. She watched the reflection of the mini-lights in pools of green. He didn't blink. This was a strange moment for Madison. She'd never felt lips on her own, except when she was a tiny child. Was it fear of being rejected? Fear that she might love and he'd leave her?

Those fears faded from her thoughts. She did not blink this time. She didn't try to pull away again. If this was going to be her first kiss, she welcomed it. Her insides changed the first day she met Rick Malone, and excitement raged when they were close. But they'd never been this close, or her this ready, this needy.

But something became obviously wrong with this perfect moment. Sounds were coming from under the wooden bridge, little snickers from little boys who had slipped out of bed and hidden by the creek.

Madison grinned, "Rick, do you hear someone laughing?"

"I thought it was you. Well then, let's see who we can find!" Rick stepped off the bridge and the twins took off running back toward the house.

Holly ran out on the back porch. "Harry and Hugh, you're in big trouble! Your daddy is looking for you!"

The boys stopped in front of their mom and looked up at her. Harry began to cry.

"Aw, don't cry. You're not in that much trouble." She wrapped her arms around their little bodies and guided them through the back door. "I'm sorry, Rick. I'll tie them in their beds this time," She called before she shut the door.

Rick looked up at Madison, still on the bridge. "Guess you got your wish." He held out his hand and she walked toward him, but the moment was gone.

# 27

H ey, Sheriff," Holly giggled. "What are you doing?"
       "I still make you laugh?" Madison asked.

"Oh, no, not you! It's just that I can call my best friend Sheriff. You know me, I'm easily entertained."

"So am I, evidently. I still grin when I think about it. Anyway, I was sketching a couple of ideas to run by Henry, about my addition to the cottage."

"That's why I'm calling. Henry was wondering if you had time now for him to bring some ideas for you to see."

"Really? Sure, this is perfect. Are you coming too?"

"No, I need to get the twins bathed and put to bed. They stayed up much too late last night. But wasn't that a fun wedding?" Holly sounded sincere, and almost in tears.

"Yeah, I only wish that Drew had been able to walk—and I wish he were able to take Nell on a honeymoon. Oh, I just wish that had never happened!" Now Madison was on the verge of tears.

"I know, me too. But Nell is such a good sport. She's taking good care of Drew. Even the nurses are impressed, and coming every other day now. She does all his cleaning, meds, and everything he needs anyway. They will continue his therapy. It's only three days a week. He's determined to get his mobility back."

"I've noticed. Gosh, Drew has strength. I'm not sure I could be that optimistic," Madison said. "Send Henry on out; I'm eager to talk to him."

Henry's truck rolled up in front of the cottage while Madison waited on the porch swing.

"Welcome, my friend. What have you got to share?" She asked.

"Good ideas, I hope!" Henry slammed the truck door. He stepped up on the porch, sitting next to her on the swing. "I want to show you this one first." He pulled one photo from a group of his sketches. "I saw this one myself and took this picture on my phone. It's on the road to Middleborough, Kentucky. I had to stop and capture the idea."

Madison examined the picture, then stood and walked around the side of her house. "This one is on the opposite side from where I wanted it, but that's not a bad idea. Except that I don't want to cut down this dogwood."

Henry joined her. "Oh, no, I wouldn't either. That tree has been here as long as I can remember." He pulled Madison by her arm and walked to the north side of her house. "This is begging to have a garage. Look how much space you have."

Madison nodded. "Let me see what you've sketched."

Henry pulled out three more sheets of paper. "This one has a screened breezeway, but that kind of limits the breeze. This one is open; not suitable for winter, but at least it's cover for a rainy day." He pulled the last one from behind those two. "I saved the best for last; this is my favorite."

Madison looked at a complete transformation of her small cottage. The front porch continued all the way around the left side, leading to a covered deck. She noticed that the measurements of the deck floor were 24'x24', with a built-in rock fireplace along the back. On the right side, she saw a door to the kitchen. To the left was a two-car garage with old-style barn doors. The roofline mirrored the house's roof angle, and was to be of silver tin.

"This is nice. I like the barn doors, except that they won't open automatically in a downpour."

"Sure they will, when I build them," Henry said. "And I'd like to use old barn planks for the wood. I can get those from the Pippin place; I'm gonna tear down that big barn of theirs, with the option to keep the lumber."

"Oh, that's good."

"Show me what you came up with," Henry suggested, and they walked back to the front porch. "I definitely want to increase the size of your porch."

"Yeah, that's a must. I do like the deck idea too, especially off the kitchen. A fireplace is excellent for cooking outdoors." She picked up her sketch and handed it to him upside down. "This might not be historically correct, but I'm not planning on ever selling this place. Who cares, if I can get this kind of upgrade?"

Henry turned over the sketch. A broad smile spread across his face as he studied her drawing, and he pulled a final paper from his portfolio. "I'm surprised to see you and I think so much alike."

Madison took his paper, surprised by what she saw. She looked up into his face, smiling with excitement. "This is remarkable. Almost exactly what I was thinking, only I like yours better."

Henry's sketch showed a closed in access connecting the kitchen to a two-car garage with a second story, all the way to the south side of the kitchen. It made an open deck with spindle railings above the back of the existing cottage.

"A master suite," Henry said. "You might want a larger bedroom one of these days."

"Oh, Henry, this is it! When can we start?" Madison threw her arms around his neck.

"Do you want old wood, or should we cover the whole house in vinyl siding? That's practically maintenance free, but the old barn wood can be painted just like the cottage. It's all about what you prefer. But if I have to tear that barn down first, it will be a while before we begin."

Henry explained all the pros and cons, answering her questions. After lengthy discussion, they decided on a new structure with vinyl siding. He told her he could start as soon as he got the permits.

Madison called Holly to tell her what an amazingly talented husband she had, and as they talked Rick beeped in. "Holly, I need to take Rick's call, so I'll call you back later."

"Hello, Rick."

"Hey, have you heard from Monique?" he asked.

"Nope, not in a couple of weeks. I'm sure she's busy setting up her new store."

"Oh, that's right! She was moving it here. Do you know the address?"

"I know she told me, but I can't remember the street. There's a PetSmart in the same strip mall, if that tells you anything." She listened as Rick spoke to someone in the car with him.

"OK, I know where it is. Thanks, Madison." Rick started to hang up.

"Wait, why do you need Monique? Is there news of Michael?"

"Doctor Michael Ross, you mean?" Rick laughed. "You bet there is, and it's good news, too. Monique is going to want to hear this."

"Well, tell me! And how did you know Michael is a doctor?" she asked

"He gave me as a reference when he went to court. The judge called me to say he'd been cleared of any suspicion and let go. I think he's coming to Knoxville to find Monique."

"That *is* good news. So, do you have Monique's number?"

"No, but I have Claudia's. That's nearly as good. I'll call you later, OK?"

"Sure. Thanks, Rick. I have something to tell you, too."

The next day, Madison was up early and dressed to go into her office when Mr. Olsen tapped on the cottage door.

"Hey Mr. Olsen. Is anything wrong?"

"Well, this morning when I opened the store, I noticed my back window was open. There are small footprints, maybe the size of a young boy or a woman. I think somebody got in the store last night, but nothing is missing."

"I was just about to go to my office. I'll go with you to the store and have a look." Madison and Bud walked to the hardware store alongside Mr. Olsen.

He walked straight to the back of the original part of the old building and pointed to the window, still open. "See? They didn't even bother to close it."

"Maybe it was this morning, as you were coming in. Might have heard you and not had time to close it," Madison said. She took her phone from her back pocket and snapped a shot of the footprints on the window sill. "They look just like the ones Rick and I found at Drew's apartment."

She went outside and around to the open window. Mr. Olsen was inside. "Is this crate always here?" She pointed to a wooden box on the ground.

"No, never seen it before." Mr. Olsen answered.

Madison went back inside the store. She looked at the display of handles thoughtfully. Finding a short ax handle, she suggested he put it in the window to keep it from being raised. The lock was not keeping this little someone out, not even in her jail or Drew's apartment. "Apparently, our little villain knows a way to open these locks."

"I don't want to get no little kid in trouble; I ain't pressing charges, since nothing's missing. Thanks, Madison." Mr. Olsen took the wood ax handle from her and wedged it into the closed window space. "Yeah, that ought to take care of the problem."

Luckily, the field was in need of mowing. In the high grass, all she could see was where long strides had bent the grass down. Madison followed the trail until she lost any signs someone had walked this way, in the rocks on the steep hill behind the jail. She stood staring up into the thick underbrush for a few minutes. *I wonder if there's a way into the tunnels from up here. It sure would make for easy hiding, if he could get below ground from right up there.*

She walked back to her office, unlocked the door, and looked at the bathroom window. *The nail is still in place.* "So far, that's holding. But that means the young boy is either sleeping in the woods, getting into the tunnels somehow, or..." she thought for a while. "The vacant building that used to be Doc's office connects to the tunnels, too, and the town council plans to turn it into a museum. I'd better check it out."

Madison put a note on the door saying she'd be back in fifteen minutes. Then she walked past Olsen's Hardware, the foundation of the old dental office, and to the front of the old wooden structure. The door was locked. The windows on the side facing the hardware were secure, and the back door was safe. She moved around to the side facing the barber shop. She found a stack of rocks piled up, and a window overhead was partway open.

Mr. Olsen had keys to all the buildings in town as the mayor, so she went to the hardware to get the key. Mr. Olsen said he'd go with her, in case someone was lurking in the shadows.

She turned the key in the lock and opened the door slowly. Naturally, the door creaked, since the building had been vacant a long time. She and Mr. Olsen walked from room to room, looking for any sign that things were disturbed. In the room where the high window was open, they found a cabinet slid underneath the window and muddy shoe prints on the wall.

Mr. Olsen looked in the bathroom. "Someone has used this, and the water is shut off. I'll turn it back on to clean out the commode. Poor fellow must be desperate for a place to sleep." He went outside, Madison following.

"Mr. Olsen, I have an idea who it may be. I've not spoken about it to anyone else. I found a bulletin from Smyth County Virginia about a nine-year-old boy who went missing in February. I called last week to see if they'd found him, and the deputy told me they had not. There are no clues; he just vanished from his school one afternoon. He's an orphan, and had been living in a foster home with several other kids. The deputy says he's small for his age, and he thinks was bullied. I think he might be our culprit."

"Could be. Poor kid, how'd he make it all the way down here? And why stick around this town?" Mr. Olsen went into the bathroom and flushed the commode a couple of times. "Not much chance of freezing now, so I think I'll leave this water on."

The two walked back to the hardware store. Mr. Olsen had a customer, so he went inside. Madison waved and went on to the jail.

*How can I catch this little guy? I need to think of a way, before he gets hurt or somebody shoots him.*

In Knoxville, Rick drove into the shopping center parking lot, where he found a sign: OPENING SOON – NIQUE'S BOOKS AND CARDS.

There was white paper over the windows, covered with artwork. There were drawings of birds, other animals, and blooms, as well as poetry, and each illustration was signed by Monique Morrel. Rick tried the door; finding it open, he walked in. Claudia looked up from a piece of paper on the display case.

"Rick! How nice to see you." She walked to greet him.

"Claudia, how's it going?" he responded, with a hug.

"Going well! We're planning to open next month," she said.

"Great! I'll try to make the party. You will send me a text, I trust."

"Oh, yes. I was looking over my list when you came in."

The tiny bell on the door jingled, and they both turned to see who was coming in.

"Shannon, I'm glad you came in. Claudia, meet Shannon Westcott, my training partner."

"I've heard a lot about you and Monique. It's nice to meet you, Claudia."

"Glad to meet you too, Shannon. Are you a native of Knoxville?" Claudia asked.

"No, I'm from Kentucky, but I'll be a resident here for a while. I'll be a regular customer, too. I send cards for any and all occasions."

"Welcome! We need lots of those customers. Bring your friends." They all laughed.

"Where is 'Nique?" Rick asked.

"Ah, you caught the nickname. I thought it was catchy. That's what Jewels called her," Claudia's eyes became misty.

"Really? That might not be such a good idea." Rick rested his arms on the display case. "When I went to Clewiston to see what I could dig up, I discovered a couple of suspects that might have had something to do with the boat explosion. If they knew about Monique, she could be in danger, now that the story ran in the papers again. Did you advertise under this name locally?"

"Yeah, it was in last week's papers, and again this week. We've already had some very interested callers." Claudia gasped. "What if they were calling her for some nefarious reason?"

"They asked for 'Nique?"

"No, they asked for Monique. I only assumed they figured out her name." Claudia put her four fingers on her lips. And then she said, "Oh, dear. I never even thought..."

Rick placed his hand on Claudia's shoulder, "It might be nothing. Don't worry, but was it a man or a woman that called?"

"Both, on two different days. Might have been the same voices both times. They didn't give me a chance to tell them that we plan to open June fifteenth."

"I was hoping to talk with her."

"She's down in Atlanta today, finishing up some business," Claudia said.

"Has she talked to Michael recently?"

"Why would she, and how could she? I thought he was in jail."

"They held him as long as they could without charges. I thought he might come here."

"If she talked to him, she didn't tell me. And now with these other people, I'm apprehensive," Claudia said.

"Shannon, on opening day, I'd like for you to come in and work with Claudia. Just refer any questions to her, but be here to watch the people coming in. And keep your gun out of sight, OK?"

"Sure, I'll be happy to." She gave Claudia her cell number. "Call me when you're sure that will be your opening day."

Claudia added Shannon's number to her phone's contacts. "I'll call you soon."

Rick and his partner started to leave. Claudia said, "Oh! Rick, wait; remember the day we met for breakfast in Atlanta, and I said I had some other business? Well, I recalled that the first week Jewels and I met, she gave me something to hold. It's been decades, and I forgot all about it until that day. I've looked at it and can't figure out why it's important. But I want you to take a look. Jewels assured me that someday Monique might find it relevant." She pulled a small box from under the counter and handed it to Rick. He opened it, and saw a satin-lined box with barrettes inside, like a small child would wear. "Do you mind if I take this to the lab?"

"No, of course, do whatever you need to. Monique doesn't know about it yet."

Rick took the box, and on the way out he suggested she keep the door locked.

* * *

Monique's phone rang. She didn't recognize the caller's number, so she ignored it and continued driving out of Atlanta with the rush hour traffic. After a while, her phone rang again. She noticed it was Rick. She pushed the button on the hand's free device and said, "Hi, Rick."

"'Nique, how are you, Girl?"

"I'm good. What's up?" she answered.

Rick talked to her for a while, nothing in particular, just casual conversation about her store, and he told her about Nell and Drew getting married. Finally, when he ran out of other things to say, he asked, "Have you heard from Michael?"

"Michael?" she replied.

"Yeah, Michael Ross. I know he's been released. Did he call you?"

"Um, maybe, but I don't answer my phone when I don't recognize the number calling." She took a deep breath. "Looks like I've got a message from a call I let go to voicemail. Let me pull off the highway. I'll see who the message is from."

Rick waited. He and Shannon pulled into an empty parking lot. When Monique came back on the line, she said, "No, that wasn't Michael. Some guy wanted to talk to me about my store."

"Did he give you a number to call back?" Rick asked, as casually as he could

"No, just said he'd be in touch. Rick, the CID shows a blocked number."

"Turn your phone off until you get back into Knoxville. Will you do that for me?"

"Rick you're scaring me. What are you not telling me?"

"Just do as I asked, please. Don't stop anywhere, come straight back to Knoxville. Have Claudia call me when you get here. We need to talk, but not over the phone."

"OK, if you're sure I'll be OK without my phone." She hung up and steered her vehicle back onto the highway.

Rick and Shannon were eating dinner when he got a call from Claudia, telling him that Monique was back at the hotel and she was a nervous wreck.

"We'll be right there, Claudia. Keep her in your sight and let no one in the room." He asked the waiter to give them two to-go boxes. Rick was not about to leave Olive Garden's chicken fettuccine behind. He killed his glass of wine and paid the check.

They drove across the river to the Comfort Suites on Alcoa Highway. On the fourth floor, he tapped on their door. Claudia let them in after checking the peephole. She introduced Shannon to Monique, then sat on the sofa with Monique. The TBI agents sat in wingback chairs by a window overlooking the Tennessee River.

Rick explained about his visit to Clewiston, Monique's hometown. He told her that Sean Martin had been suspicious of two men he passed on the rim canal the day her folks' boat blew up. Sean had identified the men from a text Rick requested after headquarters ran down one man's driver license.

Monique wiped away tears and asked him to tell her everything he knew about those men, and also Michael.

On their way out of the hotel lobby, Rick asked at the front desk if anyone had called or come in asking about Monique or Claudia. The lady checked for notes and found none. He instructed her to call his cell if anyone did. "If anyone comes looking for them, call nine-one-one as soon as they're out of sight. Under no circumstances are you to give anyone information about them or their room, or even acknowledge they are guests."

"No, Sir. That would be against company policy. We'd never do that."

# 28

Once he was back in his apartment, Rick put his fettuccine in a microwaveable bowl. He opened a bottle of red wine while it heated, and called Madison.

"Hello, Rick," she said.

"Hey, Maddie. Are you busy?"

"No, just sitting on the porch with Bud. What are you doing?"

"Eating my lunch, a little late. I might need you to help me kill this bottle of wine."

"I have confidence in you, Rick. You can do it." She laughed. "But I wish I was there."

"Me, too," Rick said very softly. "You could drive over for the weekend; I'd like to have company for my birthday."

"I've got some things going on here. Why can't you come to me?" she teased.

"I have things going on too. I can come for the day on Sunday, if you aren't too busy then."

"Well, if that's the best you can do, I'll take it."

They talked for a while, until Rick had to excuse himself. Someone was at his door. "I've gotta go," he told her, but not who was at his door or where he needed to go. He had chosen not to say anything about the conversation with Monique and Claudia.

Madison lay in her bed listening to the rain, wondering where the young boy was sleeping.

She got up to make a cup of Sleepy-Time tea, which usually helped her relax.

But until that happened, she had an idea. Bud watched her for a few minutes, and then went back to her bedroom. He must not have had an insomnia problem.

A young boy slept under the bridge over Cold Water Creek on the edge of town until the water rose too high due to the unrelenting rain. Walking in darkness along familiar paths, he made his way to the woods behind Madison's property. Soaked to the skin and chilled, he dreaded going into the tunnels. But cool as they were, at least they would give him a dry place to finish out the night.

*Maybe, if that nosy sheriff hasn't closed it off, my loft is still open. I can get out of these wet clothes and sleep.* He knew the way blindfolded. However, he tripped in the dark wet mud and nearly fell. His light battery, dimmed from constant use, hadn't illuminated the square plastic object. He took it with him and continued to the secret opening to the tunnel. Finally, he climbed the ladder to the loft and opened the container. He was happy to find a flashlight first thing. The brighter light revealed what appeared to be someone's lunch: a peanut butter and jelly sandwich, potato chips, and even a carton of milk, in a Tetra Pak.

He quickly removed his clothes, hung them on the ladder and wrapped one of the blankets around himself before eating his feast. He had eaten the sandwich and chips before he thought to dig deeper. Under an envelope, he found the Chocolate Chip Cookies. *Gee, what a treat!* He ate the cookies and finished the milk. He was feeling sleepy but thought he'd open the envelope. It wasn't sealed, so nobody would know. He read:

> *Hello there,*
>
> *My name is Sheriff Madison McKenzie. I know you've seen my office, as well as most of the buildings in our town. You are not in trouble; nothing was damaged. You don't have to fear me; I'm just worried about you. I feel like you're hiding because you fear someone. I can help you, but you need to tell me your problem.*
>
> *In an attempt to gain your trust, I'll tell you my story.*
>
> *When I was six, my aunt told me that I was adopted. I was living a lie. I felt that I must not be worthy of love, because my birth mother hadn't loved me. One day my dog dug up a skull, and that developed into an all-out search—which turned up a total of seven missing women's skeletons. One of them was my birth mother. She hadn't abandoned me; a trusted family member had murdered her.*
>
> *That's what attracted me to law enforcement. In fact, at the age of twenty-one, I tracked down my mother's killer. So, I'm sure you too can overcome whatever is haunting you. I can help you, you just have to let me. Now, please tell me your story.*
>
> *Sincerely,*
> *Madison*

His hand shook from cold when he reached to unfold the second sheet of paper. It was blank, with a pen clipped to it.

He laid his head on a roll of straw and thought about what he should do. Was she trustworthy? Or was this a scheme to catch him and return him to his hometown? He wondered what he could write to make her understand. He drifted into a dream state and dropped the pen and paper.

Madison found the square plastic container on her porch two days later. She opened it and found the envelope with a neatly printed note that read:

> *Ms. Madison,*
>
> *My name is Nick Cameron. I ran away from my foster parents because the other kids hated me. The bigger boys were mean. Everyone at school hates me. Nobody likes me. I had to leave.*
>
> *I walked most of the way to TN, and then hitched a ride to the top of the mountain with a trucker. He said he didn't want to take me across the state line, and made me get out. I saw a guy in an old pickup truck, so I walked down to the old road. I hid under a tarp while he fished. He drove to the end of town and parked at that trail going down by the bridge. When he was out of sight, I slipped out. He never saw me. Nobody saw me. I found a way into the cave under your jail.*
>
> *Only it wasn't you, it was a man named Sheriff Perry. I didn't try to hurt him; he saw me trying to get out that door in the basement. I ran like the wind and nearly got seen by a feller in a red Ford truck. Honest, I didn't do that to the sheriff. He just fell on his own. I might have seen him die, but I swear I didn't touch him.*
>
> *Thank you for the food. I love peanut butter. And that was apple jelly, I know because it's my favorite. I won't bother you anymore, Ms. Madison. I'm on my way out of town.*
>
> *Your friend,*
> *Nick Cameron*
>
> *P.S. Please don't try to find me. I ain't going back to Smyth County. I got an uncle somewhere in NC out near the islands. I'll find him. I know he won't run me off.*

Madison dropped the container and note, running from her cottage, to the woods. She had to find that secret entrance and talk to Nick. She couldn't let him run off thinking that he watched Sheriff Perry die. How could a nine-year-old boy ever get over those thoughts?

Rick called Madison's cell phone and the office number for at least the tenth time. He decided he'd try Mr. Olsen at the hardware store.

"Olsen's Hardware Store, Mayor Olsen speaking."

"Hello, Mr. Olsen. I'm Agent Rick Malone with the TBI."

"Well, Rick, I know who you are. What can I do for you, Son?" Mr. Olsen was cheerful.

"I've been trying to reach Sheriff McKenzie all day. She's not answering or returning my calls. I hated to bother you, but since she's next door..."

"No problem, Boy! Let me run over to her office. Hold on for a second," he said. "Rick, are you there? She's not there; her Blazer is in her driveway, and Bud is on the porch. Let me see if she's at home."

Rick listened, but the line went dead. He waited for what seemed like ten minutes, and finally, his cell phone rang. It was Mr. Olsen.

"Sorry, Rick. My store landline didn't reach all the way to her cottage. The door is unlocked, but she's not there. I asked Bud, but he didn't tell me anything." He laughed, then said, "But I did find a note on her porch, laying on the floor like it fell out of her hand and she hadn't stopped to pick it up. Want me to read it to you? I had to come back to my store to get my glasses so I can read."

"If you think the note is important, go ahead," Rick said.

Mr. Olsen read the letter to Rick, and said, "Well, I'll be. I wonder who this Nick guy is, and why he writes like a kid."

"Because he's a child," Rick tried not to show his concern, but he was irritated. "I'll be there in about 90 minutes, Mr. Olsen. I'm going to call Henry to see if he can help. I'll talk to you in a while." He disconnected the call and looked up Henry's number.

Holly answered, "Hey Rick. Do you need to talk to Henry? He's out in the garden. That's why I answered his cell."

"Holly, have you seen Madison?"

"No, and she hasn't called all day, either."

"Will you take the phone to Henry? I have to talk to him," Rick said.

"Sure, I'm walking out there now. Harry, run and tell Henry to come to the phone." She already sounded out of breath. "Sorry, Rick, I've gained more weight with this baby than I did with the twins, so I can't do anything fast anymore."

"That's OK, Holly. I hated to ask you to get him. I can't find Madison, and she's not answering her phone. I want Henry to go to her cottage and the jail, to see if he can tell what's going on."

"OK. Here he is, Rick."

"Hi, Rick, what's the matter?"

Rick explained as quickly as he could. He asked Henry to call him from Madison's office. "I'm on my way. I'll be there in an hour."

Henry pulled in at Madison's, surprised to see Bud outside. The door was open, and there was the plastic container, laying on her porch. It was turned up sideways like it had been dropped. Henry walked through all the rooms of Madison's cottage, with Bud right next to him. "Buddy Boy, I sure wish you could talk. She'd never go off and leave you outside. And her Blazer's parked out there."

Not seeing anything else that seemed out of place, he went to her office. As he was checking there for some clue to Madison's whereabouts, Mr. Olsen came in the door with the note in his hand.

"Rick told me you were coming. Here's that note. I found it on the porch next to her chair."

Bud whined when he smelled the note and the container.

"Bud, do you know where Maddie is?" Mr. Olsen leaned down to pet his head.

Henry picked up her jacket from the back of the chair and held it to Bud's nose. "Smell, Bud; Madison. Find Madison, Bud," he said.

Bud walked through the rooms of the jail. Not seeing her, he went out to the sidewalk. He sniffed the ground several times before trotting back to the cottage, then he ran straight toward the woods.

Henry followed. He called out to Mr. Olsen, "Tell Rick when he arrives. See if you can round up some volunteers."

Henry ran through the brush until he found Bud sniffing an area where it looked as if there had been a scuffle. He saw tracks leading toward the River Road, going up the hill. "Bud, find Madison." He tried to point the dog in the direction of the footprints.

Bud kept sniffing the rocks and the bushes. Henry heard him growl, and just then a small boy came out of the dense brush.

"He won't bite me, will he?"

"No, I don't think so, unless you are a bad person. Are you, Nick?"

The boy kept his eyes on Bud and nodded his head.

"Have you seen the sheriff? She's missing."

"Don't let him bite me! I'm not bad; Ms. Madison wouldn't let him bite me. Please, Mister."

"Ah be quiet, Bud. He ain't going to hurt you. Come here, Kid." Henry held out his hand. "Did you see what happened to Ms. Madison?"

Nick stepped around Bud and came up to Henry. "There were two men dressed like that friend of Ms. Madison's. You know, in dark suits, and they wore sunglasses just like the Men in Black."

"Had you seen them before?"

"No."

"Where did they come from?"

"Over that hill. I heard a car speed away after they picked her up."

"The two men picked up Madison?"

"One did; he was a big guy, like a wrestler or a football player. The other guy was smaller, like you. They ran off that way. I tried to follow, but I slid and cut my hand on a rock." He had a dirty rag wrapped around his left hand.

"Let me see," Henry said firmly, and pulled off the cloth. The cut was deep, and blood ran all over his hand as he held the boy's. He grabbed a handkerchief from his overalls and said, "This is clean. I just put it in my pocket, but haven't used it." He wrapped the hanky tightly. "Now, run back to the jail. Tell Mr. Olsen I said for him to call the doctor to help you, and tell Rick which way I went. He'll be here shortly. He's Madison's TBI friend. You got all that, Nick?"

"Yes, Sir. Be careful; that small man had a big gun." Nick ran toward the jail.

Henry and Bud hurried up the hill.

# 29

Rick's SUV had barely stopped before he jumped out and ran into the jail. Mr. Olsen told him that Henry had gone after Madison. The doctor walked up with Nick at that time. "Hey, Rick. This boy got a deep cut. I had to put in ten sutures. He's brave, though. Didn't say a word, not even when I numbed it," Chip said.

"This is Nick, the boy Madison tried to rescue. He witnessed her abduction," Mr. Olsen explained.

"Tell me what you saw, Nick." Rick bent to look the boy in the eye. "She's important to all of us. We have to know what happened."

Bud burst into the room and ran straight to Rick, jumping up in excitement. Henry came in behind the dog. He was dirty and breathing hard.

"They got away in a Suburban, or some other big SUV. There are a lot of tire marks. It looks like they've have been watching for a while. One was a heavy smoker. I picked this up." Henry had used a toothpick to drop a cigarette butt into his bib pocket. "I haven't touched it, just the toothpick," he carefully fished it out and held it toward Rick.

"Nick, can you describe the men? I mean, besides their size and sunglasses?" Rick asked.

"I'll try. I draw pretty well."

Rick looked at Henry, and they both smiled.

"Here, sit down and do what you can. I'm going to go and make a mold of those tire prints. Mr. Olsen, can you stay with him?" Rick asked.

"Sure, just let me run and put a note on my door, and get my phone. Be right back, Nicholas," he said, then rushed out the door.

Rick and Henry got into the black TBI SUV. Henry directed Rick around the hill by road. They found the tracks and made molds of them. Rick scanned the area for any other signs of the men. He found an empty water bottle and picked it up with gloved hands, dropping it into an evidence bag. They noticed prints where the SUV had backed into the brush.

"Bet they've been here for a couple of days. Maybe someone at the restaurant will remember seeing strangers," Henry suggested. "I'll go and talk to them, if that will help you, Rick."

"That would be nice. I need to get photos of these tire prints to my office in Knoxville as soon as the molds dry." The two drove back to the jail and Henry crossed to the restaurant.

By the time he returned, Rick was looking at the sketches Nick drew. "Any luck?" he asked

Henry shook his head. "No strangers have been in yesterday or today."

Bud lay under Madison's desk. He raised his head with every movement, whining when he didn't see Madison.

"Poor fellow, why wasn't he with her?" Henry patted his knee, a signal he used to call Bear and Bud.

Bud lowered his head, ignoring Henry's signal.

"Nick, I want you to look at these photos on my phone." Rick held the phone so that the boy could see the faces.

Nick jumped to his feet. "That's them! That's the men that took Ms. Madison!"

"When I studied your sketches, I thought it was too much of a coincidence, how much they favored these photos." Rick looked at Henry. "They're the two with the Chicago Mob suspected of killing Monique's folks in that boat explosion."

"How can that be?" Henry asked.

"Obviously they've tracked her here since the story hit the newspaper." Rick pulled up his contacts and pressed a number.

"Claudia, is Monique with you?"

"No, I haven't seen her today. She had some printing to pick up. Is something wrong?"

"Try to get in touch with her. I'm sending a team to get you. Lock the store and go with them. I'm texting you their photos; don't let anyone else in the shop. Someone has Madison. We believe it's the same men to blame for Monique's folks' death. You might be in danger, too; you were friends with Jewels."

He hung up, then called and spoke with someone at TBI Headquarters for a while.

After hanging up, he questioned Nick. "I've read your note to Madison. So you *are* the young man missing from Smyth County Virginia. Where are your parents?"

"I don't have any. We were living with some nice people, but they couldn't adopt us. So they split us up. Robbie was younger and cuter; he got adopted, but nobody wanted me. I guess 'cause I'm two years older." Nicholas scuffed his shoe across the floor.

"Robbie? Is that your brother?" Rick asked.

"Yeah, he's a lot smaller than me."

"Where is he now?" Rick put his hand on the boy's shoulder.

"I don't know. The agency moved me to a different home, and told me I'd never see him again." Nicholas blinked away tears.

"Well, we'll see about *that*," Rick said. "Is his name Robert Cameron?"

"No, he was my half-brother. His last name is Lucas."

"Henry, do you have something a big boy like Nicholas can do to help you around the farm for a while? I'd like to change his luck." Rick winked at Henry.

"He looks healthy, but can he work?" Henry shoved his hands into deep overall pockets.

"Oh, yes, Sir. I sure can work."

"I don't know; I have a garden needing attention, livestock to feed, and I have twin boys that could use some company. It would give their mom a break. She's an excellent cook, but if she chases them all day, we might not get supper." Henry rubbed his neck. "That's a lot of responsibility."

"I can do it, Mr. Henry; I promise I can." Nick stopped just short of begging.

"Henry, looks like you've got a good farm hand here. Tell Holly hi for me, and not to worry. I'll find Madison and get her back here." Rick ruffed up Nicholas's hair. "Behave yourself. I'm counting on Madison's trust in you."

"Ms. Madison was the first person to believe in me. I want you to bring her home safely," Nick extended his hand for a handshake.

Rick smiled as he grasped the boy's small hand. "I'll do my best. Will you take care of her dog, Bud?"

"Oh, yes, Sir. I love dogs!" Nick dropped to the floor and put his arms around Bud's neck.

Rick parked in the front of the white TBI building. He grabbed the evidence bags and went inside.

"Rick, Madison's phone came on for a few minutes, then it went off again.

I'm trying to locate her." Corina stood behind her desk.

"As long as the battery is up, you should be able to track her."

"Except when there's no signal. I'm guessing Madison is in the mountains and moving. I'm keeping a constant watch on it."

"Good work, Corina. I'm taking this to the lab. Is Jan still here?" Rick asked.

"Yes."

When he entered her lab, Jan met him with a puzzled look on her face. "How can this be? The prints you texted me are a perfect match to the guys you learned about in Florida."

"I know. The witness was able to ID them. He's a great sketch artist. I need to recruit him." He leaned in close to look at the latest information on Jan's screen. "What's this blue line?"

"Places I've been able to pin them. I noticed they started moving this way a couple of days ago. I was just about to notify you when you sent me this print."

"So they went through Knoxville, and then straight to Cold Creek. That means they've lost Monique. They haven't learned about her move here. I thought for sure they knew..."

"Maybe they do, and they know about the connection to you and Sheriff McKenzie. How else can they flush Monique out, but by taking a hostage?"

Jan was on a trail that Rick hadn't wanted to consider. The sinking in his gut told him she was most likely right. He dropped onto a stool, quietly processing what Jan had said. Madison's abduction was personal; the Mob was not ignoring his interference in the Florida job. Indeed, they wanted Monique dead, and maybe Claudia too.

"Rick! Are you OK? Did you hear what I said?" Jan raised her voice.

"What?" He couldn't let his personal feelings for Madison show, or the team would relieve him from this assignment. "I was trying to think of where they might take her. Close to Knoxville, but out...somewhere they won't be seen. A cabin, a campground, off the beaten path. Gatlinburg is full of holes to hide out. And there's little chance her phone will lead us to her, due to poor reception in those mountains." He shoved the door open and walked into the hallway. "Call me if you see any movement."

"They won't go anywhere on the main roads. This week is the Classic Car Show. You know how that can be, with all the cars and traffic. If they know anything about Pigeon Forge and Gatlinburg, they'll stay on all the back roads." Jan called out to Rick as he disappeared down the hall.

He raised his hand to signal that he heard her.

Madison felt stiffness in her neck and pain in her shoulders. She was on the floor of a moving vehicle, blindfolded. Her hands were tied behind her back, and her feet were tied together at the ankles. What was going on? How did she get in this position? All she remembered was that she had to find Nick, and tell him the sheriff was alive.

Her head felt like someone was pounding on it with a mallet; a dull thud beat in her forehead. She breathed deeply, listening for sounds around her. Voices... Two men were talking, but she couldn't make out their conversation. She lay still, not sure if they could see her. At least one was smoking, maybe both. The windows were down; she heard the rush of air blowing through the vehicle. The road was curvy, and rough at times. From the sounds of the engine, she thought they were in the mountains.

The vehicle slowed to a stop, then started out again, turning left. Madison heard a car horn, and one of the men yelled, "Idiot! Learn to drive!" She didn't recognize his voice. The vehicle was traveling slower now; there might be more traffic on this road. In a while, she heard one of the men say, "Ooh, that's beautiful! Think I'll pull off and take a picture with my phone."

The second voice said, "No! There's too many people around. Have you forgotten what we have in the back of this Suburban? Someone could see her."

"I guess you're right, Rod. Better keep going. That was a lot of water coming over the falls!"

"Shut up, Idiot! Don't use my name!"

Madison realized Rod was the passenger. And they had just passed a sizable waterfall. She thought of places near Cold Creek, but couldn't tell how long she'd been unconscious. *North Carolina has a lot of waterfalls near Brevard, and that's a curvy road.* But she couldn't be sure.

Since she was in the back of a Suburban, there must be a seat in front of her. She tried to push to see if her head bumped anything. She inched forward. *Yes, there's the back of the seat. OK, they can't see me unless they stop.*

She took a chance and wriggled to see if she could change position. That's when she felt her phone in the thigh pocket of her cargo pants. The thought gave her a feeling of hope. She knew if the battery held up, Rick could track her.

The vehicle stopped again. Madison stiffened, hoping they would not check on her. The passenger said, "What do you want?"

"Bottle of water, and a Snickers bar," the driver replied.

She lay very still, knowing Rod might walk past to look in on her as he went inside the store or a gas station, wherever they were. Footsteps on gravel were easy to make out with the windows down. He stopped, but said nothing, and walked away from the Suburban. The driver began fiddling with the radio, switching from station to station until he came to a hard rock song. She listened to him patting his hand in rhythm on the steering wheel. The song went off and the DJ spoke, identifying the station as WKNX FM, out of Knoxville, TN. A heavy metal instrumental song came on, and Mr. Driver turned the volume up. When Rod returned, he shouted, "Turn that down! She'll wake soon enough. With that noise, it'll be sooner!"

The Suburban backed up and then pulled forward with a jolt, rolling back onto the road. Madison's body hurt from laying on the hard surface, covered only with thin carpet.

The men didn't talk for a long time, until Rod finally said, "Turn left!" The vehicle slid to a stop, backed up, turned left, and sped off again. "Drive on through the campground; we'll see a jeep trail going up the mountain side. You'll probably have to switch to four-wheel drive. There, see that sign? Water Tank Road. We go that way. The cabin is a couple of miles up," he said.

Madison tried to loosen her hands, but it was no use. She was tightly secured. Same with her feet, so she'd wait for her chance.

The SUV turned right, and in a short distance left again. Madison felt the wheels drop into the ruts of a dirt road. They were on the Jeep trail now. She could tell by the angle that they were climbing a steep hillside, and this was an incredibly rough road. Where into the backwoods were they heading?

# 30

Rick's desk phone buzzed. He pushed a button and listened to the voice of Corina, "I'm getting a signal from Madison's phone again. I'm able to tell they are west-southwest of Gatlinburg, and moving."

"Southwest... Hmm, let me know if they stop or you lose the signal," he said.

"OK, I will."

Rick pulled up a map on his computer. He zoomed in to see the terrain on the southwest side of Gatlinburg. "Four forty-one is the only paved road crossing the mountain. But what's in here?" He zoomed in more as Jan entered his office.

"Nothing in there but hiking trails," Jan looked over his shoulder at the map. "I've hiked all that backcountry. No vehicle is going in there."

"What about Elkmont?" He pointed to a short road turning off Fighting Creek Gap Road. Just below it was Little River Road. "There are cabins there."

"Yes, but there's a campground and a clubhouse: people around, you know?" Jan said.

"There are some Jeep trails, too. I've seen them come out of the mountain covered in mud and buzz right through the campground. And that's where they're heading! I'd bet my life on it." Rick slammed the cover on his laptop. He grabbed keys from the top drawer. "That author's cabin, further up Jakes Creek. I've never been to it, but there must be a trail because I saw where some artist spent time there recently, and he didn't backpack his canvases in. He used a four-wheel drive!"

"What's the name of it?" Jan asked.

"Corina will know. Get hold of Rodriquez and Crews, have them meet me at the cut off to Elkmont," Rick ordered. "And they better wait for me! Get Gillette and Sams to meet me there. Tell them to be in four-wheel drive vehicles," he shouted to Corina, passing her on his way out the door.

Jan returned to the lab and called Rodriquez and Crews. She gave them instructions and clarified that they had to wait for Rick at the cut off for the road, since he had to drive the farthest.

Then she checked her computer for a cabin near Elkmont. "Corina..." she called over the phone's intercom.

"Yes, I've got Gillette and Sams heading that way," Corina answered.

"What's the name of that cabin? Could he be talking about Mayna Treanor-Avent?"

"Yes, that's south of Elkmont. Is that where he thinks they're heading?"

"That's what he said. I don't know about that area. I just do the hiking trails."

"I've been up there looking for it, but never found it. Wonder how Rick plans to find it."

"Hey, I've never known Rick to go on a wild goose chase. And he's motivated. I think he's in love with Sheriff Madison McKenzie," Jan said.

"Oh, I'm sure of it," Corina laughed. "I hope the feeling is mutual. I'd hate to see him get hurt."

The Suburban lunged one last time and came to a stop. Madison let out a cry when her head banged against the seatback.

"Sounds like our passenger might be awake," one of the men said.

"Stay here while I take a look around." She recognized Rod's voice. So, the passenger was going to tend to her.

Madison heard the rear door latch click, and a rush of air blew across her face. She felt a hand grab her leg and pull her toward him.

"Ow!" she cried.

"Yep, you're awake now, aren't you, Sheriff?" The strong hand grabbed her arm, lifting her off the carpet. Suddenly she was sitting up on the edge. "I'm going to untie your feet. Don't you dare try anything, or I'll knock you out."

She shook her head from side to side and made a muffled sound.

He pulled the rope away, causing the skin on her ankles to sting. She wasn't sure her feet would hold her when he pulled her out of the vehicle and her feet landed on hard ground. He held on to be sure she wasn't trying to run.

She took a step and then he pulled her next to him. She felt his hand guiding her as he walked. She stumbled, but his hold kept her upright. The sun felt hot on her face, but a fresh wind blew. They were in a clearing; she was aware of sunlight all around her. Soon they walked into a shaded area.

"Step up," he commanded. The man held her up when she didn't raise her foot high enough, and her leg struck a solid object. "Higher," he scolded.

She tried a second time and hit the same spot. Suddenly, she felt him lift her into his arms and step up onto a porch. She recognized the sound of his heavy foot. He took several more steps before dropping her onto a soft surface. Her leg ached.

The man named Rod came over to where she sat. "Are you thirsty?"

"Yes," she answered.

"Drink." She felt a cold, wet bottle against her lips. She sipped, but the water dribbled down her chin.

"If you'll loosen my hands, I won't try to run. My arms are aching."

Rod didn't say anything. He rolled her over sideways, and she felt the ropes released from her wrists. She lay there for a moment before she tried righting herself. Pulling her arms back to the front of her body gave her excruciating pain. Especially her left arm. She sat up and with her right hand, squeezed her shoulder, moaning in pain.

The big man placed his fingers in the joint and pushed quickly. Madison felt it pop. She gasped, but the pain lessened immediately.

"Must have been out of the socket," the man commented. He rubbed the muscle of her shoulder for a minute. "You'll be OK."

She sat without talking, waiting for the bottle of water. Finally, she felt it against her right hand. She took it and drank a big swallow, then another.

"Why did you take me?" she asked.

"We need you," Rod answered.

"Why? Do you know how much trouble you're in, kidnapping an officer of the law?"

She heard both men laugh. Rod said, "We've been in trouble before. You, little girl, are not going to intimidate us! We've got bigger fish to fry." He laughed again. "Take her upstairs."

"Uh, it's awful hot up there." A new voice in the mix, younger, answered from the other side the room.

"I don't care, that will feel good tonight when the sun goes down. Now take her up to the loft," Rod said.

Madison leaned her head toward the sound of the other guy's voice. *Who is this? Does he live here?*

"Brute! Now!" Rod's voice sounded sharp, like he meant business and wasn't taking any pushback from anyone.

All of a sudden Madison was tossed over the shoulder of the same man who had pulled her out of the Suburban. She smelled his strong odor, and felt the strength in his body. Holding her with one hand, she realized he was climbing a ladder. She was indeed going into a loft or attic. The heat hit her as soon as he dropped her onto a mattress on the floor. He said nothing, and after he had disappeared, she pulled the blindfold off her eyes.

The loft was open to the room below. Madison heard voices, but didn't lean over the edge to try to see any faces. She looked at her wrists; one was nearly bleeding. It was the same with her ankles; the left one had dried blood on it and the right was shiny, just short of drawing blood. They both stung. She looked at the mattress. It appeared to be clean, maybe even new. She lay down on it and blinked away tears of pain.

She didn't know what was in store for her, but Rod said they needed her. *That means they're going to entice someone else to come for me. Rick is the only person I can imagine. But why go to the trouble to take* me? *Why do they want Rick? Surely they don't think we're a couple.*

The thought of Rick coming for her caused her stomach to flip-flop. *How will he find me?* That's when she remembered her phone. She took it out of the thigh pocket on her cargo pants. She powered it up and hoped for a signal. There was none, unfortunately. Too far off the cell tower path.

Madison put the phone back in her pocket, turned off. She had only 40% power, so she didn't want it to search a signal and run down.

Rod's loud voice erupted again. She could tell he was arguing with the brute. She wondered why the third guy was there. In a few minutes, she heard the men go out to the porch, and only one set of footsteps came back into the room below. She waited to see who was with her and who was leaving.

She heard noises coming from below. It sounded as if someone was banging pans together. Or maybe hitting cans on the pans. Was someone fixing some food? She hoped so. She was feeling hungry. And what about her water? She looked around, and there at the top of the ladder was the bottle. She reached over and brought it to where she could lean against the wall. She thought she'd better drink it sparingly, in case she didn't get more for a long time.

The smell of food wafted to her nose. *What is it? Chili? Hotdogs?* She didn't care; she'd eat whatever he gave her.

About that time, she heard the ladder bump; someone was coming up. The smiling face of a young boy appeared. He had light skin, and long blonde hair pulled back into a ponytail. "You hungry?" he asked.

"Yeah, I am." She stayed where she was, on the far side of the loft.

"I'm Austin. And you're Madison, right?" he set a plate of beans and two hot dogs down on the floor. "You still got some water?"

"Yeah," she nodded.

"I'm not supposed to talk to you. I'm here to guard you, to keep you safe."

"Where'd they go?"

"Not sure, probably to eat some good food in Gatlinburg," he said and started back down the ladder.

"Wait, have you eaten?"

"No."

"Bring your plate up here and keep me company," she said.

"OK, but please don't let them know I talked to you. Those men won't pay me."

"Oh, I won't say a word, I promise."

Austin sat on the end of the mattress and ate his hotdogs and beans. He also brought up a big bag of potato chips. He opened them and offered her the first ones.

"Thanks, these are the kind I like," Madison said as she dipped her hand in and brought out a bunch, dropping them onto her plate.

"Mine too," he said. Then he brought out a handful.

They didn't talk, they just finished eating. Then Austin went back down the ladder, pausing to say, "I'm going to get some wood from out back. I think we'll need a fire in the fireplace tonight." He stopped at the door and looked up to the loft. "Madison, you won't try to get away, will you? I just want to keep you warm tonight."

"No, I won't try to run, I wouldn't know where to go anyway, and it's nearly dark."

She heard his boots thumping across the porch. And after a few minutes, she heard him on the steps, stomping back across the boards and through the front door. His arms were filled with logs and smaller sticks, all of which he dropped to the hearth. She heard him stacking the smaller pieces. In a moment, she smelled smoke.

"I got a good fire going now, Ms. Madison. We won't get cold. The way the wind is blowing, I think it's going to rain." Austin went back out to the porch and came back with a second armload of wood.

Madison knew her chances of getting away would be slim when Rod and Brute returned. She thought she'd see how far he'd trust her. "Austin, what am I supposed to do when I need to use the bathroom?"

"Um, there's an outhouse. I can walk you out there, I guess. You want to go before it gets any darker?"

"Please. I'm coming down."

"OK. I've got a flashlight," Austin answered.

The two walked out onto the porch, down the steep steps, and around the back of the cabin. Up on the hill at the edge of the forest stood a slim building, with a crescent moon carved into the wooden door.

Austin shined the light ahead, showing the path so she wouldn't stumble.

"Let me have the light, to check for snakes." She took the heavy flashlight from his hand and went inside, checked all the corners, and overhead. Then closed the door. After a few minutes she said, "Aw, there's no paper. Can you run and get a couple of paper towels from the cabin?"

"OK, stay there, I'll be right back."

"Madison," Austin called out as he approached the outhouse. "Here, I brought some paper." She didn't respond, so he knocked on the door. "Madison?" No answer from her so he opened the door.

"Oh, no! Ms. Madison, please don't do this. I trusted you. Where are you?" He heard an engine sound. It was the Suburban. "They're back; please come out. They'll be so mad at me. You might get hurt out there in the woods."

Brute clambered around the side of the cabin and up toward the outhouse. "Austin," he called.

Austin stepped toward the beam from Brute's penlight. "Right here."

"Where's the girl?"

"Using the bathroom," he lied.

"Come on out, Madison. You ain't staying in there all night." Brute pounded on the door.

Still no answer from Madison. He jerked the door open, shining his light into the empty outhouse. Austin rushed up close to look in, like he didn't already know she had escaped.

"Oh my God, where'd she go?" Austin sounded convincing, he thought.

They returned to the front of the cabin, where they met Rod standing on the porch.

"She's gone!" Brute said, as he climbed the steps.

"How?"

"He let her go to the bathroom, and she slipped away in the dark."

"Oh, he did, huh?" Rod pulled a semi-automatic pistol from his waistband. "Slipped away, in the dark, did she?" He pointed the gun at Austin.

"Well, she took my light to look for snakes. She shut the door; there was no way she slipped past me. She just vanished," Austin said.

"Inside," Rod backed up, still pointing the gun at the young man.

Austin and Brute walked up the steps and went inside. Rod joined them and pointed the gun at Austin's head. He fired; Brute lunged at Rod, knocking the gun away. But it was too late for Austin. He fell to the floor, motionless.

Brute picked up the gun, turned, and went out to the Suburban. Rod followed, getting in on the passenger side.

Rick, Rodriquez, and Crews parked at the end of Water Tank Road. Gillette drove up in a four-wheel-drive Jeep with the top removed. Sams sat next to him. The other three jumped in the back, and they headed up the primitive road toward the cabin. The headlight beams bounced up and down between the ground and the trees. Rick nearly fell out. Rodriquez caught him with one hand and pulled him back.

"Thanks, man. I thought I was a goner," Rick said.

Gillette stopped, saying he could smell smoke.

"We should walk in from here," Rick said.

Rick pointed out tracks imprinted in a shallow muddy spot. "Somebody's been up here in a vehicle recently."

They continued to the cabin. Crews took the lead, going into the cabin first. "Clear," he called. "Got a guy with a GSW to the head."

Rick signaled the others to go around the back. He joined Crews, who was at the top of the ladder by then. Rick felt for a pulse. "He's alive! We gotta' get him out of here." He turned to the small microphone on his shoulder. "Need a bus to meet us at Elkmont Water Tank Road, stat! One GSW to the head, bringing him out in the Jeep. No sign of Madison."

Rodriquez, Gillette, and Sams came up on the porch. Rick instructed Gillette to run for the Jeep, and told Rodriquez to carry the young man out. "Got an ambulance meeting you at the bottom. Take it as easy as you can."

Sams climbed into the back to hold the patient's head, now wrapped in a towel Rick had found in the cabin. The rest of the guys walked off the mountain.

Rick felt defeated, and he hated that feeling. He thought it made him look weak. At the same time, he felt angry; the bad guys had scored because he and his team had been two steps behind them.

By the time they reached the paved road, the ambulance was gone. Rick leaned his elbows on the Jeep. Crews ran toward him from the direction of the campground.

"Rick, we caught a break." He stopped to catch his breath. "The office at the campground uses security camera. They showed me a black Suburban that hadn't registered, and had no business in here. It went up and back out twice. The last time was just a few minutes before we arrived. Couldn't see the tag, but it had two guys in the front. It looked as if they were alone."

"Why bring her all the way up here for six hours, just to shoot someone else and leave again?"

"Maybe their plan went sideways," Crews said, "and they left because they thought the boy was dead."

"Get a team up to that cabin. If Madison was there, she left us something behind. Find it!" Rick jumped into his vehicle and drove away.

* * *

Throughout the night, Madison moved slowly along the edge of the creek, following it down the mountain. She knew it would lead her to people. She only prayed those people would not be Rod and Brute.

She came to a bridge crossing the creek. She saw a sign that read Jakes Creek, and on the trail coming uphill to the bridge was a marker showing .7 *mile*. The trail made traveling so much easier, and it followed the creek.

Light in the eastern sky promised daybreak was near. The trail became a road, which passed in front of some houses—old abandoned houses. Houses that had not heard the laughter of kids and their families in decades, houses that smelled of mold and mildew wafting through their broken windows. Vines clinging to rotting wood was the only life they held.

The houses stood sadly among overgrown landscaping, and there were steps leading down to the tumbling flow of Jakes Creek. Once this had been a popular setting in the cool foothills of the Great Smoky Mountains, but now the roofs swagged in humiliation, discarded like old news. *What is the story on these old houses?*

A movement out of the corner of her eye drew Madison's attention away from the sad houses to a parking area. She noticed a park ranger unlocking the bathroom doors in a concrete block building painted dark green.

She waved her hand and called out, "Hello."

He waved back and answered, "Good morning."

As she approached, she said, "I'm Sheriff Madison McKenzie—"

"Thought you might be. You got away from those two fellows last night, didn't you?"

"Were they caught?" she said in a high-pitched voice.

"Don't know. But the young boy they shot and left for dead, wasn't. He's at the hospital in Knoxville, thanks to those TBI agents.""

"Austin was shot? Oh no! It's my fault. They blamed him because I got away."

"The TBI guys are all gone now, too. But we've got a car at the office you can use to get into town. I mean, if you're not hurt." The ranger looked her over.

191

"Guess you been in the creek; must be pretty cold. Come on; I'll take you to the office and get you warmed up. Bet you could use some coffee and a bite to eat."

"Thank you; I'd appreciate the loan of the car. I'll be OK 'til I get to the hospital. Do you know which one they took him to?"

"University Hospital, I heard them say." He climbed into a green truck, and Madison got in on the other side.

When they reached the office, they went inside to get the keys.

"Can I use your phone?" Madison asked.

"Sure, help yourself."

"Aw, the numbers are all on my phone, and my battery is dead. Do you have a phone book?"

The woman behind the counter pulled a rumpled old phone book from a drawer. "It's old, but most of the numbers ought to be the same."

Madison called the first number for TBI. She asked to leave a message for Agent Rick Malone. "Yes, thank you. Let Agent Malone know that Sheriff McKenzie called, and I'm heading to the University Hospital. Let him know that my phone battery is dead."

"Oh, he's going to be glad to hear that you're OK. I'll call him immediately."

Madison took the keys to the older model four-door Ford, painted green, just like all the other vehicles in the park.

The ranger gave her instructions as to where she could leave the car; he'd send someone to pick it up. He offered her a cup of coffee with a lid. She took it gratefully, and thanked him and the woman.

# 31

Madison turned left onto Fighting Creek Gap Road, as the ranger had instructed. She thought she recognized where she was when it became Little River Gorge Road. When the road intersected the Laurel Creek Road, the way to Cades Cove, she was positive.

"Oh, my goodness. As many times as I've been here, why have I never noticed this Elkmont resort? And I thought I was an observant person."

There were a couple of cars slowing in front of her. They took Cades Cove Road, and she signaled that she was turning right to go toward Townsend. As she made the turn, a car coming out from the Cades Cove Road rammed into her. The green Ford slid off the side of the road into the grass. The other car, a black Suburban, backed up and rammed her again, this time shoving her over the edge of the bank toward the Little River.

At this bend of the River and Laurel Creek junction, the river is anything but little. The car slipped slowly toward the deep water, jerking as it caught on some rocks. She held on and hoped it wouldn't go into the water. One more large rock and the momentum caused it to tip over, going into the river upside down.

With the windows down, water rushed in rapidly. Madison released her seat belt and sunk to the headliner of the car. When the bubbles settled, she noticed out the passenger side she could see into a culvert that looked about four feet across. Laurel Creek rushed out, causing turbulence. Her breath was desperate to escape; she pushed off the seat and out the window, swimming toward the culvert. Madison noticed a rope whipping in the current that was secured to the pipe. She swam with all her might to reach the lifeline. The current pushed her back toward the car. Even the car began moving down the river. Madison had to surface, and for a split second, she saw people on the bank looking down toward the car. She gulped in as much air as she could and dove again. This time the rope was within her grasp, and she pulled herself toward the pipe. The force of the water pushed to wash her body away with the swollen Laurel Creek. She fought to pull herself into the tunnel. In the mouth of the opening, she spotted a boulder the size of a basketball. She pulled herself past it and got her head out of the water. The rock was holding firm, but she couldn't stay there long. Her strength was nearly drained, and the cold water numbed her body.

She turned her head to see that the car was upright and floating downriver with the rapids. That gave her hope that the men would believe she was still in the car. Or at least, that if her body had washed out, it had been carried downstream, too.

After a while, Madison managed the strength to crawl toward the other end of the pipe. She felt exhausted, but realized her only chance was to get out on that side of the road. Maybe no one was looking for her there. What were the odds?

Just when she could no longer feel her knees, she reached the end of the culvert. The water seemed to have slowed down. She couldn't see anyone from just inside the pipe, so she lunged, one last effort to escape the overwhelming force. Her legs refused to hold her; she grabbed a rock and held on tight. A hand reached down and grasped her arm, lifting her out of the water. She was aware that the sleeve was khaki; hopefully, it was a uniform of some kind, and not her captors.

She lay on the bank in the sun, breathing heavily. The silhouette of a man knelt next to her. He removed his hat, and she saw that it had a shiny emblem on the front. He was a state trooper.

"Oh, thank God!" she whispered.

"Lie still. Get your breath. You fought hard to come out this direction, against the current. I guess you didn't want those two men to see you." He smiled and sat next to her on a flat rock. "Name's Bill. Would you happen to be Sheriff McKenzie?"

"Yes," Madison managed to answer weakly.

"They took off when I came on the scene. That was smart of you, but I don't see how you did it."

Madison sat up, "I almost didn't make it. And you sure saved me right there. Thank you."

"You'll be OK, I'm sure, but I'd like to take you to the hospital to be checked out."

"I was on my way to the hospital when they shoved me into the river." Madison felt her numbness fading and her energy returning.

"Just sit here and let me move my cruiser over. I don't want anyone to see you, if possible. In case your friends return."

Madison nodded.

Bill wrapped a blanket around her and helped her into the back of his cruiser. "Probably be best that you lie down in the seat until we get clear of here."

Trooper Bill got on his radio and told the person on the other end that he wanted an unmarked unit to come to Townsend and arrest the men in a banged-up Suburban. He said to Madison, "I didn't want to let on that I saw them, but we just passed those two. I'd say they're watching for me to leave. That's fine; my buddies will get them."

In just a short distance, he pulled off the road and stopped. "How are you feeling?"

"I'm dizzy." She sat up cautiously.

"I was afraid of that. Do you want to move up front?"

"If you don't mind. I think I'll be better off sitting up straight now."

The officer opened the front and back passenger doors for her, then helped her move up front.

"I can watch you better this way anyway."

The drive was long, and Madison felt like she had water in her ears—and her lungs, too. Aching all over, she'd be happy to get checked over at the hospital.

Trooper Bill pulled up to the emergency room and ran in to get a wheelchair. He wheeled Madison in and explained to the nurse what had happened to her. He went back out to move the patrol car while Madison waited to be seen.

Madison asked the nurse to call Agent Malone to the ER. In just a few minutes, he came into her examination room.

"What happened?" Rick looked at Madison's clothing, alarmed.

"Where do I begin?" Madison shook her head.

"I know who kidnapped you. We found the young man they shot at the cabin—"

"Is Austin going to be OK?" she interrupted.

"He's unconscious, in a drug-induced coma until the swelling goes down. They shot him in the head?"

"Yeah, the ranger at the campground told me. It was all my fault. If I hadn't run away, he wouldn't have gotten in trouble. He's not such a bad person; they just hired him to guard me."

"I know. The boy's mother is here. We found his ID in his pocket, and called her in. The doctors say it was a glancing blow; it didn't penetrate to his brain. He should be all right in a few days."

Rick put his hand on her cheek. "Now, tell me how you got away."

Madison told her story of the outhouse, and how she ran when she saw her chance. Following the creek down the mountain had been slow going, and she'd ended up at the parking lot, where she'd encountered the ranger. "Oh, he must have told them what I was driving. How else did they know it was me in the forestry service car?" She continued the story with the black Suburban hitting her and pushing her off the road. Madison didn't go into the details of how she got out of the river.

At that point, Tennessee State Trooper Bill walked into the exam room. He asked if she'd rather he come back at a later time.

"No, it's fine, you can get the information you need from me now. Bill, meet Agent Rick Malone of the Tennessee Bureau of Investigation. Rick, this is Bill."

"Bill Conway," he introduced himself and shook hands with Rick. "How do you connect with this case?"

"I'm after these two bad guys; they abducted Sheriff McKenzie from Cold Creek." Rick showed Bill the photos of Rod and Brutus on his phone.

Madison looked at the photos. "How did you know it was them?"

"They're the same two who are mixed up in the murder of Monique's folks," Rick said.

Madison sunk lower onto the table. She had a lot to process.

"Sheriff McKenzie is a smart lady. Did she tell you how she got away the second time?" Bill asked.

"No," Rick said, staring at Madison. "What did you do?"

The nurse returned at that time with a doctor, who asked the men to leave the room so that he could examine her.

Agent Malone and Trooper Conway sat in the ER waiting area. Bill filled Rick in on how he discovered Madison. The Trooper got all the necessary information from Rick for his report on the crash. He had to go, so he told Rick to have Madison call to let him know what the doctor said.

Rick waited until the nurse said he could come back, and wasted no time returning to her side. It was just the two of them now. Madison lay flat on the table. She informed him the doctor wanted to admit her for observation because of the amount of water she'd ingested.

"I'd rather go home."

"I'm sure you would, but you need to stay." He leaned down to kiss her forehead. "Don't argue, please. I can't lose you, Maddie. If the doctor's worried about water in your lungs, don't try to ignore him."

"OK, OK, I'll stay. I don't feel so great anyway," Madison smiled at Rick. "Where will you be?"

"Well, Bill sent a team to find these guys. I'd like to follow up with him. And I'll have a talk with that ranger while I'm at it. Do you remember his name?"

"His shirt had Jones appliquéed on the pocket, but he didn't tell me his name."

"You'll be safer here anyway. I'll post a guard outside your door, just to be sure. Oh, and you need to call Holly."

"My phone! I drowned it!'" She tried to reach her thigh pocket.

Rick grabbed Madison's hand and retrieved it himself. He opened the battery compartment, and water dripped onto the floor. "Hmm, that's not a good sign. Here, take my spare. I'll pick you up another one soon as I can."

"Thank you, Agent Malone. I can buy a phone when I get out of here," she frowned.

"At least use this one tonight. Henry and Holly's number is in it." He kissed her forehead again and left the room.

Madison drifted off to sleep while she waited for her room to be assigned.

After a while, an orderly woke her as he unlocked the wheels of the gurney she lay on. She looked above her head to see a smiling young man with dark blond hair. He rolled her into the hallway and said, "We're taking a trip to the fifth floor. You all set to go?"

"I guess."

"I'm Joey, and I'll be your driver, Ms. McKenzie. Oh, forgive me: Sheriff McKenzie! I'll be sure to watch my speed and obey all the traffic signs." He chucked almost under his breath.

"While we're at it, let's take a side trip to the beach. I could use some sun and surf." Madison laughed along with Joey.

"Wish I could, but my shift ends in a few minutes. You are my last ride today."

"Just my luck. At least take me to a warm room. I'm still cold from that icy water." Madison shivered.

"Oh, I'm sorry, why didn't you say something?" He veered to the right and entered a side hallway, stopping in front of a door marked *Employees Only*. He stepped inside the linen closet and grabbed a couple of blankets. He spread one quickly over the single sheet covering her, and put the other on her chest. "I got you an extra. It can get chilly on the fifth floor in the middle of the night."

"That feels better already. Thank you, Joey."

A short red headed nurse at the nurses' station spoke up as they approached. "Is that Sheriff McKenzie?" she asked.

"Yes, Ruth. And I loaded her up with blankets. They let her freeze in the ER," Joey said, as he rolled on past the station.

"End of the hall, on the left. We're all ready for her." Ruth ran on ahead and opened the door. She held it as Joey pushed Madison inside.

"Here you are, Madison. Can you slip into the bed?" Ruth stood on the other side, holding a folded sheet.

Madison sat up with Joey as support and slid onto the hospital bed. "Gee, I hadn't realized just how sore I am," she said.

"Well, you were in a horrific crash, after all. The seatbelt alone can cause all sorts of bruises as the car flips. I'm not the least bit surprised that you're sore." Ruth said, "I read your chart. That cold river water must have been difficult to endure, too. I'd be surprised if you *weren't* hurting."

Nurse Ruth and Joey tucked her under the sheet and first blanket. "Do you want the second blanket now?"

"No, the one is fine for now. I'm warmer already," Madison smiled when Joey waved to her as he left the room.

"You've missed lunch, but I'll be happy to bring you a snack. What do you like?" Ruth wrote on her chart as she asked.

"Just a hot cup of tea would be perfect, if you can get that. And an extra pillow?" she requested.

"Yes, of course. I'll be right back." Ruth placed the chart in an acrylic bin attached to the foot of the bed before leaving the room, quietly closing the door behind her.

Madison located the remote for the TV. She scrolled through channels, looking for The Weather Channel or some news. Not finding either, she settled on the Travel Channel, leaving the volume muted.

Ruth returned with the pillow tucked under one arm, carrying a tray with a mug, short stainless-steel pitcher of hot water, and a package of shortbread cookies on it. She reached into her pocket and brought out packets of sugar and a couple of pink artificial sweetener packets. "I love shortbread with tea, so I brought them in case you do feel hungry before supper." She glanced at her watch. "They'll serve it in about four hours."

"Thank you, Ruth. I appreciate the tea and cookies," Madison said, as she put the pillow behind her head.

"You should get some rest. After supper, your doctor will be in to talk to you. We don't have any medicine orders as of now. We're just observing you for now."

"Yeah, I get that. I'll try to catch up on some sleep. It was a rough twenty-four hours," Madison closed her eyes as she remembered the events.

"I'll put a note on your door. That way they'll know not to wake you unnecessarily." Ruth patted Madison's arm. "I'm on duty 'till 8:00 this evening. Let me know if you need anything. And I do mean anything!" she stressed, turning to leave.

\* \* \*

By the time Rick returned, Madison was eating supper. She held a cup of fresh fruit in her left hand and a spoon in the right. The waterlogged patient ate the fruit and a container of Jell-O, then pushed the tray table away.

"Have you eaten?"

"No, but I'm OK. I'll get something later," Rick answered without looking away from the meatloaf.

"You might as well eat this; they'll just throw it away." She handed him the fork.

"You might get hungry later on."

"And if I do, you'll go downstairs and get me some yogurt or something. Right?"

"Uh-huh," he nodded, accepted the fork, and pulled the food toward him. "I'd hate to see this go to waste." He dug into the scalloped potatoes first, then ate a scoop of English peas. "This is delicious; you should at least try it."

"No thanks; you'll enjoy it far more than me," she said. "Is there anything that you won't eat?"

"Not much." He took a bite of the dinner roll. "Seriously, this is good food for a hospital. You don't usually recognize the food, let alone like the taste of it. But this is real, and good food."

Later, Madison flipped through the TV channels again. Finding the Travel Channel was still the only decent option, she turned the volume up just enough to hear—but not loud enough to disturb the sleeping Rick. Even the attendant removing the empty try hadn't awakened him.

Except for Jess, her daddy, Rick was the only man Madison had been around while he slept. She noticed how his eyes darted from side to side under his closed lids. *Do you ever rest, Rick? Your eyes say that even in your sleep, you are watchful of your surroundings.*

About an hour passed, with Madison amused by the Booze Traveler until she heard a slight tap on the door. "Come in," she whispered.

Patrolman Conway stuck his head in the door. "Am I interrupting?" He asked.

"No," Madison answered.

The tall patrolman stood close to the head of her bed. He whispered as Rick slept, "Is Malone your bodyguard?"

"No, we've been friends for a long time. He's family."

"We didn't get the men in the black Suburban. I wanted you to know."

"Thanks. What about the ranger? I know he had to tip them off; no one else knew I was in the forestry car."

"I think Rick's team handled him today."

"I'm worried about Austin, the young man. That same ranger was the person who told me he was here in the hospital. What's to stop them from coming to get him here?"

"The two agents I have posted at his door," Rick spoke up. "Conway, what are you doing here?" he asked, standing up to stretch.

"I'm here to check on the beautiful sheriff. How about you? Sleeping on that side the bed, in the corner? You could at least drag your chair to this side, so the bad guys have to go across you to get to her."

Rick walked around the bed to shake hands with Conway. As they parted, a man came into the room and introduced himself as Dr. Roland. "I'd like to talk to my patient for a couple of minutes, gentlemen."

Both law officers stood their ground, in front of Madison. "You got an ID, Doc?" Rick asked, his hand sliding to his shoulder holster.

Trooper Conway already had his hand on the holster on his hip. "Madison, do you know this doctor?"

"He treated me in the ER. His name is Roland, but that's all I can say for sure." She laughed, "You two are a bit paranoid, aren't you?"

The door opened again, and a technician wheeled in an EKG Machine. "You two will need to step out, please." He looked from Rick to Conway and back to Rick. The technician was a large man, resembling a wrestler—or at least a UT tackle.

Not wanting to cause any trouble for Madison or themselves, Rick and Conway walked into the hall.

Dr. Roland explained his concerns to Madison as he listened to her heart. "At first, I thought you might have water in your lungs. But it hasn't gone away, so I doubt it's water. The only other thing it can be is an arrhythmia. That's why I want to run an EKG. Nothing to be alarmed about," he said.

It took the technician a while to hook up all the leads and set the machine.

Dr. Roland questioned Madison.

"You said you felt dizzy in the ER. Have you experienced it before the crash?"

Madison nodded.

"Often?"

"No, but when I get busy and don't take the time to eat regularly, I get a little light-headed."

"Have you ever passed out?" he asked.

"Not recently. But last night when they injected me with that drug, I was dizzy when I woke up. I just assumed it was from the drug."

"It might have been, but that's pretty well out of your system by now. And I can still hear the irregular heartbeat," Dr. Roland said. "Do you ever drink those energy drinks? Or those little shots of five-hour energy?"

"No. I don't even drink sugary sodas! I drink water or unsweet tea most of the time."

The doctor nodded. "Good."

With the EKG completed, Dr. Roland said, "I want you to see a specialist. I'm also ordering a CBC with a thyroid panel, so you'll need to fast after midnight tonight."

"OK, I haven't had any bloodwork done in a long time." Madison readjusted her gown and pulled the sheet back over her legs.

"I'll see you after we get the results. Then I'll make the appointment with a specialist." Dr. Roland turned to go. "I guess you'd rather see a doctor in Johnson City, wouldn't you?"

"Yes, it would be much easier for me," Madison smiled as the doctor nodded.

Rick came back into the room, followed by Patrolman Conway.

"What was that all about?" Rick asked.

"He detected an irregular heartbeat. Maybe an arrhythmia, nothing to worry about," Madison could not look Rick in the eye as she answered him.

"My younger brother had that happen when he was a student at UT. He downed those energy drinks like crazy and ate poorly during finals week, causing a potassium deficiency," Conway said.

"Madison doesn't drink anything like those energy drinks. She doesn't even drink sugar in her tea." Rick ran his hand down the back of her hair. "She's a fanatically healthy eater. Pretty much a vegan."

"No, I'm not." She cut her eyes at Rick.

"Well, I guess I might as well head out. It looks like the night shift is here to stay." Conway looked disapprovingly at Rick. He handed Madison a business card. "Call me to let me know you're OK after the bloodwork results, will you?"

She took his card and looked into soft brown eyes. "OK."

Rick dragged the recliner toward the door side of the room. He had to face it toward Madison so it would recline all the way. "I didn't want to be an obstruction here, but he did have a point. Not only will the nurses have to walk around me, but if someone who shouldn't be in here tries to get to you, I'll take a bullet for you." He didn't laugh when he said it.

"Are you worried that they might come in here?" she asked.

"I would never have believed they would kidnap you in your back yard. Better safe than sorry."

"So you plan to stay there all night?" She sat up straight.

"Do you have a problem with me being here? Maybe you'd rather have that Patrolman Conway guard you. I mean, he did save your life, and I couldn't even find you." Rick dropped into the recliner.

"No, there's no one I feel safer with than you, Rick Malone." Madison stared at him as though she might cry. "I figured you knew that."

Rick stood up, leaned in close and whispered, "I thought I did too—until that guy started giving you options. For a minute, I thought you were going to ask him to stay."

"You're *jealous!*" She laughed and fell back against the pillows. "Aw, poor Agent Malone thinks Super-Trooper is a threat."

Rick jokingly lunged toward her, placing his hands on her neck with a comically villainous leer. "No, I'm not, its concern for your welfare, not jealousy."

Just then the door opened, and Jess and Shirley walked in. "I thought you were guarding our daughter, Rick, not here to take her out." Jess slapped his big hand on Rick's back.

"Hey, Jess, Shirley, it's good to see you," said red-faced Rick, backing away from the bed.

"Why didn't you tell me you were back in town?" Madison reached to hug her folks.

"You've been hard to reach, my dear. We heard you dunked your phone in the river," Jess said, then kissed the top of her head.

"I'm so glad to see you're smiling." Shirley hugged Madison so tightly she forced a cough out of her daughter. "Are you sure you weren't hurt?"

"That hug made me realize how badly my body aches," Madison replied.

"I'll just go outside and let you all have some space," Rick moved toward the door.

"Nonsense, Malone. We want to see you too, boy." Jess slapped the TBI Agent across the back again.

"Momma, I'm sorry we didn't get a chance to visit the weekend of the wedding. And then you all left again so quickly again. You look great," Madison said.

"Thanks, and I feel like a new person! I still have some toning, but at least I can walk comfortably."

Shirley's doctor had instructed her to lose fifty pounds to keep her heart functioning. Once she started dieting and exercising, she realized she wanted to lose more like 75. That would put her back to the weight she was when she fell in love with Jess. Owning and running the restaurant had made it easy for her to continue gaining, once she reached middle age. It wasn't until she had a scare, thinking it was a heart attack, that she faced it. Her weight was affecting her life. That's when Jess realized that he had to get her out of the restaurant to help her change her habits. They leased Shirley's Restaurant to friends, and Jess took Shirley to Hawaii for a long-belated honeymoon. That had been four years ago.

"Tell us about your Alaska trip," Madison coaxed, knowing that was all Jess needed to change the subject.

"I'm sorry we were late returning. We just couldn't pass up the last-minute opportunity to go on that cruise around the Aleutian Islands." Jess leaned against the wall next to the head of Madison's bed. "Did you tell Rick about that?"

"I don't think I ever had the chance." Madison looked toward Rick. "They got picked for a free cruise."

"No, I hadn't heard. But that's the best excuse for coming home late that I can think of," Rick said. "Before you start the details, let me grab another chair from the hallway. There's one right outside the door."

Rick carried a brightly-colored upholstered chair in and set it next to Madison for Jess to sit down. The orange and yellow stripes fit the festive atmosphere of the reunion. Shirley relaxed in the recliner as Rick settled onto the foot of Madison's bed. Locating the remote, he turned the TV off.

Jess talked, and Shirley added commentary where she wanted to color up the story. It was evident that the cruise had been one of the highlights of their vacation. With the cool spring temperatures, the couple had really enjoyed their spacious and elaborate room, most days ordering room service. There had been some sunny days, which allowed them to watch the beluga whales up close. Jess had some amazing photos, including selfies with Shirley, the whales surfacing behind them.

"Listen, I'd hate for you all to drive the two hours back to Cold Creek tonight. I'm staying here, to make sure Madison doesn't have unwanted visitors. My housekeeper was in today, and she always changes the sheets. There's no reason you two can't stay at my apartment. That way, you can come back in the morning, too." Rick stood up and stretched after Jess told his daughter that they had to go.

After some argument and discussion of why they should stay, Shirley told Jess that she was exhausted and the idea of sleeping at Rick's place made good sense to her. With concise instructions, Madison's folks left, promising to come back and join her after breakfast.

"Call when you get there," Rick said, and followed them out into the hall.

Madison was wide awake from the excitement of Jess's stories. "So, Rick... When are we going back to Alaska to see it like tourists?"

"Someday, Sheriff McKenzie. But in the meantime, you have a job in Cold Creek. Or have you forgotten?"

"No, I love my job. I'll gladly step down when Drew is ready to return, but for now, I'm happy with what I was elected to do. And I'm willing to get back to it." She lowered the head of her bed to an almost flat position. "You ready to guard me while I sleep a while?"

Rick walked closer, leaned down and kissed her forehead. "Good night, Madison."

As she turned her back to the door and the recliner, she thought of how safe she felt in his care. She went to sleep, dreaming the kiss on her forehead was on her lips instead—but sadly, she felt that Rick looked at her as the little sister he never had.

# 32

Instead of the lab tech waking her, Madison awoke to a scuffle at the door inside her room. She pulled the chain for the nightlight over her bed and saw that Rick was struggling with a large man she didn't recognize. From her perspective, it looked like Rick was at a disadvantage. Madison grabbed a small fire extinguisher off the wall and clobbered the stranger over the head with it. He dropped to the floor with a thud.

Rick wasted no time securing the man's arms behind his back with handcuffs. Madison asked, "Are you OK?"

"Yeah, thanks. Get the nurse to call security up here, and then get your clothes on. You're going with me."

Madison ran into the hall and down to the nurses' station calling, "Hello? Where are you?"

A plump nurse in purple scrubs came from a back room. "What's wrong?"

"Call security; Agent Malone fought off a man who meant me harm. He's secure now, but Rick needs backup. And hurry!" She ran back to end of the hall.

In moments, three security guards came into her room, tasers in hand.

Rick asked them to help him move the man to the hallway and call a doctor in to check his head.

Madison retrieved her clothing from the cupboard and went into the bathroom to get dressed.

Through the door, she heard loud voices. *Rick's crew must be here to haul him away.*

She hurriedly buttoned her shirt, pulled the sweatshirt over her head, and returned to get her shoes from under the bed. Bending to tie her shoes caused excruciating pain in her back. *I must remember to get Dr. Chip to x-ray my back.*

Rick came in. "My guys took him away. The doctor says he'll need a couple of stitches from your attack. Way to go, Sheriff! Very resourceful." He held his hand up for a high-five.

"I could see you needed help. He *was* a brute, wasn't he?" She smiled and heaved a big sigh of relief.

"I thought you didn't know the guys who kidnapped you," Rick commented.

"I only saw one of them; he was a small fellow."

"Well, this was the other one, and his name is Brutus—known as 'the Brute,'" Rick laughed.

"That's what Austin called him, but I didn't know it was his real name." Madison frowned. "Have you checked on Austin?"

"He's OK. Security called the third floor to be sure." Rick glanced around the room. "You ready to get out of here?"

"What about my bloodwork?" No sooner had she spoken than the phlebotomist came through the door.

"Let's get this done. Agent Malone doesn't like our facility."

Madison sat in the recliner while the man took several vials of blood from her arm. "That ought to do it. Dr. Roland will be in touch with you—if he can find you." He laughed and left the room.

"Where are we going?" Madison pulled her sleeve down.

"First, we're going to get some breakfast. I've called it in, and we'll take it to my place. Shirley and Jess are up and ready to take you back to Cold Creek."

"I'm ready for that." She walked out of the hospital next to her best friend.

\* \* \*

Back in Cold Creek, Jess rolled slowly into Madison's driveway. "Get a change of clothes. We're going out to Henry and Holly's place; they can keep an eye on you better there. No one can approach their house without arousing Bear and Bud."

"Sounds like you and Rick have this all planned out."

"No, I planned this. With Rick in Knoxville, I had to help someway 'til you're feeling well enough to go home."

"Thank you, Dad. I hope we hear something from Dr. Roland soon. I've never felt quite like this before. I'm as dizzy as can be." Madison opened the door, but didn't get out.

"I'll get your clothes. What do you want?" Shirley jumped from the front seat and took charge.

"Anything, just so it's comfortable. I don't want a uniform. Oh, and my New Balance shoes are next to my dresser. Be sure to get a couple of pairs of socks, too." Madison slumped back into the seat of Jess' new Ford F150. She laid her head against the headrest.

Jess's phone rang. "Dr. Roland, thanks for calling. She's feeling worse."

He listened for a few moments, then said, ""No wonder! Yes, I will. OK, I'll call you after Madison has taken the first dose. Thank you, I appreciate it."

"What did he say?" Madison leaned forward in the seat.

"You have a potassium deficiency, and it's causing your irregular heartbeat and dizziness. Your doctor called in an emergency prescription to our pharmacy. As soon as I get you settled at Holly's, I'll go and get it."

"Potassium deficiency," she repeated. "And that's why I feel so bad?"

"Guess you'll have to Google it. He said for you to eat a couple of bananas every day for a week, besides the medication he's called in."

"I love bananas. I'll make a list for you to pick up at the supermarket. Is that OK?"

"Yeah; he also told me some other things to get for you." Jess started the engine as Shirley climbed back into the truck.

"I got everything you should need here in this bag," she said, settling a large canvas bag on her lap.

"Dr. Roland called." Jess told Shirley what the doctor had said.

Holly ran from the front porch to meet them as soon as they crossed the cattle guard. Bud and Bear ran ahead, beating her easily. Jess parked the truck in the circular drive and helped Madison out, holding her arm as she walked up the front steps into the yellow two-story house.

Bud waited until everyone was inside the house to come up and lick Madison's hand. He whined and lay on the floor beside the chair Jess had seated the patient in.

"Where do you want me to take her? Upstairs?" He asked.

"No, I'm putting her in the room where Drew and Nell were. They went to his apartment, you know," Holly said.

"How?" Madison sounded puzzled. "Is he able to walk?"

"No, Henry installed an elevator in one of the apartment's closets. And it works great! He has a locking compartment in the lower level, like a mechanical lift. He got it from that old mill in Johnson City. It was in the part they're tearing down."

"Oh, my goodness. Henry is the most enterprising guy I've ever met!" Jess commented, "OK, let's get you to bed so I can go to Erwin."

"Henry's in Erwin right now. What do you need?" Holly quickly pulled her cell phone from her jeans pocket. "I'll call him."

"Let me talk to him," Jess reached for the phone.

Madison was surprised that Holly had rearranged the room and changed the bedding and curtains. She had even put Bud's bed next to the queen bed where Madison would sleep. "This looks nice; thanks, Holly," she said. "You didn't have to work so hard."

"Aw, it wasn't hard. Besides, the twins helped me," Holly giggled.

"Holly, I want to see your boys. Where are they?" Shirley asked.

"With Henry, but they'll be back soon. I have super on, and I want you and Jess to stay and eat with us." Holly hugged Shirley. "I'm happy you two are home."

"I've missed your laugh, Holly. Nobody enjoys a laugh as much as you," Shirley said.

"And you look fit, Shirley," Holly hugged her again.

"Oh, I feel so much better. Why didn't I listen to my daughter when she tried to get me to run five years ago?"

"You didn't need to run then, just walk. And now you can start running with me, as soon as I get my energy back," Madison plopped onto the bed. When she bent to untie her shoes, she gasped in pain.

"Let me get your shoes! Here, lay back!" Holly cried.

"I'm OK, I just have a catch in my back," Madison resisted the urge to lay down.

"Did the doctor take any x-rays?" Shirley asked.

Madison shook her head. "I'll go see Chip in a day or so."

"I'm getting a cold pack. You probably have a pulled muscle," Holly ran out of the room.

Shirley bent to remove her daughter's shoes. "I'm just thankful we got back so I can help take care of you. And that I feel like doing it."

"I'm thankful you feel good too, Momma."

Bud jumped up onto the bed next to his master. Or in their case, his friend. He and Madison had been inseparable for six years. He hadn't liked the times that she spent away at school, so when he could lay beside her, he made that fact known. He nudged her arm, lifting it enough to slip his head under it.

"I know, my Buddy missed me. I love you, Bud. You knew something was wrong. Didn't you, Boy?"

Holly returned with the cold pack and placed it under Madison's lower back. "You've missed Bud, but no more than he missed you. Bud didn't want to leave your yard. He kept running back to where he smelled your scent. Henry finally had to drive his truck over and pick him up to bring him out here. We watched him like a hawk, thinking he might try to slip back and look for you." Holly turned down the bedspread so Madison could lay on the fresh sheets. "Is this comfy?" she asked.

"You know it is," Madison laughed.

The women spent the rest of the afternoon talking, while Jess went out onto the porch to wait for Henry.

Rick phoned Jess. "I got Madison a new phone. I'll bring it out tomorrow; I'm taking a few days off to spend there in Cold Creek.'

"She's with Henry and Holly. It's safer than her cottage, and Holly loves fussing over folks. Shirley has a couple of doctor's appointments, and we'll be in Johnson City a couple of days this week. I thought this was best."

"Good idea, Jess. I'll see you tomorrow." Rick disconnected the call.

Dr. Roland called Jess first thing the next morning. Jess explained that he had taken Madison out to stay with friends, where she'd be safer, in case the other fellow was still after her. He told him that the dizziness had subsided within a few hours of the first dose of potassium. Dr. Roland was pleased to hear the news, and advised Jess that Dr. Hardin's office would call in a few days to set up the appointment for Madison.

Things were going better with each hour for Madison, and she was beginning to feel the effects of the supplement and Holly's cooking.

Rick surprised her with a new phone, new number, and a lovely bouquet of yellow calla lilies. He even brought a pot of pink calla lilies for Holly.

"I got the potted lilies for you, Holly, because I want to see them blooming in your English Garden next spring, after your little Mattie is born," Rick accepted a tight squeeze from Holly.

"Oh, Rick, you're amazing!" Holly said.

"Yes, he is." Madison smiled as she buried her face in the bouquet of her favorite blooms.

"I need to run back to my car for a moment. Are the twins up yet?" Rick asked.

"Yeah, they went out early with Nicholas and Henry. Those boys have become Nick's shadows. Where ever he goes, there they are—right there under his feet! Henry thinks it's a good thing, but I'm worried," Holly said.

"Why?" Rick cocked his head. "He hasn't done anything to them, has he?"

"Oh, no. Nick adores the twins. But how will they handle him going back to Virginia?"

"Ah, I see," Rick looked toward Madison. "What if someone here in Cold

Creek took him in, and he didn't have to go back?"

"Could we do that?" Holly's face brightened up.

"Would you want to foster him?" Madison set her flowers on the table. "You and Henry did take the foster parent classes before you had the twins." She looked at Rick.

"I've already spoken to Henry, and he's all for the idea. I guess it's up to you, Momma." Rick put one hand on Holly's shoulder.

Tears had been welling up in her eyes, and now they cascaded down her cheeks. She swallowed hard. "This house has been filled with laughter ever since the twins were born. But adding Nick has made such a difference. He takes charge as soon as they are awake. He makes them dress and brush their teeth, and he checks to see that they've done a good job. He helps them pick up their toys and clothes. He is a Godsend! I am in awe of the love that young man has to offer. I'd not only foster him, I'd adopt him in a heartbeat!"

By now Holly was a blubber of mush and tears. Madison hugged her and shed a few tears of her own. Rick took this moment to slip back outside to bring in another surprise.

Nicholas and the twins came onto the back porch. They had been up at the barn helping Henry feed the animals. Removing their boots had become a ritual. Madison watched as Nick put his upside down on a bare tree branch next to the steps. Then Harry put his on another branch, and Hugh started into the house. Nick stopped him with a gentle hand. He pointed to the muddy boots sprawled on the floor. Hugh ducked to pick them up and walked to the edge of the porch, adding his to another branch.

"Now that's a terrific idea. Who came up with the boot tree?" Madison turned to Holly. "I should know: Henry, of course."

"No, Nicholas came dragging that in after his first day in the garden. Nick asked Henry if he could use his post-hole digger. Henry told him where to find it, and to be sure to clean and return it to the same spot when he finished. I guess Henry figured out what Nick was up to. Anyway, that little guy spent nearly an hour digging and burying that dead tree, making sure it was sturdy before he cleaned the tools and carried them back to the shed. The twins and I wondered what was going on, but Henry said for us just to watch." Holly took a deep breath.

"He sat on the steps and removed his boots, knocked them together, then placed them that way on the branch." Holly propped her fists on her hips. "The twins didn't even have to be told! They went out and got their boots and did the same thing. Nick was pleased when Henry got his boots and put them on the top branch. It's as if they think alike, Henry and Nicholas."

"That was such a good idea. I wonder where Nick came up with it," Madison said.

"Henry says he has a sharp mind, and that he'll do what's needed even before he tells him. Henry is crazy about the boy. We all are."

Rick came back into the house carrying a large box. Madison and Holly were curious, but he wouldn't tell them what was in it. "We need to wait for the twins."

Holly returned to the kitchen and Madison followed her. Rick carried the box to the back porch. "Here they come," Holly pointed out the kitchen window.

"Let's watch from here," Madison said.

The twins ran faster when they saw Rick. Nicholas slowed, as if he wanted to run the other direction. Henry came up behind him. He put his arm around the boy's shoulder and walked slowly with him.

Rick greeted the twins with a big hug, lifting them both off the ground. He waited for Henry to introduce him to Nicholas. Rick extended his hand, But Nicholas stood firm. Henry said something to him, then Nicholas reached out to shake Rick's hand.

The women realized Nicholas was afraid Rick was there to take him away. They both rushed out to the porch.

Rick stood close to Nicholas and told the twins to open the box. They scrambled to pull the tucked flaps, but their little hands weren't strong enough. Rick told Nick to give them a hand.

The three boys managed to open the flaps and began pulling out rope, swing seats, and finally a tire swing. Nick looked at Rick, recognizing the objects and what they meant. The joy on his face gave Madison a feeling of pride in Rick. She walked up next to him and put her hand in his. He squeezed it gently and held on. They didn't look at each other, but Madison was sure Rick felt what she was experiencing.

"All right," Henry clapped his hands and said, "where can we put these swings?" He looked straight at Nicholas. "I know you've spotted the perfect tree on the edge of the woods. You told me about it. Show Rick and me where it is."

"We'll need a ladder, a machete, and some pieces of an inner tube," Nicholas started toward the tool shed. "Come on guys, give me a hand."

The twins took off after him. They had a leader, a big brother with a powerful mind that knew how to fix things. In a couple of minutes, Henry and Rick joined the boys.

Madison and Holly sat on the porch swing and watched the guys all walk into the edge of the woods above the creek. At least from her perspective, things were looking better—not only for Nicholas, but for Rick and Madison's unspoken relationship as well.

211

# 33

Madison returned to her responsibilities as sheriff of Cold Creek the next week. Her first chore was not a chore at all. She was looking forward to talking with the sheriff in Smyth County Virginia.

"Good morning, Sheriff McKenzie. How are things in Cold Creek?"

"It's been a stressful week, but things are all good now. How are you?"

"Good."

"The reason I'm calling is to let you know I found Nicholas. He's OK, he's great, actually. I want to know if we can begin procedures to keep him." She waited for his refusal.

"Well, this is fantastic news, Madison."

"Really? You mean it is possible to adopt Nicholas?"

"He's had some tough breaks. Nick's a good kid. Why, if I weren't so near retirement, I'd have taken him into my home. He deserves a real family. Who's wanting to adopt the boy?"

"We have a family, friends of mine, who live on a farm just outside town. They have twin boys. They've all grown attached to Nicholas. Holly and Henry are wonderful folks, and they've had the fostering classes. They will do it either way, but eventually, they do want to adopt him into their family."

"I tell you what, I'll make some calls. See what the judge says, and I'll get back to you as soon as I can give you a definitive answer."

"That sounds good, Sheriff. Thank you," she replied. "Oh, I need to give you my new cellphone number," she added.

Madison was closing up the office for the evening when the phone on her desk rang. She thought of letting it go to the answering machine, but unlocked the door to go back inside instead. She hurried back to the desk and answered.

"Sheriff McKenzie."

"Hey, Madison. I'm glad you answered. I've been calling you for a week. What's happening?"

Madison recognized Monique's voice. "Oh, I am so sorry. I had to get a new cellphone, and Rick thought it was best if I also had a new number. I would've thought he'd give it to you."

The two women talked for a while, then Madison told Monique she'd need to call her back after eating. It was getting late, and the restaurant would close soon. Monique asked Madison to please not forget to call from her new cell; that way she'd have the number. Madison agreed, and hung up the landline.

After she had ordered a to-go box at the restaurant, she went to her cottage to eat and feed Bud. While she ate, she called Monique's number, and in two rings Monique answered.

"Hey, thanks for calling back. I was anxious to tell you about Michael, but when I heard your story, I completely forgot 'til you had to hang up."

"What about Michael?"

"He's all right; they cleared him of any connection to the deaths of the women. They told him he was trespassing, though, and couldn't live in the valley anymore. He went back to Baltimore to settle things there. He's a doctor, you know, and he said he had to face his fears there before he could go any further in my life. Madison, he's thinking of relocating to Knoxville!" Monique sounded as if she were jumping up and down.

"Wow, wouldn't that be nice? You will keep me posted, won't you?"

"Of course!" Monique said. "And my friends, the hikers, are planning to stop in Cold Creek to see you when they reach Tennessee. You aren't far off the trail, are you?"

"No, it's no more than a half hour walk. Do you know when they will reach this area?"

"They're kind of slow. I think they're enjoying the scenery way too much. But that's all good. Diane was excited when she learned I'd moved the store to Knoxville."

"How is Claudia?"

"She's good. She's in Kentucky for a few days, with her grandchildren," Monique said.

213

"I'll come down to visit you two soon. I want to see the store."

"Oh, perfect. We're having our grand opening week after next. Why don't you come then?"

"Sounds good. Why don't you call again soon and remind me what days? I'll see what I can work out." Madison hung up the call and turned to Bud. "I'm ready for some sleep. How about you?"

Bud stood up and stretched his back legs, one at a time. He yawned and walked to the front door.

"Ah, you need to go out. OK." She opened the door and went out onto her front porch. The street lamps glowed in the evening dusk. She looked up and down the sidewalks. It gave her a feeling of the old western towns you see in cowboy movies, with the raised wooden walkways. A few years ago, the council members had discussed replacing them with concrete. But the expense was not worth the loss of the old-fashioned charm to most, so the idea was defeated. Madison loved the peaceful look of her hometown. She felt proud that she was the person responsible for keeping it that way.

Bud jumped back up onto the porch, and they went inside. The sun was setting on another strange day in her life. It seemed like there were a lot of those now. More and more, she wondered if she'd made the right decision, taking the summer off from school and taking this job. She'd seen more violence and death since than she'd ever seen in class. Was that her destiny, to be surround-ed by death and mayhem? She certainly hoped it was not a sign of her future.

\* \* \*

The next morning, Madison and Bud ran their usual loop early. On the way back her cottage, she detoured to Drew's apartment. Bud barked, recog-nizing where they were. He ran up the steps. Nell leaned out of a window and called down to her, "Try the elevator."

Madison went into the garage portion of the building and saw that Henry had done a remarkable job installing the freight elevator. She pulled the rope for the gate to lift and stepped inside. In a moment, the compartment moved upward. Nell stood at the top next to the shrunken kitchen and lifted the gate. There was no other place Henry could make it work.

"This is helpful. And I am so happy that Henry rescued the elevator from the old General Mills building in Johnson City. That's special; it's a dinosaur, but nonetheless a treasure," Madison commented. "I hope I'm not interrupting anything, stopping by this early."

"No, we were just having breakfast. Want some?" Nell ushered Madison to the table.

"Hey, Drew. I'm happy to see you up and about. How are you feeling?" She bent to hug the former sheriff, seated in a wheelchair at the small table.

"I'm better each day. Thank you, Maddie. I'm glad you stopped by, I've missed you."

"I've been kind of busy," she laughed. "Did Nell tell you I got in some hot water?"

"I heard it was more like *cold* water," Drew teased, placing his hand on hers as she sat across the table from him. "You do know how to get into some deep..." he stopped. "My wife wants me to stop using my favorite four-letter word."

"Uh-oh. That means I'll have to, also. It'll certainly be better, in the presence of the new little girl coming into our lives soon."

"You both could use some scrubbing up on your habits. And so could Rick!" Nell added. "By the way, I hear he has been spending a lot of time in Cold Creek lately."

"He has a surplus of vacation time; he could leave work for six months and not use all the days."

"I'm glad to see he's spending time here, with you," Drew looked sharply at Maddie.

"He likes the peaceful atmosphere here," she said defensively.

"Here Maddie," Nell handed her a steaming cup of coffee, then sat down to finish her meal. "Have a biscuit?" She passed a plate covered with a paper towel.

"Oh, yes. I love your biscuits." Madison lifted the towel and picked up one of the smaller homemade biscuits. "Pass the butter, Drew."

"And I know how well you like the strawberry freezer jam." Nell slid the wide-mouthed Ball jar filled with bright red temptation close to Madison's hand.

"You know me too well, Nell. But this will be my desert for the day," Madison laughed.

"Poor Bud, you made him stay outside." Drew looked at Bud, who lay by the door.

"He's resting. We've been for our run already."

Nell got up and opened the door. ""You are allowed in our house, Bud. Come in, Drew wants to see you."

Bud walked over to Drew and nudged his hand. Drew patted the top of the dog's head. Then he took a strip of bacon from his plate and gave it to Bud.

"You spoil him!" Nell said.

"And you act surprised. That's why you opened the door. You knew Drew would give him bacon," Madison shook her head. "Some people don't get as much love as this dog."

"I better get going," she stood and started for the stairs. "I've been trying to call Rick, but I can't get an answer.

"I thought he was going to Nashville with his partner. You know they're an hour behind us," Nell said.

"Partner?" Madison wheeled around. "He didn't tell me he had a partner. When did this come about?"

"This week, I guess," Nell said. "He's bringing her here on Sunday."

"Sunday is his birthday," Madison said, as she and Bud went down the steps.

"Hey, Maddie, I think this all started innocently when you first got kidnapped. Ben and Margie had everybody meet at the restaurant for cake and coffee while we waited to hear back from TBI. Rick said he loved her carrot cake, and told her his birthday was soon and she could bake another one; she fancied the idea of a party to cheer him up. I'm sure he feels obligated to bring his new partner," Nell wrung her hands.

"Oh, sure! That's fine," Madison lied. "Who am I to say who he spends his birthday with?"

Bud ran across the field, racing Madison to her cottage.

She went inside and didn't stop to feed Bud, she just got straight into the shower and lathered up like a mummy. The lavender foam wasn't working to rinse away her anxious mood as it had in the past.

She dressed and returned to the kitchen. "Oh, I'm sorry Bud. I should have been thinking of your hunger instead of my feelings. That's jealousy, and I have no right to be jealous. What on earth is wrong with me, anyway?"

All day, Madison had felt like she was missing something. She couldn't concentrate on what she needed to get done. Mr. Olsen came in to see what she was doing.

"I wondered if you could give me a hand. I have misplaced my keys. I opened the store, and the phone rang as soon as I came in. I ran to answer it. I must have put the keys down somewhere along the way, but I can't find them."

"Sure. I can't concentrate on anything here at my desk today, so I might as well not be in here. Let's go see if the two of us can retrace your steps." She and Mr. Olsen went next door to the hardware store.

"I walked inside and hurried to the counter." He shuffled, but it was nowhere near what Madison called a run.

"How long did you talk?" she asked.

"Just for a minute. It was Henry, wanting to know if that part for his tractor was here."

"Did you have to go and look?" Madison asked.

"No, I knew it wasn't. I went to turn the lights on." He took a couple of steps toward the switch.

Madison walked behind him. She looked on all the surfaces, then asked, "Would you have dropped them into your pocket?"

"I checked all my pockets. Not there."

"What do you do every morning, things you don't have to think about?"

"I go over there and turn on the AC unit."

They walked to the back room. Madison looked around. Every surface was cleared and clean. "You are so well organized and neat, Mr. Olsen," she said.

"I like to keep everything in its place."

"Where do you usually put your keys?" she asked.

"Next to the cash register. Got a little box I keep my keys in."

"Show me, as if you just came in and the phone wasn't ringing," she said.

Mr. Olsen walked to the register and put his hand on an old cigar box. He opened it to show her there was nothing inside. Madison stood next to him and looked around. All she saw was an empty trash can.

"Did you take the trash out last night or this afternoon?" she asked.

He stood quietly for a while. "I took it out after I turned on the AC. I empty it into the bigger trash in the back room."

They returned to the back room. Madison looked at a pile of receipts and some crumpled up papers in the top of the trash can. She looked around for an empty box, spotted one, and began taking handfuls of paper out, putting it into the empty box. If the keys were in the small can, Madison knew they would fall all the way to the bottom. She kept digging until she heard a metallic sound hit against the side of the metal trash can. She stuck her hand all the way into the bottom of the papers and came up with the keys.

"I'll be. I missed the box and put my keys in the trash. Lucky I only put paper in there. I burn it about once a month, out back. It would have been a while before I found them, if I ever did, on my own. Thank you, Madison."

"You're welcome. I'm glad I could help." Madison returned to the sheriff's office in time to hear the radio transmit an alert. "Sheriff McKenzie, Washington County SO is in pursuit of a suspect driving a Toyota Corolla, blue in color. The suspect turned off I twenty-six at Clearview Road, heading up old twenty-three southbound. The subject is armed and considered dangerous."

"Sheriff McKenzie to Washington County SO, I'll keep an eye out."

In a couple of minutes, the radio transmitted again, "Washington County SO, suspect veered off at Rice Creek Bridge, heading toward Cold Creek. Coming to you, Sheriff."

"Ten-four."

Madison knew if he was trying to outrun the WCSO, he was moving fast. And she had to move faster.

She jumped into the Blazer and set her blue light on top before speeding out of town to the east. Henry had left an old dozer by the side of the road back in the winter, after he plowed snow off the road. Madison parked her Blazer, lights flashing, at the beginning of the curve. She ran to the dozer sitting in the old logging road.

Remembering Henry told her he'd hotwired the dozer for the last ten years, Madison climbed the tracks to the driver's seat. Underneath the steering column, she saw two wires, and a third was wrapped around the ignition switch. She touched the two wires to the third wire, and the Caterpillar roared to life. She looked at the levers, hoping to find one that could make it move forward. Thanks to the luck of the draw, the hulking machine crawled backward. She quickly moved the lever into the opposite direction. It lunged forward and went into the road. She stomped the brake and clutch at the same time, and shut the engine down. She jumped off the back side of the tracks and climbed the hill a few feet off the road to watch for the blue Corolla. In less than five minutes, she heard sirens and car tires squealing as cars slid through the curves. She pulled her gun and waited. A blue car darted around the curve, not even slowing for her Blazer. By the time he saw the faded dozer, it was too late. The car slammed into the metal tracks and the back wheels came off the ground. It made one of the loudest bangs she'd ever witnessed.

She watched for movement and slipped slowly up to the driver's side of the Corolla. The suspect was stunned, fighting the airbag that had ballooned into his face.

"Hands where I can see them!" Sheriff McKenzie shouted.

The man turned toward her. She saw his face was bloody and his nose crooked. "Hands up! Now, where I can see them!" she commanded.

His left hand came out the window, but she couldn't see the right one. She pulled the slide back on her Sig. "Last warning!"

The man struggled to get his right hand where she could see it. Finally, she saw his hand was empty. She jerked the door open with her left hand, still pointing the Sig at him. The airbag began shrinking. "Step out of the car slowly." She backed away. "Don't even think of running. I'm a great shot, and I'd love to blow out your knee!"

The suspect was making an attempt to get out as the WCSO cars arrived. The first officer, Madison recognized as Sargent Masters.

"Is this the suspect you're looking for?" She never took her eyes off the man. "I think you need to call an ambulance for him. He's had a bad jolt!"

"Dang, Madison! You did the right thing!" Masters laughed.

Several other county deputies joined them. Masters cuffed the suspect, and another officer took him to his cruiser and put him in the back.

"How did you manage this so quickly?" Masters asked.

"Been parked her since the last snow. I was just lucky that it started up. I hope it isn't hurt. Not sure Henry would forgive me," Madison holstered her pistol and walked closer to inspect the dozer.

Masters walked next to her and slapped her on the back. "I'm sure glad I thought to call you. We've chased this fellow through Washington, Carter, and Unicoi Counties for the last hour. He robbed the One Stop over near ETSU. Shot one of the girls behind the counter, but she's going to be OK."

"Glad I could help, Sargent. I didn't want him racing through our community, and this dozer came to mind. I barely had time to get it in place." Madison walked down to her Blazer. She called Henry and told him she'd like for him to ride out and check to see if the dozer was OK. She left her blue lights on until the wrecker came up from Flag Pond to get the Corolla.

After the wrecker had loaded the smashed-up car, the deputy drove away with the suspect, and a line of cars had formed near her Blazer, Henry arrived. He looked at the tracks, and seeing no visible damage, he backed the dozer off the road. "I was going to try to get my trailer out here and load it up, but my flatbed trailer has a flat."

"I'll get a rollback to take it in and get it looked at for damage, then the rollback can deliver it to the farm for you," Madison said. "I've already talked to Samson. He hauled the Corolla away. He's coming back in a bit to load up the dozer."

"Thank you, Maddie," Henry placed his arm around her shoulders. "I can't imagine that car hurting the dozer, but it's a good idea to have it checked. If you need to go back to town, I can stay and wait for Samson," Henry said.

"You sure? I know you're always busy."

"No, I'm fine. I'd like to talk to Samson anyway."

"OK, I do have some important paperwork waiting on me." She got into her Blazer and drove back to town.

Madison reminded herself to wash her uniform pants; these were dirty from crawling on the dozer tracks, and a clean pair was necessary for tomorrow. She parked in her driveway and called Bud, who was lying on the sidewalk in front of the sheriff's office. As the water filled the washer, she went through her pockets to remove any tissues or paper. That's when she ran across the business card from the state trooper who helped her out of the water in the culvert. She stared at the name: *William (Bill) L. Conway.*

*He was nice looking, and a good man too. He wasn't wearing a wedding band, but you never can tell these days. So many married men don't, for whatever reason. Henry doesn't wear one unless he and Holly are dressed up to go someplace. I understand that; he's a farmer, and in contact with a lot of machinery. Jess didn't wear one in the kitchen of the restaurant when they ran it. Mr. Olsen always has his on his finger.*

"Oh, well. Anyway, I promised him I'd call to let him know how I was doing. It won't hurt to call, even if he is married. Right, Bud?"

She dunked the khaki jeans into the soapy water and shut the lid. "Why are you looking at me like that? If I want to talk to a handsome guy who may have saved my life, it's my privilege," she said and walked through the kitchen. Bud followed her back over to the office.

A fax was coming in, and she read it as it printed.

*Sheriff's Office, Smyth County VA*

"Oh good, Bud, this is about Nicholas."

She pulled the paper from the tray and sat down in the tired leather swivel chair. She read and picked up the phone at the same time.

"Hey, Holly. I have some good news from the sheriff in Virginia.""

"Wonderful, let's hear it!" Holly squealed.

Madison read the legal document to her.

"As soon as Henry gets back, we'll swing by and sign it so you can fax it back to the sheriff!" Holly was always easily excited, but this was extreme enthusiasm on her part.

"I'll be right here." Madison hung up the phone and glanced at her watch; It was 1:45. *Hmm, Trooper Bill should be on duty by now.*

Bud stood up, stretched, and walked to the front door. He seemed to be expecting someone—but then he walked back to a different patch of the floor, lying down again.

"You're as miserable as me. I'm sorry, Bud. Go back to sleep." She walked out onto the porch.

Ben stood outside the restaurant and waved to her. "You are coming to the party on Sunday, aren't you?"

Madison stepped onto the street and crossed to where Ben waited. "What party?"

"Oh, I thought Nell would have told you by now. We're giving Rick a little birthday party. He's done so much for our town, and for you. We thought it would be a good way to thank him. I bet he doesn't get a birthday cake and a surprise party thrown in his honor often."

Ben opened the screen and went inside. Madison followed.

"Hey, Maddie. What will you have?" Margie called from behind the front counter.

"Nothing now, Margie. Thanks," she answered.

Ben and Madison sat at the counter on the newly recovered swivel stools. "Do you like the colors Margie chose for the stools?"

"Yeah, turquoise is one of my favorite colors. And it goes nicely with the Coke red. Looks like a retro soda fountain," Madison said.

Ben jumped up and hurried to the wall beside the front door. "And how 'bout this upgraded jukebox? It plays without adding coins. And it's fill of all the oldies songs." He pushed a couple of buttons, and Roy Orbison's "Pretty Woman" began playing.

"Oh, I love it!" Madison joined Ben at the jukebox.

"Go ahead; it will hold up to fifteen selections."

She studied the song titles and continued with *The Best of Roy Orbison*, picking her favorites from that album. Margie joined them and asked Ben to dance.

"Ah, that's another idea," he said. "We should move some of the booths into the other room and make a dance floor."

They laughed together, picturing the restaurant as a dance hall.

Madison walked back across the street just as Henry's truck pulled up in front of the jail. "That was quick!"

"We were ready to go when you called. I just had to hunt down the twins. As usual, they were with Nicholas. He is a Godsend!"

"Yes, and he will be happy to hear your news. Unless you've already told him," Madison whispered.

"We thought we'd give you that honor." Henry opened the back door to the truck and the twins jumped out followed by Nicholas.

"Oh my, look how tall you are getting! You're up past my knees now." She knelt down to hug each one separately. Then she stood and opened her arms wide toward Nick. "Don't I get one from you?"

Nick rushed into her arms, burying his head in her shoulder. "You will be happy to hear that we heard some good news from the sheriff in Virginia," Madison said. She pulled back and looked into Nick's face. "You are staying with the Jacobs. They can start the paperwork to foster you, and then in six months they will be able to proceed with the adoption."

Nicholas' eyes filled with tears and he tried to speak, but all that came out was a blubber. Finally, he wiped his face on his sleeve and said, "Ms. Madison, how did you do that?"

"I told the sheriff to work it out. We were not returning you under any circumstances!"

Henry joined the hug, "And we were willing to hide you in our corn crib if they came looking for you."

"Oh! I don't know what to say..."

"Words are not necessary, Honey. Your face is reward enough," Holly said, crying, standing next to her husband.

"Let's get these papers signed and returned before they change their minds," Madison walked inside with her arm around Nick's shoulders.

The couple signed the bottom of the document, and Holly turned to hug Henry, choking out, "Thank you so much..."

"I thought this was posed to be good news," Harry said.

"Yeah, so why's everybody crying?" Hugh asked.

"Because it is such a happy occasion. These are tears of joy," Madison explained.

The twins looked at each other and ran out the front door.

"Don't go far, boys," Henry called.

"I'll go with them, Hen—Dad?" Nicholas stepped close to Henry.

"Yes, Son. You can call me Dad." And then the big man hugged the little boy.

He patted Nick on the back and sent him running after his brothers. He turned to Madison and asked, "Did you find out anything about his brother?"

"They haven't gotten back to me, Henry. I promise I'll let you know the minute I hear anything." Madison turned and walked to the fax machine.

It was after 4:00, so Madison sat behind her desk and pulled Trooper Conway's card from her shirt pocket. She punched in the numbers on her cell and hit send.

"Conway." She heard his voice.

"Hello. It's Sheriff McKenzie."

"Madison, how nice hearing from you. How are you feeling?"

"I'm doing well, thanks. The potassium made all the difference. The irregular heartbeat has subsided. I feel great."

"Oh, what a pity. I hoped it was me that made your heart flutter."

"Aw... "She felt her cheeks burn. "Maybe that's what kickstarted it."

"I'll accept that. So, is your buddy Rick there with you?"

"Oh, no. Rick's in Nashville, I think. I don't keep that close tabs on him."

"Really? Does that mean you are free to have dinner with me?"

Madison fanned her face. She wasn't accustomed to this heavy flirting.

"Are you still there, Madison?"

"Yeah, I was checking my calendar," she nearly laughed at herself.

"How about this Sunday? I could come to Cold Creek, and you could show me around your town.""

"That would take all of two minutes." Madison gulped in air and strangled herself. She coughed and tried to cover the phone. But she kept coughing.

"Get your breath, Sugar. I don't often have that much of an effect on women these days." He paused to let her recover. "Are you OK?"

She cleared her throat, "I'm sorry, I do that sometimes. I hate it, it's embarrassing, but I can't help it. It has nothing to do with you."

"Ouch! That hurts."

"I didn't mean to hurt your feelings..."

"I know, you're one of those girls who is just too honest for your own good. Aren't you?"

"I guess I am," she answered. "So, here goes some more; Conway, are you married?"

He laughed. "No. I knew that's what you thought. I got close a couple of years ago, but it didn't work out. I wasn't willing to take a desk job in her daddy's bank."

"Can't blame you for that. Who wants to sit behind a stuffy desk?"

"Well, you are, from what I can tell. If your town is that small, I can't see how you have much crime to deal with."

"Not really, but I stay busy." The desk phone rang. "I'm going to have to take this call. I'll call you back later this evening, if that's OK?"

"I can hardly wait," Bill Conway answered.

Madison tried to compose herself before she picked up the office phone. "Sheriff McKenzie."

The phone call took several minutes, then Madison walked out into the street. It was evident that she would have to get an air conditioning unit installed if she was to spend her summer in that office. The steamy conversation with Bill hadn't helped any.

Later that day, Holly and Henry stopped by her cottage on their way home from Johnson City. The kids piled out and ran around the yard with Bud. Henry walked around the side of the house, looking at the roofline. Holly and Madison sat on the porch swing.

Holly told her how much fun the twins had helping Nicholas pick out his clothes. And she admitted to crying most of the day. "He's such an appreciative child. He's never had more than one pair of shoes or boots at a time. He had two shirts and one pair of jeans to his name. You should have seen the way he looked at me when I nodded in approval at not just one shirt, but at all of them. I just couldn't help crying. No kid should have to grow up that way these days," she pulled a handkerchief from her pocket and blew her nose.

"Sweetie, you are pregnant. Your hormones are crazy right now. But I can understand, I'm nearly as bad as you. But not for the same reason," Madison looked down at her bare feet.

"What's wrong?"

"I'm losing my mind, I guess."

"Rick hasn't called you, has he?"

Maddie just shook her head, and tears rolled down her face.

"Oh, Maddie. It's OK. You're crazy over him, and now that you know he has a female partner, you're worried. It's normal. Don't feel bad about being jealous. You love the man."

"Do you think so?"

"Of course. I've seen it for years! What's holding you back?" Holly put her arm around her best friend.

"I don't know. Throwing that handsome Bill Conway in the mix, how am I supposed to sort this out?"

"Is he that handsome?" Holly giggled her best Dolly impression.

"Yes, and he asked me to have dinner with him. He wants to come here—on Sunday."

"Aw, shit!" Holly said and then clasped her hand over her mouth. "Oops!"

They were both laughing when Henry walked back to the house. "What did I miss?"

"Nothing! Absolutely nothing, Henry." Madison stopped laughing long enough to say.

Henry asked Madison if she was ready to begin the construction job on the cottage. She agreed that it was time, and told him she'd set up an account at Lowe's the next day, so he could pick up supplies as he needed them.

The sun was setting when Madison thought of calling Bill. She suddenly felt a twinge in her gut. Was she scared of what she needed to do? Or would that kill her chances with Rick?

"Hello, Sugar. How was your day?" Bill answered his phone.

"My day was," she paused, "how shall I say it...fruitful?"

"Good! No bad guys in your jail cell?"

"Oh, no. Deputies took him to Washington County. I'll tell you about that later," She laughed. "We had a joyful time here in the jail today. My best friends, Holly and Henry, are going to adopt a runaway kid who broke into every building in our town and caused havoc for me for weeks. He witnessed my abduction and reported it to Henry, though, so I've forgiven him. Besides, I don't think this cell could hold a nine-year-old boy."

"Seriously? You are pulling my leg, aren't you?"

"No, I'm telling you the truth. Nicholas is a runaway from Virginia. He spent February, March, and April sleeping and eating wherever he could hide. I figured him out and was just establishing contact when those thugs nabbed me."

"I gotta meet this kid. What about Sunday?"

"Tell you what: I just learned that the people at Shirley's Restaurant are throwing a surprise birthday party for Rick on Sunday. Why don't you come early? Let me show you our town, and we can attend the party together. I'd like for you to meet my friends. The whole town will be there."

"Hmm, let me think about that."

"What's the matter, Bill? Can't you stand a surprise party for Rick? Or is it the fact that you'll have to meet the whole town?"

"I'll see you by ten. How should I dress for this occasion?"

"Casual, comfortable... We aren't hicks, but we don't put on airs, either," she said.

"Is this a gift party?"

"I don't plan on giving him anything." Madison thought of how curt she sounded. "We don't usually exchange gifts. I mean, we're all adults here."

"I see. So, tell me how to locate you once I'm in the big city of Cold Creek."

"I live in the little white cottage next door to the old jail, across the street from Shirley's Restaurant. They're all on Main Street. You can't miss it."

"I look forward to seeing you on Sunday. And Madison, if you get over whatever it is that's put the burr under your saddle, just say so. And I'll stay away."

"I guess I deserved that, but no, it isn't something I can share with you. Not yet, anyway."

"You want to talk about it? I've got nowhere to go and nothing to do until Sunday." The kindest voice came across the line.

"How would you like to meet me in Morristown at Cracker Barrel for supper tomorrow night?" Madison had said the words before she realized it.

"I have an even better idea. A friend of mine has me house sitting for her in Asheville for the week. Why don't you drive over here, and we can go to lunch at the Grove Park Inn tomorrow?" Bill suggested.

"OK, that's even closer to me. What about work?"

"I've taken some vacation time. Wheezy is in Europe, and this is a good time for me to let new friends into my life. What do you say?"

"There isn't much going on here. I guess I could get away for a few hours. How will I find you?"

"Do you know Asheville well?"

"Well, kind of..."

"You know where the Grove Park Inn is?"

"Yeah."

"Do you know the Fuddruckers Restaurant on that road?"

"Yes, I've been there many times."

"Meet me there. This house is a little hard to find."

"OK, how about eleven o'clock?"

"How about ten? They have lots of trails to walk at the Grove Park."

"OK, ten o'clock it is, in the parking lot of Fuddruckers. I'll see you in the morning."

"Good night, Madison. I am looking forward to getting to know you. You aren't like any other sheriff I've ever met."

"I should hope not!" She laughed and hung up the call.

Madison was up early the next morning. She waited until 7:00 to call Holly.

"Hello, Maddie. Did you see the Channel Eleven News? You were on there."

"What? No, I didn't see it."

"It was Sargent Masters. He talked about how you are the one that stopped that robbery suspect with the bulldozer. Didn't you see the TV crew out there?"

"No...you mean on the scene?"

"Yes. You and Henry were looking at the tracks of the dozer when he started rolling the film. I guess he arrived with the wrecker."

"I didn't even notice them. What did the news say?" Madison wondered if he made her look like a hero or a nincompoop.

"Oh, he praised you for being so intelligent and thinking that quickly. Henry even talked to the reporter. It was, oh I can't remember her name. You gotta get the *Johnson City Press*. It's in there too." Holly was enjoying her friend's fame.

"I wondered if I could bring Bud out to play with Bear and the boys."

"Oh, yeah, anytime. You know you don't even have to ask."

Madison told her friend about her late-night phone call, and that she was going out on a limb to find out how she felt about Rick—who, incidentally, *still* had not called.

"Have you tried to call him?"

"I've never had to leave a message before. He always sees he's missed a call, and he calls me back."

"Try again. You were in a sketchy signal area. Maybe Rick never even got your call."

Madison agreed to call Rick again, and told Holly she'd be on her way out to bring Bud in a few minutes.

The phone rang several times, and Rick answered. "Hey Madison, what's wrong?"

"Does there have to be something wrong for me to call you?"

"Well, no. But there usually is," Rick sounded as if he was whispering. "How are you feeling?"

"I'm good, Rick. How's Nashville?"

"Same as always. Busy, busy!" Rick laughed. "Who told you?"

"Does it matter? You didn't feel it was important to tell me, or to let me in on the secret that you have a new partner. So what does it matter, Rick?"

"OK, I was afraid you wouldn't understand. I didn't want this partnership, but my superiors don't let me choose. I can tell you've already formed an opinion, and that's exactly why I haven't called."

"You know that's crap, Rick! It isn't like we're a couple. I called you because I wanted to tell you happy birthday. I just haven't talked to you in nearly a week." Madison let her statement resonate in his head.

"I'm sorry. I should have called you. I was wrong to try and keep it from you."

Madison heard him take a deep breath. "Don't mention it. It doesn't matter to me either." She hung up the phone and drove out of town toward Asheville, after dropping off Bud at Holly's. She stopped by the Wolf Laurel Store to pick up a Johnson City paper before she hit I-26. Sure enough, there on the front page was her photo with Henry, the dozer still blocking the road, and the wrecker hitching up to the Corolla.

As she took the left lane and headed toward downtown Asheville, she was still upset, and she was early. She didn't want Bill to see this mood, so she called him. When he answered, she tried to tell him she had business that was keeping her from coming to meet him.

He didn't buy that. "What's wrong? Did you talk to Rick and change your mind?"

"No, I didn't. Change my mind, that is. I'm in Asheville early, and I don't want to take out my anger on you. I'm heading back to Cold Creek. Goodbye, Bill."

"Please don't!"

Madison didn't hang up; she listened, and he convinced her to come to Fuddruckers and meet him.

Her mood lightened when she showed Bill the photo on the front page of the newspaper. They laughed, and she told him how it had happened. Laughing with him gave her an uplift that she thought was better than being alone today, and letting Rick's actions eat her up. She had no right to be upset with him; she had no hold on him, and he had no hold on her. She was free to spend her time with whomever she pleased, especially a handsome trooper like Bill Conway.

They walked from Wheezy's house to the Grove Park Inn—it was that close. Madison listened to Bill tell her about his friend, whom he adored like a mom. An eccentric old maid on a tour of Europe, she had no family. Somewhere along the line when he'd helped her out of a burning car, she'd latched onto him as an adopted son, and she never let go.

"She's the age my mother would be, if Mom were living," he explained.

Madison walked and listened without comment. She was afraid she'd say something cruel and out of character, so she kept quiet. They walked until nearly noon on the trails. When Madison felt weak from hunger, she took hold of his arm and said, "I need to eat."

"Of course." He held her hand and walked straight to the Veranda Restaurant. They took a seat in the shade.

"What do you need immediately?" He leaned close and whispered to her.

"Orange juice," she answered.

When the waiter approached, he requested two oranges juices, with an extra glass of ice and some bread.

The waiter returned quickly with the beginning of the order, and handed them menus. "Let me know when you're ready."

"Thanks, I will."

Madison drank some juice and took a bite of bread with honey butter. She rested her head in her hand, resting her elbow on the table. Bill buttered another bit of yeast roll. He encouraged her to eat it, then lifted her juice to her lips. She took the glass and immediately dropped it. Bill placed his napkin over the spill and held her hand.

"No worries, I have another one." Bill held it to her lips and she drank several sips. She felt embarrassed. But he was gracious enough to care for her, so she accepted his kindness. Maddie had eaten an entire roll and drank the rest of his OJ when the waiter approached.

"Can I suggest the chicken salad croissant?"

"Two of those, with a side of bananas and other fresh fruits?" Bill requested.

"Absolutely." The waiter hurried away.

"Any better?" Bill whispered.

"Yes. Thank you." She shook her head, complaining, "I thought this was behind me."

"Don't talk; eat this other bread, if you can." He put the roll in her hand. "My mom was diabetic. Have they checked you for high sugar?"

She shook her head. The soft roll went down nicely. She felt better quickly. "I'm the opposite."

The waiter returned in under five minutes with a lovely spread of freshly cut fruits, lemon slices on bananas, fresh strawberries, blueberries, pineapple wedges, apple slices, and Brie. Between them, he set a platter of chicken salad croissants, drizzled with honey.

Bill picked up a slice of banana on a salad fork, then lifted it toward her lips. Madison took a bite and then took the fork. She speared another banana slice, then an apple with Brie. Bill waited for her to recover before he took his eyes off her.

"You didn't eat dinner last night, or breakfast this morning, did you?"

Madison's eyes met his. *Warm brown, the color of the honey on the bread,* she thought.

After a long slow luncheon, the two walked to the pool next to the spa. Madison thanked Bill for his attention, his care, and she assured him this did not happen often. She was ashamed of herself.

"Love will do that to you," Bill murmured. "I can attest to that." He rolled his eyes. "It's something you can't control, and you can't hide it, either. I'm here for you, under any circumstances."

"This isn't fair to you." She breathed deeply. "I won't pretend Rick didn't hurt me, but it's my own fault. He hadn't encouraged me in any way. I just did this on my own."

"No, you *did not!*" Bill sounded stern. "I saw him at the hospital. I heard his voice when he speaks to you. He was so darn jealous of me showing up at the hospital, he was green!"

Madison laughed. "Not the Rick I know. He's never even kissed me."

"Then he's a bigger fool than I thought." Bill leaned in closer. "You are as rare as that lovely flower, the lady slipper. They are difficult to find; they don't transplant well from the wild, and you can't keep them in a vase. They die almost instantly."

Madison held her breath, her mouth open. "What did you say?"

"The white lady slipper. Have you ever seen one?"

"No."

"Neither have I, and I've searched. Lady slippers are the elusive gem of the forest's bulbs. Granny told me if I ever found one, I shouldn't pick it. She told me to just enjoy it in the wild."

"This spring, we were in a case in North Georgia, where pink lady slippers grow. But we never saw any white ones. Where did your granny say you'd find them?"

"She didn't know. She died before she ever saw them. But she'd seen them in a book about wildflowers of Virginia. I've always wanted to find them." Bill bowed his head and closed his eyes. "You are the closest I've come to finding one."

"Bill, don't. I'm in a bad place in my life right now. I could destroy your kindness, your heart, and I don't want to be responsible for causing you pain." Madison put her hand in his. "We should go. I need to get home."

"Stay with me?" He looked into her eyes with the strongest persuasion she'd ever felt. "The house has lots of rooms. You can sleep anywhere you wish. I won't intrude. But I want to spend the rest of the day with you."

"Bill, no. It won't work. I can't. I'm not sure how I feel about Rick. So how could I know how I feel about you?"

"I'm not asking you to love me, just spend time with me." His eyes darted back and forth between hers. "I'm not asking for anything but your company."

"OK. If you understand that I might get up in the middle of the night and drive home."

"Don't you mean, get up and run?"

* * *

The next day, Bill followed Madison to her cottage in Cold Creek for Rick's surprise birthday party. After walking up one side of Main Street while telling him a brief history of the buildings, then back down the other sidewalk, Madison walked with Bill to Drew's apartment.

Drew was practicing walking with a walker. Nell called out for Madison to come in. When she saw Drew on his feet and Nell supporting him with a back-strap, she offered to help.

"Thanks, this is our last pass. I'm ready to rest in the recliner," Drew announced. "Who do you have with you?"

"This is Bill Conway, the trooper that saved me from a cold drowning. Bill, this is Nell and Drew Perry."

They exchanged handshakes, and Bill assisted Drew to the recliner. Nell sat on the arm of his chair, while Madison and her new friend sat on the loveseat. Drew and Bill hit it off immediately, with shop talk about strange encounters on the job. Drew shared that he had started out as a state trooper in Florida, before he heard of the opening in the little town of Cold Creek while up here on a fishing trip.

Madison was surprised, and told Nell she'd never known that Drew had been a state trooper. Nell knew; she knew just about everything about her husband.

"I need to get out to the farm and pick up Bud. He'll probably need a bath after romping in the fields and mud with Bear and the boys." She stood, asking, "Will you be coming down for Rick's party?"

"Wouldn't miss it," Drew looked up at his wife with a telling grin.

"We'll see you over there."

On the drive out to Henry and Holly's farm, Bill asked what Drew was referring to when he said, "Wouldn't miss it."

"Well, Rick is bringing his new partner, and I'm bringing you to the party. That's all. Two new folks in town on the same day. We're a small community, as you've seen."

"Are your folks going to be there?"

"I don't know. Shirley and Jess went to Kingsport with another couple for a funeral. I'm not sure when they'll be back."

Madison turned onto the gravel drive leading across the cattle guard and onto the circular drive of the Jacobs lovely home. As usual, Bud ran to intercept the Blazer. When the vehicle stopped and the passenger door opened, Bud rushed in—only to back up immediately. He had anticipated Rick, but seeing a stranger, he wasn't sure whether to bark or run. Madison hurried around the other side to introduce Bill to Bud.

"It's OK, Bud. Say hello to my friend."

Bud sat quietly for a short time, then raised one paw toward the new man in Madison's life.

"Aw, now that's a good boy." Bill knelt down and extended his hand but did not look eye to eye with Bud. After a couple of seconds, he shook the dog's paw. "Hello, Bud. I've heard a lot about you. You must be a smart dog."

Bud barked one soft greeting, and then he backed away.

"He's not accepting me completely. He and Rick must be good buddies." Bill smiled at Madison. "I'll win him over. I love dogs."

"He's a smart one. He already knows you like him. He's withholding his opinion on you, for now."

Everyone parked their cars on the back side of the church so Rick wouldn't suspect anything when he drove into town. Madison's Blazer was in her driveway. Bill's was in the back of the jail. Henry and Holly parked behind the hardware store.

Rick pulled in beside the restaurant, next to Ben's truck. He and his new partner walked into Shirley's.

"Surprise!" No less than twenty-five voices yelled.

Madison stayed behind Shirley and Jess. Bill stood next to her. Henry and Holly, along with Ben and Margie, met the two at the door for introductions.

231

Nell pushed Drew's wheelchair into the mix.

Rick introduced Shannon by saying, "Everyone, this is Shannon Parker, a temporary pain in my rear and one of the bravest TBI agents I've worked with."

Jess stepped aside and Madison moved forward, holding hands with Bill as they approached. "Rick, you remember Bill Conway. Shannon, I'm Sheriff Madison McKenzie, and this is my friend, Bill, a Tennessee state trooper. Welcome to Cold Creek."

Madison leaned toward Bill, watching Rick's face. He shook hands with Bill, but said nothing. He didn't even look at Madison—but she was looking Shannon up and down.

She sized her up as *overdressed, petite body, bleached-blonde, and her perfume is overwhelming.* Her make-up stopped abruptly at the jaw, and her lipstick was pink, clashing with her orange crop top and matching skirt. Her six-inch wedge sandals looked out of place for the occasion. *Tennis shoes and a racket would go with that look.*

Luckily Ben and Henry had a plan for Rick, so they were able to distract him as Madison and Bill mingled with the guests. Ben led Rick to the jukebox and asked if he would pick out some songs to start the celebration. Henry went to the kitchen to get the cake: three boxes covered with fondant. A blow-up doll was ready to jump out as soon as Henry pulled the string.

Bill whispered in Maddie's ear, "Relax, Sugar. I got you. You're shaking like a leaf."

"I'm fine. Which Shannon ain't!" Madison said sharply, but in a quiet voice.

"No, she ain't," Bill winked at Madison.

Henry was in position. The twins pulled on both Rick's arms, wanting him to come and see the cake. As soon as he approached the table, the top blew off, and the joke blow-up doll sprang out. Everyone hollered and laughed. Rick appeared shocked at first, then enjoyed the fact that his friends of Cold Creek cared enough to go to all that trouble.

"Thanks, that was quite a surprise," Rick laughed with Ben. "Your idea or Henry's?" he asked.

Margie brought out the three-layer carrot cake with candles burning. "Grab the fire extinguisher," she yelled. She gave Rick a hug as soon as she put the cake down. "Thank you, Rick, for everything you've done for our town. And Happy Birthday!"

That was the cue for the guests to sing happy birthday. Shirley and Jess brought out the ice cream.

After the cake and ice cream were all gone and the guests began to disburse,

Rick abandoned Shannon and followed Madison to the kitchen as she carried a tray of dishes.

"So, you and Conway are an item now. And you had the nerve to get angry at me for my partner. You disappoint me, Maddie. He's obviously just after one thing."

Madison wheeled around to face Rick. "At least he noticed that I am a woman!" She pushed past Rick and went back into the dining room. It was all she could do to keep away the tears. She nodded to Bill that she was going out the door.

Bill shook hands with Jess and Shirley and excused himself. He joined Madison in her cottage. "Sugar, I think it is time for me to go. Thanks for a lovely weekend." He pulled her into his arms. Call me?" He leaned in and kissed her with the heat of passion unmatched by any movie she'd ever watched.

Madison held her breath even after he pulled away.

"Breathe, Sugar. Breathe," he squeezed her close again. "You weren't kidding that he's never kissed you. Has anyone?"

"No." Madison could barely speak. She leaned her head back to look into his face. Bill couldn't resist, he kissed her again, and this time she kissed him back.

# 34

The weekend had been very emotional for Madison. She felt like staying in bed but with the sun shining through her window she felt guilty. As if by power of thought, Bud barked. She drug herself out of bed, dressed and went into the living room. Jess walked up on the porch and she saw that Henry's truck was pulled up next to the house. He was unloading a ladder.

She went onto the porch and gave Jess a hug. "I guess you heard what we have in mind."

"Yeah and I like the sound of it. This cottage is special, but you do need more room. And of course you need a garage to put your new vehicle in."

"What new vehicle?" She laughed.

"Honey, that Blazer is over ten years old, things are going to start to break on it. You need a better mode of transportation. The Sheriff gets a car or whatever they want, as part of the package. You know that."

"I do, but it seems like a waste of money when my Blazer is in good shape."

"Let me give Henry a hand. We need to do some measurements."

"I need to get to work on trying to locate the adoptive family of Nicholas' brother. So I'll be at the office if you need me." Madison called Bud and they stopped by the restaurant for a breakfast-to-go.

She checked records of adoptions on the computer for Smyth Co. VA. No one named Robby Lucas. So she called the sheriff that had helped her get Nick's paperwork going.

A lady answered the Sheriff's phone, "Sheriff Whaley's office."

"Hello, I'm Sheriff McKenzie in Cold Creek, TN. Is Sheriff Whaley in?"

"No, Ms. McKenzie, can I help you with something? My name is Sarah."

"Sarah, what can you tell me about Nicholas Cameron's younger brother?"

"He didn't have a brother. He was an only child. I mean he had lots of boys he lived with in foster homes, but no blood kin," Sarah said.

"Did you know his mother?"

"Yes, Sheriff. Nichole and I were pretty good friends in high school but she dropped out when she got pregnant. She never married and far as I know, and never told anyone who Nicholas's father was. When she first dropped out of school, rumors said it was one of our teachers' baby. But I think she would have told me if she really knew whose it was. I think she just lost her way and got into trouble with a couple of boys from the college. She was drinking a lot at that time."

"I wonder why Nicholas would make up such a story," Madison said.

"That's not uncommon for foster kids."

"Oh, I see." Madison thought for a minute, "Does Nicholas look like his mother?"

"No, she was a blonde with blue eyes. He must look like his daddy," Sarah said.

"Do you have a child from the foster families called Robby Lucas?"

"Why, yes. He was adopted out to a couple in North Carolina. Let me look here in the files. Yes, here it is. He went to a home in Spruce Pine. Their name is Scott, Alex and Andrea Scott. I have a phone number for them. You want it?"

"Sure, thank you." Madison recorded the number and then she asked, "Do you have a photo of Robby?"

"Yes, I can fax it to you."

"That would be very nice. Thank you, Sarah. You have been very helpful." With that Madison hung up the phone and waited for the fax.

As the photo printed out, she saw a resemblance to Nicholas. They had the same eyes and they both have two dimples in their cheeks. Even their noses look to be the same. She looked at the facsimile a long while as thoughts raced through her head.

*I forgot to ask Sarah what ever happened to Nick's mom.*

She hit recall and when Sarah answered, Madison said, "I'm sorry to pester you again. I wondered if you could tell me what happened to Nichole."

"Yes, she was killed in a car crash when Nicholas was just four years old. Strange circumstances too, a single vehicle accident. The car went over a cliff and burned. Never did even figure out what happened."

Sarah had been full of information. Not what Madison thought should be working the phone of a Sheriff Office.

The phone rang back and Madison saw that it was Rick's cell number.

"Sheriff McKenzie," she said coolly.

"Ouch," Rick said. "This is Agent Malone, waving a white flag."

Madison couldn't help but grin. She knew it would resonate in her voice, "What are your terms of surrender?"

"Whatever it takes," Rick breathed deeply.

The air between them was silent and then Madison said, "I'll forgive you, if you'll forgive me."

"That works!" Rick sounded like a pup that had just been scolded and then given a pat on the head.

"I saw you in the News. Knoxville is calling you the Bad-Ass Sheriff who knows how to stop a fleeing suspect."

"Did you see the photo?"

"Oh yeah! Your method was pretty extreme, but it got the job done," he said.

"I could only imagine him speeding into Cold Creek past the playground full of kids," she paused for a moment, "Not on my watch."

"You know he'll probably sue you," Rick chuckled.

"Hey, bring it on. I had my Blazer parked in the westbound lane with the blue lights flashing. He chose to ignore my warning. That's on him! I'm just sorry I couldn't get the dozer out of the road in time."

"That's your story and you're sticking to it. Good Girl!" After a moment of silence, he said, "Will you have dinner with me?"

"Yes."

"What evening is your calendar open?" Rick asked.

They discussed the matter and settled on a date and time. The air between them was cleared. Madison felt she'd done a suitable job of letting her feelings be known. Either he'd be more approachable or he'd shut down any flame that might flicker. But it was a place in their lives they had to get through. She felt as though she'd been promoted to womanhood. But are they friends or something more? That was yet to be determined.

Madison researched the phone book for Spruce Pine and was surprised that she located a different number for Alex and Andrea Scott. She called the new number first.

"Scotts residents," was the answer when the ringing ceased.

"Hello, this is Sheriff McKenzie in Cold Creek, TN. I would like to speak to Mr. or Mrs. Scott."

"I'm sorry Madam and Sir are not in at the moment. Would you like me to take a message?"

"Yes, please. Ask them to call this number," she gave out her cell number.

And after disconnecting the call she tried the second number.

"Switzerland Inn, how may I direct the call?"

"Alex or Andrea Scott, please. This is Sheriff McKenzie."

"One moment please," the voice sounded polite and professional.

"Alex Scott speaking."

"Hello Mr. Scott. This is Sheriff Madison McKenzie of Cold Creek, TN. I'm calling about your son, Robby."

"What? I don't have a boy named Robby."

"No, maybe not now, but you adopted a young boy whose birth name was Robby Lucas. I want to meet with you and your wife concerning this adoption."

"Um, how about you and I meet first. Can you tell me if there is a legal issue with the adoption? Because Sheriff Whaley assured me there were none."

"I'd be happy to meet you somewhere, just the two of us. What is convenient for you?" She asked.

"How about tomorrow morning? I have business in Asheville, say around 10:00 a.m.?" he suggested the time, "Are you familiar with Merrimon Drive?"

"Somewhat,"

"There is an exit, New Stock Road, where Merrimon becomes Weaverville Rd."

"I know that exit," Madison said.

"On your right, there is Granny's Kitchen. They have marvelous breakfasts. How about meeting me there?"

"That makes it easy for me. I'll see you in the morning, Mr. Scott."

Madison hung up from their conversation and thought of his words, "How about you and I meet first." *I wonder if his wife knows all of what has transpired.*

Madison collected the information she'd printed out about Nicholas, Robby, and their mother. If she was mother of both the boys, Madison wondered if Alex is the father. Had Nichole had a baby by the same man twice? And if so, was he behind her accidental death? So many scenarios played in her mind. Meeting with Alex alone might not be such a good plan. The more Madison thought about it, the more she worried. What if she had someone meet her there but not join them? What if that someone was Law enforcement? What if she called Bill?

"This is Bill, leave me a message." Madison listened to his voice mail.

After the tone she said, "Bill, I hoped you might still be in Asheville. I'm meeting someone in a restaurant in the morning. This someone might be Nicholas' father. He might also behind the death of Nicholas' mother. Will you call me back?"

Almost immediately, Bill called. He told her how dangerous her idea was. He tried to dissuade her from the plan but soon realized he was wasting his breath. So they agreed that he would get to the restaurant early and sit close to the door. Madison felt better with a backup plan. But what if she was wrong? In a way, she hoped she was. But if she was right, and her hunches usually panned out for the worst, she could open a can of worms that can't be recapped. But she was willing to test the theory. She would not accuse Mr. Scott, but seeing him for herself might be all she needed to douse this idea. If Sarah was telling her the truth, it would mean Alex had been a student of the college or a professor. It had been Madison's experience that where there are rumors there is often truth.

Madison took the exit onto Weaverville Road. She turned right and spotted a small white building with a red roof, Granny's. *Surely this is not it.* The drive way went around the tiny building. It was a drive through or eat outside only. She noticed Bill at a picnic table as she pulled into a parking space next to another car. There were two more cars in the back of the building.

She waited in her vehicle for a moment, anticipating a text from Bill. Sure enough, a text came through.

*I'm the only customer here. You might want to wait a bit.*

*Ok*, she replied.

Just then a Lincoln Navigator pulled into the drive. He drove slowly past Madison's vehicle and continued on around to the other side to additional parking spots. A tall slender man got out and walked up to the window in front of Granny's. Madison watched as he took a seat at a picnic table as far from Bill as possible. She noticed he was drinking a cup of coffee he ordered from the window. She walked toward the tables. Wearing her Sheriff Uniform and her gun belt and holstered Sig in plain view, she knew he would recognize her if indeed that was Alex Scott. As she neared Bill's table the other man stood and waved to her. She ignored Bill and walked past to the second table.

"Sheriff McKenzie, I'm Alex Scott." He extended his hand and shook hers briskly. "Can I order you a coffee?"

"Thank you, Mr. Scott, with two creamers." Madison sat down to stop her knees from shaking. She kept her back to Bill.

"Alex, just call me Alex," his smile was captivating.

Madison studied his features. She knew instantly that she had seen those brown eyes and that narrow chin on Nicholas. Even his hair looked the same shade of brown and that smile brought two dimples to his cheeks.

Alex walked away and returned with a coffee, two small tubs of Coffee-mate and a stir stick with a napkin. "Here you are."

He sat opposite her and sipped his coffee, "I'll warn you this is hot! But with your creamers that should cool it a bit."

"Yes, I can feel it through the cup. She removed the lid and poured in the creamers, stirred and left the top off.

"What is it you want to know?" Alex's eyes met hers and he didn't blink.

"How is your son adjusting to his new life?" She asked.

"Tommy, is doing great! We have him in Boy Scouts, he plays soccer and baseball, well T-ball for now. He is on the honor roll in his studies, he's well rounded and enjoys all kinds of sports even in winter." Alex took a cleansing breath.

"That's wonderful. I'm happy to hear he is doing so well. Do you happen to have a photo of him on you?"

"Yes, I do," he removed his wallet and flipped to a photo of a darling young boy, looking similar to the fax she'd received from Sarah.

"Oh he's adorable and he has your dimples," Madison handed the photo back and smiled sweetly. Inside she was angry to the point of feeling sick.

"That's his latest school photo. Yeah, I'm very proud of my son," he dropped his head and the smile fell away. "At least he feels like he is my son, even though he's adopted. The dimples were the decision makers for my wife and me. We had interviewed boys from here to Washington DC, and when we saw Tommy, we knew immediately. That was our boy."

"Were you and your wife unable to conceive?"

"Yes, Andi had an accident as a young girl and she could never have a baby. We'd been married three years when we decided to adopt. It took us four years to find little Tommy."

"You were a student at Virginia Tech when you met her weren't you?" Madison was fishing.

"Yes, and she was on the facility. We never dated until she took the job here at the Swiss Inn. She's manager over the restaurant."

"From teaching to managing a restaurant. That's a switch," Madison said.

"Not really, she is a Chef and she was teaching cooking classes."

"Aw, I need to get to know her. I could use some classes in cooking," Madison laughed deliberately to let Bill know the conversation was going well.

Alex laughed with her. But then he said, "You haven't told me why you wanted to see me. We've established that we can afford to give Tommy a good home and he's adjusted well. Is this a well check from Human Services?"

"In a way," Madison changed her attitude. "Did you know a woman when you were in school, by the name of Nichole Cameron?"

She leaned forward, both elbows on the table. Alex swallowed hard and sat speechless for a few minutes.

"Was she also a student?" He furrowed his brow. And then he purged his mouth as if thinking very hard.

"Yes, but not in VA Tech. She was in high school."

"Then I wouldn't have known her." He said and looked her in the eye again.

"She was Tommy's mother." Madison propped her right hand at the top of her Sig. "She had an older son too. He's 9 now. He and Robby, Tommy..." she lifted her shoulders, "they are brothers. Did the foster parents ever tell you he had a brother?"

"No. He had no siblings. I don't like what you are insinuating." He stood.

"What am I insinuating, Mr. Scott?" Madison stayed seated, but moved her hand slightly toward her Sig. "Only than they might have told you there were two boys. There's nothing against the law in not wanting but one."

Alex sat back down. "They didn't tell us about him if they knew of another. That's not against the law either."

"Can I get a DNA test from you, Sir?" Madison stared him down.

"Why?"

"Why not? Do you have anything to hide?"

"No, and if you want any more information you need to go through my attorney." Alex's hand shook as he pulled his wallet out again. He handed her a business card. "His number is on here. Don't call me again. Or I'll report you for harassment." He got up and left the table.

Madison watched as he walked quickly to his Navigator and drove away. Then she picked up his cup and poured out the remaining coffee. She pulled a baggy from her pocket and placed the cup into the clear plastic bag.

Bill got up and walked to her side. "Are you okay?"

"I might fall down if I try to stand. My legs are shaking. But I got what I wanted." She sipped some of her coffee.

Bill sat beside her, his feet facing opposite of hers. "Just sit here and I'll keep you company until you feel like getting up. I heard some of the last couple of comments he made. You really rattled him."

Madison nodded her head. "I'm afraid I was right about him. He's either Nick's father or this is a miracle match. Because Robby and Nicholas are brothers. She pulled the fax of Robby out from her pocket. "What do you think?"

"Oh my, this could have been Nicholas just a couple of years ago. I think you're right." He shook his head. "Tell me what else you have to go on."

Madison explained the story of how she and Nicholas met, how she made him trust her and the story he told her about having a little brother somewhere in North Carolina. She even told him how freely she got the news of the boys' mother's death by suspicious circumstances and the names of the couple that adopted little Robby.

Bill agreed that she had a strong case and he offered to check into Nichole Cameron's accident. After all, traffic was his specialty.

"You have to agree to meet me in Rogersville for dinner when I have something for you," Bill teased.

"I'll even buy you dinner," she said. "Just don't make it on a weekend. I'm going to VA over a weekend to see what I can find out about Nichole Cameron."

"I'd be happy to join you," Bill's voice had a tempting tone to it.

"Thanks, but I'll do this on my own."

Madison drove back over the mountain and stopped at Holly's to get Bud. She saw Nicholas and the twins on the swing. She waved and watched the boys playing. She wondered if she is right about Alex, if he is the father of both boys, then there is a chance that Robby will be without a home. Unless his Mom is innocent. She could keep him, but would she? If her husband's guilt is revealed, she might not want anything to do with the boy. If she was in on the deal, she could also be arrested. Madison didn't like the idea that she was apt to upset Nicholas and Robby's lives.

She decided to talk to Rick about it. At first she thought of telling Holly and Henry. But with Holly's delicate condition, that might not be advisable. Yeah, she could talk to Rick about anything. That was the way to begin.

Bear and Bud came running from the back of the house. She knew where they'd been by the mud on their feet.

Holly came out the front door. "You might want to use the water hose at the side of the house. They followed Henry into the hog pen to see the new piglets! They smell to high heaven," she said.

"I can smell them from here! Oh, Bud, come here. You've got to have a bath."

Nicholas came to see Madison so he volunteered to wash the mud off Bud.

"Holly?" she didn't even have to ask, Holly just waved her hand. "That's fine. He can wash off too after washing the dogs. Come on in Maddie."

She went back into the house to check on supper. Madison smelled the aroma of Holly's tomato sauce.

"Can I invite myself to supper, Holly?"

# 35

Meanwhile in Knoxville Rick got a notice that the second of the two men who abducted Madison was apprehended. "Yes!" He slammed his fist down on top of his desk.

He speed dials Madison's cell number.

"Hello, Rick."

"Madison, they caught Rod! The other bad guy. You can breathe a sigh of relief."

"Thank you! That makes me feel a lot better! Where was he?"

"Somewhere between here and Chicago is all I know. At least he's back where he belongs."

"Good. Say, I'm eating supper with Holly and family. Can I call you when I get home? I have something I need to share with you."

"Sure."

"Okay, thanks for calling. I'll talk to you in a while." She slid her cell phone back into her pocket and made the announcement, "Rick says the FBI caught the second of the bad guys who abducted me."

"Wonderful," Holly said.

The boys chimed in and made all kinds of sound effects, imagining what it was like to take down the bad guy. Henry had to call them down and remind them not to play at the table. Nicholas smiled at Madison and then went back to emptying his plate of spaghetti. Holly reminded the twins that if they couldn't eat all their supper, they couldn't have desert.

Hugh said, "What's for zert?"

"I'm not telling. Just finish your supper," Holly said.

"I think its peach cobbler," Henry sniffed the air as though he could smell it.

"Yum!" Hugh dove into the spaghetti and cleaned his plate.

After cobbler and ice cream, Nicholas took the twins upstairs for bed. They gave hugs all around and disappeared into the magical world Holly and Henry's home has become.

"He is a God-send." Holly settled onto the porch swing next to Henry.

Madison sat in a rocker with Bud and Bear at her feet. "I'm amazed and happy for you two. Who knew how your lives would evolve into so pleasant a surrounding. Henry, you are special and I'm glad I'm counted among your friends."

"What have you been into, Maddie? You didn't dip into the recipe in the basement, did you?" Henry laughed.

"No, you keep the door locked," she laughed with him. "I hope I'll have a life similar to yours someday. But if I stay in Law Enforcement, I'm afraid that's out of the question. It would not be fair to leave a child with a sitter while I'm out there risking my life." She took a deep breath and let it out loudly.

"Then don't stay in that line of work. It's simple." Henry looked sternly at Madison. "Didn't you tell me that trooper friend said yours was the life he'd like?"

Madison nodded. "But, I'm sure he makes more money than our sheriff salary can offer."

"It isn't always about money, Honey," Holly said. She looked up at her husband. "Is it, Henry?"

"That's right. You ought to give him a chance at least to consider the idea. We are only a couple of months away from an election."

Madison nodded but said nothing. She sat silently with her friends thinking of what she wanted, what she needed, and what was within her control.

As soon as she and Bud arrived at her cottage she called Rick. They talked for over an hour as Madison explained her suspicions and what she'd done. Rick thought that her facing Scott with the accusation was pure risky. When she told him she was not alone, he was quiet for a while and then he said he had to get up early in the morning and needed to go to bed.

"Rick, you are my future, not Bill. The sooner you get used to that idea, the better off we will be as a ...what? What is our relationship? Can you define it? For me it's like trust in my faith. I can't explain my belief or my feelings about h, but I feel secure. I used to feel secure in us. But now I don't know. I know that I love you. But is it the same love you have for me?"

"I'm not sure anymore either, Maddie. Yes, I know that I love you, and is it the love like Henry and Holly feel? I guess there is only one way to find out." Rick didn't put it into words so Madison did.

"You are free to go with anyone you please. I'm not getting mad or confronting you ever again. Good night, Rick."

Her hand shook as she put down the phone. She felt as if her heart would burst. Tears fogged her vision as she undressed to get in the shower. The shower was the soothing cleanse she needed tonight. She knew there was a decision to be made. Could she walk away from Rick Malone and not miss him? Or was it like when Jess and Shirley go on one of their trips? When they leave she misses them, but they always come back. What if Rick didn't? What if she spent more time with Bill? He already told her that she and this job was exactly what he wanted out of life. Was that just an example he was comparing her to?

Holly followed her heart and her gut, loving Henry when no one else even liked him. She stuck with him through thick and thin; now her life is amazing.

Why are adult decisions so difficult to make?

Loud cracks of thunder woke Madison. Lightning lit up the sky above the mountain. Bud whined as if he was scared. She patted the side of the bed and he jumped up and into her comforting arms. She knew he acted this way as a puppy, but had not seen him afraid of lightning in recent years.

"What's the matter, Bud?" She felt him shivering. "It's not cold in here. What do you sense that I don't?"

Another flash of lightning lit up her room and the thunder cracked at the same moment. The storm was right on top of them. She got out of bed and walked through her cottage to be sure all the windows were down. She looked out the front door and saw that the trees behind the restaurant were blowing as hard as she'd ever seen. The sound of thuds on her roof she recognized was hale. She shut the door and moved to the window. Hail bounced off the wooden sidewalks like ping-pong balls. Another flash of lightning and she watched a large tree fall beside the restaurant. The roar of the wind caused Bud to run back to the bed room. When she went to comfort him he was under her bed.

*Maybe we're having a tornado.* She grabbed her radio and listened for weather alerts. Sure enough, they were under tornado warnings in Unicoi County. She needed to notify others, but how? Cold Creek had no alarm system.

She speed dialed the Jacobs phone. Henry answered and Madison told him to get his family into the basement. Next she called Nell and told her to get Drew to the main level of the building. She called Ben telling him and so on, she called everyone she could think of off the top of her head.

The wind grew louder and stronger. The old Oak beside her house scrubbed the metal roof of her cottage. She thought of the tunnels, that's the safest place, but all the entries have been closed up except the entrance to the caverns.

"The jail, at least it has a basement. Bud!" she yelled, "Come!" She and her dog ran out into the pelting hail to the sheriff's office. She opened the basement door and Bud ran down without being told. She grabbed a flashlight and shut and locked the door as she followed him.

Even from the basement she could hear the wind. Bud scratched at the iron bars leading to the tunnels.

"It's sealed off now, Bud. We can't go down there anymore. We're safe here." She knelt to hug him and then they both sat on the cool concrete floor.

After a while, the wind stopped howling so she and Bud went back upstairs and onto the street. She looked first to see if the cottage was still standing. It was, but the Oak had left a large limb draped across her kitchen. She walked over to check the restaurant. It looked fine, narrowly miss by the tall evergreen that fell from the hill behind it.

The hardware was intact and so was the museum. She and Bud walked the full length of town. The church was fine even though a big Poplar sprawled across the parking lot. She called Henry. He said they were fine, only a lot of hail damage on his truck. But he was heading up to check the barn and the outbuildings.

She called Mr. Olsen and heard his phone ringing behind her. She turned to see him walking up the street from the hardware. "Are things alright at your house?" Madison asked.

"I'm glad you called. We were asleep. Good thing you woke us, the wind took our roof off the bedroom. We had gone into the cellar. Everything okay with you?"

"Yeah, I've got a tree limb on my roof over the kitchen. But I haven't gone inside to see the damage yet. I was just heading over to check with Nell and Drew." Madison kept walking as Bud ran ahead of her straight to the garage where Drew's apartment was.

"Nell?" She called out.

"We're fine, we're here," she rolled Drew's wheelchair out from the shadows of the side door. "Are you okay?" Nell asked.

"Yeah, but we have damage all over town. I'm checking homes now," she turned to go down the street to her parent's home. They are out of town but she could only hope their roof was intact and no trees down. Their house was fine and so was the house next door. She asked everyone she ran into to call family or friends in the area to make sure they were okay.

By the time the sun came up the town's residents all gathered at the restaurant where Madison was forming a plan. She asked for anyone who needed help to sign up on the tablet of paper she was passing around.

"And write what type of damage you have so we can get the worst done first." Madison had still not been to her own home to check the damage.

"What about yours, Madison?" A man from the back of the room spoke up. "I don't see your damage noted on here. You know there is a huge limb from that old Oak on your cottage, right?"

"Yes, I know, but I haven't been back to check. Bud and I went to the basement of the jail," she said. "Which reminds me. I want some ideas of how many folks don't have a place to go. We can use the basement as a shelter in the future. And I want ideas of what kind of an alarm system we need to come up with."

Her phone rang and she walked outside to talk. Since she was out, she continued over to her cottage. The tree limb had not hurt the structure, only the roof. The new ceiling which Henry had put up five years ago was fine, but she feared it might leak if they had more rain.

She returned to the restaurant adding her name and damage at the bottom of the page. At that time Henry walked in. He talked to Mr. Olsen and several of the town's people and then he came to Madison. Nicholas was right by his side.

"I brought my chain saws, where do you need me?" He asked.

"Look over the list," she handed him her tablet. "See who needs you first." She walked up to Nicholas and gave him a hug. "Glad to see you're here to help. That's the way we do things here in Cold Creek. We help each other. So thank you."

"Can you make a copy of this?" Henry asked.

"Sure. I'll make a couple, you can allocate the work. You're a good leader."

She, Nicholas, and Henry walked across the street to her office. She ran off some copies from her fax/copy machine. Henry went straight to her house.

"What are you doing?"

"Just removing the limb and putting on a tarp so the under structure doesn't get damaged. I am going to remove this part of the roof for your add-on anyway," Henry answered. "See if there are any 30 foot tarps left at Olsen's."

"Okay." She turned to go toward the hardware. And that's when she realized Bud was not with her. "Henry, did you see Bud when you came into town?"

"No," he started up one of his chainsaws.

Madison walked into the hardware store. She figured the crowd was gathering the tarps. So she went to where they were all standing. There were only a couple of tarps left. She took hers and left a note for Mr. Olsen. *Catch you later, one 30ft tarp, Your Sheriff.*

Outside she looked up and down the street. She called Bud's name and whistled. But he didn't come or bark. So she took the tarp on to Henry and helped him drag the pieces of the Oak limb to the side of the creek.

"When all the repairs are done, I'll cut this for firewood for you. You'll want it when the addition is done, I've added an outdoor fireplace and bar-beque pit." Henry told her as he removed the last section of the branch. "We'll let the leaves dry and then I can cut it into firewood size."

"Thanks, Henry. Now I need to go and look for Bud. Last time I saw him was in the restaurant. I hope Ben isn't filling him up on bacon," she laughed.

Bud wasn't in the restaurant, so she went toward the church, where the majority of the town's people were cutting up the Poplar tree and piling it in the vacant field next door. Madison asked if anyone had seen Bud. No one had, so she went to Mr. Olsen's house to see how many were helping there.

Six men had already strung tarps over the missing roof area. Henry arrived to measure and make note of the necessary lumber and items they'd need. Some of the men with flatbed trucks were gathering information and heading to Lowes in Johnson City.

Just at that time the police chief in Greenville called Madison's phone. He was looking for volunteers to meet him down in Camp Creek area to assist with search and recovery. The storm had leveled many homes and several folks were missing. Madison said she'd send as many as she could.

She made the announcement about the missing and several men walked away immediately to go and help the community of Camp Creek, in the next county over. At least Mr. Olsen's house was dried in and he had all the help he'd need to replace his roof.

Madison told everyone she ran into to watch for Bud and let her know if they see him. He's not one to run off and she was worried.

Ben was trimming the evergreen tree beside the restaurant with a small chainsaw. She offered to help him drag away the cut branches. She heard what she thought was an injured animal, "Listen, Ben. Shut off your saw a minute." She walked closer to the trunk of the tree. Bud crawled out from underneath the heavy branches fully loaded with greenery.

"Bud, what are you doing in there?" She looked him over. She knew he had been inside with her when the tree fell, but why would he crawl under it?

"Ben, there's something or someone under this tree." Madison began lift-ing the branches that she could, and looking beneath. She heard whining again. "It's right under here." She called Ben to bring the saw. "Let's remove some of these and see what's under there."

Ben started his saw again and carefully cut away the top branches. Eventually they could see under and there were three tiny pups. Their eyes closed.

"They must have been born last night," Ben said. "Just one more branch, Maddie, here's the mother. I'm afraid she's hurt."

Maddie called Doc Edwards. "Can you come to the north side of the restaurant? We need you to check a patient."

In just a few minutes Chip ran around the side of the building. "Where is the patient?"

Madison was on her knees beside the mother dog. "She's here."

Dr. Chip knelt down. He was shocked to see the patient was a dog. But, the kind man he is, he began checking to see if there were signs of life. "She's hurt badly but she's alive. Can you cut the tree trunk away?"

"My saw is too small. Henry has a bigger one, let me go find him." Ben jumped up and ran toward Mr. Olsen's house. In a while he returned with Henry and a couple other guys. Henry cranked his saw up and made short work of the trunk while the other guys and Ben used branches like poles to hold it off the dog. When the weight was removed she tried to stand. Doc held her so she couldn't and soon she relaxed. Ben brought a blanket and they eased her onto it and moved her to the back porch of the restaurant. Doc stayed with her, trying everything he could think of. But without x-rays, he couldn't be certain of her injuries.

The pups needed to eat, so he placed them next to Momma dog and she allowed them to nurse. Chip stayed with them all day. That night Ben said he'd stay with her. In the meantime folks dropped by to see the brave momma who had given birth while pinned under the tree. By the next morning she was strong enough for Doc to move her to his office.

He x-rayed her chest where the tree had her pinned. There were no broken bones, miraculously she'd escaped any internal injuries. Doc kept her on low dose pain meds and antibiotics for five days. She was up and walking as if nothing had happened. The pups were growing. Everyday someone brought her food they'd cooked themselves or milk from their cows.

The only male pup had a blue ribbon on his neck with Mr. Olsen's name on it. One of the females had a pink ribbon with Nicholas' name. Doc told the towns people that the last one is his. She was going to be his office guard.

Ben and Margie brought her some ribs with lots of good meet on them. Since Margie had boiled them to soften the bone, Doc said it was okay to let her have them. Margie named the momma dog, Shirley. It seemed fitting to name her after the restaurant. Since no one had claimed Shirley, Margie and

Ben agreed to keep her.

By the end of that week all the repairs had been made to the houses except Madison's. Henry planned to start work on it that next Monday. There had been no deaths from the storm, not even in Green County. Six people had been injured but all were cared for and the homes would be rebuilt or replaced with modular homes.

# 36

Madison returned her attention to her work over the next few days. She braced herself and called Rick about the DNA results.

Rick told her that Alex Scott was a match to Nicholas. Now all that was left was to comb the remains of the car in which his mother died. If the Virginia Bureau of Investigation couldn't find a connection, Rick knew Madison would not be satisfied. And he knew she wouldn't let it go.

So, he took the time to visit the VBI in Roanoke himself. He stressed to them that two young boys' lives were hanging in the balance. If a murder had been committed, they needed to investigate Alex Scott.

The wheels moved slowly, but after a long wait, he got a call one Friday morning. Agent Collins revealed there was evidence of an incendiary device. He ordered the exhumation of the victim for another autopsy.

During the process, Sheriff Whaley admitted that he'd suspected Scott. But he had threatened to harm Nicholas if Whaley pursued the case. Sheriff Whaley encouraged the boy to run. He just hadn't expected him to surface so close to home. The sheriff was arrested and turned state's evidence, so charges had been dropped. However, he could not work in law enforcement ever again.

Madison had made all the difference, and Rick wanted to be the one to tell her. And he would do it in person.

He drove into Cold Creek early on Saturday morning, parked next to Madison's Blazer. He noticed that it had gotten a lot of hail damage from the storm. He walked up on the front porch, but didn't have to knock. Bud barked from inside the cottage.

Madison opened the door, letting Bud out to greet Rick. The dog wiggled all over as he had as a puppy.

"Madison, I have news for you," Rick said.

"You could have called. You didn't have to drive all this way," she walked away from the door, leaving it open.

Rick opened the screen and went inside. "Got any coffee?" He asked.

"Sure, have a seat," she walked into the kitchen and returned with a mug of black coffee. She handed it to him and sat in the rocker, across the room.

Rick explained about the phone call, and handed her the envelope with the DNA results.

Madison acted cold and uncaring. Rick felt that coming to see her might have been a huge mistake. He drank the coffee while she read the pages.

Madison looked up with a smile on her face. "I was right," she said.

"You usually are."

"I appreciate that you brought the information," she stood up. "Has Scott been arrested?"

"Not yet. The DA is working up the case, and expects to charge him next week."

"Do they know if his wife was in on the murder?" Madison asked.

"No, but they have exhumed Ms. Cameron's remains. They're looking for signs that she was dead before the car went over the cliff. If she was, then they will proceed with charges. That's all I know for now." He stood up facing her. "The VBI was impressed with you." He turned and started for the door.

"Rick. What do I tell Nicholas?"

He turned around to face her. "I wouldn't say anything yet. Let the law do their work. If Mrs. Scott is charged, we can tell the Jacobs they can adopt another little boy." He turned away and walked out the door.

"Don't leave," Madison said. "stay and talk to me for a while. I miss you."

Rick stood on the porch. "Don't ask me to stay and then run me off again. I can't lose you over and over..." His voice cracked.

Madison rushed into Rick's arms. "I'd never ask you to leave. I just need to know how to deal with you."

"Maybe we talk too much, Sheriff McKenzie." Rick swept Madison off her feet and carried her into the living room. "You want to know what how to deal with me? Love me, Madison. The way I've loved you for five years."

# 37

Henry had worked only a week on the makeover of the cottage. Madison was happy with the new roofline over the kitchen. It was raised to allow for extra supports. That raised the inside dimensions of the laundry room, which had resembled a lean-to off the south side of the kitchen wall. He was able to add an outside door so she could also use it as a mudroom. Considering the muddy messes she and Bud got into at times, the mud room was a welcome idea to Madison.

The second week, it was time to lay the foundation for the garage and second-story master suite. Madison thought that losing one large branch of the old oak had been a blessing. The view from the street was more open now; she would be able to see Shirley's Restaurant from her upstairs bedroom.

Madison barely went to the sheriff's office while Henry and two other men worked. Her curiosity was so overwhelming that Henry put her to work removing cutoffs from his lumber. Bud even got into snagging the smaller pieces of 2x4s and dropping them next to the mounting pile of discarded materials.

Shirley, the momma dog, left her pups on the porch of the restaurant to get into the fun. She and Bud were great friends since he'd saved her from the downed evergreen. They were similar in size, but nobody could agree on what breed Shirley was. Finally, Ben settled it by declaring that she was a cur hound. It didn't matter; the entire community had fallen in love with Shirley and her pups.

At the end of the day, Henry looked at their progress and the pile of scrap material, and concluded that they would need to have an autumn bonfire. That sent Madison's mind into planning mode. She'd invite the entire community, especially the kids, and she'd supply the hotdogs and marshmallows.

On Friday of the second week, Rick showed up just after noon.

"Henry, you're working twenty-four seven on this, aren't you?"

"Just about," he met Rick with a welcoming handshake. "I've had some great help."

"Madison told me that everyone around town has helped in some fashion. I get the idea they love her as much as I do." Rick glanced around the area, "Where is Maddie?"

"She ran an errand for me. I need some larger nails for the gun before I can attach the supports for the second level."

"Good, that gives me time to plan my attack," Rick reached into his pocket, bringing out a small silver box. He opened it and revealed a dazzling emerald-cut diamond engagement ring.

"Oh, Man!" Henry looked approvingly at the stone. "That's got to be a couple of carats."

"Too much?" Rick quickly asked.

"No, it's gorgeous. Maddie will flip out and say it's too much, but what woman wouldn't love to have that rock on her hand?"

"Phew," Rick let out a sigh of relief. "I thought of letting her pick it herself, but I knew she'd be too conservative. When I saw this, I knew it had to be the one—just like when I saw her years ago, and knew she was the one for me."

"Congratulations, my friend. You two seriously deserve one another. And I mean that in the most respectful way." Henry put his hand on Rick's shoulder. "When I designed this addition, I had you in mind. Seriously, I hoped you two would need this as a future home. Glad it's worked out that way."

"Well, she hasn't said yes, yet," Rick shared a nervous laugh.

"She will."

Bud came running from the back of the restaurant, greeting Rick with what can only be called brotherly love. He wriggled all over, and Rick dropped to his knees to hug him. Bud barked a couple of times, and from the same direction he'd come, Shirley ran almost up to them. When she stopped short, Bud nudged her closer, as if to introduce her to Rick.

"So, this is the love of your life?" He laughed. Rick extended his hand slowly toward Shirley. She reacted guardedly, and Bud stepped up beside Rick and whined. Finally, Shirley lowered her head and bumped her nose against his hand. He slid it up over her nose and petted her head, then scratched behind her ears. "She's a lovely lady, Bud." He took his hand away and stroked Bud's neck. "Good job, Boy."

The dogs followed the two men as Henry walked Rick through the plans, and they toured the construction site.

"I like the idea that the structure connects with the upper hallway. Where do the steps come out in the cottage?" Rick asked.

"They come down here," Henry stepped close to the outside wall of the old structure. "Enclosed stairs ascend to a split-level landing. Steps lead that way, through the existing wall and into the kitchen, here, just between... Well, it's where the little bar is now. She'll lose the bar." Henry turned to face the front of the garage. The second set of the final four steps come to an outside door, leading to the lanai between the old and new structure."

"That's a good idea. It'll be great in warm weather, yet remain closed off against the winter cold; I like it," Rick said, staring at the imaginary space.

"The fireplace/fire pit will be here. I have a guy who does the most beautiful stonework you ever saw; Joe Terranera is going to build that for us."

"What about the floor? Stone?" Rick followed with his questions.

"Yes, Joe has some left over from his house. He thinks it's enough, and if not, we'll cross that gap when we come to it." Henry laughed.

Rick gave him a sideways glance. "Have you seen this stone?"

"Yes, and don't worry. You'll love it. Joe only chooses the best and the prettiest."

"Can't wait to meet this guy, Joe." Rick moved toward the area of the three-car garage. "Are you sure there's room here for three bays?"

"Yep, unless you plan on bringing home a bus," Henry laughed.

"Not a bus, but I see Madison's Blazer got hail damage. I plan to get her into a new SUV soon," Rick said.

"Good luck with that," Henry closed up his tool box and loaded it onto his truck. "If you two don't plan on somewhere special for supper, come on out."

"Oh, I've got something planned. But if that doesn't work with Milady, I'll give you shout." He turned toward the construction, and quickly back around to catch Henry before he drove away. "Um, let's let Maddie give Holly the news, OK?"

"Yeah, sure! Besides, I don't want her knowing what a big rock Maddie is getting. We have our tenth anniversary coming up next month, and I don't want to sell the farm to get her one to match," Henry laughed and waved good-bye to Rick.

Rick followed Bud and Shirley to the back porch of the restaurant to meet the pups. There he saw Henry's handiwork; a mini restaurant design dog house. The puppies were roaming all over the porch. He noticed the ribbons with names on them. Mr. Olsen's read, *Hardware*. One of the pink ribbons had *Nikki* printed on it, and the other pink ribbon read *Stella*.

Rick felt happy that all three pups had homes. He watched them romp on Bud when he lay down next to Shirley. Rick thought of how Bud had grown so attached to this female and accepted her family. He wondered if the dog's relationship would still be as close with Maddie.

He heard a truck approach across the street. He went to meet Madison getting out of Mr. Olsen's truck. "I didn't even ask Henry what you were driving."

"Mr. Olsen needed a few things, so he told me to use his truck." She climbed out, throwing her arms around Rick's neck. "I didn't think you'd be here this early. I haven't had a chance to get my shower and dress."

"Good, I'll help."

"Oh no, you won't. You can unload the truck," Madison tossed the keys to him. "The nails are Henry's, and then you can help Mr. Olsen with his items." She disappeared into the cottage.

Rick put the nails under the tarp on the concrete inside the construction zone, then he moved the truck to Mr. Olsen's Hardware Store.

"Howdy, Rick. I see you got volunteered to bring my stuff. I'll give you a hand. Those boxes will be heavy."

The two men used a dolly to move the boxes inside. Rick offered to distribute them to the areas of the store where they needed to be unpacked.

"That's OK. Thanks, but I have a young man coming in tomorrow to put them into my stock. We'll let him do the hard part," the old mayor laughed. He followed Rick onto the sidewalk. "I gotta ask you something. I know it ain't none of my business, but you and Maddie have been close for so long... Are you ever going to pop the question, Son?"

Rick grinned as he pulled the small silver box from his pocket. "As a matter of fact..." He opened the silver box, showing Mr. Olsen the aquamarine lining and the glittering diamond ring.

"Well, I'll be darn. You are as smart as I figured you were! Congratulations, Rick. I'm happy for the both of you. She's getting the one man I approve of."

"Thanks, Mayor. Now if she just says yes, I'll be happy."

"She's way ahead of you, boy. Why do you think she is adding on to the cottage?"

"I hope I'm the one she has in mind. A man can never be too secure, you know."

"Well, I guess you got a little jealous when than good-looking state trooper feller came into her world. Glad to see you ain't waiting too long to speak up."

"Keep your fingers crossed for me, will you?" He stepped off the sidewalk and headed to the front porch of the cottage. Just as he got there, his phone rang. The caller ID said it was a Virginia call.

"Agent Malone," Rick answered. He listened for a couple of minutes, then thanked the caller.

Just as he sat down, Maddie came onto the porch wearing a brightly colored sundress with spring blooms of pink, purple, and blue. Her hair was pulled up into a French twist. She wore a pair of low-heeled sandals with straps that matched the colors of the dress. Her face glowed with a touch of make-up.

Rick stood up, walked close and pulled her into a hug. "You are beautiful! Have I told you that lately?"

"No, but I'm happy that you noticed." She leaned in and kissed him.

Rick took her hand and led her to the porch swing. She sat, expecting him to sit next to her. Instead, he knelt on one knee in front of her. "Madison, you are the most amazing woman I have ever met." He slipped his hand into his pocket and brought out the silver box, opening it as he said, "Milady, will you be my life partner? Will you do me the honor of becoming my wife?"

Maddie's eyes welled with tears as she stared at the ring. Blinking several times caused a waterfall of droplets on the front of the sundress. She looked from the diamond to his eyes, then answered, "I can never imagine any man in my life but you. Yes, Rick Malone, I'll be your wife." The tears continued to fall.

Rick took the platinum-set emerald-cut diamond ring from the box and placed it on her finger. A perfect fit on her slender tanned finger, the stone looked even larger than he'd realized.

Madison wiped her cheeks with her right hand as she admired the ring on her left. "It's so flashy, so extravagant. Oh Rick; I love it."

Rick squeezed her to his chest and laughed. "I thought you'd hate it for its size. God, I'm so glad you like it." He moved to sit next to her on the swing. They embraced for a long, unhurried time, just breathing in the clean mountain air.

In a moment, they became aware of an audience clapping from the sidewalk across the street, at Shirley's Restaurant. Madison turned her head to see Mr. Olsen, Ben and Margie, and Nell and Drew. They continued clapping as Maddie and Rick walked hand in hand across the street to join their friends. Nell was first to hug Maddie. She too was in tears, and Margie joined them, also crying. Rick accepted the men's handshakes.

Mr. Olsen said, "We couldn't wait. She's our daughter; the whole town raised this one. We aim to share in her happiness."

"And it's a good thing she said yes, because I hate seeing a grown man cry," Drew caught Maddie's hand and pulled her close for a hug from the wheelchair.

"I got lucky," Rick said. "She called the ring flashy and extravagant, but she loves it!"

"You had to outdo me," Drew said, admiring the ring on Maddie's hand.

"Let me see that," Nell pulled the hand from his grasp.

"Let's not fight over it," Margie squeezed in between Nell and the wheelchair. "Wow! No woman in her right mind would turn that proposal down. Smart move, Agent Malone!"

"Thanks for your approval. I appreciate it, folks. Now, I have an evening planned, and it's time to get on the road for our reservation." Rick pulled Madison away from all the well-wishers.

They headed out of town and turned onto Clear Branch Road. Madison glanced at Rick when he took the southbound ramp instead of driving toward Johnson City. "Asheville or the Outer Banks?" And then she laughed.

"Only Asheville tonight, Milady. I'm saving the OBX for our honeymoon." He smiled at her and reached for the hand he had just put the ring on. He kissed it and added, "I might have to hock the ring to afford a honeymoon."

They both laughed all the way to the North Carolina state line.

"Just before you came out of the cottage a while ago, I had a call from the Roanoke Coroner's Office," he said, and glanced at his bride to be. "Gosh, you sure are beautiful!"

"Oh, come on. I know that isn't what the phone call said," Maddie giggled.

"No, they learned that Ms. Cameron was dead before the crash: poisoned."

"Oh, no! Poor Nicholas. He was right to run." Madison sunk lower into the passenger seat. "What can we do?"

"We? Nothing! The police in Virginia are going to take Scott and his wife in for questioning."

"What about that sheriff?"

"He's cooperating, but maintains his innocence. He knows more than he's letting on; they'll get him to talk now. He could be looking at accessory to murder."

Madison sighed "I knew all along, something wasn't as simple as they made it out to be."

"Oh, hadn't you better call Holly? I mean, the whole town knows we're engaged."

"Yes! Thanks for reminding me."

As they came into cellphone range going down the south side of the mountain, Madison placed a call to Holly.

"Get your sewing machine dusted off, Holly. I need you to make my wedding gown."

Rick heard Holly's squeal. He watched the smile on Maddie's face as she talked to her lifelong friend. They carried on with silly girl stuff all the way to the turn onto Charlotte Avenue. She told Holly that they could make plans later; now she needed to get off the phone. Rick turned right onto Macon.

"The Grove Park Inn?" Madison's eyes were as wide as when she'd seen the ring.

Rick just smiled and kissed her hand again.

The Grove Park Inn had long been Madison's favorite historical attraction. Jess had taken her there when she was a young girl. They walked the hallways and read the history of how the inn was built, looking at all the photos posted on the walls. She fell in love with the history of NC after that first trip. She kept the fact that she and Bill Conway had visited recently on a need to know basis. And on this special evening, Rick had no need to know!

Rick and Madison got out at the front door, letting valet parking take his SUV. Rick held her hand as he escorted Maddie into the lobby. "We have a reservation for seven o'clock. Let's check in, then walk around some. We're a little early," he told her as they walked down the long hallway off the right side of the lobby.

The fireplaces that face each other with rocking chairs and comfortable couch seating between them were cold, but had mini lights to brighten them. On a cold day, the walk-in size fireplaces burn small trees, logs 6 feet in length, warming the atmosphere. Between Thanksgiving and Christmas, the long hallways are lined with variously themed evergreens decorated to the hilt. Many folks visit just to see the decorations.

They arrived at the Veranda Restaurant to check in for the evening buffet, and were seated immediately. "I didn't think we'd get to sit this early; it's another half hour 'til our reservation." Rick commented.

The hostess answered, "Agent Malone, we're pleased you chose our dining for your special occasion. Congratulations to both of you." She led them to a window facing west. "We get some awesome sunsets this time of year. I hope you'll enjoy your evening. Matt will be your server. He'll be with you momentarily." She stood by as Rick seated Madison, then handed him a wine list. "The first bottle is on the house, Sir. Please choose one from our list."

Rick looked over the list and said, "We'll have the house semi-sweet red. We're not exactly big wine connoisseurs."

"Sir, may I suggest this one? It's my personal favorite. I don't like the expensive wines so much myself. This one is right in the middle, and perfect for this occasion."

"Thank you, I trust your judgement. We'll have that one." He smiled and the hostess walked away. "Did I sound too ignorant?"

"No, Rick. You were amazing. And I get the feeling she gave an honest suggestion."

The nice young hostess returned with the slightly chilled bottle. She presented it to them, opened it, and poured the first taste to Rick. "What do you think?"

"That's good," he said. "Thank you for your recommendation."

The hostess smiled at them both and poured up the glasses. She placed the bottle to Rick's left. "Your server will be right with you."

Madison tasted the red wine. "I like this."

"Good evening. My name is Matt, I'll assist you with your dining tonight. I see Rosanna has served you her favorite wine. I like it too. The buffet begins with the salad bar, to your front and right side." He waved his hand, palm up. "Can I get you coffee or water?"

"Water please, for both of us," Rick looked at Maddie.

"Yes," she answered.

"Then help yourselves to the salad bar at your pleasure, Sir, Ma'am," he bowed and then stepped away.

Madison took Rick's arm whispering, "This is so elegant."

"Only the best for my love," Rick kissed her forehead.

During dinner, rain began to fall softly on the golf course below the window. "Aw, I was hoping we could watch the sunset," Maddie sighed.

"Sometimes clouds give you more color for the sunset. Don't give up hope."

Just at that moment, the sun broke through. The rain faded away, and the sky turned golden.

"What did I tell you?" Rick put his hand over Maddie's.

"How did you know?"

The happy couple watched as crimson worked into a layer and the golden sun dropped behind a purple veil of distant mountains.

"Is there anything else you want? Or need?"

Madison drank some iced water and then said, "Carry out service?"

"You mean, me carry you out?" he laughed and stood. "I thought you might wheel me out in a wheelchair." He linked arms with her, and they strolled onto the open veranda. "It's a lovely night. Let's walk a while."

"Sounds good to me." Madison smiled at her man. She felt the same flip-flop inside as she had the first time she looked into his emerald green eyes.

The ascending rock stairs led to lower levels, and finally a waterfall at the area around The Spa. Rick knew there was an elevator in the hallway to the right. He wasn't planning to climb back up all those stairs, so he led her past

The Spa into a dark hall with lighted alcoves cleverly cut into the rocks. Soon, they came to an open room with an elevator.

"Ah, we won't have to climb back up those stairs to the main lobby after all." Rick pushed the up button. They were the only ones on the elevator, and when it stopped on the third floor, she didn't say anything—but looked closer at the numbers on the control panel. Then she stepped off behind Rick.

"Are we lost?" She asked.

"Oh, dear, and I've heard there is a ghost in here" the lady in pink." Rick shivered.

Madison slapped his shoulder and walked onward. The hall seemed endless, but eventually they came to a glass door overlooking some stairs.

"I know where we are. This area is where the Gingerbread House Contest displays at Christmas," Madison said.

"Yeah, I know." Rick pushed open the door and walked across a small lobby to another elevator. He pressed the up button again.

Madison stepped onboard and watched as he selected the main lobby button. "You have been here before. I didn't even know how to get back to this lobby."

"I've been here many times. The Gingerbread House Contest has always been a favorite of mine. I can't believe I never brought you here."

"You mentioned it once, but I think they held it somewhere else then. Remember, at some Conference Center?"

"Yeah, must have been when they changed over to Omni Grove Park Inn."

As they entered the lobby, they saw a young man building a fire in one of the enormous fireplaces.

"Can we sit for a while?" Madison asked.

"Sure," he smiled and chose a double rocker. "Maybe we can make plans for our wedding date. I mean, this is a romantic atmosphere."

"Yeah, it is. I wonder if anyone ever gets married in here."

"They do. Would you like this for a destination wedding?"

"I'm sure that would be too expensive." Madison took a deep breath. "I know the rooms are expensive. Unless... Maybe we could have our wedding here, and everyone else drives home after."

"Now, is that nice? Get our friends and family drunk at the reception, and then let them drive home?" Rick leaned in close and stole a kiss.

A voice behind them cleared his throat, "Excuse me. You two look jubilant. May I take your photo?"

They turned to see a young man with a large camera.

"Sure, why not? We just got engaged." Rick stood and pulled his wallet out.

"Will you take a couple, so we can use them for our invitations?"

"Yes, Sir," the young man said. "I'm a wedding photographer. I do it all, invitations, DJ for receptions, everything. Here's my card."

Rick accepted the colorful business card, reading *Sound Professionals & Lighting*.

"I noticed your profile looks stunning with the flames as a backdrop. Do you mind?"

"You're the pro, whatever you suggest," Rick said, and sat back down next to Madison.

After a thirty-minute shoot, Gerad showed them his shots, and they chose the ones they liked.

"How fortunate that you happened to be here," Madison said.

"I just photographed a private party in one of the restaurants. When I saw the glow on your face, I had to ask."

"Thanks. You are very good at your job."

"Well, Ma'am, it's my hobby." Two deep dimples showed as he smiled. "I'm a teacher."

"Then you need it for an extra job! Teachers don't get paid enough!" Rick said.

"Unfortunately, they don't."

The happy couple walked outside with their photographer and a new friend. Rick handed Gerad his business card, with instructions to send the package to Cold Creek Sheriff's Office.

"OK," Gerad looked at the card. "TBI? I thought you were the sheriff."

"No, she is," and they all laughed.

"Now *that's* different," Gerad said. He offered his hand in a friendly shake. "Sheriff Madison, I'll be in touch. Just don't forget to let me know your date. That's pretty important, you see."

Rick's vehicle arrived in the valet line, and the driver handed him the keys. He tipped the boy, and they waved good-bye to Gerad.

As they drove across the mountain back into Tennessee, Madison thought of how happy she was when they were together. If she ever had a hint of a question, this evening removed any doubt that they loved each other.

Monday morning, Madison was eager to get to her office and check her schedule for the day. If she had no calls or appointments, she'd start her list for the invitations. As soon as she sat down with pen in hand, the phone rang.

"Sheriff McKenzie," she answered the phone. She waited for a moment, then she said, "Hello, is anyone there?" She checked the CID. It read *Blocked number.*

She hung up the phone and dismissed it as a wrong number. Back to the list. She began with family, making notes of whom she'd need to get addresses for from Jess and Shirley.

"*Oh, no!* Jess and Shirley!" Bud jumped up from his nap and looked toward the door. He looked back at Madison.

"I forgot to call them!" She laughed at Bud. She tapped the first speed dial on her cell, and soon heard Jess's voice on the other end. "Hey, Dad. How are you two?"

"Good, how's my girl? What's up, I didn't hear from you over the weekend," Jess said.

"I was busy...getting engaged, and celebrating with Rick!"

"Really? Thanks for forgetting your folks. When is the big day?"

"We haven't decided yet," she said. "Where is Momma?"

"She's out walking. I expect her back anytime now."

"Why aren't you walking with her?" Madison asked.

"I stepped on a nail, and plunged it right up through my shoe and my foot. Had to get a tetanus shot. My foot is pretty sore today, so I didn't want to walk."

"I'm sorry, are you OK?" Madison turned into mush whenever something happened to her folks. "When are you coming home?"

"We'll be there in about a week. We're really enjoying this RV. I think we might get one for ourselves."

"Sounds like fun. Might as well, as much as you two enjoy traveling." Madison heard a noise outside. "Well, tell Momma I'll call her back tonight. You can tell her I have a beautiful ring."

"OK, Honey. We'll talk to you later." Jess hung up his phone.

A woman dressed in dark hoodie and jeans walked into the sheriff's office. Madison hung up the phone. She turned to ask the woman if she could help her.

The woman walked closer and pulled a revolver from beneath her sweatshirt. "You the sheriff?"

"I am. And who are you?"

"You've caused me a lot of trouble, sticking your nose into other people's business. You might think you're taking my son away from me, but you aren't." She walked close. "Put your weapon on the desk, carefully."

Madison stood motionless for a moment. "You're Mrs. Scott. You or your husband killed to get that little boy. The law will never let you keep him. You might as well hand me your pistol." She didn't bat an eye.

The woman pulled the hammer back, "I'm not joking, and I *will* shoot you!"

"No, you won't. That would take guts, and you don't have them. You're the one who poisoned Ms. Cameron. Did your husband or the sheriff cover up your mess?" She still had not gone for her gun.

"Don't try to psychoanalyze me. Drop your weapon. I'm warning you."

In a flash, Madison saw a form come through the door and grab the woman from behind. They both fell to the floor. Madison pulled her gun and pointed it at the woman. She was struggling with someone smaller than her, but Madison couldn't get to the revolver. She didn't dare shoot; she might hit them both, at this distance.

The woman elbowed the person on her back and pulled loose. She jumped to her feet and aimed at the boy on the floor. Madison shot the revolver from her hand at the same moment the woman pulled the trigger. Mrs. Scott was knocked backward, flying off her feet. Madison saw that the boy was Nicholas, and he was bleeding. She stepped between him and the woman, who was trying to get up.

"Don't move!" Madison kicked the revolver further away, still aiming her Sig at the woman. "I'll blow your head right off your shoulders if you even breathe too deep." She stooped down to check for Nicholas' pulse. He was alive. She motioned the woman toward the open cell at the back of her office.

Mrs. Scott moved slowly, leaving a trail of blood. "I'm bleeding!"

"So? If you're still alive after the boy is tended to, I'll get the Doc to look at what's left of your hand. Now shut up, or I'll shoot you just to put you out of pain." She slammed the cell door and turned the key, pulling it out as she rushed back to Nicholas.

"Madison, I heard a shot—Oh my God! What's happened?" Mr. Olsen stood in the doorway. "I'll get the Doc."

Madison knelt beside Nicholas and put a towel on his shoulder, applying pressure. The pain caused his eyes to open.

"Lie still, Nicholas. The doc is on his way. I have to keep pressure on it so that the bleeding will stop."

"That's the woman who took my brother. I saw her the day our mom died. Is she gone?"

"She's in my jail cell. Just be still, Nick. Don't try to move or talk."

Dr. Chip ran into the office, and in a second he had Nicholas' shirt off his chest. He applied a white bandage to the wound, saying, "Hold this, Madison." Chip pulled a syringe from his black case, using the fluid in it to wash out the wound. "This has to come out."

"Mr. Olsen, back your truck over here. Madison, put something on the tailgate to cushion his little body. I've got to take him to my office."

They all quickly got into urgency mode.

"What about me? I'm bleeding here," the woman yelled.

Doc looked at Madison; she shrugged her shoulders. They ignored the woman and helped Nicholas to his feet. Madison laid a blanket on the tailgate of Mr. Olsen's truck. Doc helped him lay on the blanket.

It caused Madison pain just watching the boy. Doc walked behind the truck as Mr. Olsen drove at a snail's pace toward Doc's office, just a couple of buildings away.

Madison had time to run back into the jail and look at the woman's wound. She handed her a clean towel and told her, "Sit down, and stop bleeding all over my clean office! Get this through your head, woman: I don't give a crap about your hand!"

She walked out and joined Doc and Mr. Olsen. They put Nicholas in a wheelchair and got him on a stretcher inside the operatory.

"I'd better call Henry," Madison said. "Oh, that woman in my jail has a severe wound. She's missing a couple of fingers now. Just in case that makes a difference." Madison said.

"She shot this boy?" Doc asked.

"Yeah," Madison replied.

"Then she can wait. I can't help her anyway. After you call Henry, you might want to call the Smyth County Police, maybe the Virginia Bureau of Investigation" he suggested.

"Good point." She stepped outside to call Henry.

In a matter of five minutes, Henry was in town at Doc's office. "I didn't tell Holly."

"Good. She doesn't need to be upset."

They sat in the waiting room while Doc took the bullet out. Madison explained to Henry what had happened, and asked why Nicholas was in town. Henry told her he wanted to ride his new bike to show her.

"Aw, and he saw her and saved me. What a sweet boy. I hope his brother is as good as Nicholas." Madison stopped, hoping Henry might not have caught on to what she said.

"What do you mean? I didn't know Nick had a brother."

"Don't tell Holly. That's why we've kept it from you." Madison faced telling Henry the entire story now. *Maybe this is for the best.* Henry could make the decision and not upset Holly.

"Why, we wouldn't hesitate to pick up that little boy. You know us, we take in all strays. Yes, if it comes to that, I want his brother too. How long has it been since they've seen each other?"

"I'm not sure, but I think Robby was only three or four the last time Nick saw him. Now he's seven. Only they don't call him Robby. They changed his name to Tommy," she said.

"Does Nicholas know?"

"Not unless he figured it out today. I haven't told him anything."

Just then, Doc came in. "He's going to be just fine. I'll keep him here for a while, just to be sure there's no further bleeding or reaction to the medicines. You can both come in and see him."

Madison and Henry walked in to see Nicholas barely awake. The bed was cranked up to an elevated position.

"Hey, how are you feeling?" they both asked at the same time.

"That's the woman who took Robby. What did she mean, you trying to take her son away? Is she the person who adopted him?"

"It's complicated, Nicholas. But if Henry says you're big enough to hear this, I'll tell you why she was here today."

"Nick can handle it." Henry held the boy's hand.

Madison explained how she had investigated what he and the Smyth County sheriff told her. She also said that Rick had reopened the investigation about their mother. In a short while, Nicholas was sound asleep.

Doc and Madison went to the jail to check on Mrs. Scott. Henry stayed with his son. He called Holly and told her he was all right, no need for her to worry. Doc said Nicholas could come home later that evening. Holly trusted Henry's judgment, and promised not to ask questions until he was home.

Madison spoke with the law office in Roanoke that was handling the Scott case. They asked her to have an officer of the law to bring her to Virginia, and they would have one of their officers meet them halfway.

Madison called Rick to let him handle the transporting. He told her he'd do it himself, and asked her to ride along with him. That would give them a chance to talk about the evidence he'd received from Claudia.

She agreed to ride with him. She was responsible for the woman's injury, which was causing Mrs. Scott a tremendous amount of pain and anguish. The trip was difficult, but it only took three hours to reach the meeting place, where another agent took the prisoner.

On the drive back to Cold Creek, Rick told Maddie that the barrettes had both Monique's and her birth mother's DNA on them. Also, Rick had been curious about the box itself. Why use a box twice as large as it needed to be, just to store some small barrettes? They did not appear to be of any value. Jewels had entrusted them to Claudia almost immediately after meeting her. There was more to this than meets the eye.

He tore the lining out of the box and discovered an underlying motive. Jewels had been concealing a tape, for a small voice-activated recorder. When Rick finally managed to round one up that worked, he heard a shocking story.

Jewels had realized early on that she'd married a deceitful man. She knew enough about his lifestyle to know she could never get away. So, she hid a small recorder to get any conversation she could on tape, just in case he ever threatened her. She was implementing his gangster tactics on him for her defense. After she'd presented him with evidence that could get him in trouble with the mob, she told him if he wanted to stay with her, he had to leave his line of work. That's when he took the job in the forestry service, and they moved to the Appalachian region. And that was the reason he was able to give her a child.

They made a truce, and she agreed that if she was able to raise her as their child, they had to disappear again. After they had moved to South Florida, Jewels realized she was trapped. She made the tape thinking that when Monique became an adult, she might want to know who her family had been before she came to live with them. Jewels also realized that the Mob would never stop looking for them—another reason to pass the tape off to a stranger. She had only hoped Monique would figure it out if something happened to her and her husband. She made the right choice giving it to Claudia, a trusting and worthy friend.

Madison listened as Rick told the story. Finally, she let out her breath. "That's a lot to take in. Are you going to tell Monique?" she asked.

"I'm going to give her the recorder and let her listen to the tape if she wants to. But I'll leave it up to her." Rick pulled into a diner, explaining, "I'm hungry, and I haven't seen a Cracker Barrel."

Meanwhile, the Burnsville Police Department had been responsible for picking up Tommy Scott at his school. They would hold him until children's services could decide who had a legal right to the boy.

Once again, Henry and Holly were chosen to foster the child, even though they were out of state. The fact that the DNA of the boys matched made a difference to the judge who ruled on the case. In less than a week, Robby his big brother were reconnected.

Nicholas wasn't sure his brother would remember him, he was so little when they took him. But as soon as the social worker brought Nicholas into the room, Robby ran to him.

Nicholas was sore from his surgery, and had to ask his little brother not to squeeze him so hard.

"You were shot? Can I see?" Robby's reaction was a little unsympathetic, until he saw the wound. Then he felt bad and began crying.

"I'm OK, Rob..." Nicholas stopped. "What do you want me to call you?"

"Robby is my name. I never liked the name Tommy. Do I have to keep that name?"

"No, Honey," the Social Worker said. "If you want to use Robby, it is your choice."

"Robby Lucas Cameron is my name." No one argued with the little boy.

\* \* \*

Rick felt a bit left out of Madison's life, so he suggested they go ahead and get married. He had enough vacation to spend at least a month in Cold Creek, and that was after a two-week honeymoon. But Madison talked him into waiting for the end of the year. The addition on the cottage would be complete, most of the holidays behind them, and the town would've had time to elect another sheriff.

"What do you mean, I'm going to be the next sheriff of Cold Creek?" Rick surprised her with this statement.

"I've already discussed it with the mayor and some of the town council," Rick said.

"'Is that right?" Madison rarely found herself in this position; she was speechless.

# 39

Rick was back in Knoxville, awaiting orders on a case in Memphis. He called to tell Madison that Shannon had been reassigned to Nashville, so she had no more reason to worry; his partner was no longer around.

"Say hello to Elvis for me. Will I see you this weekend?" She asked.

"I hope so! I'll call you every day."

Madison had some phone calls to make, so she got busy at that first thing. She liked getting the things she least enjoyed out of the way early in her day. Just as she made the last call, she heard a loud siren.

She ran out onto the street to see everyone else was out on the sidewalks, too. The sound was coming from the museum. Madison joined Mr. Olsen, and both walked over to the old wooden building. It was one of the few original structures from the 1800s remaining in Cold Creek. The sound wound down, and everyone took their hands off their ears.

Doc Chip stepped out of the front door. "You said we needed a siren, Sheriff McKenzie. Now we have one, and I'll take responsibility for warning folks about storms or fires, whatever the emergency. When I'm not going to be in town, I'll make sure I appoint someone to stand in for me."

"This is great. I doubt even Mr. Olsen can sleep through that sound!" she exclaimed, and the crowd laughed. "Seriously, I think this is an excellent precaution to take, for all our residents. And I will do the same; for those of you who don't have a basement, the jail basement will be open as shelter during any storms. I'll make sure that if I'm out of town, someone else will have a key.

Let's give our respected doctor a round of applause." She clapped her hands and began a loud uproar for Doc.

The folks slowly scattered, and Madison returned to her office in time to catch a phone call. "Sheriff McKenzie," she said.

"Hello Madison, it's Monique. Are you busy today?"

"No. Are you in my neck of the woods?"

"Yeah; can I buy you lunch?" Monique asked.

"Sure. When will you be here?"

"Oh, in about a half hour."

"Great! I'm in my office," she said. See you soon." After hanging up, she took a stack of completed paperwork to the file cabinet. She was just finishing with them as Monique and Dr. Ross walked through the door.

"Hey, there, Michael. It's good to see you." She walked over and offered her handshake.

He pulled her close and hugged her instead. "Aw, we're better friends than that."

"You're right," she said, and gave Monique a hug too. "So, what's the special occasion?"

"We wanted to share some news with you, in person," Michael said

"Come over and sit down," Madison ushered them to a couple of wingback chairs in front of her desk. "Can I offer you something to drink? Coffee or water?"

"No, thank you," they both said.

"This is a new addition, Monique said, settling into her chair. "And a lot more comfortable than the hard, straight-backed chairs that were in here."

"Yeah, it's the woman's touch." Madison laughed.

"We were able to prove that Monique is the daughter of Lynda and Larry Morrel of Knoxville, so she stands to inherit their estate. I'll let you tell her the other good news." Michael looked at Monique.

"Dr. Ross took a job at UT Medical School in the Surgical Department, and he has asked me to marry him."

"Oh, Monique, that's wonderful! Congratulations on both accounts, Dr. Ross."

"Thank you, Madison," he said, looking at his fiancée again. "And we would be proud if you and Rick would stand up with us."

"What about your friends, the hikers? Wouldn't that be their place?" She felt a little awkward.

"Coach is going to give me away. Diane will be my maid of honor, and I want you to be my bridesmaid. And Michael wants Rick as his best man. Steve and Clark will be Ushers."

"When is the wedding?" Madison asked.

"October the twentieth, it's a Friday. It will be in Knoxville at the First Baptist Church on Main Street, not far from Calhoun's on the River; that's where we'll have the reception."

"Sounds like you've been busy. I'll talk to Rick, but I don't see any reason why we won't be able to do that. You'll let us know the colors or when to get the dress, and a tux for Rick?"

"Oh, I will. I'm looking for the dresses in Atlanta, but they'll be sent to Knoxville to try on. We don't have to make a trip all the way to Atlanta for fittings." Monique's face glowed with happiness.

"I'm happy for you two," Madison said. "You know, Rick and I are getting married, too, but most likely not until January. We don't have any plans set in stone," she said.

"So where do you want to go for lunch?" Michael asked.

The girls both laughed. After all, it was Michael's first visit to Cold Creek.

They drove off the mountain down to the Mexican restaurant in Unicoi, near Walmart. As they were ordering, a heavy rain began. It continued falling, and the parking lot soon looked like a lake. They reordered on their drinks to wait out the storm, but it seemed to be unrelenting. They gave up after a couple of hours and ran to the car.

Michael drove back onto I-26 heading southbound. As they started up the mountain, he noticed the sign for Rocky Fork State Park. "Say, that's nice, that you have a state park this close to Cold Creek."

"Well, it's not there yet," Madison said. "I mean, it's there, and it's a beautiful creek, but there hasn't been much progress yet. I don't understand why they put the signs out so early. Campers are always stopping in at the office, wanting to know how to find it and why they didn't see anything when they were up there..."

"They put the signs up before it is open?" Michael asked.

"Uh-huh," Madison said. "You can take the old road at the next exit, if you want to see what I mean. There is a trail you can hike, but that's all for now. Don't misunderstand, it is beautiful!"

The old road snaked up the mountain alongside the creek, which looked more like a river escaping its banks in low lying areas, thanks to the downpour. The three gawked at a garden space with three-foot tall corn stalks bowing with the flow of the fast-running water. Around the next curve, water ran across the road from the hillside.

Monique asked if they should turn back. Michael observed that he could still see the yellow lines in the center of the road, so he pushed forward, slowly. As they approached the small bridge where Rocky Creek crossed their path, they saw a felled tree bobbing toward the bridge. Michael stopped in the middle of the road.

"Is this the turn to go into the state park?"

"I don't recommend we go up there right now," Madison said, feeling fear for anyone who might be caught outside in the downpour. People were already coming in to hike the Rocky Fork trails. What if there were cars and hikers stranded up there? She kept her feelings to herself and suggested they continue up to Cold Creek.

The tree barely had clearance to pass under the bridge. They waited and watched anxiously, then continued up the mountain, southbound. The rain-swelled runoff lessened as they neared Cold Creek, causing a sigh of relief for all.

Michael and Monique said their goodbyes to Madison and headed to Asheville.

Madison called Henry. She advised him that she was going down to Rocky Fork to check the situation. "Bud will be at the store with Mr. Olsen and Hardware," she laughed. "I'm beginning to think Bud believes he's the daddy."

"Maybe he is, Maddie. Denny was a doctor of dentistry, not a vet. Since she did his surgery, I wouldn't bet his neutering worked. You know?"

"Ah, that never occurred to me—but you're right," Madison agreed.

Sheriff McKenzie threw a few items in her Blazer and went back down the old road to Rocky Creek. Water was now lapping the bridge, but she crossed anyway. She drove up the narrow, curvy road, with barely room to pass another vehicle. When she came to the bridge where Rocky Creek curved under the asphalt, she stopped to examine it before driving over. At the moment, the bridge appeared secure.

With the creek on the right side of the road, she could tell the hillside on the far right had been eroding where it was the steepest. The wall at this point was a creek-carved rock cliff, extending high above the water level. She felt the minor erosion was not that important in this area. However, as the rocky wall lessened and actual earth replaced the solid wall; that was another question. A shallow hollow open to the creek brought a flow of water not typically present on the scene. Madison drove on, judging that amount of runoff not a threat at this point.

Another curve, another bridge, and the water switched under the road once again. This bridge stood well above the water and looked passable. Up ahead, Madison knew there was a turnoff to the left where there could be a future road, or maybe just a trail ascending another hollow. This was the main fork of the creek. Water gushed out engulfing the temporary parking lot of freshly smoothed earth in the hollow opening. She drove up the steep incline, rolling past an old apple tree. Halfway up this stretch was a driveway, angling toward the top of the hill behind her. As many times as she'd driven this road, she'd never seen the gate across the drive opened; nor was it today. She went on to the sharp curve to the left, where a small wooden structure stood on the right hillside. She noticed drainage under the house had eroded the cabin's supports. Since no one had lived in it for decades, she ignored it for now.

Rain continued to fall as hard as it had when they were at the restaurant in the valley. Finally, on the top of the ridge, she turned her Blazer into the cemetery on the right side of the road. Just beyond this point was a junction of two roads. Edwards Branch Road edged its way along the ridge a short way before it dropped off toward some homes scattered down the hillside. She wasn't sure where the road to the left ended up; she'd never traveled it. Today was not going to be her day to venture up there, either.

While she watched clouds hover along the distant ridges and blanket the valley below, she took in the one view to the north from Rocky Fork. Then she heard a car approaching from behind.

It was a small, red four-door, and she noticed a couple of children in the back seat. She waved as they passed, heading down Rocky Fork Road. *Gosh, I wouldn't bring my kids out in weather like this. My kids...* she smiled as she looked down at the diamond on her hand. *Rick and I will have children, maybe two or three...boys! But all daddies want a girl, so she should be first.*

Madison looked one more time at the view, then backed her Blazer onto the road and drove slowly back the way she'd come. As she approached the old house, now on her left, she slammed on the brakes, watching as the house gave way to the force of the water and crunched onto the roadway and over the bank. She considered backing up the hill to the cemetery and heading off Edwards Branch Road.

That's when she thought of the red car with kids inside. The debris from the old house had plunged 75 feet to the creek bed below, splintering like toothpicks. A layer of mud replaced the water running across the road in front of her. She put the vehicle into 4-wheel drive to continue. The Blazer's tires slipped sideways toward the cliff, so she turned the wheel into the slide. The movement brought the back end up the hill, giving it more traction. She let the SUV idle slowly along the slippery road, not touching the gas. Continuing down the hill, she kept watching for debris from the house. Not seeing any, she stopped short of the bridge. Just then, a wall of boards and brown water approached, carrying

272

with it another small outbuilding picked up along the way. The muddy mess from the other side of the cleared field had grown to nearly ten feet, and was about to collide with the debris at the bridge. She gunned the accelerator to cross the bridge and continued down the road, trying to stay ahead of the wave about to overtake her and everything in its path.

Suddenly, she saw a flash of red slide off the road into the ditch ahead. The car with the kids in the back had wedged into the hillside. Madison pulled alongside them and put her window down. No one was hurt, so she said she'd try to push the car out, if the driver wanted her to.

Fear in the young woman's eyes assured Madison she was doing the right thing. She backed her Blazer up and bumped the back of the red Chevy. She feared it would ruin the bumper and the trunk, but she pushed anyway. The light car was soon free of the ditch, and the Blazer climbed out with the help of the four-wheel drive. The car drove on ahead of her.

Madison felt like she was driving too fast, but there was nothing she could do to stop the woman without endangering her vehicle. She stopped to disengage the four-wheel drive and started forward again quickly. She glanced in her mirror, seeing a wall of muddy debris engulf the bridge.

In the next curve, a log had washed into the road. The red Chevy was blocked, and the woman had pulled over to the edge of the road. Madison re-engaged the four-wheel drive and pushed the log off the road. She then motioned for the car to stay behind her, and led the way. The wall was catching up to them at an alarming rate; the woman saw what was coming and raced around Madison.

Madison watched helplessly as the car hydroplaned where the water was now over the road. The creek was moving the car toward an enormous boulder. She pulled her Blazer off the side of the road as close to the hillside as possible, and raced toward the car. One child, who appeared to be a teenager, got out on the passenger side; the driver was trying to open her door. Madison reached the car and pulled the back door open, unfastened the seatbelt of the older child, and lifted her from the car. The car lurched closer to the boulder. Madison told the teenager to climb the hillside as high as she could, and hold on to the trees with the child.

She returned to the car and helped the driver, now out and pulling on the back door. The water's depth was increasing. Madison rushed to the other side and climbed into the back seat to get the screaming toddler out of the car seat. The driver held on to the boulder for a few minutes, but then lost her grip and was swept away. Madison finally released the latch holding the baby, and exited the car with him in her arms. She climbed the hillside to where the two girls clung to a sturdy pine. The teen grabbed the baby and Madison slid down the hill, running to the car as it floated toward the boulder. How was she going to get across the water? She paced back and forth until she heard the crashing of the wall behind her. She raced up the hillside to escape the onslaught, just as the debris reached the red car. She prayed the lady was somewhere out of the path of the debris, further down the creek and still alive.

Madison held the toddler to try to stop his crying. She was cold, and knew that he must be. Bending over his body to block the rain, she hoped the warmth of her body could warm him. The teenager told Madison the other children were her niece and nephew, and the driver was her sister. She tried not to cry, not wanting to alarm the little girl any more than she was already. It wasn't easy, considering they'd watched her wash down with the flood water.

"Maybe someone on the other side helped her," Madison tried to give the girl some hope.

They shivered for a long time before the rain subsided, and the water dropped as suddenly as it had risen. Madison was amazed that the SUV was still sitting where she'd left it. She'd thought the wall of debris would dislodge it, but it hadn't touched her trusty old Blazer.

She placed the little girl in the backseat and belted her in best she could. The teen held the baby in the front seat. Madison moved slowly through the shallow water on the road all the way to the old highway. At the bridge, she noticed a car upside down wedged against the bridge. Traces of the debris were scattered all over the road. *It must have been quite a sight to see when that wall came out of the hollow.*

There were a couple of cars parked on the road a short distance from the bridge. Madison recognized Henry's truck. An ambulance pulled away with its lights flashing, heading toward Erwin As Madison parked next to Henry. He saw her and rushed over from the bridge.

"Are you OK?" he asked.

"I'm cold, but we're all OK." She got out of the vehicle, and Henry handed her some blankets from in his truck. She gave them to the girl in her Blazer, then she and Henry walked away to talk. Maddie asked, "Did the ambulance have a young woman in it?"

"Yes; we pulled her from the water. I thought sure she was dead, but the EMT felt a pulse, and they're taking her to Erwin Hospital. Are those her kids?"

"The little ones are; the teenager is her sister." Madison turned to go back to the Blazer. "I'll take them to the hospital."

Madison drove the old road to Clear Creek Road, then she followed the ambulance onto the interstate and to Erwin, at the base of the mountain.

She parked at the rear of the hospital, watching as the attendants unloaded the woman from the ambulance. They hadn't run the siren and driven at emergency speed; Madison was worried about what that might mean. The patient was either deceased, or doing well. She hoped it was the latter.

When she saw the oxygen mask was still on the patient, they all got out of the Blazer and walked in behind the EMT crew. The victim raised her head slightly and waved to her family.

"Let's park you all in the waiting room, and I'll go find out how she is," Madison said. The oldest girl, whom she now knew as Candi, took the baby from her and kept her wrapped in one of the blankets. The toddler stretched out on a blanket on the floor watching cartoons that she'd noticed on the TV high in the corner. "Are you warm enough, Candi?"

"Yes Ma'am, thanks."

Madison went through the double doors marked *Employees Only*. A nurse held her hand up as if to stop her passing, but then she saw Madison's badge. "Oh, excuse me, Sheriff."

"That's OK. I want to inquire about the ER patient just brought in. I have her children and younger sister."

"You're the woman who saved them; sure, come this way." The nurse led the way to a room with the curtain open, which buzzed with people working on the lady.

Madison recognized one of the EMTs, so she stepped over to greet him. "How is she?"

"Amazingly good: I couldn't believe they pulled her from that muddy water alive, let alone not choking. I'm pretty sure she has at least a broken arm, and maybe a little water in her lungs, but she's doing well."

"Thank goodness; I thought we'd seen the last of her. Is it the right arm? I watched her crash into a huge boulder, and then she lost her grip and disappeared from my sight."

"Yes. So you're the woman who saved her kids."

"I was there," Madison shrugged. "I watched her get swept away, but she's much more petite than me. I guess my big feet held me down."

"Well, that was a good thing. Where are the children? I'd like to take a look at them, too," he said.

"In the waiting room. And I think that's a good idea. The baby was pretty traumatized, but he did watch his Mommy get washed away."

The EMT walked to the waiting room with Madison, who introduced the children and Candi. The baby had fallen asleep. He took the little boy into his arms gently and listened to his heart and back, then handed him back to

Candi. Then he sat on the blanket next to the toddler.

"Who are we watching?" he asked.

"Goofy," she giggled.

"Oh, I love Goofy! Do you mind if I watch with you?"

She shook her head and smiled at the young man. After a few minutes, she got up and sat on his lap. "Where's Mommy?"

"She's right down that hallway," he pointed. "A doctor wanted to check her arm. Did you ever hurt your arm and need a doctor?"

She quickly shook her head, never taking her eyes off the TV and Goofy.

"Well, she might get a bandage on it, and then she'll be out here with you. OK?"

This time she nodded her head.

"Are you hurt anyplace?" he asked her.

"I got this boo-boo." She showed him her elbow.

"Let me see that. What a booboo! Do you want a Goofy Band-Aid on it?"

"Uh-huh," she said.

The big EMT dug a Disney band aid from his pocket and put it on the bump on her elbow, then he kissed it.

"Candi, did you get any scrapes or bangs?" he asked.

"No, I'm OK."

"I'll go back and see how the x-ray turned out," he slid the younger girl carefully out of his lap, got to his feet, and walked down the hall.

"Do you have someone we can call to come pick you up?" Madison asked Candi.

"Mom lives here in Erwin. I tried to call her, but it went to voicemail. She'll call back when she gets home." Candi checked her phone.

"Doesn't she have a cell?" Madison asked.

"That is her cell. She might be driving, and she won't answer it if she's driving."

"Good for her."

A slim woman with graying hair burst through the ER doors and glanced into the waiting room. "Candi!" she yelled. "Where's your sister?"

Candi stood up and greeted her mom with a hug. Her mom took the little boy, who was waking up. "She's with the doctor; she might have a broken arm."

Madison stood, extending her hand. "I'm Sheriff McKenzie. I brought the kids and Candi in, following the ambulance. The car was destroyed."

They shook hands, and the woman asked if she could see her older daughter, Cathy. She gave the baby back to Candi and followed Madison to the ER exam room, where Cathy was having a soft cast put on her right arm.

After explaining that the sheriff had saved her sister and kids, Cathy told Madison that they would be OK now, and if she needed them they'd be at her mother's house. Madison took down the information, address, and phone numbers, then returned to the waiting area to say goodbye to Candi and the kids.

When she reached Cold Creek, she stopped by the hardware store to get Bud. He raced her to the cottage, full of energy as usual. She went straight to her shower, washed her hair, dressed, and then went to the kitchen to make a pot of tea.

Her phone rang just as she was drinking the first cup. It was Henry. "Good job, Sheriff. How is the patient?"

"She's OK, all but a broken right arm. Even the doctor was amazed she had no water in her lungs, and no more injuries."

"Her car didn't fare so well; it's still wedged under the bridge. They have to wait for the water to go down to wrench it out. Then they'll have to inspect the supports under the bridge. What a mess!"

"Did you see the house? You know where that came from, right?" Madison asked.

"Oh, was it a house? The only one up that creek I can think of was hanging on to the right side like a mountain goat. Guess it got washed out, huh?" Henry was familiar with the area.

"There's a new creek up there today."

"Good for those folks you decided to go up and check out the situation. It could have been a recovery situation, instead of rescue. You did well, Maddie."

"All in a day's work, my friend," she said.

Madison didn't want to think what could have happened to them if she hadn't seen what happened. Those babies were so adorable, and it made her wonder what her own children might look like.

"Madison, did you hear me?"

Henry's voice snapped her out of her daydream. "I'm sorry, what did you say?"

"Holly wants to talk to you," he said. Madison heard him laugh and tell Holly, "I'm not sure she's listening."

Holly and Madison talked for a while. Madison asked how the brothers were doing. Holly told her that it would break her heart if they had to be separated again.

"They love each other, but the twins are showing signs of jealousy," Holly whispered.

"They'll be OK, just give them some time."

"Henry said the weather forecast says we should have a beautiful day tomorrow, so he's anxious to get back out to work on your house."

"Oh, good. I know the weather has halted progress for a while now. At least we haven't had any more tornados. That flooding of Rocky Fork was scary today. You should have seen that house, rolling across the road and down to the creek. I've never witnessed anything like it. Oh, that reminds me; I need to call the courthouse before they close. I want to find out who owns that property."

"All right, I need to finish supper anyway. I have five hungry boys now," Holly laughed like it was delightful to feed so many.

*She's such a perfect mother, wife, and friend. I'm very lucky to have her in my world.*

Madison looked up the number and called the records department for Unicoi County. She spoke with a polite, helpful lady who agreed to fax the information to her office. In only a few minutes, the fax machine printed out a map. Madison located the area where the house used to be. She concluded that it belonged to a family named Ervine. The second fax showed the upper portion of the connecting land, and she saw that the Ervine name was connected to several parcels of property in the Rock Fork area.

"What am I thinking?" she said to herself. "I bet all I need to do is talk to Johnny Lynch. He was involved with this project since day one. He should have all the answers I need." She had spoken to Mr. Lynch previously about the state park, and he was very helpful.

She tried calling his home number, but it went to voicemail. Then she remembered she had his cell number— "Oh, but that was on my old phone: the one I drowned."

Madison and Bud loaded into the Blazer, and she drove down the mountain into the lower Unicoi valley along the old Erwin Highway. Mr. Lynch, a talented artist, displays his works at The Farmhouse Gallery and Gardens.

Madison enjoyed the feelings of calm and tranquility as she drove across the iconic Covered Bridge leading to his home and the surrounding gardens with multiple structures. Folks gather for events like the Fiddlers Festival & Antique Car Show, weddings, family reunions, and blue grass music. Lynch and his wife, Pat, make BBQ and wood-fired loaves of bread for sale, as well as keeping the blacksmith shop busy making various handmade gifts. Wildlife includes peacocks, buffalo, the occasional white-tailed deer, and ponds with nesting ducks and geese.

Mr. Lynch crossed the drive as she approached. She stopped next to him, and they talked until he invited her to park and come into his gallery. She viewed his lovely wildlife watercolors on display while he returned a phone call.

"Sorry to hold you up. What can I do for the new Sheriff of Cold Creek?"

He swiveled an old leather-armed desk chair to face her.

"I need some names of landowners up at Rock Fork. It made sense to me that you must know all about them."

"I heard about you saving those kids up there. It is a blessing that things turned out good. It could have been a disaster."

"I'm thankful, too. I don't mind telling you I was doubtful at the onset." Madison felt that dread return each time she thought about what she'd witnessed.

"I have a plat map with all the names. I can run you off a copy, if you'd like," Johnny said.

"That's exactly what I need. Thank you."

Map in hand, Madison walked outside with Johnny. They watched a peacock dancing in his full temptation plumage for a moment.

She thanked him again, and studied the map before she drove away in her Blazer. Thirty minutes later, she sat on the road where the red car had been wedged. The Chevy had since been removed, and things appeared as if nothing had happened.

A call came over her police radio; she recognized the code as a domestic disturbance, and pretty close to her current location. She answered the county dispatcher, saying, "Sheriff McKenzie, Scott. I'm on Rocky Fork, I can take that call."

"Ten-four," he answered.

Madison drove to the top of the hill, passed the cemetery, and made a right turn onto Edwards Branch Road. The address was the first on the left. She noticed a house on the opposite side of the road, too. She pulled into the address on the left. A woman and a young boy stood on the carport.

"Evening," she said, as she got out of her Blazer. "I'm Sheriff Madison McKenzie. You called in a report of possible assault?"

"Yes, Sheriff. I'm Beth Oliver, and this is Bobby. It's his folks. They fight a lot, but this time he thinks his mom is hurt. They live across the road," she pointed a shaky hand toward the house across the way.

"Bobby, how was your mom hurt?"

"Daddy shoved her, and she fell over my bicycle. He drinks too much. Momma just came in from work. She's a waitress at Maple Grove and was late, so Dad got mad. She had to work a shift for a girl that didn't show up for work. He always accuses her of running around. My mom doesn't fool around. She's a hard worker, and even brought supper home because she was late."

Bobby appeared to be about ten or eleven. Madison noticed that his eyes were red and his face streaked with dirt, as though he'd been crying. "Does your

Daddy ever hit her?"

"Sometimes," he answered.

"Has he ever hit you?"

The boy took a deep breath, and tears began to flow again. He wiped his nose on his shirt sleeve and didn't say anything, but he looked up at his neighbor.

The woman said, "Go ahead, Bobby. Tell Ms. McKenzie. She can help you and your mom."

"Yes, I can, Bobby. Nobody should be bullied. Not at school or at home. He doesn't have that right. You can tell me; if you don't, I can't do a thing to help."

"Last weekend he hit me with his belt. It left a bad bruise, and it hurt a lot." Bobby looked at the ground. "He slaps Mom a lot, and kicks her."

"OK, Bobby. I'm going over to your house to see if they will talk to me. You stay inside with Mrs. Oliver." She looked at Beth. "You two should stay indoors for a while. Is anyone else here?"

Beth shook her head.

"Is there anyone else at your house, Bobby?"

"No, Ma'am."

Madison left her Blazer in the Olivers' drive, but she brought the map she'd gotten from Mr. Lynch. Looking at it as she walked to the door, she knocked, waited and then knocked again, louder this time. In a moment, she heard footsteps. A man opened the door, barely a crack.

"Hey, are you Mr. Sullivan? I see here on my map that you own this property, and it borders the Edwards' property. Right?"

"Yeah..."

"Oh, I'm sorry; my name is Sheriff McKenzie. I'm trying to find the folks who owned that little house that used to be on the right side the hill coming up Rocky Fork. You know, the one that washed away this week?"

"So? What's it got to do with me?" the man opened the door slightly wider.

Madison noticed a woman leaning against the wall in the room behind him. "I need to know where to locate the Edwards, because that little shack was on their property. Can you help me?"

She looked past the man to the woman who stepped out of sight into the door of another room. "Is your wife an Edwards?"

"Yeah, she was. Her folks own that land. But they ain't here."

"Can you tell me where I can find them?" Madison asked.

"In that cemetery at the forks of the road."

"Oh, then your wife owns it now. I need to speak to her. Mrs. Sullivan?" She called out.

"She's not feeling good. You need to leave," the man stepped onto the stoop and pulled the front door to behind him.

"I'm sorry to bother you when she's not feeling well, but I have to get a sign-off about the property. Please ask her to come to the door. It will only take a second."

The man studied her as if he was trying to decide if he should run, or call his wife to get rid of this annoying woman.

"I'm not going away until I talk to your wife. I think you know that, so don't stand in the way of the law, Mr. Sullivan, or I'll feel you have something to hide other than the fact that you've consumed a couple of beers." Madison lifted her jacket and put her hand on her holstered Sig. "Do you understand what I'm saying?"

At that point, the man backed against the door. His left hand reached for the door knob behind him. The door opened, and he called out, "Kelly, come here and talk to this lady."

The woman limped to the open door. She held a dish cloth in her right hand. She blinked away tears. "Hello, Sheriff. I had a double shift at work today; I'm beat," she said, faking a smile.

"Oh, I know you. You work at Maple Grove. I'm sorry to bother you. Are you sure that's all that's wrong with you, Kelly?" Madison asked.

"I'm just tired," she repeated.

"Why are you limping? There's blood on your leg. Did you fall over something?"

"Yeah," she laughed. "Bobby's always leaving his bike laying around. I tripped over it, that's all."

"What's wrong with your hand?"

"Nothing," she lied.

Madison reached out to touch her right arm. She took the dishcloth from her hand and saw that her wrist was swelled and badly bruised. "You must have fallen on your hand. Looks to be broken," Madison managed to step between the man and his wife. She nudged Kelly off the stoop and into the yard. "I'll call an ambulance for you. That's the best way to get your wife's fall looked at, Mr. Sullivan. You understand, don't you?"

"She doesn't need an ambulance; I'll take her to the doctor. Come on back in here, Honey. I'll get you to some help."

"Do you want to go with me to Mrs. Oliver's house, Kelly?"

"Yes," she said, not looking at her abuser. It was painful, but she walked away from her husband. "I think Mrs. Oliver can help; she's a retired nurse."

"That's fine, I'll give you a hand here," Madison moved to Kelly's left side and supported the woman as she hobbled out of the yard and across the street.

"Bobby told me what happened. Do you want protection from your husband?" she asked as they walked up to Mrs. Oliver's drive.

"He's getting worse every week. He hurt Bobby last weekend. I can't put up with him hurting our son."

"No, Kelly, and you shouldn't put up with him hurting you, either. Women don't have to live like that these days. The law is on your side. You can get an order of protection, and we can remove him from the house. He has to take steps to work on his problem if you take action to protect yourself and your child. I'll drive you somewhere, if you want."

"I've made up my mind; this is the last time he's going to hurt my son or me."

"Good for you. I'll be glad to take you to the county courthouse. We can get you some help there. Do you want Bobby to know?"

"Yeah, he's involved now too. I think he's known for a long time; he always tries to protect me. But last week was the first time Buddy hurt Bobby."

Mrs. Oliver said she'd take care of Bobby. After a quick exam, she told Madison Kelly needed stitches in her leg, and a doctor should check her arm. When Madison and Kelly came back out to get in her Blazer, Buddy stood in the driveway with a rifle.

"You're not taking my wife, Sheriff. Kelly, get away from the car. Get Bobby and come back home." He swayed back and forth in a drunken stagger, nearly falling. He caught his balance and pointed the rifle at the Blazer. "I said, come here!" he yelled.

Madison stepped away from the driver side. "Put the rifle down, Buddy. In your shape, you couldn't hit the broad side of a barn—but I can. You don't want your family to watch me shoot you down in front of them, do you?"

"You ain't gonna shoot." He stumbled forward. "Kelly, you hear me?"

Madison pulled back the slide on her Sig, chambering a round. "Buddy, are you a betting man?" Her voice was calm.

"What?"

"I'll bet you that I can put a shot within an inch of your foot. You want to see me prove it?"

"You ain't gonna shoot." He laughed and staggered backward.

Madison squeezed the trigger, and dirt flew up less than an inch from Buddy's boot. He looked down, almost in shock. Then he sighted down the barrel of a shaky rifle. Madison fired again, putting a bullet in his right shoulder. It knocked him backward; the rifle dropped to the ground. Buddy lay in the middle of the road, yelling incoherently.

Madison rushed to him, aiming her gun directly at him. "Buddy Sullivan, you are under arrest for attempted murder. You have the right to remain silent. Anything you say can and will be used against you in a court of law. You have the right to an attorney. If you cannot afford an attorney, one will be provided for you. Do you understand the rights I have just read to you?"

"You shot me!" He lay flat on his back.

"I warned you. Now lie still, while I check the wound. Were you going to shoot me?"

"Damn straight! No woman playing sheriff is telling me what to do!"

Madison saw that her aim was true; she'd just grazed his upper arm. She turned toward Mrs. Oliver, who was now standing next to the Blazer. "Do you have a dressing you can put on him?"

Kelly remained next to the Blazer and stopped Bobby from running to his dad. "He had it coming, Bobby. He isn't hurt badly. Sheriff McKenzie had no choice; he was going to shoot somebody. Now, we have to be strong."

Bobby buried his face in his mother's breast. "Why did he hurt us?"

"He's an alcoholic. Alcohol makes him a different person. He's not the man I married, or even your father, anymore. But if we can get him some help, the good man we love will come back."

An ambulance arrived on the scene and loaded Buddy into the back.

"I'll give you a ride so that you can see a doctor, if you'd like," Maddie said as she walked up to Kelly and Bobby. "I'm sorry you had to see this, but don't worry, he's going to be OK."

Bobby wiped his face and stretched his hand out to Sheriff McKenzie. "I don't blame you, Ma'am; he's not himself. You could have killed him, but you chose just to wound my Dad. I thank you for that."

Madison accepted the young man's handshake. "You had to grow up too quickly, all of a sudden. You'll be OK too, Bobby. Just remember, the law is always on the side of the innocent and the good."

He nodded.

Mrs. Oliver returned from her house. "Thank you, Madison; I'll take Kelly and Bobby to Erwin. You did a good job handling this incident. I knew you would. I've known you most of your life. You come from good people, and so do Kelly and Bobby. I'll take care of them."

"Thank you, Mrs. Oliver. I know you, and my folks are your friends through their church. I'm glad you called for help for your neighbors. That's what we need to do, stand up for each other."

She waved goodbye, and drove toward Erwin to check in on her prisoner.

The EMTs were unloading him as she arrived at the ER. She'd radioed ahead to be sure a deputy from the county police department met them there.

The ER doctor looked at the wound, and said, "You're an excellent shot, or this is a very lucky man."

"I hit what I aim for, Doctor." She stepped out of the room while he dressed the wound.

The deputy told Madison he'd bring the prisoner to the jail, if she wanted to go on and get the paperwork done. She agreed and drove the few blocks to the county lockup.

An hour later, with all the legal papers filed, Madison thanked the deputy for his assistance and went to her Blazer for the thirty-minute drive to Cold Creek.

She'd had a long day and was ready to relax. Bud greeted her with his all-over wiggle.

"I have a good job, Bud, but it takes me away from you too much. I won't be the law in Cold Creek after Rick and I are married."

She lay down that night with prayers for Bobby and his mother—and for Mrs. Oliver, who loved her neighbors. She asked a particular intervention for Buddy, so that he could get well and return to his family.

# 40

R ick woke early the morning of his trip to DC. He didn't much like returning to the city he'd grown up in, but this time it was on business. There
was a mandatory training seminar, and this was his last chance to take it if he
wanted the promotion he was due. Schooling had never been his favorite pas-
time, but this was at least a subject he was interested in, and DC was closer than
the previous two locations. January's seminar had been held in San Francisco,
and the other was in Dallas, Texas. Washington DC would be just about an
eight-hour drive for him. He'd asked Madison to go along, but she had obliga-
tions to Cold Creek.

"Good morning Milady." Rick listened to Madison's soft breathing when
she answered the phone. "I'm heading your way; got your suitcase packed?"

"Rick, we've been all through this. I have too much going on here," she
said.

"I know, but that doesn't stop me from wanting you with me."

"What time are you leaving?" Madison yawned into the phone.

"I'm coming up on I twenty-six now. This is the closest we'll be until the
weekend," Rick said.

"Aw, you're making me feel bad."

"Nah, I know you have responsibility. I wouldn't be going either, if I had a
choice."

They talked for a few more minutes, then Rick said goodbye. He planned to
stop for breakfast once he got into Virginia. He was watching for a Cracker Barrel.

Madison was wide awake, so she dressed in running clothes. She carried her shoes to the door, sitting on the steps to put them on. Bud came out behind her, wiggling all over, showing he had missed their early morning runs.

They walked to the playground to warm up, and as the eastern sky began to lighten, they headed up the climb through the evergreens. Madison felt the burn, too much of it; she was obviously out of shape. This course had been their daily routine before she left Cold Creek to go to UT. Bud was just a pup then. She wondered if he felt a difference after not running every day. *But I guess he's stayed in condition by running and playing with Bear while I was walking to and from class*, she thought.

Reaching the top of the mountain, at the ridge where she walked to cool down, she saw the trees had grown noticeably taller. Cold Creek was nearly hidden. Like everything else in her life, even the mountain changed. Bud slowed to sniff something, so she stopped to see what he'd found. There were deer tracks, lots of them, and they looked fresh. Not only deer had been through the soft soil, though; she noticed bear tracks, too.

"Bud, we might have more wildlife on the mountain now. I hope we don't surprise a momma bear." She petted his head, and he took off again. "You could rest a while, Bud."

But he was gone, so Madison pressed on. She didn't want to stay still too long. As she rounded the turn where they would run downhill toward home, she heard a loud growl. "Bud!" she yelled. "Bud, come!"

After hearing another growl, she saw Bud scurrying out of the underbrush. His side had four distinct claw marks, and a lot of blood. She caught up with him and checked to see how deep the scratches were. "You found her, didn't you?" Examining his side, she decided it was only a swipe, not deep cuts, but she didn't want him to run anymore. She held his collar and made him walk alongside her until they were clear of the thick underbrush.

When she turned Bud lose, he continued walking slowly beside her. At the creek, he lay down and panted hard. The cold water must have helped him feel better, because he got up in a moment, shook off, and continued to her front porch.

Henry was getting his tools out of the back of his truck as they returned. "Back to your running routine, I see."

"Yeah and we ran across a bear. I'm afraid she wasn't happy with Bud being there. Will you look at his side?" Madison sat on the porch next to Bud.

"This was a young bear. Momma would have taken not only the hair, but skin and some muscle too, all the way to the ribs," he said. "If you get me some white rags, I'll patch him up, but you ought to get Doc to give him a tetanus shot—and maybe some antibiotics."

Madison ran into the cottage and returned with a couple of old white towels and some Betadine. "He washed off in the creek."

"That's good; the water washed any dirt out. He'll be fine."

"I'll walk him over to see Chip. Thank you, Henry."

Later in the day, Madison got a call from Scott, the county dispatcher. He said he'd received a call from a motorist passing through on the old road, reporting a car driving erratically. The caller doubted it would make all the curves. Since Madison lived just a couple miles off of old 23, Scott thought she'd be close enough to check it out quickly.

"Sure, Scott, that's my territory. I'll give you a call on the radio when I check it out."

She drove out of Cold Creek in the Blazer, with her blue light flashing on the dash. Driving close to the edge of the curves so she could look over the edge, she hoped no one would come around a curve speeding. She came to a right-hand curve with a deep ravine off the left side. Madison didn't want to drive on the wrong side into a curve, so she pulled off onto the shoulder of the road, facing traffic. With no guardrail in this section, a car could easily go over and not be visible from the road.

As she drove slowly, watching over the steep drop, it occurred to her that if a car had gone over, she might not even be able to spot it in the dense underbrush. At that moment, she heard a loud engine revving behind her. She looked back, and saw a high-lifted off-road truck coming through the curve, straight at her. She mashed the gas to try to avoid the truck, but her tires spun in the grass on the shoulder. She felt the truck ram her, and it kept pushing as she slid over the bank.

A couple of young saplings held her for a moment, but the truck rammed her again, shoving her vehicle over into a roll. Now upright again, the momentum of the Blazer cleared its path. It mowed down small trees, picking up speed as it plowed through vines and brush. Madison's instincts were to lay over toward the passenger seat in case something punched through the windshield. The sounds crashing around her brought back the memory of Sam's plane crash in Alaska, with her in the back seat. She felt every jolt of all the stumps or rocks the Blazer encountered. Finally, it shuddered to a stop against a large walnut tree.

She listened as the swishing of branches stopped. Then there was silence. Madison was afraid to sit up, afraid of how her body felt, afraid of what she might see outside her vehicle. Whoever ran her off the road might be coming down the hill to finish the job. She felt for her Sig. The holster was empty.

When she'd leaned over on her side, it must have fallen out between the seats. She unhooked her seatbelt, sitting up enough to look for the pistol. There it was, on the floor of the passenger side—just out of reach. She had to slide into the other seat to get it. Outside crackling sounds made her think someone was indeed making their way down to her. How far had she fallen? Would they actually walk that far, just to see for themselves?

Carefully, she pulled up the handle on the passenger side to open the door. Amazed that it opened, she climbed out. She reached back inside to get the portable radio, which had also fallen into the floor. She pulled the plug of the blue light on the dash from its charger. Without the blue shield, it doubled as a flashlight. She thought about anything else she might need. The sun had vanished from these thick woods, and soon it would be completely dark.

In the back of the Blazer was a kit with road hazard preparations. She didn't want to carry the entire bag, but she'd get the flares. They might come in handy. With every step, she thought she heard sounds further up the hill. Then she heard voices. Was someone coming to rescue her, or—she didn't want to think of the other option.

After getting the flares, she closed the back quietly. Maybe she'd climb the hill in a different direction and wait to see who came. As she began climbing, she realized she felt dizzy, with nausea coming on. She hurried to find a thick patch of rhododendron to hide in and observe whoever was coming. The voices seemed to get further away; or was she losing consciousness? She checked the radio. "Scott, can you hear me?" There was no answer. The signal could not get through, this deep in the hollow between the mountains.

\* \* \*

Madison awakened with a start. She heard a crackling noise, and saw a glow. Her Blazer was burning! She felt the urge to get out of her hiding place, but then she thought better of this idea. There hadn't been any sparks or smell of gasoline. She'd hunted for a place to hide for only a moment. How long had she been out?

She sat low, waiting and watching, sickened to see her Blazer go up in flames right in front of her. Had it been her imagination that she thought she heard voices? Her body must have taken some hard blows as the vehicle rolled over. She probably had a concussion, like from the plane crash. At least she was alone. Bud had not been with her.

Bud... Oh, he needed his food, and the medicine. Would Henry have thought to give it to him before he went home? Would he remember to put

Bud in the cottage? Would Scott remember that she'd promised to check back with him?

Madison closed her eyes, leaning against the trunk of the old growth rhododendron. Each time she'd tried to get up, she got sick at her stomach. She decided she'd stay still until daylight. Maybe by then, a rescue party would come.

Back in Cold Creek, Henry loaded his tools and put Bud inside the cottage. "Tell Madison she can't be staying out after dark like this, or I'll take you home with me." Henry had watched how Bud's side was swelling. He felt Bud's nose, and decided he'd leave Madison a note, and take Bud home so he could keep an eye on him. Henry knew how to nurse sick dogs. He'd had more than one coon hound that had tangled with a bear.

At the close of his shift, Scott was surprised by his granddaughters, who came to get him and take him to a surprise birthday dinner. He instructed the on-duty dispatcher to pay attention for Madison to check in, once she got back in radio range.

As the evening shift wore on, calls came in reporting a train wreck, which had set fire to an empty warehouse close to the tracks. Also, several small houses were in danger from the tanker cars, which were hauling some flammable substance. The town of Erwin was a buzz of activity, with all the fire departments throughout the county coming on the scene from all directions.

Ambulances had been called from Washington County. Even though there hadn't been many crew members on the train, one of the buildings involved was an office, with twelve railroad employees. The injuries were minor, but most required transporting to the hospital. The ER at Erwin Hospital could not handle them all, so some went to Johnson City.

To add to the overload of so many emergency vehicles in town, the residents who wanted to see what was happening compounded the traffic problem, causing multiple fender benders. Every deputy, state trooper, and city police officer had to be called out.

Westbound traffic on Interstate 26 slowed to view the carnage in the valley below as soon as they topped the hill, coming off the mountain from Sam's Gap. Soon a domino effect of crashes brought the interstate to a standstill. Carter County had to send troopers to help with the traffic flow.

No one even missed Sheriff McKenzie up in Cold Creek. Mr. Olsen closed the store and walked home before dark. Ben and Margie had a private party of thirty people in the side room of the restaurant, so they hadn't had time to miss her coming in to eat. Sometimes she ate at her cottage, so even if they hadn't been busy they might have thought she was at home.

Rick called Madison's cell, and it went straight to voicemail. He called the landline at the sheriff's office, but only heard her voice on the answering machine. Rick left her a message there, too. Just before he turned out the light to go to sleep, he called Henry and Holly's home phone.

Henry told Rick that he had brought Bud home with him because of the injury from the bear. They talked for a while about the construction, and then he hung up. Rick tried Madison's cell number one more time. Still no answer. "She's probably let the battery go dead," he said aloud, and switched off his light.

Madison woke with sunbeams stabbing like swords through the dense overhead canopy. Her head hurt. Her neck hurt. Her stomach was empty, but it hurt too. She still felt dizzy, and knew she needed water. The sun was directly overhead, she realized. *That means I slept for nearly twelve hours. I guess no one came looking for me. Why didn't Scott send someone to look for me?*

She crawled out of her hiding place, then walked around the Blazer, looking at the burned-out metal carcass. It saddened her, thinking of all the times Bud rode with her. He surely would have been hurt this time, if he'd been along.

Madison felt she could not make it up the steep hill to the road. In the daylight, she could see it was very far, and straight up. She looked down the hill. There was a semblance of a game trail; maybe deer used that path to go to water.

She walked a few steps and slid down. Not wanting to add to her injuries, she found a tree branch to use as a walking stick. Soon she thought she could hear water flowing. It must be a small stream, because Rocky Fork was the only big creek she was aware of in this area of the county. She kept moving down the hill, and sure enough, a rocky creek bed ran between the two hillsides, cascading over the steep terrain. She found a place where she could lay down and scoop water up with her hand. It was cold and clean tasting. She drank what she estimated to be about a cup. As much as she wanted to drink more, she knew she should take it slow and wait until she was further down the hill. Following the creek, she had to cross to be able to pass some places. Madison continued back and forth, walking on whichever side had the least underbrush.

The thick woods opened to a cleared field. Although not in crops now, Madison thought it looked like there had once been furrows from plowing. Maybe she was close to a farm. In another 100 yards, she found the remnants of an old barn. It was now mostly just piles of logs and tin. Further down the creek, she came across a springhouse. The water flowing through the spring was clear, and tasted good to her. She continued, coming to a shack much like her cottage had looked before she and Jess updated it with a new roof and paint for the weathered boards.

Hers was built in the late 1700s. Madison wondered if this old house was also from that period. She went inside. Most of the floorboards were rotted, so she stepped carefully, walking only on the main timbers, which were hand-hewn logs like the ones underneath her cottage. The rooms were set up the same as hers had been: two bedrooms, a small kitchen, and a living room with fireplace. She'd had Henry remove the wall between her two bedrooms so she could have a larger bedroom. At some point, Shirley's family had added a bathroom. This house did not have one. There was no doubt she'd see an outhouse someplace.

She looked at the wood burning stove in the kitchen. With the sky showing through the roof, there was nothing left to shield it from the elements. It was a rusted shape vaguely resembling the old one Henry had taken out of her cottage. There were no cabinets' a small table with legs rotting away stood askew in the corner. The back door, where her cottage had an updated laundry room, used to open onto a small back porch. The frame of logs left a faint footprint on the ground. Madison observed a copperhead among the timbers, so she went back to the front door and left the shack to nature.

After the forest had thickened again, she stayed close to the creek and trudged through thickets of wild rose bushes. She smelled iris blooms. Looking up the hillside, she saw headstones. It was a small cemetery. She climbed the hill to see if she could read the names.

The largest of the markers was hand carved. Moss grew on the letters of the name. She scratched it away with a stick. Her fingers traced the carvings; I-R-V-I-N-G, and the years 1897 and 1937. The remainder was too shallow and eroded; she could not read it.

Only one other headstone had dates she could make out. They were 1852–1853: a baby, and there was no name. The other three stones were small, just foot markers with no carvings. *The whole family is buried here.* She tried to note the dates so she could look up the name Irving when she got home.

Madison found a patch of blackberries. She braved the high weeds to pick some and ate them in seconds. With purple fingers, she continued going down the creek. Her head still hurt, but she was not feeling sick any longer. Maybe the berries helped. In the quiet of the woods, Madison heard a tune. It wasn't until she remembered her phone in her back pocket that she realized what it was. She touched the screen to see if there was by chance a signal. The tune was her phone signaling that the battery was going dead; there was no signal. She shut it off to preserve what little charge it had for when she came to a place where she might get a signal.

By late afternoon, she figured that she had covered maybe ten miles. Still, she'd not seen one house, no signs of a road or any hint of civilization. *Where on earth does this creek come out?*

Another hour passed, and she still heard no sounds of life. Was she going to spend another night in the woods? Surely Rick would have called Henry and Holly if she didn't answer her phone. Surely Henry was out looking for her.

Henry had an appointment in Johnson City, and left the house at 8:00. One of the twins was sick and stayed in bed, so Holly sent the other boys out to check on the dogs as soon as they ate breakfast.

After Henry's appointment, he went to Lowe's to get more drywall for the construction job on Madison's cottage; he also had three 5-gallon buckets of paint mixed while he was there. By the time he got home, it was early afternoon, and he was hungry.

Holly had lunch on the table, and as he sat to eat she ran back upstairs to check on Hugh. He was sleeping finally, so she felt relieved and went back to talk to her husband.

"Did you hear about the train wreck in Erwin last night?" Henry asked.

"No, was it bad?"

"According to the talk in Johnson City, it escalated to the point that every emergency vehicle, fire truck, ambulance, and police car in three counties was involved," he explained.

"I guess that's why Madison hasn't called to check on Bud," she said, then sipped from a glass of iced tea.

"You haven't heard from Maddie?" Henry dropped his fork. "Have you tried to call her?"

"No, I've been busy with the boys, and Hugh just finally went to sleep. I'll call her now." Holly pulled her phone from her apron pocket. Without talking, she hung up. "It went straight to voicemail."

"I'm going to town to see what's going on with her," Henry said as she slid his chair back and slapped his cap on his head. He got straight into his truck and headed to Cold Creek.

It was nearly 3:00 when he pulled in between Madison's cottage and the jail. Seeing no sign of the Blazer, he went to the hardware store. Mr. Olsen met him, asking if he'd seen the mess in Erwin.

"I saw it from the interstate. It's still smoldering. Mr. Olsen, have you seen Madison today?"

"No, I figured she went out early to see what she could do in Erwin."

"Was her Blazer here when you opened up this morning?"

"No; come to think of it, I didn't see it."

"I'm going over to ask Ben if she was there when they opened this morning," Henry said as he walked out the door.

"Morning, Henry," Ben said from behind the counter.

"Ben." He nodded his head. "Was Madison's Blazer in her driveway when you opened up this morning?"

"This morning? Hmm... Hey Margie, was Madison in here today?"

"No, haven't seen her since yesterday. Come to think of it, I thought she went out early this morning. We opened at five thirty, and her Blazer was already gone," Margie said.

"What time did you close up last night?" Henry asked.

Ben answered, "Late; we had a party of thirty in the side room. It was the class of nineteen ninety-seven, having a class reunion. We didn't get cleaned up and out 'til nearly ten. I remember thinking that Madison was out late. No lights on in the house, and her vehicle wasn't there."

"Something's wrong. Madison would never go twenty-four hours without checking on Bud. Especially after he got swiped by a bear yesterday morning. I took him home with me; she's not experienced at nursing a sick dog like I am. I thought she'd call when she came in and found him gone. I left her a note. But that's just not like Maddie."

"Where'd she go, when she left after Bud was hurt?" Ben asked.

"I don't know; she just said Scott had called her to check on a report of a possible drunk driver. I need to call Scott."

"Here's a phone book. He's a city dispatcher, isn't he?" Ben asked as he flipped through pages.

"No, county. Sheriff's office on Love Highway," Henry answered.

Ben located the number and read it off to Henry. He keyed it into his phone and hit send. "I need to speak with Scott; this is Henry Jacobs."

"Scott speaking. How can I help you, Henry?"

"Have you seen or heard from Madison today?"

"No, and I left straight from my shift last night before all the uproar began. She was supposed to check in. Let me call Bayne and see if he talked to her. Hold on, Henry."

In a minute, Scott returned to the phone and said he couldn't find anyone who had heard Madison check in. With all the excitement of the train and the interstate traffic, no one had even thought about her not completing the call he'd sent her on.

Scott notified deputies in the area to check the old road. Henry drove up to the area where the erratic driver was reported. He went to the top of the mountain, and back down on the old road. There was no sign of her Blazer anywhere. Henry stopped to ask folks who were outside their houses, in case any had noticed her Blazer in the area yesterday.

No one remembered seeing her. Henry drove back up the mountain, this time driving on the shoulder of the road. He watched for any signs of tracks. Just before sunset, he stopped at a farmhouse, where a man and his wife were sitting in rockers on their porch.

"Howdy, how are you?" Henry asked as he stepped from his truck.

"Mighty fine, you?"

"I'm worried about Sheriff McKenzie. She drives a black Chevy Blazer, an older model. She would have had her blue light on the dash flashing. Did you see her at all yesterday evening?" Henry was feeling anxious. This behavior was not in Madison's character to make her friends worry.

"No, can't say as we did. But we were in the garden out back 'til dark. We sat here on the porch 'til late, after. We saw something burning right after we sat down. It was a bright glow, but nothing compared to that train wreck in Erwin, from what I heard," said the old fellow.

"I heard an explosion, but George can't hear; he just saw the glow," the old lady said.

"Can you give me any idea where the light might have come from?" Henry got a sick feeling in his gut.

"Yeah, down in that holler, almost at the end of the curvy part of the road. It's awful steep, down that left side. If a car went off there, you'd never see it. Unless it was what exploded and burned." The old woman got up from her rocker and pointed up the mountain. "Follow the road 'til it curves right and looks over that cliff. I hope she weren't in it when the car blew up."

"Thank you. And please, when you see a deputy come up the road, wave him down and tell him the same thing you just shared with me, will you?" Henry jumped into his truck and spun out from the gravel on the side of the road.

He called Scott's number again and told him that something blew up, and he was afraid it might have been Madison's Blazer. He asked if Wings Air Rescue could get in the air to help look. He gave Scott the best location he could figure, according to the mile markers.

Madison had gotten tired enough to lay down in a bare spot next to the creek. She was feeling sick again, and couldn't make her feet walk any further. Madison unhooked the spotlight from her gun belt and checked the battery. The light was still bright. She set it down next to her head and closed her eyes for a short nap.

The sound of a helicopter woke Madison. It was dusk, but not quite dark. She shined the light into the air. The 'copter kept going; it seemed to be heading to the top of the mountain.

*Maybe they'll at least spot the Blazer.* Madison tried to stand, but her legs were not holding her weight. She heard the helicopter again, but it circled further up the mountain. "Yes, that's where the Blazer would be—but they can't even tell what kind of car it is from the air."

She waited and listened. One pass, she caught sight of the helicopter again. She turned the light on and shined it directly at the chopper. Then she thought of the SOS signal. She'd learned it in a survival class in Knoxville.

Madison tried the signal. She kept flashing the light on and off, repeating SOS. She only hoped that whoever was in the air could see it.

After a few minutes, she stopped hearing the sound of the helicopter. The sun was below the mountain, but it wasn't completely dark up there, even though it was down where she was—nothing but a speck in a forest of hundreds of acres of dark woods.

Henry heard someone calling his name. He was almost back up the hill after climbing down to the Blazer. By the time he got to the roadside again, he was out of breath. Scott and a deputy stood next to his truck.

"It's her Blazer, burned to a crisp. I can't tell if there is a body in it, but I don't think so."

"No, Henry, she wasn't in it. The helicopter spotted an SOS signal. They landed and sent a couple of deputies in on foot. We'll hear something soon. She followed the creek down the mountain. We'll get her out of here before long."

Madison felt another night in the woods might mean that Bud would go without food for a second day. She hated that her job put him in danger, but he would have been in worse danger if he'd been with her yesterday. She reached into the creek for another handful of water to cool her mouth. She thought of dehydration. *Can't let that happen. After all, I'm practically lying in a clear creek full of spring-fed water.* She made herself drink again and again until she began to feel more energetic. Maybe she hadn't been taking in enough. At least with the water, she was not going to die of thirst.

Each time she dozed and roused again, there was less and less light. She turned the spotlight on and shined it all around her into the darkness. *Is anyone out there?* She heard a dog barking. *Wow, now I'm hallucinating. I thought I heard Bud.*

Then she heard branches breaking from up in the valley, small ones. *Maybe it's a stray dog.* She was having a hard time keeping her senses about her. Exhaustion was overtaking her determination to stay awake.

The sounds were coming closer. *That bark, that's Bud! That's my rescuer!* "Bud! Here, Bud!" she called out.

The barking became more frequent and excited. She turned on the spotlight, and there he was, crossing the creek where she'd crossed an hour or so ago.

"Bud," Madison managed the energy to stand. The wiggly dog jumped up and put his paws on her chest, nearly knocking her down. She hugged his neck and fell to her knees. "Oh, Good Boy! You found me. Bud, I love you so much."

She picked up the stick she'd used as a staff and crossed the creek to the cleared field. With the spotlight in her hand, she looked up the valley for Henry, figuring he must have brought Bud to track her. Just then, two men in blue and white uniforms emerged from the tree line. Bud raced to them and back to Madison, yapping excitedly.

Then she realized the helicopter had landed in the clearing of the old farmhouse, and they'd been the ones who brought Bud. The two men met her with a hug, and one gave her a drink. He told her it was for energy, and that she'd better drink it. The other man radioed the 'copter. "Pete, we have her. She's about a mile south of where you're sitting. We have a large cleared field where you can set down. She has a bright spotlight, look for that."

Madison pulled five flares from the thigh pocket of her pants. "Here, these might help him locate us."

The two men hurriedly set the flares in a circle, giving the pilot the perfect lights to land by. In minutes, they heard the helicopter approaching the makeshift landing zone, and it touched down right in the center. Madison walked between the men with one holding on to each arm, Bud leading the way. He was the first to jump onboard.

"Sheriff McKenzie, I believe you've got a real rescue dog there for a partner. Bud needs a badge and a vest."

"Yes, he does. He's my hero, for sure!" she said, and they helped her into the back of the chopper.

One of the helicopter crewmen got on the radio to Scott. "We've got her onboard. She's fine, just hungry and tired. We'll be landing at the JCMC in seven minutes."

"You hear that, Henry? She's OK, and on the way to the Med Center to be checked out. You might as well meet them there. They have a four-legged passenger for you."

"How did Bud…" Henry laughed. "They stopped and picked him up, didn't they?"

"Yeah. It was Mr. Olsen's idea. He loves that girl, and he knew if anybody could find her, it would be her dog!" Scott slapped Henry on the shoulder and got into his truck.

Henry got into his truck and drove toward the interstate. He called Holly to let her know that Madison had been found, and he was on the way to the Med Center to see her. Next, he called Mr. Olsen. "That was a great idea you had. Bud tracked Madison, and she's OK, just exhausted. The helicopter is taking her to the Med Center to get her checked out. Will you let Ben and Margie know?" Henry asked.

The helicopter crew stood next to the helipad. They had Bud posing for pictures for Channel 11 News. Henry waited until the camera crew moved away before he walked closer. Bud saw him and ran to meet his friend.

Henry put Bud into his truck, lowered the windows halfway, and told him, "On guard, Bud." That was the signal Madison used when she wanted him to stay in her vehicle while she was away.

Inside the ER, Henry found the EMT who had been on the helicopter rescue crew. He thanked him and inquired about her welfare.

The doctor came out from behind a curtain. He'd overheard Henry's question. "She's going to be OK. Got a bad concussion, and she will need bed rest for a while. But that's one strong woman."

"Yeah, she is," Henry agreed.

Henry's phone rang; it was Rick. "Hey, Rick. I was just about to call you. Your lady is OK; she's at the Johnson City Med Center. Doc says she has another concussion, but she's going to be OK, with some bed rest and a little TLC."

Henry explained what had happened and where they found her, with Bud's help. Rick said he was in Roanoke, on the way to Cold Creek.

"I thought you had to complete that training session," Henry said.

"Milady is far more important than any promotion. Besides, I aced the test, and the instructor signed me off. I can get an additional nineteen hours in Dr. Baker's class at UT."

"Well, that sounds like more fun anyway. So, you're going to be a couple of hours, I guess. I might have Maddie at my house by then. Why don't you call me when you get to Bristol?"

"Will do. See you in a while," Rick said.

"Rick, you are welcome to stay with us. I know Holly is going to want to fuss over Maddie, and not let her go to her cottage."

"Thanks, Henry, I appreciate that. Tell the boys to save me a bunk."

# 41

Holly ran down the steps as Henry's truck drove up. She went to Madison's door, opened it, and hugged her before she could get out. Bud raced onto the porch, but Madison told Henry not to let him in the house.

"He might have ticks; I had some on my legs. He'll need a bath."

"I'll take care of our boy Bud. Now, you just go on in and don't worry. Let me be in charge of things. Go on, now," he shooed her up the steps.

Holly helped Madison get into a tub bath so she would feel more comfortable, and she could look for additional ticks. Not that she didn't trust the nurse who had checked her over, but she wanted to know for herself. Ticks are bad in all the woods, and it was a simple matter to remove them before they got too stuck on the skin.

The bath had been soothing, but it had also given Madison a case of the munchies. Holly told her she'd fix anything she wanted, but all Maddie could think about was a glass of milk and graham crackers.

They sat in the kitchen while she ate her late-night snack. Henry joined them and said that Bud was clean. No pests, and he'd had a warm bath. He and Bear were playing on the back porch until he dried off some.

Madison noticed that Henry kept looking at his watch. "Are we expecting someone, Henry?"

"Well, I thought Rick might call. He knows your phone went dead, and he was going to call mine. Maybe he fell asleep," Henry teased.

"What if I call him?"

"That won't be necessary," Holly looked out the dining room window. "I'll bet that's him driving up in the yard now."

Sure enough, they heard the dogs racing around the house barking, announcing "We have company!" *From Bud's happy yapping, it has to be Rick.*

Holly insisted that Madison stay seated and let him come to her. She finished her milk and crackers while she waited. Her heart pounded with both dread and excitement. She knew that Rick would fuss about her leaving the site of the wreck. He always said, "It's just like in a plane crash. You never walk away from a downed aircraft. The vehicle can be found easier than one lone person on the ground, wandering in the woods."

But Rick Malone surprised his fiancée. He walked straight to her and bent to hug and kiss her without a word of criticism. "I'm so happy that you weren't hurt any more than the concussion. I'd have never forgiven myself for not stealing you away to go with me to DC."

"Truthfully, I guess I could have gone with you, but I don't like the idea of being in the same city as President Trump these days. Someone just might try to blow the government up, and I don't want to be there if that happens."

"You've been watching too much TV!" Henry said with a chuckle.

"Madison has had a long two days. I think she needs to get to bed. You can stay in the room with her, Rick, we have a comfortable chair in the sick room. But if she falls asleep, you better let her sleep. I'm sure she needs it." Holly pulled on Henry's arm, and they went toward the stairs.

"Are you hungry, Rick?" Madison asked.

"No, I went through a fast food drive-thru. I'm fine. But I would like a beer; do you think Henry has any?"

"Look in the refrigerator and see."

Rick escorted Madison to the room on the main level, affectionately known now as the sick room or recuperation room. He carried a bottle of water and a beer.

Madison explained what she remembered about the incident. She read his emotions, fluctuating between anger and pain. "Well, look at the bright side. My Blazer will no longer be questionable; it's out of the picture entirely!" She burst into tears.

Rick held her for a long time, standing in the center of the room. He finally insisted she lie down, and he pulled the chair up close to the bed. Rick turned the overhead light off, the ceiling fan on, and opened the blinds to allow the moon to shine in. "I'll tell you a story," he said, holding her hand.

Madison didn't hear the end of the story. She drifted to sleep in the safety of her furry hero guarding the porches, her heart protected by the lawman sitting next to her bed, sheltered in the home of her best friends, filled with love.

She dreamed of a lovely wedding in the hidden valley, joined by friends standing next to the cascading waterfalls, surrounded by white flowers, in the place where lady slippers grow.

The End

# About the Author

Bev Freeman was born in Virginia, living in the Appalachian Mountains until her teens when her family relocated to Florida. Missing the mountains, the tumbling streams and changing seasons birthed a love for writing, giving her an escape, for at least short stays.

After high school, life and a career in the dental field got in the way of returning to the mountains. She married a Floridian and raised a son.

However, the year 1993 brought shattered dreams and a divorce, so she followed her family back to the Appalachian region. In 1996, she married a local God-fearing man and ever since, life is beautiful in Tennessee with two spirited grandsons living close by.

Retirement offers days free for writing stories of unique characters set in her beloved mountains, making local history and legends come to life. A member of The Lost State Writers Guild, Bev attends yearly writing conferences and workshops surrounding herself with authors and writers.

She and her husband, Bill, enjoy weekends touring the backroads of the beautiful Blue Ridge and Great Smoky Mountains on their Goldwing, with similar cycle-loving friends.

You can find Bev on Facebook and the fun world of Pinterest.

# Coming Soon

## Return to Walker's Mountain

Based on a true story. I was 12 when a friend told me the story of her Dad, Mom, and Grandmother murders. The older sister hid with the two sibling under their grandmother's bed, the only reason the kids survived. Her story made such an emotional impression on my childhood, that I felt like I had to include this tragedy in my third novel. Due to their young ages, the children were not told the fate of the man who killed their family.